Meg Henderson was born in the Townhead area of Glasgow in 1948, the youngest and only girl of three children. Thereafter she lived in the Blackhill, Drumchapel and Maryhill areas of the city. She gratefully left her convent secondary at sixteen, and though writing had always been her main interest, she spent some years working within the NHS before going to India with Voluntary Service Overseas. On her return she married, went to live on a Scottish island and became an adoptive and a foster parent. Over the years she had 'kept her hand in' by writing the occasional newspaper article and when she gave up fostering she decided to write full-time. She now lives with her husband, three children and three cats on the East Coast of Scotland.

Finding Peggy:
A Glasgow Childhood

Meg Henderson

CORGI BOOKS

FINDING PEGGY
A CORGI BOOK : 0 552 14185 2

First publication in Great Britain

PRINTING HISTORY
Corgi edition published 1994

13 15 17 19 20 18 16 14 12

Copyright © Meg Henderson 1994

'Mexicali Rose', music by J. B. Tenney, words by
Helen Stone. © 1925, M. M. Cole Pub Co, USA. Reproduced by
permission of Francis Day and Hunter Ltd, London WC2H 0EA

Set in Linotype Plantin 11/12pt by
Hewer Text Composition Services, Edinburgh.

Corgi Books are published by Transworld Publishers,
61–63 Uxbridge Road, London W5 5SA,
a division of The Random House Group Ltd,
in Australia by Random House Australia (Pty) Ltd,
20 Alfred Street, Milsons Point, Sydney, NSW 2061, Australia,
in New Zealand by Random House New Zealand Ltd,
18 Poland Road, Glenfield, Auckland 10, New Zealand
and in South Africa by Random House (Pty) Ltd,
Endulini, 5a Jubilee Road, Parktown 2193, South Africa.

Printed and bound in Great Britain by
Cox & Wyman Ltd, Reading, Berkshire.

FOR

Nan, Peggy and George Clark,
Peggy's children and grandchildren,
and
The Clarks and the O'Briens

Also for my husband Rab, who knows why,
and our children,
Euan, Lisa and Debbie.

Acknowledgements

Willie McIlvanney
for years of encouragement and arguments.

Lynne Reid Banks
for years of encouragement and nagging.

John Saddler
for recognising the story before I did.

also

Bill Black, Radio Clyde
Dr A. Cameron MacDonald
Sean Damer
Tony Martin
The School of Scottish Studies,
Edinburgh University
Marion Zekulin
and my cousins:
Anne Caldwell
Vicky Clark
James Kelly
Nessie Robertson

Prologue

My life has been shaped by two women, who, in my child-hood, instilled in me the values I still live by: my mother, Nan, and her sister, my Aunt Peggy. Although these days I earn my living as a journalist and TV documentary maker, working and mixing with media high-fliers and household names, I was born and brought up in the poorest and toughest areas of Glasgow. As I was growing up I wasn't aware of how much Nan and Peggy had influenced me, but the truth is that I bear their stamp, and the older I get the clearer this becomes and the more grateful I am for it.

We were three sides of one tightly-bound triangle from the day I was born, so that it was impossible to think of one without the other; prick one and we all bled. Nan and Peggy were bright, vivacious, vital women, always on the verge of laughter or tears and usually both. They lived on their emotions and acted on instinct, they knew no other way. When I think of them today I picture them laughing helplessly and holding on to each other for support, their faces awash with tears as they struggled to remember why they had been laughing in the first place. Somehow I always picture them laughing.

Nan and Peggy Clark were strong women in that they believed in things, they had ideals and shared a dream of how life should be. This dream was entirely non-political, but it was in essence what started the Labour Party, though I'm sure they would not recognize what has evolved as the Labour Party today as anything to do with them. They believed completely that people were good and honourable and that everyone was of equal worth; indeed it never occurred to them that this wasn't universally accepted. Looking back there was something naive about that, and given the hard lives they had it is difficult to understand how they could have sustained such a belief. But there is something heroic and admirable about it too, painfully so, as my story reveals.

Peggy's sudden death at the age of thirty-six brought an end to the family as it had been; unable to deal with what had happened the Clarks simply fell apart. My mother became a recluse within months and my childhood ended abruptly as I had to take care of her. I never knew the exact details of how Peggy had died, except that there had been something especially awful about it, and the family found it too painful to explain.

It seemed that Peggy, so long an intregal part of me, had simply vanished without trace and even mentioning her name was frowned upon by the Clarks. Losing her devastated and scarred my life and with my mother's withdrawal I was suddenly alone for the first time, one fragile side of the triangle that had existed for ever. Within a short time Peggy's children went into care, and added to the confusion and the grief was guilt. We all felt it but were unable to express it because none of the Clarks connected anymore.

Much of my adult life has been spent fostering and adopting sometimes very damaged children and I can now see why I did that. When asked I would give what I truly believed were my reasons and I would use all the correct sociological jargon to explain. But the truth lies in the events of my childhood and in the guilt about Peggy's children. I was trying to reclaim her children over and over again.

All through my life I kept Peggy in my mind and in my heart. Though I knew she was dead, the Clarks' reaction had blocked the normal processes of grieving and healing. No one had ever explained her death to the child I was then, so how could I truly believe it? That was why in some secret place inside me I kept alive the fantasy that one day I'd look up and she'd be there beside me again, as she had been when I was a child. As time passed and I married and settled down, I realized that I would never find peace until I knew what had happened to her and why, and though more than twenty years had passed I managed to piece the story together. What I found out was shocking and tragic and terrible, not just because it happened to Peggy and my family, but because it could have happened to anyone. I understood for the first time how vulnerable working-class women were, and still are.

The other side of the experience, however, was that I also appreciated for the first time the extraordinary worth of the ordinary people I grew up among, especially the women, like Nan and Peggy. They are part of the unacknowledged history of working-class women. They didn't make speeches or form trade unions, they just kept their families alive against all the odds, they survived and ensured our survival.

All through my childhood I watched my mother fight highly effective campaigns to right wrongs, and to that end she valued education and knowledge. Education and knowledge equalled power, power to right more wrongs for those unable to do so themselves, power to change the way she and Peggy had been raised. Nan was the doer, the articulate, literate one, and Peggy, shyer and quieter, provided the back-up. Together they were a strong team, unable to accept that there was an alternative to what was Right, unable to refuse help to those who had been wronged. But caring exposes you to all sorts of hazards, and for the two sisters the cost, inevitably, was high.

Above all they provided me with a blanket of love and caring that has touched every corner of my life and covers me still. I didn't realize how important they had been in life, because like most people I simply accepted what I had grown up with. Until, that is, a conversation I had with a film producer I was working with. I mentioned that I had grown up in Blackhill and Drumchapel in Glasgow, two of the city's black spots and regarded by those who know nothing about life in either place as the far end of the moon. 'Well,' he said, clearly shocked, 'You've left that well behind!'

When our condemned tenement in the centre of Glasgow collapsed in 1952, three generations of my family were rehoused in Blackhill, a council estate three miles to the east of the city. It had a reputation for deprivation and violence that follows it to this day, and those sent to live there knew in advance that there was little likelihood that they would ever get out again. Blackhill wasn't so much an attempt at rehousing slum-dwellers as a judgement that they didn't matter; Blackhill was a life sentence.

With my mother, father and two brothers, I did get out though; as part of the inner city clearances in the 1950s, we moved to Drumchapel, a new estate five miles to the west. It was happening all over the country after the Second World War, vast housing estates, or schemes, were built and were optimistically regarded by the people who were sent to live in them as the first step to the good life. Extended families like ours, who had lived within doors of each other for several generations, were split up and sent to different estates, in the expectation of a bright new future. For my mother too, always chasing her dream, the move to Drumchapel heralded a better life for her children.

But Glasgow seized the opportunity to show the rest of the country how not to do it. The heart was torn out of the city as ghettoes were built to replace ghettoes; devoid of any amenities to make decent life sustainable, the new estates quickly became as rundown as the old. For the people who lived in them the situation was compounded by the loss of the support network provided by their extended families, by the loss of their roots.

My film producer meant it as a compliment that I had left Blackhill and Drumchapel well behind, but as I thought it over I saw that he was wrong. It made me think about my childhood and examine what and who had shaped it, who had enabled me to work with, and shock, film producers.

The people of Blackhill and Drumchapel remain a part of me and I of them; I have no need to leave them behind. To deny them would be to deny the two women who raised me. For now I see that without them I wouldn't be where I am today or be who I am. This then is the story of the family I grew up in and the tragedy that almost destroyed it. It's the story of my search for the truth of Peggy's death, of how I lost her and found her again. Much more than that though, it's about Nan and Peggy. Despite everything that happened they weren't destroyed; their values, their ideals have survived. And that I suppose is why when I think of them it's not sadness, sorrow or bitterness that come instantly to mind, it's that joyous picture of them laughing. They won in the end.

Chapter One

On the day I was born, so the story goes, there was a storm, so someone, somewhere, must have had an inkling. It was May 1948, I was part of the post-War baby boom and as my father was fond of relating, on that particular day, the 10th, Winston Churchill was given a medal by the Germans. I analyzed that thought countless times over the years but I never did find the connection. He was fond of linking unlikely events though, and often told me that his mother had died on his sixteenth birthday. All my life I was fascinated by that fact; even for the O'Brien clan, my father's family, it seemed a somewhat bizarre gesture for her to have made. He also liked it to be known that he had been born on the Feast of the Holy Innocents, a coincidence that was more apposite than he ever realized.

His name was Laurence Thomas O'Brien and he was called after a friend of his father's, a Frenchman who had ended up in a lunatic asylum. He would relate this with relish, then cackle madly to himself. We called my father's family 'the O'Briens', as though they were a thing apart, an alien entity to be categorized as a collective but separate genus, which they were. My father, the youngest in his family, was known to the O'Briens as 'oor Laurence', and to my mother as Laurie, to annoy the O'Briens, but to the rest of the world he was Skipper, or Skip. He had once proclaimed himself to be the Skipper of the good ship O'Brien, and the name had stuck.

My mother's name was Joan Henderson Clark, but she was known as Nan, and reluctantly as Mrs O'Brien. She wasn't exactly honoured to be part of 'they mad Irish pigs', as she called her in-laws. At this term of endearment Skip always gave another insane cackle, as though to prove her point.

Though Nan stood a fraction over five feet tall I weighed in at 10lb. 3oz., which must have been a considerable relief to her because six years earlier my brother Laurie had weighed 14lb. 6oz. Five years before that, as our brother, Mickey, liked to say of himself, the daintiest of the O'Briens had been born, a mere stripling of 9lb. 8oz.

. I was blue when I arrived, which was put down to my being cold, so I was placed in a drawer and put beside the fire. It was years before I discovered that in fact I had been suffering from a fairly common condition where the closing of a flap of skin over a normal opening in the feotal heart is delayed. But I suppose the extra heat did me no harm on a cold, windy day. Though my mother said I was born on a Monday, it was in fact a Thursday, not that she ever accepted this. She had her own thing about dates. For instance, she was inordinately proud of her fertility and was happy to tell anyone who would listen that she had been married on 17 July and had Mickey on 20 July. In an era when such things mattered, she omitted to say that her marriage and the birth of her first born had been separated by a year. My father would just smile with sly humour and never once corrected her.

She was eighteen years old when she had Mickey, after walking out of the maternity hospital at Glasgow's Rottenrow because no one was bothering with her. She walked the mile back to our house at 21 Balmano Street and had him and, in later years, Laurie Junior and me, at home among her family. Her mother, my grandmother, called Maw Clark by everyone, was at my birth, as she was at my brothers' and all my cousins' births too.

I was called Margaret Anne O'Brien. Anne was Maw Clark's name and every female child had it bestowed upon them like an indelible stamp of ownership. Call 'Anne!' at a family gathering and a stampede started, but I was lucky, it was only my middle name. I was named Margaret in honour of my mother's younger sister, but it was her 'Sunday best' name; she was known all her life as Peggy.

To save a stampede of two I was called Rita by the family. Though I tried to get an explanation of why Peggy and I had the same name but were called something else, I never got it. Whenever I asked, my mother would immediately be engulfed in a disabling spasm of laughter that would then infect Peggy, so that the two of them would cling to each other for support while furiously mopping their eyes.

Skip had wanted me called after his mother, Mary Ann O'Brien, but Nan, in another fit of logic, pronounced it 'too Irish'. The truth was that her sons had been called after the O'Briens and she was damned if her daughter would be too. Naming me was one of the small victories she delighted in winning over my father's family.

We lived at 21 Balmano Street which stood at the top of Balmano Brae, so the street was known simply as the Brae. It towered above the city centre, on top of the steepest hill in Glasgow, a grey-stone tenement four storeys high. Underneath it ran old mineshafts and train tunnels leading into Queen Street Station. Each of the eight houses was the same: a room and kitchen, with a toilet outside on a landing down a flight of stairs that was used by two families. There were no bathrooms and no hot water; kids, and sometimes adults, too, washed in front of the fire, standing in a tin bath filled laboriously with water boiled on the kitchen range. A proper bath could only be had by using the public baths a couple of miles away.

The kitchen also served as a dining-room / sitting-room and it was where my parents slept. Along one wall was a set-in bed which was covered during the day by a curtain, and there was a further bedroom where my brother Laurie and I slept and where Mickey would have slept too if he hadn't spent years in hospital. He had TB in his knee-cap and since before I was born he had been in Mearnskirk, a hospital set in the open countryside, fifteen inaccessible miles to the south of Glasgow city centre. I grew up with him only as a name. Mickey was something or someone my parents and the rest of the family visited, but no-one ever explained who or what Mickey was, let alone that he was my brother. As far as I was concerned I had Laurie, who was six years older than me, and all my cousins, that was all.

There were seven families in 21 and the Clarks lived on the top storey until the children left to get married. By the time I was born only Peggy lived in the family home with Maw Clark. Next door to them my mother's widowed sister Mary lived with her son David; and my parents, two brothers and I had a house on the first. I have very few memories of the Brae, just feelings and impressions. First of all there was the closeness; I felt that all the families who lived there, the McCreadies, the Fitzgeralds, the Turnbulls and the rest, were my family too, because I knew them equally well. So when Nan and Skip visited Mickey in hospital, Laurie and I were cared for by everyone in the Brae. And there is an impression of the old buildings crowded around 21, the winding, narrow, covered lanes, or closes, of Townhead and Rottenrow that led to cramped, dark houses with several generations of families living in them. I had aunts, uncles and cousins living all around, because news of empty houses was passed by word of mouth by families who preferred living near to each other. So we could safely walk into any house in the area, because if it didn't belong to a relative it belonged to a friend. Skip's family had stayed near by in Tarbet Street, so we lived in an area of Glasgow where both sides of our family had been for two generations. It was our own enclosed little world.

I wasn't aware of the Brae's crumbling stonework or any other negative aspect, to me it was just home. But the living conditions were unhealthy and the tenants had been waging a long campaign, led by Nan, to be rehoused. Apart from the obvious overcrowding, with most families having three or more children, there was a constant battle against the bugs that were taking over the delapidated building. In October 1950 Glasgow Corporation had shored the tenement up on one side in an attempt to arrest gradual subsidence and the tenants of 21 were told to be ready to move out at any time. To the inhabitants of the Brae this clearly meant that they would move into a better tenement *en masse*, that they would remain together wherever they moved to, which was what they wanted. They wouldn't, however, be considered for new homes, they were told in a classic example of bureaucratic speak, until they were actually homeless. As a very small child I was unaware of all this, my reality was that I lived happily in a large family that took in all the streets around the Brae.

But of course all was not harmony, no family ever is, and as I grew I became aware of the divisions and sub-divisions that made up mine. I was nearer in every way to Nan's family, the Clarks, and gradually I absorbed the rules that governed Clark life. They were a close family and outsiders were never aware, to my knowledge, of the two 'sides'. There were the 'Fair Yins', those like Maw Clark who had fair hair and blue eyes, and the 'Dark Yins', who had the dark hair, eyes and skin of Da Clark, my grandfather. The 'Fair Yins' stuck together on all counts and were favoured by Maw Clark, and the 'Dark Yins' kept to their group and had the special affection of Da Clark. Yet there was no animosity between my grandparents, in fact Maw spoke of her husband with nothing but affection; still the two groups grew into adulthood regarding each other with deep suspicion. No 'Fair Yin' ever sided with a 'Dark Yin' or vice versa in inter-family matters. Much plotting went on, discussions about the motives and actions of the others and plans to subvert them were food and drink to the Clark factions.

And they were very different in character too. For instance, Vicky, Mary and Willie, the 'Fair Yins', loved to have a good time, something they shared with Maw. They went dancing, were known to drink alcohol and smoke cigarettes; Vicky and Mary even had their ears pierced. Nan, Peggy and George came from the other side and were altogether more circumspect. The 'Dark Yins' had very definite ideas of how to behave, which meant with decorum at all times – good manners were high on their list of priorities. The most damning comment my mother could ever make of anyone was to pronounce them common, and she could encapsulate every possible shade and nuance of disapproval in to that one word.

Maw Clark was a strong personality and she cunningly ruled her children by keeping them divided. She would complain to one group of some supposed neglect or snub by the other and they would rush around competing to do things for her. If that didn't work, she had the ability to bring herself to death's door at will, which never failed to bring the entire family to her bedside. Once she had their full attention she would stage yet another miraculous recovery and my childhood was studded with her death-defying performances. There was a feeling that the 'Dark Yins' were constantly striving for her approval, which they never did get, and in the process they became do-gooders, ever ready to take the side of the underdog and to do the right thing. It was as though they felt they were out of favour because they had disappointed Maw and had to make up for it in whatever way they could.

They had a high regard for education and were always keen for their children to do well at school. They wanted a better life for the next generation, not in strictly financial terms, but in terms of status too. A good job wasn't one on an assembly line making a lot of money, it was one that allowed you to get on, to contribute something, to be somebody and to win respect by helping other people. This was directly at odds with the philosophy of the 'Fair Yins', who regarded their siblings as getting above themselves; that kind of thing wasn't for the likes of them.

The exception to the family rivalry was Willie, who outwardly qualified as a 'Fair Yin' but who had dreams for his kids too and wanted them to be bright. Despite his looks, a dark gene had inadvertently sneaked in at Willie's conception, rendering him loved but distrusted by both sides. Willie was everybody's friend, eternally stuck in the middle, though he'd go with his own group when the chips were down, always hoping not to be told any secrets because he knew he couldn't keep them. 'Don't say anythin' in front o' yer Uncle Wullie, hen,' Nan would tell me, 'It's no' his fault, bit thu'll get it oota him.'

As Nan's child I was counted as a 'Dark Yin' too. This meant that I absorbed the need to always be on my guard with the 'Fair Yins', to be careful what I told them, and that extended to their children too. It was assumed by each side that the other's children were attempting to extract information and we would be debriefed after every family gathering about what had or hadn't been said. It's a conditioning that exists still, when we're all old enough to know better, and to this day I'm more at ease with my 'Dark Yin' cousins.

As I grew the other differences became clearer too. The Clarks were Protestant and the O'Briens Catholic, that was the biggest, all-encompassing difference. Maw Clark was known to be a bitter Orange woman with an illogical hatred of Catholics, so what it must have done to her psyche that more than half of her grandchildren were Catholics can only be imagined. Of her children, Nan, George and Vicky had married Catholics, which of course meant they had to agree to their children being raised as Catholics too. I had no idea that I was a Catholic and wouldn't have understood had I been informed anyway, but from as early as I can remember I felt a tension in the family that went beyond being the child of a 'Dark Yin'.

All small children stick closely to their mothers during the first few years; fathers are optional extras, which is probably why I have no memories of Skip then. He was working as a bus conductor for Glasgow Corporation Transport Department when I was born and I vaguely remember playing with his badge. My mother and Peggy are the the ones I recall best. Their faces often merge into one as I look back, so I suppose that's how they seemed when I was little. They looked so alike anyway that outsiders were often unsure which was which, though they knew they were different people. So Nan would answer when called Peggy and Peggy would answer when called Nan, it was easier than explaining. To me they were beautiful women – whenever I hear the word 'bonnie' I think of them. They were in constant touch through what I suppose was telepathy and

I clearly remember them finishing each other's sentences or answering questions that hadn't been asked aloud. To me it was perfectly acceptable because it was there all my life. If they went out shopping alone they invariably returned with identical items and if they went out together they swapped whatever they bought anyway. This produced the characteristic Clark laughter, a helpless, almost soundless shaking accompanied by lashings of tears. They would hold on to each other and stumble about creaking with laughter, mopping uselessly at their streaming eyes. They told me endless stories of their family, the tales dissolving into the Clark laughter at the funny parts, or into tears of sorrow at the sad parts.

They had been particularly fond of their father, Da Clark, as he had been of them, and it was one of their greatest sorrows that he died before I was born. I think because we three were so close, it seemed 'no' right' to them somehow that we had no shared memories of him. Somewhere in the telling of the current story one of them would look at me, sigh and say, 'Oh, bit Da widda loved you!' and then the two of them would burst into tears. After a few minutes of communal grief one or other of them would say, 'Whit a daft perra buggers we ur! Look at the state o' us!' And they would then start laughing. This of course produced more tears and as they clung to each other one of them would say, 'Noo whit wur we laughin' at?' As though finding the cause would help them eradicate the effect. 'Look at that poor wean! She disnae know whit's gaun' oan!' But I did. I would watch them enthralled, a show in themselves that I never tired of seeing. Their performances were so memorable that Da Clark was ever-present in my life, he was real and alive to me because they kept him so.

Da Clark was the son of a Borders farmer and had run away from home when the farm horses he had cared for all his life were sold to the Glasgow Police. He was found sleeping in the hay beside the horses in the police stables in Bell Street and was promptly thrown out. For much of his teenage years he survived as and where he could, and in the process acquired 'a bad chest'. His family made one attempt to bring him home by sending one of his brothers to find him. Once released from the farm, the brother decided to remain in Glasgow too, and neither of them ever went home again. The brother worked in the Camp Coffee Factory, and though I have no memory of ever seeing him, I do recall that Camp Coffee was ever-present in all Clark cupboards.

Da Clark became a docker; I remember once seeing a photo of him at work, a tiny man with a huge black moustache, the inevitable bunnet, or flat cap, on his head and his shirt-sleeves rolled up; he hardly looked strong enough for the hard lifting that dockers had to do in those days. My mother used to tell stories of his breathing troubles, of how in summer he had to sit upright all night beside the window, trying to catch a decent breath, but still he went to work every morning. By all accounts he was a kind, if strict, father who worked hard and was fonder of his 'Dark Yins'. He fought incessantly with Willie, who being Willie never fought back, but just laughed in his good-natured way and merrily agreed that he was a waster who would never achieve anything.

The story goes that during the Second World War Da Clark lay unconscious and dying in Duke Street Hospital, with George, his eldest, still missing presumed dead. In the middle of the night the heavy tramp of army boots echoed through the hospital, coming ever nearer to the ward where the females of the family sat vigil by Da's bed. He opened his eyes, shouted 'George!' with great joy, and died before Willie walked in, dressed in his Highland Light Infantry uniform, having somehow managed to get home on leave. Strange that the one who caused Da the greatest annoyance should have been the one to let him die happy, but every time I heard this story as a child I wondered how Willie really felt about this crushing story against him.

After the war, with George safe and sound, it was Willie who took the badge and followed Da Clark into the docks. Da was fifty-five when he died, which seemed incredibly ancient to me as I listened to these stories in my childhood, but of course it was very young – and seems more so to me the nearer I get to it myself.

* * *

Another character who figured large in the lives of the Clark children was Granda Johnston, Maw's father. Old William Johnston came from Belfast, where he had been a bacon curer, but he was highly intelligent, a man of good taste and some education. He drove the less academic of the Clark children to distraction by waiting outside school to drag them to libraries and museums. He learned Scots Gaelic, for instance, and read music and became determined to teach his grandchildren whatever current interest he had, thudding them on the skull if they didn't perform well. My mother was the clever one of the family, the dux of Glasgow High School for Girls, as she never tired of reminding us. Nan at least showed some promise and he liked her but poor old Willie, at the other end of the scale, had to climb over the back wall of his school to escape from the self-appointed dominie.

From Da the 'Dark Yins' got their demeanour and sense of themselves, but it was perhaps from Granda Johnston that they got their appreciation that the way out was through learning and with that their determination that their children would be educated. Though quite why the message got through chiefly to them I cannot say.

Granda Johnston stole everything he could lay hands on as he got older and the family turned a blind eye to it. His favourite time was during the blackout, when everything walked under cover of darkness, but he didn't confine himself to it by any means. He would set out on a mass visit of the family and ask to wash his hands in each house, slipping the soap into his pocket when he was finished. Another trick was to pretend to be asleep, then when attentions were elsewhere, he would sneak whatever was on the table into a paper bag and resume his 'snooze'.

My only memory of him is of an occasion after the War when he hadn't noticed my brother Laurie in the room, lying in wait for him. As the old lad pocketed a bag of sugar, Laurie's voice rang out, 'Mammy! Granda Johnston's stealin' oor sugar again!' As he died in 1950, when I was two years old, I'm not sure if I was really there, or if I've heard the story so often that I just think I was.

Granda Johnston was a passionate Orangeman and a Past Master of an Orange Lodge, so it was partly from him that the dichotomy of my upbringing stemmed. Unlike his daughter, Maw Clark, he wasn't bitter, he was, as Nan and Peggy told me, a gentleman. By all accounts he was also a proud Scot despite being an Ulsterman. He used to sing 'MacGregor's Gathering' at family get-togethers with eyes blazing in stern defiance, ending the war song of the outlaw Rob Roy MacGregor with a rousing 'MacGreegor despite them, will flourish F-O-R-E-V-E-R!' He never seemed to notice, in his patriotic fervour, that my father and Willie were fencing around him and between his legs and arms with pokers from the fire, for the entertainment of the others.

It was Willie, naturally, who was given the job of staying with the old lad as he became increasingly confused with age, and he returned to find him dead one day. He got my father to help him lift the body and tidy the house up. All day they tripped over a box in the middle of the floor, and instead of moving it they kicked it out of the way and cursed it as they worked. They found countless sugar packets stuffed with half-crowns and when the coal had been removed from the bath, envelopes full of cash were discovered underneath. In his years of thieving from the family Granda Johnston had managed to put away a tidy sum. Then someone picked up the box from the middle of the floor, or as Willie said, 'Sumbody *honest*' and inside was a fortune in banknotes. Skip and Willie were heartbroken. If they had found it they would naturally have purloined the treasure and not been seen again for some time, instead they had kicked and cursed it all day long.

My father's family, the O'Briens, lived in Tarbet Street, behind the Brae. My grandmother, Mary Ann McCue, had been born in Scotland but her family came from the town of Carlow in County Carlow, to Dundee, where Mary Ann was a weaver. There Mary Ann met Tom O'Brien, whose family came originally from New Ross, in County Wexford. In

23

Dundee, Tom's family had run a guest-house and were quite well-to-do, and Tom was well-educated and well brought up. He was apparently destined for the priesthood, but in the parlance of the day, he got Mary Ann into trouble and had to marry her. Once married they moved to Glasgow, probably to escape Mary Ann's father, and quickly set about founding a dynasty.

Granda Tom was a studious, aesthetic soul and quite unsuited to married or family life, especially with the family he sired. I remember him as a distant, quiet little man with a permanent look of confusion on his face. He was a lithographic printer but gave this up to work as a janitor in St Aloysius in Garnethill, a Jesuit school for Roman Catholic boys. He did so for the simple reason that he wanted to be near the Jesuits, which demonstrates an astonishing lack of responsibility to his wife and the large family he was supposed to provide for.

He loved literature, art and the theatre and to escape from his family he buried himself in these pursuits and in the Roman Catholic Church. He was a devout Catholic, partly I suspect to provide some sort of order in his life. Marriage to Marry Ann was clearly not the life he would have chosen for himself and he was quite incapable of adapting to it. He was highly respected in the community and his growing brood regarded him in much the same light, mixed perhaps with a little pity. He was not like them in any way and they mostly realized this without blaming him. The exception was his son Tommy, who saw Mary Ann's health decline over her many pregnancies and blamed his father for doing nothing to help her. 'He hid nae interest,' Uncle Tommy would say bitterly, 'except when bedtime came.'

Granda Tom's devotion to the Catholic church extended to all his money, and countless black babies in Africa doubtless became good Catholics thanks to his donations. But Mary Ann suffered a slow, painful death from womb cancer when there was no pain relief available except alcohol. She was ill all during my father's childhood, and died, as he said, on his sixteenth birthday in December 1927. Her children suffered from rickets, caused by a lack of calcium in the diet, which was the scourge of working-class children at the turn of the century. Indeed my father couldn't walk until he was four years old because of rickets, and all his life he walked with a characteristic rolling gait. Uncle Tommy never forgave the Catholic Church any more than he forgave his father. 'It wis a' there if they'd looked,' he'd say darkly, 'bit they wurnae ony merr interested than him. They jist took his money an' turned thur faces in the oappisite direction.'

Granda Tom kept his distance from the entire family, and I didn't know him when I was a child, though I recognized him in the street as he hurried by with a curt nod. It probably wasn't that he was a cold man, he just had perfectly understandable reservations. He knew who my father was after all. Granda looked so like Wilfrid Hyde-White, that when I was a child and saw the actor in a film I was convinced he was Granda Tom and accepted his presence on screen without surprise; after all they were both far-removed from my life. He always wore a black suit, tie, topcoat and bowler hat and an immaculate white shirt, though my mother discovered that he wiped his hands on the shirt sleeves after stoking the St Aloysius boiler, so underneath they were as black as his suit.

He didn't have much luck with any of our family, including my brother Laurie, who failed to utter his first word to anyone for years. Once Granda Tom made a rare appearance at a family function and gave Mickey sixpence. 'And you, young man,' he said to Laurie, 'Will only get thruppence, because you won't speak to me.' Laurie was four years old and chose that moment to say his first ever words. 'Stick yer thruppence up yer arse, ya auld bastard!' Granda Tom was helped out, his saintly expression extremely compromised, and he doubtless headed for the nearest chapel to fill up again on piety. But at least it proved that the child wasn't deaf or dumb; he just didn't have anything important to say until that moment . . .

In his later years Granda Tom took to wandering the streets of Glasgow with his rosary in his hands, reciting his prayers aloud. There are parts of the city where this is not advisable, and it was obvious that something had to be done. Even in an age when caring for elderly parents was the norm, he was too far removed from his family for any of them to take him in, but none of them would take responsibility for putting him in a home either. In the end an adult grandson took matters into his own hands and placed the old lad in an old folks' home run by nuns, where he lived happily, rosary safely in hand, to the age of eighty-four. The O'Briens were very relieved to have that responsibility taken off their hands but they still roundly castigated the grandson who had put Granda Tom into the home; he had done the shameful deed, they hadn't.

Granda Tom died in 1952, when I was four years old, and I remember his funeral vividly. It was held in St Aloysius in Garnethill, and as befitted a Knight of St Columba he got the full works. Men in cloaks with scarlet crosses on the shoulders carried the coffin, and they wore large, plumed hats. One of the hats lay on the coffin too, and all around thousands of candles burned, the choir sang, the organ boomed and funny-smelling smoke made me cough. I thought I was at a pantomime and I loved every minute of it.

No one had consulted me on whether or not I wanted to be a Catholic, and as I grew up reluctantly and resentfully within the fold, I realized I had been right. It was all indeed a pantomime.

Chapter Two

By all accounts the O'Brien madness came from the McCue side, in particular from Mary Ann's father, old Hughie McCue. Skip, the youngest of ten, used to tell me tales of visits from his grandfather, visits Mary Ann would bring to an abrupt end. As soon as old Hughie arrived at the house, Skip would be commanded to escort him down to Queen Street Station and put him on the first train back to Dundee, but he never managed it. Old Hughie would go down one set of stairs to the underground men's toilet in High Street and come up the other side. Next time he would do it the other way round, so that his confused grandson could never be sure where he was. He would then bolt into the bars of the city and have a hooley, arriving back on Mary Ann's doorstep whenever it ended naturally or sometimes in the company of the police. 'Every time Ah saw him,' my father would say, 'Ah knew he wid get away frae me an' Ah wis in fur a dunt oan the heid frae ma mither by the end o' the day.'

The Tarbet Street house was more the O'Brien domain than a mere house and it was the setting for many of their ploys. They were bright, witty and inventive and none of them ever really grew up. Throughout their lives they waged a form of psychological warfare against the rest of the world, and each other in particular. It was called the Game, though family members didn't need to call it anything, it was in the blood. In the Game, points were awarded, but only when the players were family. Outsiders hadn't a hope of competing on level terms since they didn't know that the Game existed. Yet they still became its victims, even though no points were awarded for a score against a non-O'Brien.

An insurance man used to call at the house, and when he

was counting out Granny O'Brien's change he had a habit of saying "'ere noo' with some regularity. 'One, two, 'ere noo, three, four, 'ere noo,' an opportunity for amusement that the family could not pass up. One day as he counted out the money, voices came from all over the house, high voices, low voices, unearthly voices, "Ere noo,' "Ere noo,' "Ere noo,' as he counted out each penny. The little man stared at Granny, who gave no indication that she had noticed anything. Everytime he came to the house after that the house rang to the sound of "Ere noos' up and down the musical scale, and still Granny's expression did not change, though apparently she beat the hell out of those she could catch afterwards. This, of course, meant that she had forfeited the points by reacting.

"Ere noo' became a family password, almost a means of identification, and it was written on Christmas cards instead of the more conventional 'From all the family'. Once, many years later, I put it on a telegram from abroad at the end of a message saying when I would arrive home. My father was delighted; all the other words had been put in a numeral code above the written message, but the bemused international operator had been unable to find a numeral that covered it, and there it was, "Ere noo' twice.

On another Tarbet Street occasion years ago that my father loved to tell us about, a travelling salesman's luck ran out. Skip was never sure where the salesman had come from, but he was black, wore a turban and arrived with a full caseload of clothes to sell on a day when the O'Briens were obviously bored and in need of amusement. The salesman was graciously invited in. There his case was emptied, and every one of the family decked out in the contents, layer upon layer, including his turban, which was arranged decorously atop the head of Norah, my father's older sister, who had a passion for hats. Then they sat down in all their finery and took tea together, pinkies stuck out, conversing in terribly polite voices, as though the unfortunate salesman didn't exist, until there was a knock at the door and he grabbed his chance to escape. They later found his coat outside, it had been caught in the door and rather than knock again and risk recapture, he had taken it off and fled, leaving it and all his merchandise behind. The O'Briens were shocked, they had only wanted a bit of fun and hadn't planned to steal the clothes. 'Poor auld bugger,' Skip would say everytime he told the story, 'He wis likely poorer thin us tae. An' he never came back either . . .', and he would shake his head in puzzlement at the strange ways of mankind.

In the basement of Tarbet Street my father in his youth had constructed a full-size boxing ring, and one of the family's favourite leisure activities was to con people into boxing in it. It didn't matter who they were or why they were there, they would be encouraged into the ring to perform. There was also a home-made still for making hooch and they tried every possible concoction of rotgut, none of which ever had a chance of reaching maturity. It would start with the necessity to 'check oan it', and when the checker didn't return another would set off in search of him. Then another, and another, until they were all out cold beside the empty still.

I didn't realize that the O'Briens were odd and wondered why the rest of the population was so boring. The oddest, and to me the most beloved, was Uncle Hughie, very aptly named after Mary Ann's father. At the age of four Hughie was knocked down by a horse-drawn tram and his right leg was severed above the knee, except for a 'sliver o' skin'. While a pair of scissors was located to deal with the sliver, his sister, Norah, (she of the hat fetish), took up a collection from the crowd of onlookers. Norah was an accomplished actress and her tears and sobs could fool the most cynical observer. The amount of performance money raised from this joint venture remained a subject of contention between her and Hughie for the rest of their days. Whenever life was dull Hughie would resurrect the argument and aver that he had been cheated, that Norah had kept more than she had given him when as the star of the show he should have received cash that reflected his leading role. After all, he had sacrificed an entire leg in the venture.

This vile accusation always produced one of Norah's

finest virtuoso performances as the wronged woman, with much sobbing and fainting, though strictly around well-placed chairs – Norah was nobody's fool.

As the drama unfolded Hughie would accuse Norah of wilfully defrauding a one-legged man, her own brother. This was a doubly heinous crime apparently, though in ordinary circumstances it would be regarded as entirely legitimate. Norah would throw herself on the mercy of the assembled audience asking for justice, but it depended who she had cheated last whether she got justice or not on each occasion. It was a highly entertaining show that I watched many times over the years and always with great enjoyment. Norah doubtless did cheat Hughie though, just as he would have cheated her had it been the other way round. But Fate had dealt him the lying down role, and he never quite got over the unfairness of it.

Uncle Hughie grew up with one leg and one wooden crutch, and he regarded that arrangement as the norm. Two legs was, well, deformed somehow. Over the years he was fitted with numerous artificial legs by well-meaning medical people, but he never used them for their intended purpose. One he arranged on the inside of his door, dressed up in a coat, trousers and hat. This, he told everybody, was his twin brother Louis, pronounced Looey to rhyme with Hughie. They had been born with two legs between them, so Hughie had taken the left one and Louis the right. Hughie and Louis lived amicably like that all of Hughie's life, and Louis was accepted by the family and greeted as they entered Hughie's abode.

The other legs meanwhile served more mundane, though perhaps more bizarre functions. For instance, one was used as a rubbish bin. Others were filled with ashes from Hughie's fire and thrown into the River Clyde. Yet another he kept solely for visits from well-meaning social workers, in those days called almoners, who naturally came from non-working-class backgrounds. Hughie had a special leg clad in a black fishnet stocking, which he positioned just sticking out of the side of his set-in bed whenever an almoner called to offer unwanted assistance. Throughout the conversation, which was conducted by Hughie in ultra-polite mode, the protruding leg and the temptress who was supposedly attached to it, was never mentioned, though the almoner couldn't drag her gaze from it.

Hughie could move at an incredible speed with the old wooden crutch and regularly raced two-legged unfortunates for money, winning every time. He once had a fight in George Street with another one-legged man, though no one can remember what it was about. They each balanced on their one good leg and bashed each other with their wooden crutches, while a huge crowd gathered laying bets and cheering on their champion. The contest lasted for hours apparently, with rest periods provided between rounds, and as far as I know Hughie won, though how anyone could tell is a mystery. It's a mental picture that can bring a smile to my face in my darkest moments, a scene so surreal that it could only have Hughie as its author.

A day spent with Uncle Hughie was an honour and to this day I remember every one. As my brother Laurie and I walked along the road with him we had to trot to keep up, and he would lodge the crutch on an electricity junction box or a handy windowsill and suddenly pole vault into the air. He would land with a cry of 'Alley-oop!', and then continue as though nothing had happened. I can still recall the feeling of pride at being related to someone who could accomplish such public feats of silliness and was daft enough to want to. He is clear in my memory still, a small man bent over the old crutch, with the ubiquitous Glasgow bunnet, under which were two bright grey eyes that sparkled and shone with the ever-present promise of mischief, of adventure waiting to begin. I never saw him without the bunnet, and even today when I see someone wearing one I remember him and I can't help smiling.

Uncle Hughie would take us on repeated tours of old Glasgow, each time pointing out the very spot where he had lost his leg all those years ago. All the while he would be giving a gripping running commentary on the events of that day. It didn't take us long to realize that he took us to a different place every time and that he gave many, many versions of how the 'sliver o' skin' had been dealt with, each one more convincing than the last.

As well as various venues throughout Glasgow, he lost that leg in the Crimea, at Waterloo, in the Boer War and in the First World War, according to Hughie. Laurie and I fervently believed all the stories at once because Hughie did. To prove his more heroic claims he had his photo taken wearing every available military uniform. Every one was one hundred per cent genuine, after all, unlike Hughie, the camera never lied.

Hughie was the first of the family to marry, but every day he returned to Tarbet Street. As part of their ongoing psychological warfare, the others would decide that he was 'It', and his knocks on the door and face at the window would be ignored. Eventually he would be allowed in, only to be given his tea in the mug that Granda Tom used to soak his false teeth. The full points were awarded to Hughie, who would drink up the tea with apparent relish and win a dubious victory.

Hughie had newly moved into a little house on a hillside, and, so the story goes, he was touched at the offer by his brothers to decorate it for him. 'A nice Regency stripe,' he ordered, and he left them to it. When he returned they had applied the striped paper horizontally, at the same angle as the hill outside. The pictures on the walls had been papered over, as had every door, which was then carefully cut around for easy access – no one could ever accuse them of being downright *silly*. Once again, though, it was Hughie who won the points by professing himself delighted and he lived with the wallpaper unchanged for years. To this day any home decorating, be it painting or wallpapering, is known within the family as 'A nice Regency stripe', though it's possible that some far-removed relatives might have no idea where it originated.

Despite all the hilarity in Hughie's life, his wife, Maggie, died young after giving birth to five children in very quick succession. Only two made it past babyhood, the others all died from the TB that killed Maggie. Granny O'Brien was still alive at the time and she placed the two surviving girls in convent homes. One died after a fall, aged fourteen, while cleaning windows in the convent, and the other was knocked down and killed by a bus after leaving the convent when she was sixteen. I didn't know any of this when I was a child. In the mythical O'Brien world of fun, sadness was not allowed, I simply regarded Uncle Hughie with adoring affection for the magical creature that he was. It was only in later years that I realized what a sad life he must have had, though he never once showed it. He brought constant joy with his belief that growing up wasn't obligatory, despite what the rest of humanity might think.

As Granny O'Brien had made the supreme sacrifice in honour of my father's sixteenth birthday, I never knew her, but she left a legacy that's still around today. She had a very potent curse, called the Curse of Cromwell, that has to be used with caution. Once put on it cannot be removed, and if it hasn't been used for a while it can become rusty; this is not a curse with a built-in margin for error, it demands exact coordinates. As Skip used to explain, 'It kin get the wan tae the side or jist behind the wan ye waant. So ye need tae be careful.' And the strange thing is that it seems to work. I have had few occasions in my life so serious that Cromwell had to be called into action, but each time he has, some catastrophe has befallen the recipient of the curse. I use it very, very rarely these days, it's too powerful to unleash on an ill-prepared world . . .

Chapter Three

My mother first set eyes on my father when she was ten years old and he was seventeen. She was playing with a piece of chalk, writing names on the pavement. She asked him what his name was and then wrote 'Lawrence O'Brien', which he changed to 'Laurence'; they married seven years later. At first she was prepared to 'turn' with my father and took instruction in the Catholic faith. It didn't last long though; she pronounced it 'A loada noansense', and walked out never to return.

They were married at the start of the traditional Glasgow holiday fortnight, on Fair Friday, 17 July 1936, in St Andrew's Cathedral in Clyde Street, beside the river at the Broomielaw. As a result of Nan's refusal to accept 'the one true faith' the ceremony was carried out at a side altar, while a real Catholic couple had pride of place at the front altar. As a child this slight to my mother made me simmer with rage, and I never understood why my father accepted it for her, after all, he at least knew it to be an insult. My mother thought it was an hilariously funny example of how infantile the whole thing was, and I learned from her that you can only accept an insult if you have some respect for whoever gives it: she hadn't.

After the ceremony they visited Granda Tom at St Aloysius. It was a mark of how isolated he was from his family that he hadn't been at the wedding, but he was due their respect, hence the visit. He wasn't even close enough to have been displeased at his son marrying a non-Catholic, it wasn't anything that concerned him. He was stoking the school boiler and that was when she discovered the secret of his dirty shirt-sleeves. It was my mother's first meeting with her father-in-law and she said he was very nice to them,

34

wished them luck and gave them one-and-sixpence, which they spent on a wedding picture. She looks so young in it that it makes you want to cry 'Foul!'

Laurie Jnr was the most vulnerable of our family. He was born during the war, six months after my father had gone overseas with the Royal Artillery. Skip's letters home showed clearly that he wanted a daughter, and wartime communications were so bad that he didn't find out he had a second son until Laurie was six months old. The only visible proof Laurie had that his father existed was a picture of him taken in dress uniform, which made him look tall, brave and handsome. The reality arrived in the early hours of one morning at the end of the War when Laurie awakened to find a five-foot-tall and perfectly unimpressive Glaswegian in his home. Laurie then went to school to tell the teacher his mother was in bed with a strange man. When told it was his father, he replied, 'Naw it's no'! Ma Daddy's a *big* man!' Laurie never quite recovered from the disappointment and he and Skip never did hit it off. Then to complete Laurie's unhappiness, I arrived soon afterwards, the longed-for daughter, not that I ever fulfilled my parents' dearest dreams in that department. The epitome of feminine charm I never was.

When my father arrived home that night to disappoint Laurie, he had noticed banners all over the street, but it was dark and he didn't stop to read them. Next morning he was borne shoulder high through the neighbourhood and saw that the banners bore the message, WELCOME HOME OUR HERO. Uncle Hughie had spread the story that his younger brother had been awarded the George Cross. He'd even told the local newspapers. My mother, who regarded anything that the O'Briens did to each other as none of her concern, hadn't warned the returning 'hero' and my father had to endure a lavish street party, complete with speeches by minor functionaries. Of course Hughie was nowhere to be seen, though it was my father's firm belief that 'he wis jist roond the coarner, watchin' and laughin'.' The points were shared though, because my father carried it off and never, ever mentioned it to Hughie.

Always missing from our family as we listened to these stories was my brother Mickey. He had been in Mearnskirk Hospital when I was born. As Laurie and I grew up, every available penny went to Mickey's needs, he was after all Nan and Skip's first born and that is always special. It was natural and understandable that in their frustration at being unable to help him, they tried to make sure that he had whatever he wanted. So they spent long hours on public transport going to and from Mearnskirk to deliver little luxuries to Mickey, and because money was tight it was inevitable that Laurie and I got less. It wasn't Mickey's fault and neither was it Nan and Skip's, it was simply one of those things. I had no experience of any other life, but Laurie had. He was deprived of Nan's attention by virtue of Skip's return, Mickey's illness and by my arrival. Laurie had needs too and they were undoubtedly overlooked.

Laurie and I spent a great deal of time together as children during our parents' absences visiting Mickey. I have no particular memory of anything we did, I just know that Laurie was always there. Neither have I any clear memory of our house in Balmano Street, except that it always seemed full of visitors. Gradually I came to realize that this was because of my mother. She was like a magnet to those in trouble, and wherever we lived there would always be a steady stream of people at our door looking for her. It would start with a knock and a voice saying 'Is Nan in?', and in they would come, usually bearing a letter of the official and intimidating kind. This heralded the start of one of her crusades, as she read the letter to the bearer and then discussed the facts. The next thing was to compose a reply, though if she thought the situation merited it she would beard the letter-writer in his den, wherever that might be.

After the War the stock of houses in Glasgow, as in all cities, was low. Throughout the War years no new house-building had taken place and money that should have be spent on repairing those that existed went instead to the War effort. Through Nan's campaigning 21 Balmano Street had been condemned and to stop it falling down it had been shored up on one side, still there was no possibility of a new home. In truth, what the inhabitants of 21 really wanted was a replica with one or two mod cons to sprout up beside the decaying building so that they could go on living together for ever. Even with improvements the housing would hardly have been ideal, but they had no experience of anything better, except for my mother, who had worked as a maid in 'big hooses' in the city when she left school at fourteen. It was always her dream that her children would live in similar 'big hooses', but the reality was Balmano Street which was like an extended family and none of the tenants seriously contemplated life apart. But time was running out as the building continued to rot.

The final collapse came one June night in 1951, after weeks of dry weather gave way to a prolonged and heavy thunderstorm. Sand had been trickling through ceilings all day, then a neighbour asked Nan to come down to her ground-floor home. The woman's sink was disappearing into the kitchen floor, and Nan suddenly realized what was happening. Just then there was a roar like an enormous clap of thunder, and the building started to collapse. Nan ran through 21 shouting at people to get out, knocking on doors and pushing her neighbours to safety. And that is my only clear, sure memory of the Brae, of being outside in the dark with the rain falling and of being in Laurie's arms, a blanket over our heads. Inside the little cave I remember feeling no fear, though all around there was panic, with people shouting and running and the ringing bells of the fire engines, police cars and brown ambulances.

In the middle of this I have a picture of Laurie, who was only a little lad of about eight or nine. He looked totally lost, as though whatever was happening was targeted at him personally. I remember it so well because it was a look I was to see often as we grew up; the night the building collapsed was the first time I registered it. He was a beautiful child, with hair so fair it was silver and big brown eyes, but always that look, as though life had dealt him a massive, unfair and irreversible blow that the rest of us had somehow escaped.

Then Peggy appeared and took me from him, and all was well because she was there. She had been out dancing and had felt that something was wrong, so she had rushed home just in time to see my father coax her mother across an open space four floors up, where their floor had once been. The gable end had fallen into the street below and a yawning chasm had appeared between one half of the building and the other. My father had eased a plank of wood across the divide and managed to get Maw Clark halfway across before it gave way. He caught Maw as she fell, then went next door and did the same with Mary, Nan's sister, and her son David, before the fire brigade arrived.

Meanwhile, as the newspapers reported next day, my mother had got all the other inhabitants of 21 out safely, no-one was even injured. While my mother had been saving neighbours though, Laurie and I had to be rescued by firemen. She had forgotten about us, and we used that against her for years. Of course Skip had forgotten us too, but by the time we were old enough to joke about it, my father's lack of concern for his family was past a joke.

The inhabitants of the building were taken to the Poorhouse at Foresthall by bus that night, but of course Nan refused to go. Instead we stayed with her sister Vicky, the leading 'Fair Yin'; it was a family issue after all, not an inter-family one. I remember press camera lights popping and all night a clock chiming every quarter of an hour, with my parents' voices talking on into the morning light. We didn't know it then, but we had spent our last night with the neighbours of 21, it was the end of the Brae era.

Chapter Four

Blackhill. The name filled Nan with horror. She wanted her children to go up in the world, to have a bright future, to one day live in 'big hooses'. Instead, it would be Blackhill, legendary home of rogues, thieves and murderers. Nan was told by the housing officials that it was only temporary, but she wisely didn't believe them. The Blackhill council estate, or scheme, was started in 1933 as a result of the Housing (Scotland) Acts of 1930/35, with the first tenants moving in, in April 1935. Incongruously, it was built on the site of the Glasgow Golf Club, much to the annoyance of the many senior Glasgow Corporation officials who were members.

For such a prestigous site the surrounding area was surprisingly unattractive. To the south was the Monklands Canal, to the west the Corporation's Provan gas-plant and its railway link. Beside the gas-plant stood the chemical works and nearby, across two tracks, was the White Horse Whisky distillery, known locally as the Bondie. The 872 houses that made up Blackhill were carefully secreted within these borders, to hide it and its residents, who were renowned for their violence and degradation.

The people living in Blackhill were those with no choice, no hope and no power; they were simply deposited there and abandoned. They were drawn chiefly from manual labourers, which meant they were either Irish Catholics or of Irish descent, Irish being synonymous with Catholic to the Glasgow of the time. There had long been a strong anti-Catholic bias in Glasgow, and for many years Catholics were not allowed to be tradesmen. Notices would appear beside job adverts, stating that no Catholics need apply, and even without the actual words, a silent prejudice applied – despite the claims of the PR men it often still does.

Even in the fifties, time-served tradesmen were predominantly Protestant, and of course they earned more and had better job security, so it followed that they also had better homes. So there was a tradition of Catholics being slum-dwellers, and as those slums were replaced by estates like Blackhill, it was logical that Catholic manual workers would form the majority of residents. As with all generalizations of course, others were lumped in who didn't belong. There were Protestants with Irish surnames for instance, or mixed marriages, like that of my parents, or those with nowhere else to go. For Nan that was three-out-of-three, and there was certainly ample evidence to base her fears on, like *the* story about Blackhill: the poisonings of 1949.

It was New Year 1948–9, a time when there was little alcohol available, and a party was in progress, until the booze ran out. A local lad, Terry Donnelly, who worked in the nearby chemical works, led a group of friends to a vat of methyl alcohol in the factory, on the basis that alcohol was alcohol. Bottles were filled and taken back to the house where the party was being held, but methyl alcohol is a poisonous industrial substance used in the manufacture of paint. Those who drank it that Hogmanay, neat or mixed with lemonade or wine, quickly became ill. The lucky ones were blinded for life, but ten men died slow, agonizing deaths.

The incident entered into the folklore of Glasgow, and the media played its shock-horror part, so that Glasgow came to accept that it was typical of the depraved monsters of Blackhill to behave in such a way. There was no sympathy, it simply reinforced the opinions of those who regarded Blackhill as a hell-hole for the hopeless and undeserving.

Terry Donnelly was given thirty days in prison for the theft of the methyl alcohol, a sentence that was regarded as harsh and unnecessary by the people of Blackhill. Though he had ended up unintentionally hurting his own, there was nothing malicious about it, he had meant no harm and had suffered enough by the outcome, and that is still the strong opinion of those who were alive at the time. But, of course, it became the one incident that characterized the place in the minds of many, and though it happened before we moved there, that notoriety was partly responsible for Nan's fears for her family.

Once in, there was little chance of escape, because no one would willingly exchange hell for a house in Blackhill, and wanting a better life and future for your kids added no points on the housing list. After all her years of campaigning to have Balmano Street condemned, the letters written, councillors ambushed and MPs coerced, the collapse of the building had played a sick joke on Nan and we were landed in Blackhill.

No buses or trams ran through it, there was no police station, only one or two shops, no social facilities of any kind and no employment within it. In the Fifties few sociologists had identified these problems and it was generally acknowledged by those outside that those inside were a bad lot and by keeping them together the better areas of the city would be that much safer. Nowadays I look at the South African townships, the ghettoes for the black or Indian people in America and the Aborigines of Australia; places that are no more than reservations to keep them in one place and contain them for whatever the authorities may wish to inflict on them, and Blackhill springs easily to mind. It was our punishment for the crime of being poor.

There were three distinct areas of the development: Blackhill Rehousing (a coy name for slum clearance), Blackhill Extension and Blackhill Intermediate. The first two were built along the lines of the traditional tenements and each housed the same kind of tenants, while the Intermediate were four-in-a-block houses of very much superior quality, and reputation. The Intermediate area was intended for the respectable poor rather than the disreputable poor. Those who lived in the Intermediate part referred to it as High Riddrie, in an attempt to disassociate themselves from the rest of Blackhill.

We moved into the rehousing part of Blackhill, though if anyone we didn't know asked where we came from, Nan always said Riddrie. This wasn't out of snobbery, but out of self-defence. The stigma of Blackhill was indelibly and irrevocably applied to all, and its residents were routinely

41

subjected to abuse. Indeed it wasn't unusual for children who ventured the few miles to the park in Alexandra Parade, in the respectable Riddrie/Dennistoun area, to be stopped by the police and questioned, before being sent back 'tae fuck where ye belang.' So if we saw the police we ran, though we had done nothing wrong.

There was no area for children to play in, a common cry heard in every council housing scheme to this day, but the children of Blackhill wouldn't have agreed. For a start there was the canal. The last words every child, including Laurie and I, heard going out to play were, 'See an'keep away frae that canal!' This of course ensured that we headed straight for it, because it had two elements that made it irresistible: parental disapproval and the sure knowledge that water is provided on earth to be played with and in by children. We never told Nan that we played there though, we knew it would only worry her.

In those days the attractions of the Monklands Canal ran to clear water, water birds, and live fish just waiting to be caught, not to mention all manner of flotsam and jetsam that challenged us to make them into rafts. Drownings were common and were accepted by the local kids almost as an occupational hazard. After each one a petition would do the rounds of Blackhill asking for the canal to be filled in, which the children of the area regarded as a gross infringement of their rights. There was nothing to worry about though, no one with the power to do so took any notice of petitions from Blackhill, and the canal remained there to tempt the local children until it was filled in to make way for the construction of the M8 motorway. The City Fathers had their priorities after all, the safety of the local kids counted for nothing. And when they did fill in the canal it was ironic, to put it kindly, that one form of environmental pollution was simply exchanged for another, the exhaust fumes of cars, buses and lorries. In the fifties the canal was part of our daily lives, something we lived with, and we never really considered it to be the danger that our parents did, though of course it was.

The railway lines ran behind the tenements at the lower

half of Acrehill Street, and there was also one, big triangle of grass. Bordered along the top of Royston Road, it had the gasworks, chemical plant and a railway track on one side, and the whisky bond and another track on the other. In those days no one had heard of the hazards of industrial pollution and, even if they had, in the eyes of our 'betters' it would have been regarded as good enough for our kind of people. Anyway, where else was there for us to go to if we didn't like where we lived? There was a lot of sickness, mainly eye trouble, and chest infections that settled into chronic bronchitis over the years. From the whisky distillery, the Bondie, ran a small stream carrying the effluent of whatever mysterious processes took place inside, but to the children it was a burn and, therefore, like the canal a legitimate place to play. We were disappointed, though, that no fish swam there.

Trains coming from the distillery-end met up at the point with those coming from the gasworks and chemical factory track, so to get to the grassy area in the middle we had to cross the line. Sometimes a railway man would descend from his signal box and attempt to chase us off. But until he did I would lie on my back, lost in the long grass, staring at the sky above, overcome at the immensity of it and wondering where it ended, as the other kids fought and played around me. It was the first feeling I had of being able to stretch my eyes, and the awakening of an awareness that there was existence beyond the streets and houses where I lived.

We lived at 34 Acrehill Street, a long, curved street of drab, grey-stone tenements like all the others, built in rows throughout Blackhill. Nan's sister Mary, and her son David, who had lived beside us at the Brae, were at 43. Maw Clark and Peggy had a house in Moodiesburn Street, towards the better Riddrie/Provanmill end.

Like all tenements there was an entrance, the close, which connected all the houses from the bottom storey to the top, and through to the backcourt, but in Glasgow it means more than a passageway. A close is a place in its own right, it's a meeting place, a talking shop, and tenement dwellers feel a strong sense of ownership over their closes. The close at

34, leading up to our first-floor home, had a distinctive atmosphere, just as every other one did to its owners. This time we had two bedrooms, a kitchen, sitting/dining-room and an inside toilet, so the house itself was luxury compared to Balmano Street. Just inside the kitchen, on the left, was the coal-bunker, and at the top, on the right beside the sink, stood the gas boiler. It was about the size of a large oil drum, with a gas ring below, and this was where the family washing was done. Mondays were boring days, because Nan had to boil the clothes up, then rub them with Fairy soap over the corrugations of the washing board, and put them through a mangle into the sink. Then she had to rinse them and mangle them again, and sometimes again. All this took a great deal of time, and on Nan's part a greater deal of effort, and I'd hear her puffing and panting while trying to keep singing, as she always did about the house. Until the washing was safely on the line, though, we couldn't go out and I had to hang around, bored and impatient to see Peggy.

The houses of the other Brae refugees were strung out between ours and Peggy's, and whenever we passed, old neighbours would rush out for a reunion. They clung to each other like prisoners in a foreign land, which indeed they were, with Nan the only point of safety, and they could never let her pass their doors.

Before long 34 became established as the place to go when in trouble, and the familar, steady stream of worried women, clutching letters and looking for Nan became the norm. Once again I didn't realize it at the time, but I was witnessing the much-denied link between wealth – or the lack of it – and education. Most of the people who brought their problems to my mother did so because they could neither read nor write. They weren't stupid and they weren't illiterate through choice, it simply went with their abject poverty and lack of power over their own lives. It came with the territory of deprivation.

Nan would read the proffered letter or listen to the story and we would hear her say, 'Noo, that's no' right . . . ,' the words that signified the start of another campaign. As in the Brae, if the matter was relatively simple she would compose and write a reply to the hapless sender of the offending letter, but if the situation was dire she would be instantly off in search of the miscreant, to sort it out face-to-face. People, she fervently believed, were basically good, and no one meant harm to another. There was only Right, and once any minor misunderstandings were explained, Right would be universally accepted and sweetness and light would prevail. It was her mission in life to do the explaining, for the simple reason that she could.

Skip maintained that the initials, HC, in the middle of her name, were born of the panic Nan induced in Council Officials. 'They see hur comin,' he would say, 'an' shout "Joan – Holy Christ! – O'Brien!" Then they a' run away hame.' She was anybody's idea of an earth mother, plump and maternal, with soft, concerned brown eyes that betrayed every emotion, dark brown hair caught up in a bun from which it was forever threatening to escape, and she always had a child by the hand. In her battles with officialdom she used this to its fullest advantage of course, knowing exactly what kind of Blackhill representative her adversaries were expecting. The best clothes were brought out and freshly pressed, stocking seams checked for ramrod straightness, hair carefully brushed and me (the 'wean') scrubbed clean. It caught 'them' off guard to be confronted with a well turned-out, articulate and polite matron instead of the stereotype they expected from the badlands of Blackhill. She then hit them with an impassioned honesty that could melt the heart of the hardest bureaucrat, and she usually emerged victorious, with respect and dignity preserved on both sides. As the youngest of her three children I was a pre-school accomplice on her missions, and I was trained to sit quietly without interrupting and to be well-mannered when spoken to. Nan didn't miss a trick when her heart was in the fray.

Years after my mother had died, I was in Glasgow City Chambers for what I thought was the first time. It is an extremely ornate building with extravagant use made of different kinds of marble and much opulent gilding of the lily; once seen never forgotten, even if you try hard. Halfway up a landing I turned left into an instantly recognizable place:

at the top of the next flight of stairs Nan had stood shaking hands with a tall, white-haired man at the end of a meeting, and he had given me the unheard of sum of half-a-crown, which my mother had immediately confiscated and handed back to him, declaring it to be 'too much'. My father at that time would have been earning something in the region of two pounds per week, and I had been handed the huge sum of an eighth of one pound! I remembered vividly how difficult it had sometimes been to be quiet and well-mannered, especially when my mother lost me the untold wealth of a half-crown. The memory was so clear that I could almost locate the three figures in mid-air as I followed the voices in my mind, but the reason for our being there was lost, if indeed I ever knew it. Undoubtedly though it had started with that knock at the door and an anxious voice asking, 'Is Nan in?'

This was the Teddy Boy era, intensified in Glasgow by the Catholic/Protestant divide, and there were running street fights every night, so Nan enforced a curfew after dark. I grew up hearing my father trying to calm her down as the sounds of battle ripped through the darkened streets, but being used to it I fell asleep quickly; it was just another familiar part of normal life. One night, though, Maw Clark had been taken to the Royal Infirmary with one of her terminal illnesses, and by the time the family had been reassured that she would live to con them another day, it was night time.

Arriving at our close we found a fight in progress, with four Teds against one. Skip, being a street-wise Glaswegian with a well-developed instinct for survival, turned and walked back out. Nan instinctively waded in though, wielding the ever-present message bag that served as both handbag and shopping-bag for working-class women. She had made it herself at a craft class at a local school, but never had she envisaged using it as a weapon. She brought it down on whatever head was nearest, and grabbed handfuls of hair, the knives and razors flashing around her. 'Bit Missus O'Brien,' shouted one of the men, 'He's a Proddy!' not knowing that so was Mrs O'Brien, not that it mattered.

She saw them off then took the victim into our house and cleaned him up, all the while lecturing him on how his mother must feel with him mixed up in knife fights. 'Missus O'Brien,' he said wearily, 'Ah huvnae seen ma mammy since Ah wis a wean o'three.' Listening at the door I wondered what this could mean. Life was simple; fathers went to work if they had it, mothers stayed at home to look after the house and the children. So why hadn't he seen his mother for such a long time? When he'd gone I asked Nan about it and she told me with a frown that the boy's mother had run away from home leaving him behind. This made me wonder even more; what terrible thing could he have done to make his mother run away from him?

Gradually, and to her great embarrassment, Nan became known as 'a guid wumman', and our home became a haven for neglected children whose mothers were away from home, either temporarily or permanently. If a mother couldn't find her child she came to our house, knowing that the child would be there, safe, fed and cared for. Children waited outside our close for her during the day happy to walk along the long road with her to the bus-stop, where the local gangs stepped aside to let her on first, though she tried not to notice. I only really became aware that Nan was different once I started school, and realized that the other kids tumbled out at going home time and fought to have her tie their laces. 'Kin ye still no' tie yur ain laces?' she would ask in mock disapproval, and the kids would grin back at her, 'Ah don't know whit kinda school that kin be!' With an exaggerated sigh she would put down the ubiquitous message bag. 'A'right then,' she'd say, 'Gimme yur fit oan ma knee.' It had always happened, but there was one day that I looked at the scene from the outside for the first time and wondered: why Nan? I wasn't bothered by it and neither was I particularly impressed, I simply noticed it consciously for the first time. By taking up a few minutes of her time the kids weren't depriving me of anything. They only wanted to bask in a little of her warmth, and she always had more than enough of it to go round.

47

Chapter Five

We were always aware that our friends' brothers, uncles and fathers disappeared into Glasgow's notorious Barlinnie Prison. It was known locally as the Bar-L, or more confusingly given Nan's ambitions for us, the Big Hoose. One day our cousin David boasted that he knew where Barlinnie was and Laurie dared him to take us there. We walked along the canal bank and stopped opposite a café on Cumbernauld Road called the Golfer's Rest, reputed to be a meeting place for the Teds. The stark, raw brutality of Barlinnie rose before us over the trees, and even though I was only about four years old, I felt a shiver run through me; the place was so patently what it was. As we stood there, engrossed in recounting the horror stories we had heard about the place, we became aware of three men standing behind us. One was Billy Fullarton, the leading Protestant baddie, and the other two we knew by sight as his henchmen and bodyguards. 'Walk!' said Fullarton, pointing back in the direction we had come from, and with a feeling of dumb terror we were trailed all the way home by them in total silence. I felt like a puppet with slack strings, nothing in my entire body was coordinated and I was cold all over. I was only a child, but I really believed that I was about to die.

At the foot of Acrehill Street, Fullarton leaned down and stared into the deepest recesses of our young souls. 'Yer mammy's a decent wee wumman,' he said, 'She'd no' like ye gaun near that place. It's a bad, bad place. So don't go near it again, or Ah'll see tae ye. Unnerstaun'?' He then released us to walk home alone in a state of shock; we were like hostages who had expected to be shot only to be inexplicably released instead. With every step there was an urge to turn around and see if he was still there, but we resisted it rather than be killed by one more glance from Fullarton's cold, hard eyes. When Nan opened the door it was like walking into a different world, like Dorothy opening the door after the storm to reveal the brilliant technicolour of the Land of Oz. I could smell gooseberry pie which was one of her specialities and up till then had always been one of my favourites. To this day I only have to see a gooseberry yoghurt to feel Fullarton's gaze on me and the terror I felt that day rushes back.

It took me a long time to work out why he had let us walk those last awful yards home alone. Nan would have been horrified if someone like him had arrived on her doorstep and obviously Fullarton knew this, so he had simply saved her the embarrassment. He knew the difference between Them and Us and he had acknowledged it that day in deference to Nan, who was 'a decent wee wumman'.

After that, whenever our paths crossed, he would stare at us coldly as he exhaled a long, slow stream of cigarette smoke, and we knew that he knew that we would never forget. Some time later I was on my way to the dentist and was wearing a scarf around my mouth, the traditional badge of the toothache sufferer. Waiting at the bus-stop with Nan I was aware of Fullarton and his two henchmen there too. To my horror, and doubtless even more to Nan's, I saw him approach us. He put his hand in his pocket, brought out a half-crown and put it into my hand. 'Ye kin get sweeties efter,' he said, and walked back to his friends. Nan took it from me and threw it away later. 'Ye don't know who he carved up tae get his hauns on that,' she told me, 'It's tainted hen.' It was a relief to get rid of it, after all it had belonged to Billy Fullarton, but even so, I wondered if I'd ever get to keep a half-crown while Nan was around.

Fullarton's intrusion into the civilian ranks had been exceptional, because the gangs were identifiable armies and though they lived among us they never truly lived with us. There was a subtle code that we picked up, like never establishing eye contact and never, ever talking to them. I wasn't aware of being told this, it was part of a collective sixth sense that we absorbed and was as natural and essential to Blackhill children as breathing. As a result we never felt that we would be harmed and neither were we. If a fight broke out when children were around we would simply move quickly out of the way or be moved by the adults present, so that the distance between the civilians and the fighting men was always maintained. Nan though, without that instinct born of childhood experience, saw danger everywhere and was unable to distinguish between real trouble and the imaginary kind. To her every minute we lived in Blackhill was filled with potential danger, and every second that passed safely was a bonus.

Laurie, David and I once dug up a gun wrapped in oilcloth in the backcourt, a hand-gun just like the ones we saw in the cowboy films. We fought over it all day, taking turns at pretending to fire it at each other, until we reached impasse on who should get to keep it. Just like everybody else, we took our dispute to Nan for mediation. She went totally to pieces when she saw the gun. The curtains were drawn, the door locked and for some illogical reason our prize was put into the coal-bunker. When Skip came home he took the gun back to where we had found it and re-buried it, and as far as he was concerned that was the end of it. Not for Nan though; it was weeks before she slept properly again, and whenever she saw a gang member she went through the closed curtains, locked door routine all over again, convinced that we would all be murdered in our beds for finding the gun. Laurie, David and I watched over our buried treasure from various close-mouths for a while to see who might come back for it. When no one did we remembered better things to do and gave up, so we never did find out who had left it there, and for all I know it could be there still.

The hard men of the gangs made their livings outside their home areas and not by robbing or cheating their own neighbours, so they kept on the right side of them. No-one in Blackhill would have grassed on any of the gangs, and not entirely through self-interest, but also because they took care to give us little to complain about. Besides, the police were our common enemy, so there was no one to grass to.

There was a convention that men didn't swear in front of women and children, so the first time I ever heard the phrase 'Fenian bastards' was from the police. Having an ear for words I of course repeated it perfectly to Nan, keen to know what it meant. Once she recovered she explained that it meant a Catholic who didn't have a father. ''Cos he's in the Bar L?' I asked. 'Aye hen,' she replied in a distracted kind of way, 'Sumthin' like that, bit don't you say it tae thum, they might no' like it.' Later, when she thought I was out of earshot, I heard her telling Peggy, as she told Peggy everything, and the two of them laughed till they cried. Then they looked at me, and I looked at them and they laughed again, till we were all three clinging together giggling. I was laughing because I was delighted to have caused them such happiness, if only I could work out why and how I'd done it . . .

The gangs survived materially by turning over factories, shops and businesses in other parts of the city, and their only money-spinners within Blackhill were protection rackets involving the pubs and illegal bookies. There was a little money-lending, but to fellow rogues, not to the ordinary punters, and of course there was dealing in stolen property. Most of the trouble that did break out that wasn't purely sectarian, was because one lot had moved in on another's territory, or someone hadn't paid up on a deal, and in that way the violence was contained within the 'armies'.

Nan's constant fear was a thing of puzzlement to me, because living in Blackhill gave me a feeling of security and safety that I have never regained and as a child I was supremely happy there. Peggy was near enough to visit every day, and *en route* we also saw the other refugees from Balmano Street. Yet from the day we moved into the house at 34 Nan was trying to get out. She would send letters to all the council officials she had approached countless times on behalf of other people, and make endless visits to meet councillors and MPs. None of it worked of course, there were no houses anywhere except those that no one else wanted, which meant houses in the worst areas, like Blackhill. Though her affection for and empathy with the ordinary people was to grow over the years, Nan never came to terms with living there and never lost her fear of the hard men.

One of the local characters who made Nan nervous lived at the top of of our street. From a ground floor house, a man leaned on his window-sill all day, every day. He talked to all the children going to and from school and gave us thruppenny bits for the ice-cream van that stopped outside his house. Skip always spent time talking to the man, but though Nan tried she seemed uneasy. When I mentioned this to Skip, he said with a laugh, 'Yer ma's mair genteel than the rest o' us.' Years later I learned that the man had married 'a bad yin', and had come home one day to find his kids locked out in the rain and his wife locked in with another man. In the fight that followed he had killed her, but he must have been convicted of culpable homicide (manslaughter) to have escaped the noose in those days.

When I knew him he was an old man and had served whatever sentence he had been given. He had never seen his kids again, so he lived through the lives of the neighbourhood kids for thruppence a time, a gentle soul who gave out no feeling of threat or danger, except to Nan, who was 'mair genteel'. It was part of her inability to judge Blackhill accurately that she couldn't relate one hundred per cent to him, though he was the kind of underdog that she would normally do battle for. Whenever the capital punishment debate resurfaces and I hear murderers described as monsters and perverts, somehow I can't help thinking about him; just an ordinary man who had lost everything, and regretted it everytime he saw a child.

Further down the long, crescent-shaped street, round about where it curved, was a different kind of man altogether. He was the father of a mentally handicapped boy of about ten, called Bobby. I never knew exactly what was wrong with Bobby, he was just 'no 'right'; he used to watch all the other kids out of his window but he wasn't allowed to join us and he didn't go to school. For long spells we never saw him, then he'd reappear again, watching from his window. One day Nan had a deputation of women at the door to report that Bobby had been heard being beaten up by his father and was badly bruised on the side of his face. Some of the women had gone to see Bobby's father and had been sent away with screams of abuse ringing in their ears, and poor Bobby got it again. Nan went to see the local health visitor, called the Green Lady because of the colour of her uniform, but she got short shrift too, and no one thought of involving the police because we knew better than to trust them. To the police, who came from outside, everyone in Blackhill was scum, fit only to be raided and thrown into the back of Black Marias en route for the Bar L, and it was accepted that we took care of our own problems without involving them. In fact, the unspoken rule about not looking directly at the hard men and not trying to engage them in conversation also held good where the police were concerned, and however bad a villain might be, no one would ever have helped the police to take him away.

Across the street from Bobby lived a woman called Mrs Logan. Her home was like a palace, everything spick and span and displaying riches beyond our experience. While we were lucky to have lino on all our floors, Mrs Logan had fitted carpets, and a taxi picked her up whenever she ventured outside, one of the few times we saw a car in Blackhill. It was said that Mrs Logan was Billy Fullarton's aunt. So Nan and I went to see her, which was an unbelievable treat for me, because Mrs Logan seemed to have an endless supply of biscuits and cakes. When we went back next day I really thought my boat had come in, but sitting there were Billy Fullarton and his two friends and suddenly I couldn't force down a crumb of the feast Mrs Logan had laid before us.

Nan hadn't acknowledged Fullarton's presence and he hadn't addressed a word to her either. Avoiding his eyes, Nan seemed to tell Bobby's story to no one in particular. Fullarton listened, his face taut and expressionless and those hard, icy eyes staring at her. When she had finished he still said nothing. As we were leaving he put a hand on my head and I drew back instinctively. 'It's a'right wee yin,' he said

53

with what passed for a smile, 'Ah don't hurt weans. Except fur bad weans mibbe. Ur you a bad wean?' Then he laughed, which was just as well because I couldn't have thought of a reply. Afterwards, as we walked along past the two closes between Mrs Logan's house and ours Nan was shaking, and when she got inside she locked the door and made cup after cup of tea.

A couple of nights later there was a commotion in Bobby's close which we took as part of normal life at the time, but next day we saw Bobby's father badly bruised and cut about the face. He never touched the boy again, in fact whenever Nan stopped to talk to Bobby, his father was positively deferential. After all, she had Billy Fullarton at her beck and call, though she never admitted having any part in what had occurred.

To my great chagrin we never went near Mrs Logan and her Aladdin's Cave of goodies again, in fact my mother would take long detours to avoid passing the house. Sometimes in her attempts to avoid Mrs Logan Nan would get lost in the maze of backcourts and closes, and being more familiar with them I would guide her safely home. This meant clambering over middens, the three-sided, concrete structures with sloping roofs where the rubbish bins were kept. I discovered that Nan was no good at dealing with middens, and, if anything, worse at climbing or squeezing through the iron railings that separated the tenement back-courts. I remember feeling mildly embarrassed by her lack of aptitude in such ordinary skills.

Whenever we did pass her house, Mrs Logan would shout down to us to come up, but Nan always had an excuse. All those cakes and biscuits, all that luxury, was lost to me for ever. There were times when I just couldn't understand my mother; she wanted the good life for us, but whenever we got close to it she threw it away.

I can only recall actually witnessing one warrant sale in Blackhill, though I knew one was probably taking place if I saw a car. We only saw cars if a doctor, the police or the sheriff officers, or bailiffs, came calling. Warrant sales took place when someone couldn't pay a debt, and their possessions were sold off to make it up. Given the level of poverty of some families, or maybe because of it, there were fewer sales than might have been expected, because sheriff officers were reluctant to venture into Blackhill to enforce the warrant. There was never any actual violence that I remember, but the reputation of the place worked in our favour in a way and certainly the women used it to its full advantage to create an atmosphere of menace.

The goods being sold off, few as they were, often went to the sheriff officers themselves at knock-down prices, so the local women pooled whatever money they could lay hands on and bought everything up, then returned it to the victim. I didn't regard this as heroic at the time any more than the women themselves did. They knew that if their turn came next the same rescue operation would be mounted for them. It was part of the way things were to me as a small child, but looking back now from an era where nobody cares much about anyone else, and especially knowing how tight money was in those days, I admire their strength and decency in a way I feel but can't adequately explain.

On that particular day I was off school with tonsillitis, a constant complaint throughout my childhood, and I was hanging onto the handles of Nan's message bag as she and the other women made their way to the home of the hapless debtor. The sheriff officers had taken the precaution of bringing police protection with them, a move that amused the women and made their loathing of both stronger. After all, what kind of men could they be, to be afraid to face a bunch of women without bringing the police for protection? The sheriff officers and the police saw it as a demonstration of strength, but the women regarded it as an admission of fear. Nothing much happened, the goods were snapped up by the women but I can remember the tension as they stood in ranks so close that the intruders could barely move. When the sale ended the weeping woman once more took possession of her bits and pieces. As the sheriff officers were leaving the close Nan couldn't contain herself any longer.

'Excuse me!' she called after a bowler-hatted sheriff

officer, 'Ah wis wonderin' aboot yer mother. Is she still alive?' He stopped for a moment, puzzled, and stuttered that his mother was dead.

'Likely died o' shame,' Nan replied, as the other women gathered around. 'Hur wean growin' up tae dae this tae decent people.'

'I get no pleasure from this kind of thing,' the creature said, 'I am only doing my job.'

'Aye,' Nan said softly, 'Sumbody will've gied ye orders right enough. It's no' really your fault like.'

'Exactly!'

'Is that no' whit the Nazis said tae?' she asked.

'I don't need to take this from the likes of you! I fought in the War!'

'Bit oan whit side?' Nan retorted, 'Ah hope tae God it wisnae oors 'kis oor men wur surely *men*!' The other women formed a semicircle behind Nan as the police moved in to shepherd the sheriff officer towards his car. Nan reserved her fire until the car door was open and he had one foot off the ground ready to climb in.

'Ye don't seem sich a bad wee man,' she said kindly, 'Bit ur ye no' black affronted at earning yer livin' in this *durty* wey?'

He hesitated just long enough to register that her barb had gone straight home, before climbing into the car and being driven off. His chin rested on his hand and his face was turned away in an attempt to convey his complete lack of concern. But the women had witnessed that split second of hesitation as he got into the car and they knew better. Their derisive laughter rang out, and though I had no real understanding of what had happened, I knew we had won somehow; Nan had been taking lessons from the O'Briens. Yet much to my puzzlement, she hurried home, closed the door and burst into floods of tears. Then she made a cup of tea and got on with her housework, singing as she always did. I understand now, of course. She was crying tears of humiliation and rage, the tears of the helpless and powerless.

* * *

And yet despite the harshness of Blackhill life, it was for me filled with the magic of childhood. The summers were just as long and sunny, the winters as full of sparkling snow as anywhere else. Indeed, the only time I ever saw Santa Claus was in Blackhill. I slept in a bed cabinet in my parents' bedroom and on that Christmas morning I must have wakened just as Santa was leaving, because certainly I heard a noise that made me ignore my presents. I ran to the window and looked out – and there he was! He was just above ground level, guiding the sleigh through the air, laden with presents, giving instead of taking, and the sleigh was pulled by two long lines of reindeer. I tried to waken my parents but they didn't seem interested, so they probably missed their only chance to prove the existence of Father Christmas. I can still see in my mind's eye today what I saw that dark, early morning, and it really was Santa, it really, really was . . .

Chapter Six

Peggy was the only unmarried Clark, a gentle, vivacious woman with a lovely smile and quiet nature. My mother was regarded as the brains of the family, but together she and Peggy formed the core, even to the 'Fair Yins'. Peggy was less articulate than my mother, less intense, but they were two parts of one character. Nan was the doer, but only after discussing everything with her sister, including the approach to Fullarton through Mrs Logan. Peggy would never have had the courage to actually do it, but she would have agreed with the plan or Nan wouldn't have carried it out.

Nan and Peggy met every day, it would have been unthinkable not to because they needed each other, and I grew up the third part of a tight eternal triangle. Peggy's one ambition was to get married and have a family of her own, but there was a feeling about her of being one of nature's spinsters, a custom-made maiden aunt. If that was what fate had decreed, Peggy wasn't for accepting it though.

Weddings drew her like a magnet and she would stand for hours outside a church if she happened on a wedding, just for a glimpse of the happy couple, then she would smile for the rest of the day. If you saw a wedding when she wasn't there you had to recall it in great detail while her eyes misted over with the romance of it all. I used to dread being in town with her, because she would never go home until we had visited every wedding-dress shop for miles and admired every creation available. Having spent so much time in the company of Laurie I was a confirmed tomboy and very definitely not a lace and flounces child. Despite this Peggy's plan was that when she married I'd be her bridesmaid and so, she claimed, she *had* to window shop. I used to cringe at the frilly concoctions she dreamt up for me, but she never noticed, she was eternally lost in her dream.

58

Babies also left her dewy-eyed. Like my mother she had the unconscious ability to draw children to her, and Peggy hadn't my mother's experience of the reality to dampen her romanticism. Peggy wasn't interested in having a good time, she was interested only in settling down and starting a family. This naturally put men off, especially those who had returned from years of war-service and just wanted some fun.

Her taste in men was notoriously awful, and each one would be brought to my mother for approval. The waifs, the strays, the wasters, misfits and the undesirables, somehow they all found their way to Peggy and she convinced herself that each and every one was a god. Add to that list of catches the ones she fancied but never got near, all of them reprobates to a man, and Peggy's reputation as a magnet for disaster was safe for all time. I don't think she ever noticed my mother's grimaces, she was lost in her dream and adored each god who chanced along.

When each relationship failed my mother would heave a sigh of relief, until the next unsuitable match arrived on the horizon. Uncle George, the other 'Dark Yin', would seek out my mother and plead with her to put Peggy off whichever man she was seeing through her eternally rose-tinted gaze this time, and my mother would assure him it wouldn't last anyhow.

Peggy, much as they loved her, was a constant worry, she was too gentle for the world, too trusting and in need of protection. She had a heart of marshmallow and was easily moved to tears, which in turn moved my mother to tears. They'd stand there together, mopping their eyes, then the scene would strike them as silly and funny and they'd laugh, which in turn caused more tears. The vicious circle would continue until they were exhausted by it all and were rendered red-eyed and out of breath, unable to look at each other without suffering a massive relapse. Each blamed the other on these occasions, but in truth it was impossible to tell where one ended and the other began. They were equally to blame, though neither could ever explain why they were laughing or how it had all started. 'Wait a minute! Wait a minute! Whit wur we laughin' it?' one or other would demand breathlessly, which was more than enough to start it all up again. I used to watch them, holding their sides and groaning but unable to stem the laughter or the tears, hanging onto each other for support and demanding that the other 'Stoap it noo!' No O'Brien could have or would have been able to abandon themself to such glorious, all-consuming emotion and mirth.

As part of her quest for marriage and motherhood, Peggy regularly enlisted the help of Norah, Skip's sister. Norah had a strong theatrical bent, as her performances with Hughie showed, and had decided that she could tell fortunes. This she did by reading teacups, and before each 'reading' she did for Peggy she would quiz me carefully about what was happening in Peggy's life. Thus was she able to come up with amazing details, almost as if someone had told her, and Peggy believed every word she uttered. *The* man was forecast several times and he never arrived, but that didn't put Peggy off. After all, look at the things Norah knew about her . . . There must be something in it . . .

Peggy was a highly skilled welder, a trade she had learned during the War. She made tabernacles for the Catholic church, the ornate little domes that house the Eucharist on church altars. Given the bitterness of Maw Clark's Orange leanings, this of course made Nan and Peggy laugh more than anything else did. Maw had an orange pin cushion, and embroidered on it was King William of Orange sitting on his white horse. Whenever Skip went into the Moodiesburn Street house he would insert pins in strategic parts of King Billy's anatomy, which would bring Maw screaming to remove them. This always puzzled me; what else could one do with a pin cushion but stick pins in it? Was it a dastardly plot invented by the Catholic church to manufacture the pin cushions and sell them to devotees of the Loyal Orange Order, so that pins *would* be stuck in King Billy? As with all running jokes, everyone, especially the children, joined in, so that King Billy was perpetually covered in pinholes. It wasn't because we were bigoted, we didn't understand any of it. All we knew was that it was a marvellous way to greatly upset Maw Clark.

★   ★   ★

The O'Briens were regarded by the Clarks with guarded affection, as honoured guests that they were lucky to have among them. The O'Briens of course accepted this as their due, with dignity and condescension and they put their usual ploys on hold, never subjecting the Clarks to any warfare. They were family, but family once removed after all and not up to the Game. There was no enjoyment in scoring points over an opponent who wasn't up to standard. Wisely the Clarks were never sure of them, though they loved to have them at family gatherings. It was like sin by proxy, as the O'Briens did and said the kind of things that the Clarks wanted to, but never dared.

Skip, Hughie and another brother, Pat, were famed for their sand-dance, shirt-tails out, trousers rolled up and pots on their heads. They scattered ashes on the floor from the fireplace of wherever they were, and performed their master-piece in total silence, and the sight of the five O'Brien legs sent the Clarks into their usual heaving, creaking laughter. For me the delight was in seeing the Clarks all holding onto each other, tears running down their faces, totally aban-doned to their mirth. The sand-dance itself was common-place, after all I was an O'Brien and had seen it many times.

The O'Briens reserved their gentlest treatment for Peggy, who was shy with them and blushed as Hughie kissed her hand or sang her praises. There was something about her that brought out their sensitive side, and not many people could do that to the O'Briens. They would have fun with Nan by suggesting that Hughie and Peggy would make a good match, and Nan would scream with horror. 'Wan o' us bein' married intae this lot is bad enough!' she'd declare, 'Oor Peggy disnae deserve that!' She knew of course that they were having her on, but the enjoyment for them was that they knew Nan could never be entirely sure.

Clark family gatherings usually celebrated someone's birthday, Glasgow Fair holidays, Christmas or New Year, but they could just happen if enough people turned up at the house my grandmother and Peggy shared in Moodiesburn Street. A bottle would be spun and whoever it pointed to had to sing. I always sought a cave-like vantage point to view it from, usually under the table and waited for all the party pieces to be enacted. No gathering was complete without Peggy being persuaded to sing 'Mexicali Rose'. It was a maudlin country-and-western ditty about star-crossed lovers – what else would Peggy sing?

> Mexicali Rose stop crying
> I'll come back to you some sunny day
> Every night you'll know that I'll be pining
> Every hour a year while I'm away
> Dry those big brown eyes and smile dear
> Banish all those tears and please don't sigh
> Kiss me once again and hold me
> Mexicali Rose, Goodbye bye.
>
> Mexicali Rose I'm leaving, don't feel blue
> Mexicali Rose stop grieving, I love you
> When the dove of love is winging through the blue
> All the castles you've been building will come true.

The song might have been written for Peggy to sing, the sorrow for the lost love and the building of castles and as she sang, tears flowing from her big brown eyes, Skip and Willie would mime the song to the assembled company. They would swoon into each other's arms and sob sorely before riding off into the sunset around the table, as I watched their performance from underneath. By that time Peggy would have been forced to give up anyway, due to a combination of tears of sympathy for the unfortunate Rose and tears of laughter at the travesty of her sorrow being enacted. Then Uncle Willie would sing an army song about Quinn's Pub in the Springburn area of Glasgow, an establishment obviously held in great affection and built under a rocky outcrop that had been made into stairs. It was called 'Doon in the Wee House' and had to be sung whenever Willie was present, and if a do was on, Willie was there.

Doon in the wee hoose, underneath the stairs,
Everybody's happy, everybody's there.
We're a' gay and he'rty, each in his chair,
Doon in the wee hoose, underneath the stairs.

Noo Christopher Columbus sailed the ocean blue,
'Twas him that discovered America, if history books
     are true,
All honour tae Columbus, but honour I declare,
Tae the man that built the wee hoose, underneath
     the stair.

Noo when ye're feelin' lonely, when ye're feelin'
     blue,
Don't give way to sorrow, Ah'll tell ye what to do,
Jist take a tram tae Springburn, see if Quinn's is
     there,
He's the man that built the wee hoose, underneath
     the stair.

Noo when Ah'm feelin' weary, and ma bones are
     sair,
Ah won't get auld an' grumpy, like that auld
     bugger there.
Ah'll save up a' ma pennies tae buy a hurly-chair,
Jist tae tak' me tae the wee hoose underneath the
     stair.

When it came to the line, 'Ah won't get auld an' grumpy',
the entire company would rise as one, point an accusatory finger at Maw Clark and shout 'Like that auld bugger there!'
     Skip's party piece, when the other three legs of the famous
sand-dance weren't present, was to begin singing an army
song that after a few lines threatened to descend into filth
but never did, because everyone jumped up shouting and
throwing things at him. It was what could be called a performance piece, with everyone else having to take part for full
effect, but watching from my cave under the table, it always
made me feel uncomfortable. I didn't quite understand what
it was about and of course no one would explain; it was one

of those adult jokes that make all children feel slightly uneasy for that very reason. Nan sang an odd little song, given the many others she knew.

> Wance Ah hid a wee broon hen, it hid a wee broon tail,
> Ah sent it fur an ounce o' snuff an' it never came back again,
> Noo it's deid an' in it's grave fur many an' many a day,
> God bless ma wee hen, it never came back again.
>
> Ah'll hae a funeral fur ma wee hen,
> Ah'll hae a funeral, fur ladies an' gentlemen,
> Ladies an' gentlemen know ma wee hen,
> God bless ma wee hen, it never came back again.

Everyone joined in with the chorus, as they did with every song apart from Skip's, because he never got that far, but it was a strange little song for my mother to sing. Despite the tragic end of the wee broon hen it was always sung with great gusto and greeted with much cheering and stamping of feet.

These happy family gatherings showed the great differences between the two families. The Clarks for instance lived on their feelings and lacked the emotional strength of the O'Briens, though that strength was the kind that children have, egotistical and selfish. To the O'Briens, showing what you really felt or thought gave others an unfair advantage over you, so emotions were kept tightly under control. Instead they performed a comical act that kept them safe from close emotional ties, ties that I think they were incapable of forming. They concealed their feelings behind a mask of knockabout humour and it was a matter of pride to them not to shed a tear, even under the most tragic circumstances. The O'Briens believed that control was strength, but the sentimental Clarks cared and that did make them vulnerable. As they would find out before long, caring costs.

Chapter Seven

I was a toddler when I first saw my brother Mickey. He was still in Mearnskirk Hospital and children weren't allowed to visit, so I was taken to look at him, or for him to look at me, through a fence. I had no idea what I was about to see or what I should do, but I remember feeling let down by the experience.

This creature called a Mickey had been so exotic and fabulous that my parents had spent every weekend and as many days or evenings as they could, going to see it. It was talked of incessantly, it was regularly bought gifts that were beyond the dreams of Laurie and me, therefore it had to be something wondrous to behold. At last I was being allowed to see it, to be in its presence. But it turned out that a Mickey was just a big boy supported by two wooden crutches. This confused me, because I thought only Uncle Hughie had a wooden crutch, yet here was Mickey with two. He looked physically like a 'Dark Yin', the only one of our family who had all of the Clark characteristics, dark skin, eyes and hair.

I have no idea if Mickey was as disappointed as I was by that meeting but I think he probably was. His whole attitude towards me was always impatience that I did not conform to his personal standard of what his sister should be like. So we both failed spectacularly to live up to the expectations of the other. If I wanted Mickey to be a magical creature, then he clearly wanted some ideal storybook sister he could be proud of on his terms. Not of course that we ever expressed any of this, because we never became close enough to talk of such things. We just settled into a mutual dislike that grew from the seeds of our seperate disappointments at that first meeting. It was little to do with actions or words and everything to do with unrealistic expectations that were bound to be dashed.

The only truly revealing thing Mickey ever told me was that when he was in hospital he thought he came from a rich family. Everything he wanted he got, and the best of it. Nan once saved money to buy him special soap for instance, because the hospital variety irritated his skin. It came as the biggest shock and disappointment of his life to discover that we were extremely poor. I often wondered if he made the next connection, that Laurie and I had done without to keep him in luxuries, but if he did he kept it to himself. It was something he had no control over anyway, he was, after all, a child at the time.

Mickey came out of hospital for a spell while we were in Blackhill, and because of his mistaken belief that we were rich, he hated it even more than Nan did. Apart from the feeling that he was unhappy, I have very little recollection of him then. He was after all eleven years older and therefore an adult compared to me, uninvolved in my life in the streets. Most of his time he spent studying to make up for the schooling he had missed. He was very bright and was interested in electronics and Nan was determined that he should get every chance. The only memories I have of his time with us is of his head bowed over a book and the caliper on his left leg. When he walked across the floor, which wasn't often because he spent most of his time in bed, the woman who lived below complained about the noise he made. I had no particular affection for Mickey, but the woman's insensitivity appalled whatever sense of justice Nan had instilled in me. Her name was Mrs Burrell, and to this day I dislike the name.

After years of operations Mickey's knee-cap had been removed and the joint locked, so that he could not bend it as he moved. Laurie and I were used to having a fully mobile Uncle Hughie about the place so Mickey's handicap didn't seem like one to us, but Nan cried a lot, though never when Mickey was around. I couldn't understand why; after all, she hadn't done it to him. Now that I'm a mother myself, of course, I understand only too well and I wish I could reach back through all those years and give her the cuddle I didn't understand enough to give her then.

I started school at Easter 1953, just before I was five years old, joining Laurie at St Philomena's Roman Catholic school in Royston Road, though being six years older than me he was in his last year at primary school. Nan had me kitted out in a frilly blouse, Royal Stewart tartan skirt and black-patent shoes with huge buckles, called kiltie shoes. All the children cried of course; it was the generation before play schools were invented to make the parting easier. Having gone the first day I could see no reason to go back again and had to be forced.

My teachers soon discovered that I could already read and I was instantly treated like a leper. Nan was summoned to be told how displeased they were and her protests that she hadn't taught me, that I had picked it up by myself, were treated with scorn. It wasn't until my own son was learning to read that I discovered how I had cracked the code. Apparently children begin to read by recognizing word shapes, and I have a clear recollection of picking out words with double letters in the middle; I liked words like 'good' and 'week' for instance. Knowing why I learned to read still doesn't explain how I knew what those words represented. That remains a mystery still.

Knowledge was the teachers' to give however, and if they didn't give it, it was not to be acquired. I was put at a desk apart from the other children and kept supplied with books, which I suppose was a form of punishment. If it was, then it backfired badly, because to this day I can think of no finer treat than to be left alone to read books endlessly. When the school inspectors arrived I would be trotted out to read to them, thereby proving the excellence of St Philomena's teaching abilities. I have often wondered since if the teachers were stupid for thinking the inspectors were taken in by this ploy, or if the inspectors *were* taken in and were therefore as stupid as the teachers believed them to be.

One of the more absurd features of life in Glasgow, then as now, was that schools were segregated by religion. Every morning we collected David at number 43 and together we walked to school, past the little man who had killed his wife to the end of Acrehill Street to where it met Craighead Avenue. There David had to veer off to the right and go to his school the long way. David, coming from my mother's side of the family went to the Protestant school, whereas Laurie and I went to the Catholic school because of Skip. In local parlance we were, without a hint of offence given or taken, Proddies or Papes. Despite the lack of animosity over names, had David passed our school he would have been attacked and severely beaten up, just as we would have been had we tried to pass his school.

Every lunchtime there were pre-arranged fights, with a gang of children from one school attempting to invade the other, and we stockpiled clods of earth for the battle. It would start in the ritual manner, with the day's aggressors standing outside chanting a song against the other side. We would shout 'Proddy dogs eat frogs!', which for some reason was regarded as a huge insult, and they would sing the few words they knew of 'The Sash My Father Wore'. We hadn't a clue why we should take offence at this either, we only knew that we had to or the battle couldn't commence and before long the air was heavy with clods of earth from both sides. The Proddies also sang a cheery little song that we all secretly joined in with, singing it under our breaths because we knew it was a sin:

> Hello, hello, we are the Billy Boys,
> Hello, hello, we are the Billy Boys,
> Up to the knees in Fenian blood,
> Surrender or you'll die,
> Hello, we are the Billy Boys!

Again neither side knew what any of it meant, it was just another adult insult handed down to children who sang it while happily throwing clods at each other.

At the end of the day, once out of sight of our respective schools, David, Laurie and I met up again at the corner of Craighead Avenue and Acrehill Street and headed home

68

together. For us it was doubly bizarre, because David had been as close as a brother since our Brae days. Children just accept what they are brought up with and we never questioned it. That of course is the tragedy of it and how religious bigotry survives. Anyone who doubts this only has to look at the children taken to march in Orange marches, who haven't a clue what it's all about but will make their children march too when the time comes. So it was religion which drove a wedge between families and friends, and it's still happening today.

It was natural that David should want to continue playing with the children he had been playing with at school all day, and the same was true of us. Soon we were walking on opposite sides of the street, mouthing mindless obscenities at each other that we didn't understand, things we never heard or repeated within the family. We never made the connection between what was happening at school and King Billy on Maw Clark's pin-cushion, we didn't even realize it was all part of the same nonsense. Bigotry was a subject on the school curriculum, sticking pins in King Billy was a family joke, and it's very difficult to hate something that you laugh at.

Sometimes I look back to those days and I feel great anger at the way we were manipulated into expressing a hatred we didn't feel and even greater sadness for the innocent victims that we were.

The reality was that religion just wasn't for me, even at a very early age. It made no sense to me whatsoever and still doesn't. Skip took me to my first mass when I was about five years old and I found it unutterably, mind-crushingly boring. I was forced to attend mass chiefly by Nan, in a 'never let it be said that I stopped them being Catholics' way. Eventually I became impossible through desperation to escape, behaving so badly that they stopped making me go. Otherwise I might have become a serious arsonist.

Nan was delighted that I was bright at school, after all learning, education was all to her. It took her a long time to convince me that I would never be able to fly though, and I'm not sure even yet that she succeeded. Birds in the sky were like people flying to me and I simply assumed that one day I'd fly too; I was devastated when she insisted that I couldn't and wouldn't. Somewhere deep inside I think I'm still devastated. It must have induced fears in Nan that I had inherited too strong an O'Brien streak, because she forbade me from telling anyone, apart from Peggy of course, who wasn't just anyone. I wasn't hurt when Peggy laughed, she was after all a part of me, but I always felt that Uncle Hughie would have understood, so maybe Nan was right about my O'Brien streak. It was a good example of the difference between the two families: apart from Peggy's romantic castle-building, the Clarks dealt with reality and had their feet firmly on the ground, while the O'Briens dealt strictly in fantasy and understood the yearning to soar into the air.

Mickey was clever too, but Laurie couldn't read and he couldn't spell, and his writing was totally unintelligible. Letters were missing or back-to-front and always in the wrong order. He was dyslexic, but in the fifties no one in education knew anything about the condition. He had a calculator brain when it came to mathematics, but because of his dyslexia he was regarded as an idiot.

Naturally it brought out in Nan the lioness fighting for her cub, allied to her natural sympathy for the underdog, and she had another cause to fight. When he failed his qualifying test, the forerunner of the eleven-plus, he was consigned to a Junior Secondary School, where the idiots went. Nan would have none of it; she knew Laurie had a problem even if she didn't know what it was, but she also knew that with his ability with numbers he wasn't stupid. She lobbied the Education Department, harassed the school and won over a teacher to help her lobby the Education Department some more. Finally she won and six months after being consigned to the scrap-heap Laurie was sent to St Mungo's Academy instead. Once there though, with no more understanding of dyslexia than anywhere else at the time, Laurie's difficulties weren't addressed and he got no help. It was as if the authorities had relented and said, 'OK, you're in a Senior Secondary now. Be normal.' So Laurie continued to struggle, and because of the deficiencies of the system, he was made to feel responsible for his problem.

Every Saturday David, Laurie and I went to the pictures. This entailed walking the length of Acrehill Street, along Provan Road to the Rex or the Vogue in Alexandra Parade, a distance of perhaps two miles. It was an expedition that called for sustenance *en route* and for this we went to Galbraith's, a big shop near where Peggy and Maw lived, that sold chipped apples and broken biscuits. Sometimes the expedition took so long because of many detours to play along the way that we missed the film. On one of those occasions my brother Laurie gave me a black wine gum to eat that was really a slug. I ate it with relish, and he was sick; even when he did his brotherly duty by doing something nasty, Laurie was the one who suffered.

We used to sing 'The Black Hills of Dakota', as we walked along, a song we had first heard in a cowboy film. We would sing 'Take me back to the Black hills, the Black hills of Dakota', perfectly happy to accept that Dakota was the Apache name for Glasgow. Then Laurie developed a passion for toy knights in armour, and would occasionally purloin all our cinema cash to buy one for his collection. This naturally had to be kept from Nan, and to put in the necessary hours when we should have been cheering on the cowboys we went to the park or wandered the streets looking in the shop windows. To stop us spilling the beans Laurie let David and I play with the knights too. We weren't particularly gentle with them so he didn't make much out of his little scheme.

Laurie was eternally unhappy. He disliked Skip for coming between him and Nan, yet I always felt that what he wanted more than anything was Skip's approval. There was no natural meeting place between them though; Skip was unused to dealing with low self-esteem that didn't transform itself into eccentricity. Skip was an O'Brien, and that meant never admitting the possibility of being less than special. I think because Laurie wasn't like him my father regarded him as a bit of a wimp, a failure, though he never actually said so. He was not a man used to showing his feelings, if he had them, and he was embarrassed by the fact that Laurie did. I cannot recall my father ever making an encouraging or affectionate remark to his youngest son. Mickey he adored above all other human beings, and it was obvious without my father having to say so that Laurie wasn't in that league. Neither for that matter was I, but I had a different nature from Laurie, and anyway I had a close, warm relationship with Nan and Peggy.

Perhaps the seeds of my adult relationships with both of my brother were sown then. I was never close to Mickey and never thought of it as a possibility. All we now have in common is that we had the same parents and that sort of hold loosens considerably when the parents die. There's no particular bitterness, our paths simply don't cross often. As a child I was close to Laurie, but that stopped when he married and found himself a family of his own. When siblings are brought up to compete with each other they often make a sub-conscious decision to lead separate adult lives, indeed some cannot live in the same country. Looking back I think that was how we grew up, or Laurie and I at any rate, vying for attention and approval that my father could only give to one, his son Mickey. And the sad thing is, that I don't think Mickey gained anything from being the only one Skip cared for.

Chapter Eight

My father was a shoemaker – *not* a cobbler, but a time-served tradesman. Skip always made that distinction as strongly as possible, because of the anti-Catholic bias that had traditionally banned Catholics in Glasgow from being tradesmen. Uncle Hughie had been a shoemaker too and Skip had served his apprenticeship with him. There were attempts to get Skip away from the trade over the years. At the time when Balmano Street collapsed he was a bus conductor for instance, but he was what he was. Nan's official excuse for trying to convert him was to say that it was an unhealthy life, full of leather dust and noise and the wages were low; all true, but not her real objections.

He worked in a long, low, converted farm-building across the road from my school, and when lessons were finished for the day I would sometimes visit him. The farmland had been overtaken by the city, but some of the buildings still stood, and though they weren't used for their intended purposes they kept their original names. So Skip was a shoemaker in the byre and a shop beside him that sold no milk was called the dairy. His employer, Paddy Doyle, was rarely there, so Skip mainly worked alone.

I would take my books into the workshop and watch him at the various stages of mending or making shoes between reading my stories, growing drowsier in the warm, dust-laden atmosphere, lulled by the whirring machines until I fell fast asleep. He kept a yellow tin mug there for me that he had carried around the world during his sojourn with the 8th Army, and would prepare hot, sweet tea for 3 pm. He was a fine craftsman and I never tired of watching him work with the leather, selecting the quality he needed and cutting it to shape with the minimum of waste.

Then he would fill his mouth with nails and start repairing the shoes, placing each nail onto the new sole or heel and rhythmically tapping it into place.

Skip was very particular about the quality of leather he used, and if he ran out of the right kind he would set out on the rounds of the shoemaking fraternity in Glasgow, all Irish to a man. They were a close-knit group and borrowing materials from each other was common. Tools were immediately downed, wives and children called to the shop and every visit became a hooley. I used to go with him and loved the welcoming shoemakers and their families. At one time, had I found myself in trouble in any area of the city I could have gone to the nearest shoemaker and got help by announcing myself as the daughter of Laurie O'Brien.

Skip specialized in making surgical boots and shoes by hand and people were sent to him by other shoemakers. The trouble was that he couldn't bring himself to charge for the real price of the work because anyone handicapped enough to need special shoes was invariably poor, and besides, he had a boy of his own in the same position. The practical aspects of life were never Skip's strong points.

Behind the byre stood a tall, wooden building, the top half of which was the home of an Irish family called Kelly. The Kellys were a big family and countless redhaired, almost identical children tumbled from every crevice. It seemed that every day we were called upon to climb the rickety stairs to their house to admire yet another Kelly baby. The children were clean but never well-dressed and they were the happiest family I have ever seen, a living advert for large families. The railway line ran behind the Kelly house and beside it lay an old car that Nan was determined was full of rats. I could never see the connection between the car and rats, so I played in it for many happy hours with the Kelly clones. None of us had ever been in a real car, but the rat car took us to every exotic location we had ever heard of without once moving from beside the railway track.

I always wanted to walk home with Skip but he would never let me. He would send me on ahead, saying Nan would be waiting for me at home. I knew this wasn't true because

74

Nan knew exactly where I was, but I had no idea then why he sent me on ahead.

Although Blackhill was criss-crossed with railway lines there was no station anywhere near us. We treated the track like a road we had to cross, and as no buses ran through our streets people inevitably took short-cuts across the track. By getting off the bus at Royston Road, beside the chemical plant, you could cut across my triangle of grass and the track at the bottom end, thereby saving a very long walk. Occasionally someone got hit by a train, someone's man coming home from work or the pub, in the dark. It was how things were, so we accepted it. It never occurred to us that there should have been some sort of fence to keep us and the trains apart, but then we were used to being regarded as not worth the bother by anyone in authority. When someone was killed or injured, all that happened was that Nan and the local women organized a collection around the houses for the family and that was it till the next time.

Once, one of our friends was killed as we played together outside. He was a boy called Jamie Craig who was nearer to Laurie's age than mine. We were hurried away from the scene, but we had all seen enough to know what damage a train could do. His mother's greatest wish was that he should be buried wearing a suit, which we all knew was madness. We had seen him cut to bits, how could he wear a suit? Besides, a suit was an unbelievable luxury, something to aim for but rarely to achieve. Peggy, single and earning money, paid for the suit though, and as we watched the small white coffin being carried out of Jamie's close, we idly discussed the idiocy of adults with the callous logic that children have. There had been nothing left of Jamie to hang a suit on, and all around were live boys who would never have one. Soon the memory faded, as it always did, except for a vivid picture still in my mind today of Jamie's blood on the track.

The other dangers, from the gasworks and the chemical factory, were merely dark suspicions, based on the logical belief that fighting for breath was bad for you. In the fifties there was no concern for the environment and there were no filters fitted on the gasworks. Gas was made by baking coal and to make enough to cope with peak hours like lunch and tea-times, extra coal was baked for an hour or so before, with the by-products being discharged directly into the air over the houses. If washing was left out the smell of sulphur and tar clung to them, and if you were outside you nearly choked on the yellowish fumes. Everyone knew when the gasworks 'came out' and so it was routine to rush home beforehand and to close the windows until the discharge was over.

The gasworks and the chemical factory were suspected of causing the chronic health problems in Blackhill, but it didn't occur to anyone that something could be done about it. We had no idea what came out of the whisky bond either. Added to the industrial factors we couldn't prove, was the inherent dampness and poor insulation of the houses, built with the emphasis on quantity rather than quality. Glasgow Corporation was proud of the low cost of building Blackhill and we lived with the inevitable health risks that went with that priority. It was all part of what 'they' inflicted on us that 'they' wouldn't have inflicted on the richer areas of the city. But anything was good enough for those who lived in Blackhill . . .

Chapter Nine

I was about five years old when I first saw Uncle Jim, one of Skip's many brothers. In the Twenties he had been a bare-knuckle fighter of some repute, and legend had it that he kept a special pair of white kid gloves for his battles.

Jim was a tall man by Glasgow standards and that and his reputation as a fighter made him a target for every macho drunk. He was never a member of a gang and apart from one friend to watch his back he travelled alone. One night he and the friend were in a pub when the usual challenge was issued by a drunk, and the two men got up and left. The drunk followed them to another pub, and when Jim left again he trailed behind, shouting insults. When he still didn't respond the drunk dived at Jim's feet, and Jim kicked out, knocking him against the concrete base of a lamp post and killing him.

Jim was charged with murder, and Granda Tom arranged for one of his St Aloysius contacts, top criminal lawyer Laurence Dowdall, to defend him. Not only did Dowdall get him off, but the Judge praised Jim's restraint under severe provocation. He also ruled that the drunk had had an exceptionally thin skull and that this factor had contributed to his death. Not that this cut any ice with Nan, who wondered aloud what school the Judge had gone to.

Jim was the only O'Brien she actually disliked. She didn't trust him and she believed that he was no more than a thug. Skip when pressed would admit that Jim was 'a hard big man', a lacklustre defence that I took as proof that Nan knew what she was talking about. After the trial Jim went to London, saying that he would be a marked man in Glasgow, but Nan's opinion was that he knew other charges might be pending and was making a quick getaway. As she was an expert on the O'Brien psyche, she may very well have been right.

Nevertheless the myth was born of Uncle Jim, gentleman thief, and no one built myths like the childlike O'Briens, who wove mystery and romance around him in his absence. Jim, it was decided, was a master criminal in London, and every big robbery that hit the headlines was claimed in his name. Nan would give a snort of derision and say, 'Couldnae hiv bin Jim, naebody wis killed.'

Once, when he arrived unannounced and definitely uninvited at Acrehill Street, her words of welcome to him were, 'Sumbody efter ye in London?'. Jim smiled down at her with an easy charm that fooled her not a bit. He was laden down with gifts of jewellery and clothes, and I remember a beautiful dress that he brought me, even if it was six sizes too big. Once again Nan disposed of it all, saying we had no idea where and who it came from.

Like the rest of the family Jim was a born story-teller and I remember during this visit that he kept us entertained for hours with his tales, or as Nan maintained, 'lies'. He had worked as an embalmer – 'Cuttin' oot the middle man noo Jim?' – and he told us that the biggest problem was the rats. 'They'll do anything to get at the blood,' he said. 'Aye, well, ye'll know a' about that Jim,' said Nan tartly, 'Ye've hid yer ain difficulties in that direction.' Jim smiled back sweetly.

Whether Jim was an embalmer or not, the family latched onto it with gusto, never guilty of letting the damnedest lies stand in the way of a good yarn. It was decided that he embalmed only the top people, the richest, the heaviest in jewels and gems, items that of course they no longer needed, whereas Jim undoubtedly did. It fitted with the rest of the Jim myth that he never actually harmed anyone physically, though Nan of course had other ideas about that. He gave Skip two pairs of cuff-links; a gold hexagonal pair with a pattern in wine, black and white enamel, and a rectangular pair in silver, with a similar pattern in blue, black and white. They were quite beautiful and I now know that they were worth a fortune, so naturally the other O'Briens got to work on him. They laboured the point about stealing from corpses, which on this occasion was regarded as a dreadful crime, and being masters of their art they then left the thought to fester in Skip's soul, not to mention his fertile imagination.

Finally he could stand the guilt no longer and resolved to get rid of the cuff-links in a way that would bring him no gain; he must have felt very guilty indeed. He went to a Catholic church and tried to put them in the St Vincent de Paul collection box for the poor, but they wouldn't go in. He went to another church and found another box, but again the cuff-links wouldn't go through the slot, and in the next church it was the same.

Like the rest of his family Skip loved ghost stories and tales of the supernatural. His favourite was *The Monkey's Paw* by William Wymark Jacobs, where a talisman, the paw, is supposed to bring great fortune, but turns out to bring terror and tragedy instead. He felt the same about the cuff-links; in his fevered imagination they became the monkey's paw, and he was convinced that some awful fate awaited him if he didn't get rid of them. In a state of sweating fear and convinced that God himself had decided that he should be punished by having the cuff-links in his possession forever, he panicked finally and put them through the letter box of the priest's house.

In my experience, priests, despite their talk of poverty and charity, much prefer the good life. So I'm sure the recipient of Skip's largesse would have known quality when he saw it. The beautiful cuff-links would have gone no further than the priestly shirt cuffs and are doubtless an heirloom of his family today, if he isn't still living off the proceeds of their sale. Years later it emerged that they had in fact been given to Jim by a rich girlfriend, no doubt for services rendered, and that the rest of the family had known this all along. Obviously they couldn't claim the points unless Skip found this out, so they made sure that he did. But long, long after the beautiful cuff-links were irretrievably out of his reach.

Uncle Jim spent two weeks with us in Acrehill Street, during which he threw money around, mainly in the

79

direction of the pub, and I doubt if Skip was sober for two minutes together the whole time. He never offered anything towards his keep though and Nan knew that the only way to get rid of him was to demand some cash. He left one day 'to cash a cheque' and we never saw him again.

That night the London train crashed and a few days later we got a letter from Jim telling us not to worry, that he was safe – not that this was of any consequence whatever to Nan. When he got home though, he continued, he had discovered in the turn-up of his trouser leg, a severed finger. Nan was not impressed.

'Ah'll bet ye anythin' it wisnae his finger cut off though,' she said cynically. Skip, knowing a good story when he heard it, thought that this was harsh and uncalled for and wondered how she could be so hard.

Jim had enclosed with the letter a photo of himself, dressed immaculately with gold tooth gleaming and fondling a kitten. Sensing another put-down Skip supplied the punchline before Nan could, 'Probably jist before he strangled it.'

We never heard from Jim again, but like Hughie he lives on in our imaginations. Everytime a spectacular robbery is pulled off we say with pride, 'Uncle Jim!', though he would be over a hundred years old by now. More recently however, we have had to put him into virtual retirement. Crime is so violent these days and we won't have Jim connected with anything sordid. There doesn't seem the demand anymore for skilful, classy criminals like Raffles Jim, but he's probably out there somewhere yet, still trying to cash that cheque . . .

Chapter Ten

In the early Fifties the Korean War was taking young men from Blackhill to fight in the jungle. Nan used to address us on the issues, which to her were inextricably linked to the Second World War.

After six years of a war we had won, the meat ration had actually been reduced in 1947, and clothes were rationed until 1949. Sweet and chocolate rationing had been abolished in March 1949, but the public had gone slightly crazy and it was reimposed in July of the same year and didn't end until February 1953.

On Saturdays we still went into town for the weekly shopping, going to the same shops we had used when we had lived at the Brae. We spent our sweets coupons at McLellan's in George Street, a little shop at the bottom of the Brae. George McLellan thought highly of Nan and it was said that he gave her extra sweets, and though naturally she denied it, she still took all of the Clark coupons to him. My weekly allocation was a tube of Smarties. Though it doesn't seem a lot, it was no real hardship as I had never known anything other than rationing. The business with coupons gave Nan the opportunity to complain again that not only did we still have rationing, but young lads were still being called up to fight in another war.

There were constant reminders of the war overseas. From a gap in the buildings at the top of Acrehill Street, we spent hours watching a blimp in the sky spilling out tiny parachutists as part of their training for Korea. It looked so near and we tried to find it many times but we never did. The blimp tantalized us and we argued endlessly about where it actually was but all our expeditions to find it failed. The boy Nan saved from the Catholic Teds came to say goodbye before he went to fight, I suppose she was the nearest thing to a mother he really had. She cried of course, then she told Peggy and Peggy cried too, then they cried together. This gave Nan another chance to deliver an impassioned lecture on the evils of war and rationing, getting so carried away that she and Peggy would collapse in tears once again.

Like the rest of my generation I grew up with the Second World War as an ever-present feature. It's almost like a race memory I remember it so well, though I wasn't born until it was over. The sound of an air-raid siren chills me to the bone only because it did the same to my mother. Though I never heard it sounded in anger I absorbed her anxiety and made it my own. Nan refused to leave Glasgow or to have Mickey and Laurie evacuated during the War, so the sound of the siren really did mean danger to her. I can still see the German planes flying over Balmano Brae on their way to bomb the River Clyde and the shipyards in Clydebank because she described it so often and so clearly that I felt I had been there too.

As for the lad Nan had saved for the jungles of Korea, we never saw him again. But every now and again I would think about him and hope he had survived. I'm sure she did too.

Some Sundays Skip took me for a walk along the canal bank. The canal was part of my everyday playground, but the weekly walk with Skip was somehow a special treat. Laurie never came; I don't know if he was ever asked, but if he had been I'm sure he would have refused, however much he wanted to come with us. I always wore the same dress, a charcoal and blue striped taffeta creation given to me by my godparents, Auntie Annie and Uncle George. To be truthful I only had one godparent, because Skip had taken Uncle George for a drink before the ceremony and they had disappeared, so Auntie Annie took me on her own to be christened in St Andrew's Cathedral, where my parents had been married at the side altar.

Uncle George had met her when he was twenty-three and boarding a troop train and she had been only ten years old. She and her parents were seeing her brother John off on the train and the two young soldiers had struck up a friendship on the platform that lasted forever. Her name coincidentally was O'Brien, but she came from a separate, more conventional and normal branch of O'Briens. After coming through the War together George and John O'Brien had remained close friends, and given the situation at home, where as a 'Dark Yin' George wasn't exactly a favourite, he spent more time with John's family.

Da Clark, who doted on George, Nan and Peggy, had died during the War, and the two sisters had formed their own mutual support group, so in a way George was finding his own with the normal O'Briens. As he and the grown-up Annie grew closer over the years, her father refused them permission to marry unless George became a Catholic. They split up for two months before George gave in, though he paid no more than lip service to his new religion. It was the price he paid to marry Annie, that was all. Like Nan though, he was forced to agree that their children would be raised as Catholics.

Naturally George took Annie to meet Nan before introducing her to the rest of the family, and having won Nan's support there was no problem with the rest. There were mutterings of course from the 'Fair Yins', who never missed a chance to have a go at a 'Dark Yin', that a real man wouldn't have given in, a real man wouldn't have turned. None of this was actually said to George. No Clark was ever that silly.

When I was born Annie was already pregnant with their first child and Nan won a twisted little victory over my christening. She needed Catholics as godparents, which logically pointed to the mad O'Briens but she didn't want them involved if she could help it, so Annie and George were chosen. They were a glamorous couple in my eyes; Uncle George was tall and darkly handsome, like a cross between Cary Grant and Gregory Peck, and wherever he went female heads turned. Annie wore glasses and used to wonder with a wry smile why George, who was so good-looking, had married her of all people. It was as though she was ugly, which she wasn't of course.

Annie had a beautiful figure and wore clothes well, so that

83

you always remembered a particular dress or outfit when you thought of her. She also had the nicest nature, and coming from a family of such extremes on both sides I was very impressed by this. She was genuine; when you talked to her you didn't have to work out the politics or the psychology of the situation first. Though this was refreshing when you got used to it, it was also a little confusing. She was an O'Brien after all, and O'Briens just weren't like that.

Because George was tall in a city of small men he had to keep his temper in check; a big man can do more damage than a small one. So there was always a feeling of tension about George. Like all the Clarks he had deep emotions, but somehow he couldn't risk letting them go for fear of who knows what. All through my life I can hear Annie's voice at moments of family tension. 'Watch George!' she'd shout, a warning that the big man was nearing the end of his tether. It was Annie who softened him and made him sociable, she was a gentle soul with a talent for smoothing out his awkwardness, and they were very obviously happy together. Whenever they came to visit I would wait for them at the bus stop, to bask in the glamour of walking beside them and showing them off as my relatives.

Peggy had a new boyfriend, or rather an old one for the second time. The family had breathed a sigh of relief the first time Jim McAvoy had disappeared off the scene. Now you could almost hear them collectively breathe it back in again. Soon she announced that she was marrying him, after a courtship that had tested the family's lung control and nerves to the limit.

If the Clarks didn't fit the public perception of Blackhill inhabitants, then the McAvoys did. They were, in the opinion of the family, a feckless bunch of lazy wasters who dabbled in petty crime, lacking the organisation or application for anything else, and Jim was the prime example. Like Nan, Peggy was a giver, and givers tend to marry takers. McAvoy was a charmless drinker and gambler who seldom worked, and he certainly wasn't what Peggy deserved. But at thirty-two she must have felt time

84

running out; Fate was winning, and so she took what no one else wanted. 'She should dae better,' Nan told the family firmly, 'Bit she won't.' As the two of them sat stitching hats for the wedding, with me in between them, they discussed the family's antagonism endlessly.

'They'll never like him Peggy,' Nan said, 'If ye take him ye take him knowin' that.' And take him Peggy did, one cold March Saturday in 1953, with her favourite niece waiting outside St Paul's Church in Langdale Street, clutching a silver horseshoe and shivering in the chill wind. I couldn't go into the church because I was a Catholic, and it was a known fact that no Catholic could enter a Proddie church without suffering some unspecified but dire consequences.

Instead of the frills and lace she dreamed of, Peggy wore a grey suit with a pink blouse and hat, and she was solemn as I handed over the good luck charm, expecting a smile. McAvoy put his arm around me and I instinctively shrugged it off and clung to Peggy. The wedding reception had a desperate air of forced joy, as the Clarks tried to look as though they had wished for this dream match for years. I can see them yet, looking at Peggy with concern and sorrow when her attention was elsewhere, and smiling when she turned in their direction.

McAvoy didn't warrant the same consideration; he was already in no doubt about how they felt. From that day, to the anguish of the Clarks, whatever had lit Peggy from within grew dimmer, as though the deal she had made with Fate to escape from spinsterhood had required her to surrender the very brightness of her soul. Within a year she had given birth to a stillborn son. The umbilical cord had been around the baby's neck, and I heard Uncle George saying to Nan, 'Ah wish it hid been roon' McAvoy's neck instead.' 'Wheesht Geordie,' said my mother quietly, as though she was calming a distressed child, 'it disnae help son.'

We were still close though, because Peggy and McAvoy lived with my grandmother. Nan and I still saw Peggy at some time every day, and as Peggy opened the door my mother's first words were always, 'How is she the day?', meaning what kind of mood was Maw Clark in and how much trouble was she causing? Peggy's usual response was to raise her eyes heavenward; Maw Clark could give a new meaning to difficult without even trying. We would spend some time talking, catching up on the huge changes that must have taken place in the twenty-four hours or less since we had last met. Then I'd leave Nan and Peggy talking and go out to play.

My first task was to decide if I was yet up to jumping down the back stairs. There were eight of them outside Peggy's house, leading down to the backcourt, eight steep stairs, and jumping them was a test of honour for me and all my cousins and all the Moodiesburn Street kids. The back close, the rear exit to the tenement at the bottom of the stairs, was narrower than the stairs themselves, so a misjudged jump could take you straight into the wall. Even if you judged it right, the stairs were slippy and you could end up slamming into the wall anyway. Having thought it all through and chickened out once again, I'd run down through the backcourts, past the air raid shelters to the playpark beyond, with its slides – one long, one short – a roundabout, three swings and a maypole that had no ropes. Beyond that was a stretch of grass beloved of the local dogs and then the pond, where I could catch fish and watch the swans. A single track road with a pavement at one side separated the pond from St Philomena's, our school, but curiously we only associated the park and the pond with visits to Moodiesburn Street and rarely went near it at any other time.

Nan and I tried to pick a time of day for our visits when McAvoy would be out and we would leave again before he arrived, partly because Nan knew how the sight of the Clarks annoyed him and so Peggy suffered, and partly because we really didn't want to see him either. So life went on in Blackhill, and even if the horizon was clouded by the unwelcome arrival of McAvoy and the subtle change in Peggy, the essentials for existence were still comfortingly in place. Then came the night that started Nan's big push to get out of Blackhill once and for all.

During the War metal railings had been removed from all over the country to be used, it was said, to make munitions. We now know that after collection the metal was simply dumped. It was just a government propaganda scheme, designed to make those at home believe they were contributing something to the War effort apart from their menfolk, and even Blackhill was included. A nine-inch wall ran around every tenement, studded with the remains of the railings that had once stood there. They had been intended to enclose gardens, but, in fact, they only surrounded a muddy space between the pavement and the buildings.

One evening I was sitting on the wall with a friend, exchanging scraps. It was early evening, the safe time, because the Teds usually went into battle during the hours of darkness. Then someone ran down the street shouting, 'Thur's a man comin' wi' his heid in his hauns!', an interesting proposition, and I was fully expecting to see a ghostly figure with his head tucked underneath his arm. As he staggered into view we were all disappointed to recognize him as a very much alive Ted, his hands covering his face. Every few steps he would stop and bellow, 'Youse wimmen get they weans oota the wey!'

Adult hands grabbed children along the route and took them inside houses, and from behind someone's net curtains I watched him as he staggered past where I had been sitting, only feet away. His hands were holding his face together where the blades had slashed him repeatedly, and blood pouring from between his fingers ran onto his shoulders and chest and flicked onto the road. When it was obvious he wasn't being chased by whoever had carved him up, we were released, feeling cheated as we luridly examined the grotesque red paperchase he'd left behind. We were greatly put out that an event that had started with such high expectations had collapsed into the mundane.

For Nan it was the last straw and it reinforced her greatest fear that her own kids, especially Laurie, could be caught up in the violence. From then, her battle to get out moved up a gear. Getting a house somewhere else wasn't that simple of course, because of Blackhill's reputation. So there was an obstacle course set up: if you wanted a house in a better area you had to apply to the Council, and the Factor was asked to provide a reference. Without a Factor's reference you could give up any ideas above your station. The letting department sent a Housing Visitor to inspect your home as part of this procedure, and a form was filled in, giving the Housing Visitor's opinion of the general condition of your home, the state of your furniture and the 'type of person' you were. The scale ran from very good, through good and fair to poor, and Nan lived on her wits while this process was gone through.

Looking back it's hard to understand why we put up with such indignities. But the system was supported by the ruling Labour administration, and the Party of the People made sure it didn't stop there. There was also the constant threat of the 'Green Lady' health visitor, who had the power to knock on any door at anytime and inspect your home. At the first sight of a Green Lady in the vicinity the bush telegraph swung into action, sending all the women of Blackhill on a furious tidying spree, in case the Green Lady picked on their house and gave a bad report because something was out of place. The Green Ladies were forever trying to outsmart the women, because if you wanted to avoid a visit you took yourself off as soon as the bush telegraph sounded its warning. So the Green Ladies often came on a Monday, washing day, when they knew that the majority of women would be tied to the boiler, washing board and mangle for many hours. This made them doubly unpopular of course, the last thing any woman wanted or needed was an interruption on washing day.

Another good time was Friday afternoon, when the women were waiting for their men to come home with their weekly pay packets so that they could do some shopping. So again the last person they wanted was the Green Lady arriving to take up their time instead, and of course they couldn't refuse to let her in. There was a children's street song that we used to sing about not being able to find 'a bonnie laddie tae tak' me awa' ', the first line of which was 'Queen Mary, Queen Mary, my age is sixteen.' So powerful were the Green Ladies that I thought the line started with 'Green Lady, Green

Lady', and I sang those words for years without questioning them.

Then came the news that we had passed all three elements of the obstacle course, the Factor, the Home Visitor and the Green Lady, and after five years as temporary refugees in Blackhill we were told that we would get a house in Drumchapel. Nan was ecstatic; I was bereft.

Drumchapel was part of the City Fathers' destruction of Glasgow. Instead of renovating the old tenements in the heart of the city they decided to raze them to the ground. The tenements symbolized everything that was bad about Glasgow, except to the people who actually lived in them, but there has never been a politician who listened to the people anywhere. In the Fifties in Glasgow they bulldozed away our history and background, erecting high-rise monstrosities that the people neither wanted nor needed. They created council housing estates or 'schemes', that were no more than ghettoes to replace ghettoes. Two-thirds of Pollok, eight miles to the south-west of the city, was built after the War and then Easterhouse sprang up six miles to the east, Castlemilk, five miles to the south-east and Drumchapel six miles to the west.

Our move to Drumchapel was part of a mass, enforced exodus that was happening all over the UK after the war years, but in Glasgow it was undertaken with a vengeance. In some parts of the city there were 400 people to the acre and the need to rehouse them at minimal cost took precedence over what they wanted. People who had lived for generations in cramped conditions with outside toilets and no bathrooms needed better housing, but they didn't want to leave the areas where they had grown up and the close communities they lived in. It became a common sight to see sad little groups watching bleakly as their former homes, and those of their parents and grandparents were demolished. But the politicians still knew best.

It would be over twenty years before meaningful conservation of the old buildings began and the high-rise flats, once determinedly hailed as Utopia, were blown-up, to cheers from those who had been forced to live in them. The Glasgow experience undoubtedly helped other areas of the UK not to make the same mistakes on such a stupendous scale, but the cost to the ordinary people in the loss of identity and social cohesion was enormous, and the city has never recovered.

In the mid-fifties we knew none of this, but there was talk that soon we would have skyscrapers in Glasgow, just like the ones in America that we saw in the pictures at the Rex and the Vogue. It was a time when anything American was desirable and exciting, and I listened enthralled as Nan, Peggy and Maw Clark discussed high-rise living. I saw in it definite possibilities of a reprieve, because like the Balmano Brae inhabitants, I envisaged a skyscraper being built where I lived, which meant I wouldn't have to leave Blackhill. It was the perfect compromise; Nan would be far enough off the ground to be safe from the gangs, and yet I could still be at home.

'Ah saw it in a magazine, ye hivtae use a lift tae get up an' doon,' Peggy said authoritatively, 'An' thur's nae midden, ye use a kinda chute tae get ridda yur rubbish.'

I found it hard to envisage having no middens to jump, but a chute held delightful prospects of its own.

'Bit whit if this lift thing breks doon when ye're in it Peggy?' Nan demanded, 'Whit dae ye dae then?'

'Bit they'll huv thoaghta that, therr'll be sterrs or sumthin'.'

'So ye'll hiv this lift, an' ye'll still hivtae dae the sterrs!' Nan snorted, 'An' Ah suppose ye'd hiv tae take yur turn at waashin' the lift tae! An' talkin' aboot waashin', where wid ye hing it oot?'

'Tae hell wi' the waashin', jist think, ye'd be away up there!' Peggy persisted, 'Up in the sky wi' aeryplanes passin' yur windies! Ye could wave tae the pilots!'

'Ah widnae like that!' Nan decided, 'Ah'm no hivin' nae skyscraper thanks very much! Ah'll jist hiv a hoose!' And she and Peggy laughed. I was devastated; it had all been a diversion, they were winding each other up.

'Naw, me neither,' Peggy said, 'They're mibbe a' right fur the Yanks, bit Ah cannae see thum catching oan here.'

'Ah'll tell ye wan thing,' said Maw Clark, who had been listening as intently as I had, 'If any o' yese move tae wanna they big buildin's, it's the last ye'll see o' me! Ah'll no' be comin' tae see yese if Ah hivtae use a lift!'

The same thought passed through our minds simultantaneously and I don't know yet how Nan, Peggy and I controlled ourselves. Peggy got up to make the tea, Nan went to help her and I followed, and when we reached the kitchen all three of us fell into a mutually supportive, creaking, crying, laughing huddle.

'Christ! It'd be worth it!' wheezed Peggy.

'Sshhh!' cried Nan, mopping her eyes, 'She'll hear ye!'

'Bit think o' it! Ye could be twinty stories high, an' she wid be doon below lookin' up at ye! Ye could drap things by accident like! Pails o' watter mibbe!'

'Bowls o' custard!' Nan supplied.

'Ye could even make a wee mistake an' miss the rubbish chute!' Peggy wailed, and Nan had to rush to the toilet, leaving Peggy and me to compose ourselves as best we could before we took the tea into Maw Clark. For the rest of the visit we avoided each other's eyes.

I can't pass a high-rise block to this day without seeing the phantom figure of Maw Clark, standing at the bottom looking up . . .

I put Drumchapel out of my mind for as long as possible, which was easy, because it was so impossible to believe. I kept hoping up to the last minute that the bad dream would go away, but the day came and there was the van loaded up with our furniture.

Children moving house usually have a fear that their beds will be left behind, but I hoped mine would be, so that I could stay in Blackhill. People came out of closes with presents for Nan, tins of food, biscuits, and sweeties and a few pennies for me. These were people who had very little themselves and of course Nan was so touched by this that she cried buckets; I don't think she realized till then how much a part of Blackhill she had become. Nan had started off being frightened and refusing to accept that the family had to live there, but she discovered that the women who made life bearable, even possible, who kept their families functioning against all the odds, were women just like her. Now she was leaving them behind.

The Balmano Brae refugees were in attendance too and they were almost as inconsolable as I was, but not quite. I cried uncontrollably, much to Nan's fury, partly I think because she was feeling unexpectedly fragile herself. I had never been outside the total security of Blackhill as far as I could remember, never more than five minutes away from Peggy, how was I supposed to survive hundreds of miles away?

As the bus left the city centre though, I began to glimpse another world, of trees, grass and wide roads. Along Great Western Road were huge, beautiful buildings that Nan told me were 'big hooses', not that I believed her of course. The council would hardly give one family a building big enough to house ten, and even if it did, what could one family possibly do in all those rooms?

Drumchapel was in its early stages in 1956, set in fields to one side of Drumry. Nan told me that she had come here on Sunday School picnics when she was a child, but it had been all open countryside then. Being a Catholic of course Sunday School picnics were an unknown world, a bit like the Proddie hymns we were banned from singing at school. We moved into 48 Halgreen Avenue, the top of four storeys built like an old-style tenement, but it was roomy, airy and white and it had an outside verandah, just the thing for the Scottish climate. Instead of two bedrooms it had three, so I had one to myself. I didn't think much of the deal.

It was too quiet at first; there were no gang fights and nowhere to play for a child used to second-guessing trains. I even missed the smell of the gasworks. I remember sitting on the steps at the close, unable to accept that I had to stay there, feeling totally lost and homesick for Blackhill and Peggy. I was on another continent, as far away as the people who were emigrating to Australia for ten pounds a throw. The newspapers were full of photos of them bidding tearful goodbyes to families they knew they would never see again, just as I would never see Peggy again. Part of me was missing without her; I couldn't believe that my own mother could have done such a thing to me.

I hadn't really been aware of trouble between my parents until we moved to Drumchapel, though I had a vague feeling of unease at times in Blackhill as I caught a tone of voice or a look. At family dos, as he capered and performed, the others would say, 'Leave him alane Nan, he's no' daein' ony herm,' and I used to wonder why she wanted to stop him having fun. Once we moved to Drumchapel though, like all the others who had been transported by the City Fathers and the planners, he had to travel back into Glasgow to work, adding at least two hours to his days. But he would come home later than that.

There were no pubs in Drumchapel, so he went to the nearest one before he came home, and that's when I remember the arguments starting, though there must have been others before that I wasn't aware of. Around the age of seven or so I began to realize that his drinking was different from the other men around me. Uncle Willie took a drink, Uncle George did sometimes too, though not often, but Skip drank all the time. Sometimes he came home without any wages, because his drinking money took precedence over everything else, food, clothes or paying the rent. In fact booze came before the need to breathe. As I grew older I would absorb the chronic anxiety about unpaid bills, though Nan always kept little stores of money all over the place to provide for the times he came home with little or none.

Gradually things became clearer. All those times I went to his workshop after school and he had sent me home alone, he had been going to the Provanmill Inn, the local pub beside where he worked. The times when Nan sent me with him around the other shoemakers, it was in the hope that he wouldn't get drunk with his little daughter to take care of, a forlorn hope born of her desperation. This was the start of another family myth, that Skip loved me so much that he took me with him wherever he went. To this day relatives still repeat to me this version of Nan's attempts to make him stay sober. It always ended the same, with Skip so drunk he couldn't see where he was going or stand up straight. As a child I often had to find our way home, sometimes at night, and it has left me with the ability to negotiate the city without knowing the names of places very well. In the dark I was frequently frightened, and even today I can catch sight of an alleyway in the centre of Glasgow as I pass by and it seems familiar, familiar enough to bring tears to my eyes, though I can't quite remember why.

The truth is that I didn't know Skip any other way but drunk, and as a very young child I had thought him great fun, which he was. But the other side of the amiable, life-and-soul of every party was a childish dictator, who would shout, argue and sulk, and for some inexplicable reason Nan couldn't handle these tactics. When he was late home there was never any doubt where he was or what state he would come home in, but she always feared he had fallen under a bus or been attacked. I would sit with her until we heard him falling up the stairs and trying to open the door, then I'd scamper off to bed and hide under the blankets until the inevitable row was over. I learned the art of diversion, of concentrating on something else to blot out the voices. Nan could handle the toughest bureaucrat, but she was helpless against her husband, and it always ended with her defeated and crying and him asleep in a drunken stupor; he always 'won'.

In truth, the shouting, distressing as it was, affected me less than the sight of my mother so totally vanquished each time. Everything had happened with Skip in no fit state to remember it, but Nan didn't drink and she remembered every word, as I did, and every word hurt. As the years passed I hoped rather than feared that he had fallen under a bus, and if anyone had attacked him, I wanted them to make a good job of it so that we could be free of him. The sound of his drunken falls on the stairs often reduced me to tears of rage and disappointment under my blankets. Skip was a survivor; he made it home every time.

Chapter Eleven

We went back to Blackhill every Saturday to see Peggy, the whole family assembled there and the excitement would build up all week until Saturday arrived. There was a kind of panic at first, a feeling that I would never see her again, a bit like losing a limb almost. Then Saturday would come at last and we'd set off to Blackhill.

After reassuring myself that Peggy was still there and hadn't forgotten me I would escape joyfully back to Acrehill Street to relive old times. As time passed though I found that I didn't belong any longer. I wasn't part of what was happening there every day and gradually I was losing touch with my old friends. The truth was that I had left the Acrehill Street kids behind; I wasn't one of them anymore, I was just a visitor.

So I began to stay more around Peggy's house in Moodiesburn Street, watching life go by from the top of the red-brick air raid shelter in the backcourt. I had suddenly realized that sights and sounds I'd taken for granted while living in Blackhill weren't part of my new home, and I missed them. Blackhill had a vigour and energy that made me yearn for the place even more.

In those days, before hygiene was a consideration, you could buy almost anything from a board carried around on someone's head. The baker sold cakes, buns and bread that way, shouting out as he came into the backcourt, and the fishman, the butcher and the man who sold coal brickettes too. I could earn the odd thru'penny bit by running upstairs with the goods and change to the women who had thrown down the payment from their windows. And there was Paddy the bleachman, who came around all the houses once a week selling bleach in big, green bottles shaped like whisky bottles. They cost a few pence each and were much cheaper than the kind in the shops. Every woman in Blackhill bought Paddy's bleach. Looking back, it seems incredible, given the outsider's view of Blackhill, that these people weren't attacked for the money or the goods they carried, but that wasn't a thought that occurred to anyone, and if it had happened the community would have sorted the situation out.

In the good weather a man called Ronnie McPhail came around the backcourts playing an accordion. The women would shout down requests and he'd play whatever they wanted then be rewarded with a few coins thrown from the windows. Whoever had requested the tune would start singing along, and other windows would fly open and their neighbours would join in or shout encouragement. I would lie on top of the air raid shelter, listening to the voices coming from the open windows high above, as women abandoned their housework to sing songs of grand passion or mournful romantic disappointment. When Ronnie McPhail moved on to the next street, they would be reluctant to give up the mood and a clabber, a backcourt concert, would take place.

Someone would bring down an old blanket and throw it over a washing line to form the backdrop to a stage, then the women would bring out chairs and sit like an audience at the theatre or the pictures. Everybody took their turn in front of the blanket stage, singing a song, sometimes in duos or trios, or doing a dance, and those watching from the windows joined in or sang from where they were. There was always a great deal of laughter as the women teased each other or sent themselves up, giggling at the songs of yearning romance they were singing. 'Fur coat an' nae knickers isnae in it!' they'd shout to each other, 'Ah jist look like Connie Francis, daen't Ah?', and they'd howl with laughter.

When it was coming near to tea-time, signalled by the stench from the gasworks, the clabber came to an end and the women would return to their chores, still laughing.

A clabber was a women's only do, the men had their own, quite separate pastimes, which mainly centred around the Provanmill Inn, which wasn't just a pub, but the male meeting place too. My favourite entertainment involved the drunks who took detours through the backcourts on their way home. They usually arrived after the pubs closed in the afternoon, or in the early evening if they'd been thrown out. Either way they were like lambs to the slaughter. They sang hoping for pennies, while insults and worse landed all around them. The O'Briens used to heat pennies before throwing them to drunks for the sheer pleasure of never giving a sucker an even break.

'Ah could gie ye "Ghost Riders in the Sky," ' the drunk would shout to the windows.

'Keep thum tae yersel', a' woman would shout back, 'Jist hop it Hopalong an' gie us peace!'

'Well how aboot "The Star O' Rabbie Burns?" ' the would-be entertainer would wheedle.

'Ye'll be seein' stars yersel' if ye don't get tae hell! How aboot jist buggerin' aff insteed?' would come the reply, closely followed by a pot of water or whatever unsavoury offering lay at hand. The drunk man would stagger around the backcourt, threats, oathes and missiles coming through the air at him from the windows above.

I never understood why the drunks did it, they earned nothing but a withering contempt that was always more entertaining than their singing, as the women cooperated in insulting them, shrieking with laughter at each other's attempts. I loved the drunks, not for themselves, but for the entertainment the women put on whenever they appeared.

Often though I would stay inside the house, because Peggy now had a baby son. I remember the day he was born because it was the first time I had ever been in a telephone box. The only public telephone around was in nearby Provanmill and Nan and I had squeezed into it to call the hospital. There was all the business with button A and button B, then Nan asking for the ward and for news of Mrs McAvoy. Outside we whooped and shouted with joy, Nan dabbing at her eyes with her hankie, then we rushed back to Moodiesburn Street to tell Maw Clark. We were in the house too a week later when Peggy came home with James Junior, and suddenly collapsed and was rushed back to hospital with a post-partum haemorrhage. It had happened with the stillborn child the year before and was to become the pattern everytime she gave birth. The new baby was a great novelty, of course, and Peggy seemed as relaxed as I could ever remember her. Mission accomplished: she was at last a mother.

A few months later, on Ash Wednesday, Nan and I had come through from Drumchapel to see Peggy and the baby, stopping at St Philomena's church first, so that I could have the ritual dab of ashes on my forehead. All Catholics knew that the ashes were sacred, to remove them was a great sin for which I knew I would be struck instantly dead.

Nan was shopping and I'd run on ahead because I wanted to see the baby. When I got to the house, one of Maw Clark's cronies was with her, a woman we knew as Auld Broon, and another strong supporter of the Orange Lodge. Peggy was changing the baby and suddenly Maw Clark leaned over, grabbed hold of me, snatched the dirty nappy and wiped it across my face, removing the ashes from my forehead. Then she and Auld Broon fell about cackling with delight.

Poor Peggy was embarrassed and took me into the kitchen, offering to replace the ashes with some from the fireplace, which was doubtless where the priest had got them from in the first place. But she didn't understand! The ashes were HOLY, they were BLESSED, and now I would be struck dead before finishing primary school as punishment for letting them be removed!

When Nan arrived Peggy motioned her into the kitchen and whispered what had happened, and the two of them entered into a conspiracy to calm me down by convincing me that the ashes put on my head by the priest had somehow survived. Then Nan went into the living-room and told Maw Clark off while Peggy kept me in the kitchen and gave me a special treat, some of the baby's National Orange Juice. I could still hear the raised voices in the living-room. 'It disnae maitter whit you think o' her being Catholic,' Nan was saying loudly, 'Ye've nae right tae take it oot oan the wean!' and my grandmother protesting that it had all been a joke. When we left, Nan was still angry enough to burst. I asked why Maw Clark had done it and Nan replied, 'Sometimes yer Maw's no' a very nice wumman hen, in fact maist o' the time she's no' a nice wumman! She's ma ain mother, bit she's common. Noo don't you go tellin' anybody that!'

'Dae they no' know?' I asked puzzled.

'Well yur Uncle George dis,' she replied, 'An' Peggy tae. Jist think aboot poor Peggy hivin' tae live wi' hur!'

Looking back at that incident all these years later, it was a rotten thing to do to any child, let alone your own grandchild. It taught me to keep my distance from my grandmother. Not only was I 'wan o' the Dark Yins', but I was also a Catholic, so I was learning that I was doubly at risk from her 'jokes'.

I used to hate arriving on those Saturday visits to find McAvoy there, and if he was in the house I would go out again until he had gone. I never mentioned it to anyone and never actually thought it out myself, but I just didn't like being around him. Somehow Peggy knew this and wasn't hurt by it. She would give me a cuddle and say with a smile, 'He'll soon be away oot, then it'll jist be us!'

While Nan talked to Maw Clark in the living-room I would stand beside Peggy as she made soup on the old kitchen range. These were the times I loved best, talking quietly to Peggy, just the two of us, and sharing secret spare ribs from the pot. We used to exchange little presents over the soup pot, too.

Peggy loved toffees and I remember buying her a tin for her birthday in August. There had been a choice of toffees in a tin with a battleship on the front, or some other sweets in a tin with flowers, so I made the woman in the shop empty out all the sweets and put the toffees in the flowered tin. Then Peggy and I had eaten them as the soup was made. Once she gave me a little square handbag that opened across into two triangles; I still have it somewhere. And I remember a red cardigan being handed over across the spare ribs, specially chosen to go with a black-and-white checked dress that she knew I hadn't been keen on. Eventually Nan would come in and demand in mock suspicion, 'Whit ur you two up tae then?' and Peggy and I would smile innocently and say 'Us? We're no' up tae anythin'!' through mouthfuls of spare ribs.

At the end of the evening Nan and I would take a trolley bus to High Street to meet up with Skip for the journey back to Drumchapel. Every Saturday he met old Eighth Army pals and they went drinking together, and I think Nan arranged that we met up so that she could be sure he was actually going to arrive home. She couldn't arrange what state he would be in though, and her anxiety ran through our precious hours with Peggy.

When we'd meet him Skip's moods would vary. He could be falling-down drunk and stupid, or nearly falling-down drunk and silly, and then again he could be rotten drunk and ready to fight, usually with my mother. There were pubs all along the way to John Street, the terminus for the Drumchapel buses, and it was just after throwing out time. There was a drunken fight at every pub door, so my heart was always in my throat. In Blackhill I had been protected from violence by the community and also by the men who caused it, but out in the open, in the dark, it threatened from all around.

It was always late when we travelled back to Drumchapel, arriving sometimes at nearly midnight. I hated those journeys because the bus was always full of drunks and there would be some kind of fight or someone being sick. I was terrified that my father would verbally join in a fight out of sheer cussedness, but usually he just slept. I was relieved when he did this, but disgusted too. Once we met him at High Street and he could hardly stand. We made the usual assumption, only to discover that he had stabbed himself accidentally with one of his knives at work that morning and had bled heavily; he wasn't just drunk, but weak from loss of blood. He didn't go to a doctor though. He didn't much believe in doctors.

There were no schools in Drumchapel when we moved

there. Laurie was at St Mungo's Academy by this time and had to travel as far as my father to get to and from school. Mickey was back in hospital, in Stonehouse this time, again, well outside the city. There had been no monitoring of his health after he had been discharged from Mearnskirk, despite the fact that the TB had already cost him the full use of his leg. Now the disease had moved to one of his kidneys.

Several months passed before the education department got organized. Then the Drumchapel children, including me, were bussed to and from the Marian School every day. The Marian had been founded in 1954 specifically for Catholic overspill children, as we were called. The Sisters of Notre Dame already had a fee-paying primary school in Dowanhill, and the Marian was set up alongside it. Nearby, the Sisters also ran Notre Dame High School for Girls, the top Catholic girls' secondary school in Glasgow. The bus ran through leafy avenues of quiet, 'big hooses', which seemed to confirm Nan's earnest belief that in moving to Drumchapel we had found Utopia. The Headmistress was Sister Frances Mary McNally, a quiet but imposing figure who regarded the Marian as her very own baby.

My teacher was Betty McGettigan, a marvellous woman who spoiled me for all other teachers, because she was what all other teachers like to think they are. While we worked in huge, high-ceilinged classrooms, in a class of forty-five children, Mrs McGettigan played Sibelius on an ancient gramophone. I had no idea what it was at the time or who wrote it, I only knew that quiet happiness existed in her classroom. Sibelius and Mrs McGettigan were ably abetted by the absence of boys, because the Marian was for girls only. The rooms and corridors of the school were panelled in wood just like the convent that adjoined it, and the smell of polish was the first thing you noticed when you entered. It was tranquil and orderly, and it was an extremely happy place to be in, chiefly I think because the nuns of Notre Dame genuinely liked children. It was the most civilized atmosphere to learn in and outside in the playground there were trees and grass and a cleanliness and freshness I had never known before. I discovered the existence of ladybirds in that playground one especially warm summer and I still have a fondness for the little beetles to this day, because seeing one takes me straight back to the Marian and Mrs McGettigan. However bad things were becoming at home, I had found an oasis of happiness and contentment at school in Glasgow's West End.

I was embarrassed by Mrs McGettigan's reaction when she found out that I read and wrote stories all the time. Just like flying, I assumed that everyone did these things. I read everything that was put in front of me or that I could lay hands on, and because I was busy doing so I hadn't noticed that other people didn't. It wasn't just that I enjoyed reading and writing, it all came so naturally that it was a part of me. So when Mrs McGettigan made a fuss over me it was like being praised for breathing. I thought she'd made a mistake and that when she realized this she'd be angry with me for misleading her.

She would give me a title and wait with barely concealed excitement until I had finished my latest masterpiece, then she would read it with unconcealed glee. Each time this happened I sighed with relief, then immediately started worrying about the next time, when she must surely find out. As far as I was concerned she was being extremely kind in letting me write a story, I was always grateful to be given a composition to do, so it was confusing to be treated as though I was doing her a favour.

Writing fulfilled a need. It gave me my happiest and most contented hours and made me feel really 'me', somehow. I suppose the seeds of being a loner were already taking root before I reached the Marian, perhaps in St Philomena's when I was given books to read and left on my own. Reading and writing marked me out as different throughout my schooldays. I was perfectly happy to be on my own, never needing or wanting close friends. Perhaps words were my escape from reality, just as Laurie's knights had been his. But what would I have done if I hadn't had words I wonder? How would I have coped then?

My complete incompetence with numbers saved me from

becoming really unpopular with the other children though, and I never understood why arithmetic was necessary or desirable in a civilized society; the truth is that I still don't. When it came to geometry and especially algebra I rebelled completely, refusing to accept that Y equalled anything just because someone arbitrarily said it did.

Betty McGettigan thankfully had a soft spot for creativity, and I was always aware that despite coming no higher than third in the class, and that only rarely, I was her favourite. She provided me with self-esteem at a time when I desperately needed it. I was coming to terms with the reality that I came way down my father's list of priorities, far lower than booze which came before everything else in the universe.

I made my First Communion while I was at the Marian, though not with as much gusto as the others in my class. While there were no schools in Drumchapel, lest the faithful had a chance to stray, the Catholic hierarchy built a church, called St Laurence's strangely enough. We practised making our first confessions at school for weeks, which must have been really riveting for some priest, and bravely swallowing bits of wafer in case we threw up the real thing on the day. Nan refused to spend money on a long dress, more to Peggy's disappointment than mine, so I was bought one that was short and very plain. Peggy, who naturally had tagged along on our shopping trip, was mortified; she didn't care about the occasion, she just wanted a few flounces and frills whatever it was all for. The veil was as short as possible and the head-dress plainer than the dress.

On the Saturday of the great event it was Nan who took me to St Laurence's, where all the other children were decorated like fairies on the tops of Christmas trees. They all clutched expensive rosaries in piously joined little hands and wore long, elaborate dresses under velvet capes trimmed with white fur, and they had walked proudly through the streets displaying their superb outfits. I had my coat on, buttoned up to the neck, the veil and head-dress stuffed in Nan's pocket. The only concession was a prayer book given to me by Auntie Norah, a special white one with a plastic cover made to look like marble and a little window on the front with a holy picture behind. At the last minute Peggy had given me a pair of white lace gloves, desperate for anything fancy to creep into the proceedings. When it was all over I was taken home again, my coat once again severely buttoned and my other knick-knacks concealed in various pockets.

It was left to my father to take me to a photographer for the ritual portrait, and it's no wonder I looked furtive, as though I was about to be grabbed and covered up again at any minute. Nan thought the whole thing was distinctly odd and was unable to hide it, and the cost of even a very plain rig-out must have taken a large chunk out of what little my father had handed her after his booze money had come out of it. I didn't feel cheated or upset, I never truly felt one of the faithful anyhow, but Nan was so annoyed at the whole business that it took her years to laugh at the strange little tableau we must have presented.

It was around this time, when I was about seven or eight, that Nan was diagnosed as having epilepsy, though there had been strange occurrences for a while that no one could explain. It had started a couple of years before, while we were still in Blackhill. I remember being on a bus with her one day, when she held up her hand, stared at her finger and earnestly inquired, 'Whit's that?' On other occasions, for a fleeting moment, she would seem not to recognize other familiar objects. Then very gradually she began to blank out completely for a few seconds, then for longer periods until just after we moved to Drumchapel she was having *grand mal* seizures.

During these she would collapse on to the floor, shaking and twitching all over and foaming at the mouth for several minutes, often biting her tongue or the inside of her mouth. Before the diagnosis was made she was having ten or more fits a day. Once she was put on various kinds of anti-convulsant drugs the frequency of the fits was reduced, but not completely controlled, mainly because she deeply resented having to take the tablets and would quietly cut them down or stop completely. She had very little warning of a fit, sometimes enough to call a name in a tone of voice we learned quickly to recognize, but after a time we could predict the kind of things that were likely to bring one on. If she was particularly upset, tired or excited we knew to expect a fit, which of course added another dimension to the rows about my father's drinking. There were times when I suspected him of deliberately upsetting her to bring on a fit so that he could meanwhile do what he liked without too much fuss. He was certainly childish enough to do it, but whether he was able to think up such a strategy in his befuddled state is something else.

Once, during a particularly bad argument he had raged on so much that she had had a fit. Next day, sitting in my class in the Marian, I was going over it all in my mind. Peggy was so far away and I couldn't talk to her till Saturday and my mother was at home by herself waiting for a repeat performance of the night before. I started to cry over my books and Mrs McGettigan noticed and tried to find out what was wrong. I had already learned the first rule for all families of alcoholics, that it was something to keep hidden, my own private shame, so I couldn't tell even nice Mrs McGettigan. Eventually it was decided by a process of elimination that I must be ill, and as we had no telephone at home my father was phoned at work to come and take me home. He was the last person I wanted to see, but at least he would be home sober for once. Mrs McGettigan spoke to him before we left. 'You know Mr O'Brien, Margaret is a very bright girl,' she told him, 'We expect her to take university in her stride, she's well capable of it.' He nodded and said, 'Oh aye, aye.' But even at that young age, I could see that she was trying to get something important through to him that he couldn't, or wouldn't, understand.

Because Nan's condition came on slowly over a period of two or three years, by the time she was having *grand mal* fits I had gradually learned to cope. It was simple, she had to be laid on her side for the few minutes the fit lasted and then she woke up. Afterwards she always had a splitting headache and temporary amnesia, but a couple of hours sleep would bring her back to normal. Her attitude to the condition settled into annoyance. She objected to having this nuisance thrust on her and was never reconciled to depending on the medication that eventually controlled the fits completely, but in reality it made little difference to her life. Taking my lead from her I took her epilepsy in my stride and it presented few problems.

The only reason she was ever given for her condition was possible oxygen deprivation at birth, which seemed at least possible. Like most city-dwellers at that time my grandmother undoubtedly suffered from rickets, which stunted skeletal growth, including that of the pelvis. So Maw would have endured a long, painful labour in those pre-NHS days, with no money for a doctor or the caesarian section she needed. It would have been entirely likely that at some stage the baby, my mother, was deprived of oxygen, and from the area of brain affected came her epilepsy. She refused to be called 'an epileptic', and became quite annoyed if anyone else used it as a description. 'Ah'm no' a disease!' she'd say defiantly, 'If sumbody his warts, ye don't call thum a wart, dae ye?'

Chapter Twelve

Drumchapel was beginning to grow on me. I discovered the Bluebell Woods, some distance from our house, carpeted during the spring and summer with the most wonderful blue flowers. I had never seen or smelt anything so beautiful and went on many expeditions to the woods with the other Halgreen kids, because Nan wouldn't let me go alone. Once there though I always wished I could be on my own in the beauty and the quiet. We pretended to ourselves that we were on an adventure by taking 'a picnic', which consisted of a slice of bread spread with jam and folded over. We used to take armfuls of flowers home with us, but bluebells are delicate creatures and they died quickly before we got there. We also discovered 'the Girnin' Gates', which were really no more than a large, arched stone gateway that was probably the remnant of a defunct estate. Once a rumour spread that the hands carved at the apex of the arch had been seen moving, and hoards of children gathered at the Girnin' Gates to watch for a repeat performance. It looked like the pictures we were shown of crowds at Lourdes waiting for another visitation, and just like Lourdes nothing more was seen, though those who wanted to believe still persisted in believing.

In front of 48 Halgreen Avenue was a deep valley that rose at the other side into another row of houses. On the floor of the valley ran a burn where we could catch sticklebacks, or baggominnows, called baggies for short, and on the other side of the slope stood massive trees that were just made for rope swings. Launching off from the side you would find yourself soaring hundreds of feet above the burn. It wasn't quite flying, but it was the nearest I had ever managed. No one was ever hurt seriously on the rope swing until Laurie took it a step further; Laurie always had something to prove.

He put the rope higher on the tree so that we could swing out even more, and inevitably someone fell off and broke an arm. That was the end of the rope swing. We tried leaving it till things had cooled down and then put the rope up again, but the adult bush telegraph was amazingly efficient and they quickly appeared to confiscate it.

In Blackhill I had discovered the joys of lying in the middle of the grass triangle and staring at the sky, and Drumchapel confirmed my preference for the countryside, because at first there was a lot of greenery around. Halgreen was bordered along one side by a farm complete with a field full of dairy cows. Sometimes an adventurous cow would escape into the street, even occasionally getting into a close, to the loud enjoyment of all the kids, most of whom had never seen a cow before moving to Drumchapel. It was great fun, of course, and we prolonged the entertainment by trying to return the bemused animal to the field again as slowly as possible. Because of the wandering cows, Halgreen became known as the Ponderosa, after the Cartwright ranch in the TV programme *Bonanza*.

On Sundays, Laurie and I would get up at 5 a.m. and meet up with one or two like-minded pals to go to the swimming baths in Clydebank. We had to walk about three miles in all, along part of Drumry Road, past the back of the graveyard and through bombed out ruins beside the railway line then onto Kilbowie Road. I liked playing in the ruins because the outlines of the rooms were still visible. I never thought about the people whose homes these had once been, I didn't know that the devastation had been caused by bombing because I was a Post-War child and had no experience of bombing apart from Nan's memories. The thing I noticed was that arum lilies grew all through the ruins; probably seeds had blown over from the nearby graveyard and taken root, and I remember them because I had never seen them before and they looked so exotic. Nan was none too pleased though when I took a bunch of them home to her. If poppies grew on the battlefields of the First World War it was perhaps fitting that arum lilies should grow on the scars of Clydebank, a small town that was as ravaged as any big city during the

War, because it stood on the banks of the Clyde and was the home of many famous shipyards.

We stayed in the swimming baths for hours and then walked home again, which took till lunchtime at least. Once I was thrown into the deep end by one of Laurie's pals and nearly drowned, but an off-duty policeman saved me. It was confusing to be grateful to a policeman; Blackhill had taught me that they came from a different planet and weren't to be trusted.

On Sunday afternoons my father took me to the Barras, the market place down by Gallowgate. Skip loved the bustle, the noise and particularly the bargaining. To him it was part of the Game to beat the stall-holders down, whether he really wanted something or not. Skip had a liking for bizarre china ornaments, but if some little curio caught his eye he didn't bid for it immediately – he would come back again, wearing his tattiest clothes, and try anything he thought might work to get it as cheaply as possible.

He once spotted a Satsuma-ware elephant teapot from Japan, and returned often to the stall, each time with a more pathetic performance. As the price went down so his clothes became poorer and his expression more downtrodden. Each time he sadly counted out the few coins in his pocket that were never quite enough to afford the elephant teapot. This went on for weeks, supplemented by heart-wrenching tales of some imaginary relative now breathing her last, whose dying wish for some peculiar reason, was to have just such a teapot. Eventually the stall-holder could stand it no more and practically gave it away to get rid of him, much to Skip's delight.

The main attraction for me was the possibility of seeing Uncle Hughie, whose house was within a street of the Barras. Skip would only visit him, though, if we happened to bump into him, because Hughie would undoubtedly assume points if his company was actively sought. I had absorbed all these insane, unwritten rules of the Game as I grew up, so I spent my time at the Barras constantly watching out for the figure of Hughie, hunched over the old wooden crutch, in the hope that he would happen by.

By this time he shared his house with his brother Pat, who provided the fourth and fifth legs of the famous sand-dance with Hughie and Skip. Pat was the least O'Brien-like of the family still around, and not quite up to the speed of mind their lunacy demanded. There had been a brother called John who had disappeared years before, who had been regarded almost as a changeling. He apparently hadn't a wit about him and had disapproved mightily of Hughie, so Hughie used to wait until he had fallen asleep and then paint John's bald head with black boot polish in vengeance. John eventually emigrated to Morecambe, where he married a hotel landlady, and who could blame him? He was never heard of again, so I was cheated of meeting the strange mortal who didn't like Hughie.

Pat wasn't quite as bad as John. He was at least aware of the Game but always made his move a beat or two behind the others. He was a lifelong bachelor who, it was rumoured, had had an unhappy experience at the hands of some female and therefore no longer trusted any of the species. So he had moved in with Hughie, and the two fought endlessly and happily for years. If things were dull Hughie would throw Pat out of the house on the grounds that it was after all *his* house, and Pat would then do the rounds of the family begging for their support. He would take the opportunity to go over each and every argument between himself and Hughie since the last time he had been evicted, much to the enjoyment of the others, then he would go home, by which time Hughie's mind would be on a different ploy. I always felt a bit sad about Uncle Pat because he wasn't quite like the others, but years later I heard a story from a cousin that he used to go up and down closes, removing doormats, mixing them up and putting them back at the wrong doors. So he may not have reached the heights of madness of his brothers and sisters, but I was pleased for him that he couldn't quite be called normal either.

Skip was so happy that I seemed to enjoy the Barras that he took me to his favourite place in all the world, Paddy's Market. As the name suggests, it started out as a place for the immigrant Irish to buy and sell whatever they had. It was situated in lanes and alleyways in the Saltmarket, one of the poorest areas of a very poor city at the turn of the century. I was appalled when I saw it, so shocked by a kind of poverty I had never suspected existed that I could hardly talk. The people were so poor that they were trying to sell the kind of things that others would throw away.

Skip loved it, he was at heart a street arab and he had some affinity with the people there, but I was one generation and some Clark dilution removed and I hated it. He saw it as a valid way of life while I could only see it as shameful, and my reaction was a very major disappointment to Skip. He had obviously thought at one stage that I was a *bona fide* O'Brien.

Paddy's Market is still there, in fact it has become a cult. I don't know if it's still as it was in the mid-Fifties, because I never went back. Indeed no one could persuade me or pay me enough to do so, and if I drive past it these days I steadfastly look in the other direction. Local colour it may be to those who have tried to reinvent Glasgow in recent years, but it's still shameful to me.

Drumchapel was the nearest Nan came to real happiness I think. The housing conditions and the general environment were better, at least by the standards of the late 1950s, so she had fewer problems to sort out for other people. She was still sought out by neighbours with family worries though, somehow she attracted the telling of deep personal secrets, but all she had to do was listen. She was particularly fond of the people next door, the Grimshaws, or as Skip called them, the Grimshanks. Alexa and Willie had two kids, Margaret and Alec. They were an eccentric family, but they didn't have the merest hint of malice or illwill towards any living soul. Alexa was a thin, friendly woman, always smoking, talking and rushing about, and always in the midst of some crisis that Nan had to be told about.

There was no heating in the Drumchapel houses, apart from a coal fire in the sitting-room, so if a natter was required it took place in the kitchen with the gas oven on and the door wide open to let out the heat. Nan was often summoned to the

Grimshanks' kitchen to hear the latest disaster, and always left laughing. The Grimshanks ate odd meals at odd hours and seemed to defy convention in an innocent, friendly way, if indeed they were aware of it. The house was full of all sorts of animals that Alexa had saved from all sorts of fates. Her husband worked in the Singer's sewing machine factory in Clydebank, and his hobby was collecting unusual musical instruments. He kept them in a bedroom, but he had no qualms about letting an unmusical and not very careful child spend hours torturing them.

I discovered the magic of the dulcimer in Willie Grimshank's music room, and also that I would never be a musician. We had a huge collection of old 78s, everything from Irish songs by John McCormack to opera by Caruso, and I used to spend hours singing along with them; Mario Lanza couldn't have reached those top notes without me. I then tried to pick out the tunes on Willie Grimshank's dulcimer and couldn't for the life of me understand what was wrong with the instrument that it couldn't do it.

Alexa's parents, the Dougans, spent a lot of time at Halgreen, and strangely enough they were a perfectly respectable and genteel old couple. They were as bemused by their daughter's lifestyle as everyone else was and it was hard to believe that they were related to Alexa. They never complained, but occasionally they'd catch your eye as if to check that it really was as odd as they suspected it was. Then they'd look heavenwards, shake their heads and smile slightly.

Once Alexa rescued a huge white rabbit that proved beyond any doubt that mental illness does indeed affect the animal kingdom. It went for anything that moved with fangs and claws bared, but it fitted easily into the Grimshanks' family life. All the family ran about avoiding vicious attacks from the demon rabbit, without giving any indication that they thought this was in any way odd. They would eat standing on chairs to keep out of its way, with other chairs strategically placed like stepping stones to other parts of the house. If anyone went into their house while it was loose, Alexa would shout 'The rabbit's oot!' and the visitor had to climb onto a chair too. If all the Grimshanks and the Dougans were in the house, visitors had to bring a chair from their own house, to climb on to, or wait until one became vacant or the rabbit was put back in its cage. It wasn't unusual to find the entire family watching TV or holding a conversation while standing on chairs, as though it were the most normal thing in the world, while the rabbit snarled and tried to get at them. But possibly the oddest of the Grimshanks was the son, Alec, a pleasant, cheerful boy a few years older than me, who even as a teenager took the cat to bed with him every night, dressed in a long robe. The cat that is, not Alec. It was that kind of household.

Chapter Thirteen

I was nine years old when Mickey came out of hospital again in 1957. At the age of twenty he walked with a strong limp because of the locked knee and he was now also minus a kidney, but the TB that had caused it was cured at last.

His final home-coming had been a focus for the family for so long that I was happy, but the reality didn't quite match up. It was like having another adult in the family to tell me what to do, one who had no particular affection for me as the other adults in my life had. How could he when he hadn't been around for most of my childhood? I resented his attitude and he resented the fact that I refused to accept his authority over me. Mickey was having his own problems adjusting to family life, especially poor family life, and all he did was complain and find fault with everything and everyone around him, chiefly me as I was lowest in the pecking order.

Peggy was the recipient of all my complaints about Mickey because my mother wouldn't hear a word against him. In our private chats over the Moodiesburn Street soup pot Peggy tried to get me to think about all my brother had missed and lost in his life, but I couldn't see that any of that was my fault. I thought he should think about what Laurie and I had lost because he had needed it, needed it and got it. It wasn't just the money that had been spent on him, it was also the lost time we might have spent with our parents if they hadn't been preoccupied with Mickey, spending long hours visiting him in remote hospitals. Sometimes Nan had been overcome with guilt about this and Laurie and I were subjected to 'treats' to make up. We would be taken somewhere for the day in the expectation that we would enjoy ourselves; I have clear recollections of a trip to

Edinburgh and another of a freezing day in Helensburgh, shivering in the sea to assuage Nan's needless guilt. None of this was Mickey's fault any more than it was Laurie's or mine of course, but it was a fair demonstration of the gulf between us, and not even Peggy's efforts could bridge it.

As Mickey came out of hospital Uncle Hughie went in. He was sixty-two and he had TB in his lungs, the disease that had killed his wife and three of his five children. He was in Robroyston Hospital and I wasn't allowed to see him though I never gave up trying. When the family went to visit he would take their gifts and exchange them before their eyes, so that they left with whatever the other had brought; he had an admirable way with insults.

To pass the time in hospital he declared himself to be a member of every religion that existed, and demanded to see a representative of each one. He then sent their holy pamphlets home to me; it was our joke, our way of keeping in touch, and I sent him notes and drawings via Skip.

Another gift he sent me was his prayer book, which had a crucifix inside the cover. The lower spar of the cross was loose, so that it swung under the Christ figure. I still have it; and everytime I look at it I swear I can hear him saying, 'Holy swinging Christ.'

He also used to engage the doctors in deep, meaningful discussions about the nature and cause of his illness, always ending by proclaiming, regardless of scientific fact, that 'That Mick Robés is tae blame. You find that Mick Robés an' soart the bugger oot!' No amount of detailed explanation could change his mind, and the unfortunate medics left his bedside in despair. Hughie meant microbes, but none of the learned and educated men of medicine could see that he was sending them up for his own amusement, they never cracked the Game.

About a year after he went into Robroyston, Hughie began to get worse. The report line was issued, calling all the family to his bedside to witness his impending demise. Skip was called from work and arrived with the others to find Hughie gone. Not dead, but gone. Somehow he had escaped from his deathbed and was found several hours later, sitting on the window-sill of the house he shared with Pat, as drunk as a monkey and singing 'Red Sails in the Sunset.' When Pat had arrived home to be greeted by this apparition, Hughie had demanded, 'Whaur's ma rent ya bugger?'

Still singing, he was escorted back to hospital, where the report line was hastily withdrawn. Over the months he managed a repeat performance six more times, and no one ever discovered how he had managed to cross the city with the trusty old wooden crutch safely locked up in the ward sister's office. Skip reckoned he must've bummed along . . .

Chapter Fourteen

Schools were soon built in Drumchapel, first the Proddie lot and then the Catholic ones. I watched mine go up literally in my own backyard, with no great enthusiasm I may add. It was called St Laurence the Martyr's, the same as the church where I had made my minimal first communion. The name had ironic connotations for our family of course, because Skip's standard act was that of the martyr, misunderstood by the world just for drinking all the booze money could buy until it either ran out or he passed out.

Finally the awful day came when the Marian closed its doors for the last time. The authorities came out with the same guff that they spout today, high-sounding twaddle about the good of the child and the importance of schools being situated within the community, but, as ever, the real consideration was money and damn the kids. Bussing was expensive. It was true that the Marian had only been intended to fill the gap until Catholic schools were built, but it was a good school, a happy school and that should have counted for something.

I sat at the back of the very last bus on the very last day, too blinded by tears to see the waving figures of the kindly nuns and Mrs McGettigan. Clutched in my hands was her parting gift, a book inscribed 'Special prize for composition, Margaret O'Brien', and earlier she had given a little speech as she made the surprise presentation. 'I know the rest of you will forgive me girls, when I say that my greatest joy has been reading Margaret O'Brien's stories. One day you will see her words in print and I hope you will remember that I told you so today.' I hadn't a clue what she meant.

Contained within the bright green covers of the book was

the proof that there was a happy land somewhere, and I held onto it like a thread through the labyrinth, leading home to Notre Dame. Once again adults had shattered my world, but I was determined that I would get it back together. I would hold fast to my thread and one day I would pass my eleven plus and find my way back to Notre Dame High School. That's what I'd do . . .

Meanwhile Peggy had given birth to a daughter, but there were problems. It had been a difficult birth and the child was handicapped, in fact she wasn't expected to live. A week after the birth Peggy came home without her baby and immediately collapsed with another post-partum haemorrhage. No one talked about the baby, not even Peggy, we all pretended she didn't exist. In later years I would recognize this strategy and despair of it, but it was the only one the family knew.

The child had been called Anne after my Grandmother, another appeasement. As the months passed Anne held on to whatever slim chance she had of life and her handicap slowly became clearer: she had cerebral palsy, but no one knew yet to what extent. Sometimes when we were alone I would quietly ask Peggy how the baby was – she was always 'the baby', never 'Anne' – and Peggy would whisper back 'She's a'right.' She must have visited the child in hospital but she never mentioned it, and because Nan never spoke of it at the time, it was many years before I discovered that my mother had gone with her.

If the child had died as she was expected to do, then her existence would have been kept very quietly between one or two. I suppose they thought this might save the rest of the family grief, but it didn't of course. Peggy's pain caused us all grief and perhaps if she had been able to talk freely about her baby we could have shared her pain. But the little girl survived against all the odds and came home aged ten months. Anne was an incredibly beautiful child, with fair skin, blue eyes and silvery blonde hair. She reminded me of Laurie before his hair had darkened to brown. Peggy barely left the cot for a second, her entire universe had become centred on the fragile little life that shouldn't have survived.

As Anne grew and her handicap began to unfold, Peggy would make me look into the cot. 'She's a'right, in't she?' she would ask earnestly, 'Ye don't think thur's anythin' wrang wi' hur, dae ye?' Young as I was I'd shake or nod my head as she wanted, sensing her desperate need for my lies. Over the months, as Anne made less progress than normal babies, Peggy insisted that she was 'jist a wee bit slow.' Mistaking their anguish for her only as rejection of Anne, Peggy vigorously defended the dribbling infant against the rest of the family.

As time passed too, McAvoy felt more and more intimidated by the Clarks, perhaps sensing their increasing hostility towards him and sympathy for their sister. After all, she now had a handicapped child *and* McAvoy. The Clarks 'think thur sum'dy,' he would declare defiantly, as long as there wasn't a Clark about. The family's attempts not to make their dislike of him too obvious, not to look down on him for Peggy's sake, were probably more damaging than outright contempt. Honest people, they simply made bad liars.

St Laurence's was a modern, bright, square-shaped construction, seemingly made of glass and plastic; it looked like a rather nasty warehouse. It couldn't compete with the wood-panelled Marian, set amid leafy avenues and genteel mansions, and the teachers were nothing like Mrs McGettigan and the nuns. It also had boys and a wider mix of abilities than I had been used to, a combination that brought me my first experience of the tawse.

One boy in my class of ten year olds was James Campbell, who was nicknamed Bramble, a huge boy more than two years older than the rest of us. Bramble had spent a year in a sanatorium with TB and had been placed in our class to catch up. He got no real help and in fact being with younger children reinforced his feelings of inferiority. He came from a very poor family too and the attitude of the teachers was easily detectable: he was riff-raff. Quite naturally Bramble reacted to his situation by disrupting the class whenever possible. Thus he was universally liked by the children and universally loathed by the teachers, who anyway were only really interested in the top ten or so pupils.

One day, having struggled with the mind-numbing convolutions of long-division and seen a glimmer of light, I was waiting in line to have my attempt marked. I found myself by Bramble's desk, where he sat as though on the outside looking in, making no attempt to work. 'Kin you dae this?' he asked, in a tone implying that a positive answer was tantamount to disloyalty. 'A bit Bramble,' I replied, and flushed with the zeal of having seen that glimmer, I asked 'Wull Ah show ye?' And that's where the teacher found me, doing what she couldn't or wouldn't do, trying to help Bramble break into the world of ticks. Three whacks on each hand she gave me, and as she sweated over her task I knew she was beating me with her own inadequacy and that it was a pitiful, if painful demonstration of might over right. I had the dubious benefit of a lifetime's exposure to the O'Brien view of life and though I may have had stinging hands, I knew I had won the points.

I was more popular with the boys at school than the girls. The boys involved me in their escapades and adventures and treated me as one of them, so the girls actually had little to be jealous of, not that this stopped them. To the girls any attention from the boys was welcome, be it rough horse-play or winks, because it all meant male attention. They were already conditioned to become future wives and mothers rather than people, so any male attention was important to them.

My compositions were still the talk of the place and the boys were always my supporters when marks were read out. The girls would try very hard to make their 'well dones' sound sincere, which made me laugh, because they so obviously weren't. There was a little clique of four or five girls who were always the top group academically and I was amongst them but not part of the clique. They came from the better-off families and already had fee-paying secondary schools earmarked for after the eleven plus and it annoyed them that I was bright yet uninterested in joining their gang. They were therefore delighted when a new boy, John Burgess, took over as top of the class and immediately went into competition with me for top of English, especially composition.

John was light years ahead of me in the dreaded Maths, but he could never beat me at composition and to my delight it irked him something fierce. He used up a great deal of time and energy trying, and each time he failed he showed his disappointment so openly that I almost felt embarrassed for him. Almost, but not quite. Once, to my immense satisfaction, he was unable to contain himself after losing again by just one mark and demanded to know why. Before the teacher could respond Bramble shouted ''Cos hur's is better, ya big shite!', to a spontaneous round of applause and laughter from the other boys. He received the teacher's staple punishment for any misdemeanour, three of the tawse on each hand, for which I somehow felt responsible and apologized to him. 'It wis worth it!' he said, dancing around, his hands tucked underneath his oxters, 'Did ye see his face?' Then he rolled around laughing and shouting 'Ouch!' at the same time.

Apart from Skip's drinking, Nan's belief in the magical qualities of Drumchapel persisted, she had even managed to get as near to a fitted carpet as didn't matter. It was a large square in blue, black and maroon, a colour scheme that went with nothing else, and though it lay in the middle of the living room with a linoleum border all around, she was delighted with it. A little man had come around the doors selling terrazzo doorsteps, instead of the council's nondescript wooden ones, and she had recklessly ordered one then had to scrimp and save to buy it. Halgreen may not have been the 'big hoose' of her dreams, but it was Nan's palace. She still planned a better life for her kids though, and her fantasy for me was that I'd become the private secretary to some rich managing-director then marry him. I treated this as I did Peggy's dream sequences about weddings, I winced and said nothing.

Laurie had struggled through school and left at fifteen to become an apprentice engineer in the Albion Works in Scotstoun. Nan was pleased that he'd have a trade and that he wouldn't become a shoemaker and therefore a drunk like Skip, something she had always dreaded. Mickey was working in Glasgow University, which gave Nan no end of pleasure and she tried to bring it into every conversation. Neither job brought in a lot of money, but at least Nan had the satisfaction that her sons were doing well. If that meant living with the chronic anxiety over unpaid bills, well that was something she had lived with all of her married life anyway.

Gradually the fields around Halgreen Avenue became built up with houses and the roads became the only places for children to play. The main problem with that was that the roads carried double decker buses and were barely wide enough for two to pass each other. Even the valley with the burn, the only piece of greenery left, was filled in and built on. There were few shops and no social facilities or employment within Drumchapel; it was just another ghetto, somewhere to dump those who couldn't afford anything better. The actual housing conditions had improved, but life in general hadn't, and like all the other Fifties estates it gradually went downhill. This gave the planners and the City Fathers the opportunity to wring their hands in woe; they had done their best for these people, given them inside toilets for heaven's sake, and still they weren't satisfied, still they didn't behave like model citizens! Therefore, it must be their own fault.

In the last years of the Fifties though, the worst faults of Drumchapel had yet to materialize, and Nan could see only blue skies ahead.

Once I came in from school to find her cuddling a little man, both of them in tears, and apart from the fact that I didn't know him even by sight, the scene didn't strike me as all that odd. I later discovered that he had come to fix our rented TV and Nan had been working about the house, singing, as she always did. Suddenly he had burst into tears and asked her to stop. He was a Polish Jew whose entire family had died in Hitler's concentration camps, and the tune my mother had been singing was a Yiddish lullaby he had known all his life. He was the first person I ever saw with the chilling tattooed number inside his left forearm, and for me he shrank the world and made fascism and the holocaust personal. He also became a fringe member of the family from then on, dropping in for chats and tea even when our telly wasn't on the blink.

So they came to her still, the people who needed whatever solace it was that Nan provided. Usually they found her doing her housework and singing, going from room to room carrying a shovel on which reposed a tortoise called Tormy, the last one we ever owned. Tormy was obviously a tortoise in distress because he worshipped Nan too, and he attempted to follow her on her rounds on his stumpy little legs. Despite her resistance to anything connected with O'Brien insanity, she grew fond of Tormy and felt sorry for him, but she couldn't bring herself to actually touch him. So instead of lifting him up she carted him around with her on a shovel, as he gazed up at her adoringly and gulped in that silly way that even the best-bred tortoises are apt to do. I don't think she ever stopped to consider what impression this eccentric apparition made on casual callers who didn't know us all that well, and that of course was exactly what made the rest of us smile.

We never had a pet that wasn't a tortoise; whenever we asked for a kitten or a puppy Skip appeared with yet another chelonian reptile. It was many years before I discovered why he was so fond of the little creatures. Apparently the O'Briens had two of them in Tarbet Street, and whenever Granda Tom arrived home after one of his sojourns with his aesthetic friends, Granny O'Brien belaboured him over the head with the tortoises. It doesn't take a great deal of psychological understanding to recognize the Freudian significance of Skip's fondness for tortoises, and it was the only adverse comment he ever made about his father that I know of. Tortoises of course do not fare well in the Scottish climate and none of ours lasted more than a few years. We buried them all beside the Tarbet Street originals, in the

Ramshorn Graveyard in Ingram Street, where the upper echelons of Victorian society lie at peace under metal cages to protect them from body-snatchers.

Some century in the future, archaeologists will dig up the site and conjecture about what the tortoise shells tell them about Glaswegian burial practices, little knowing it was confined to the O'Briens. One of my dearest wishes is that they should if possible be the same archaeologists who find Hughie's unwanted legs, filled with ashes at the bottom of the River Clyde – I would love to be around to hear their conclusions.

Chapter Fifteen

Peggy had given birth to another child, a healthy boy she called John, and apart from the usual post-partum haemorrhage all had gone well. She now had three children under four years of age though, one handicapped to a still uncertain degree, and Nan and George discussed the situation. After a further talk with the 'Fair Yins' it was decided that George, the eldest male in the family, should talk to McAvoy about the wisdom of avoiding any more pregnancies.

The first mistake that McAvoy made was to take George's deceptively quiet manner as uncertainty, and the second was in daring to compare himself with George. 'Ye've goat three weans yersel',' he swaggered, though George's children were each separated by more than nine months, unlike McAvoy's. His next mistake was to take George's silence for surrender instead of the gathering anger he struggled all his life to keep under control.

'An' Ah'll dae wi' ma wife whit Ah like!' the little man swaggered.

In reply George just picked him up and shook him like a rat. 'Listen wee man,' he hissed, 'You an' me ur no' the same! An' Peggy wull aye be ma sister, long efter she's your widda!' He had lifted McAvoy off the ground to get eye-to-eye contact and was holding him by the front of his jersey, which was slowly tightening around his neck. The rest was drowned out by shouts and screams, and I heard Auntie Annie's voice with the familiar warning, 'Watch Geordie!' and then my mother's saying, 'George! George son! Pit him doon! Ye don't waant tae swing fur the likes o' that insect!' I had taken refuge under the table as usual, and as George's grip was released finger-by-finger, I saw

McAvoy slowly sinking to the floor only inches from me. A long way above, Uncle George's face was ashen with rage, his hands still clenched with fury. As my eyes locked with McAvoy's I saw that he was shaking with terror, and I was glad that he knew I'd seen it.

Within months Peggy was pregnant again.

I was neither happy nor unhappy at St Laurence's; it was just somewhere to fill the time before I went back to Dowanhill and Notre Dame. I would have to sit an entrance exam and then there would be modest fees of around two-pounds per term. Skip was drinking more than ever and money was even tighter, but still I contrived not to pick up the coded messages that I might not get back to Notre Dame. I still harboured the certainty that it was only a matter of time.

I was still at St Laurence's when Uncle Hughie died in September 1958. Uncle Pat had been summoned from work by the hospital and had gone straight home to find the windowsill empty. But Hughie wasn't to be outdone; on his deathbed he informed the assembled family that if they made him die he'd get even, he'd haunt them forever. Who else but an O'Brien would believe that the O'Briens had the power of life over death?

Afterwards Skip, Pat and Norah went to St Alphonsus' down by the Barras, to arrange the funeral with the priest, who in a moment of madness left them alone in his study, along with a store of communion wine. When he returned he found Skip dressed in various vestments, marrying his sister to his brother. The 'groom' was handsomely dressed for the occasion in the priest's chasuble, the richly embroidered, sleeveless garment worn when giving communion. The 'bride', whose passion for hats was well-known, sported the black three-cornered biretta with the central pom-pom at a jaunty angle, and all three were clutching the last of many half-empty bottles of wine. The priest then sat down with this motley crew and arranged Hughie's funeral. Norah disgraced herself by falling asleep and snoring loudly throughout. The biretta slipped over her eyes, but miraculously her grip on the bottle remained strong. When the meeting was over, the three O'Briens stood up and silently divested themselves of the ritual garments, laying them neatly in a pile before leaving. The priest had said nothing throughout, which I found puzzling until Skip reminded me that he was Hughie's parish priest, so he would have been used to worse. 'Mind you,' he said disapprovingly, 'Norah ferr gave us a showin' up wi' hur snorin'.'

Skip, to whom tears were a sign of weakness, sat in George Square until he got enough control of himself to come home and tell us that Hughie had died, missing the ordinary buses and having to wait for the night service in the early hours of the morning. His eyes though were still red-rimmed and Nan spotted it instantly and maliciously accused him of crying. Skip hotly denied it of course, but the points went to Nan; she had caught him showing human emotion, crying for his dead brother, and it was one of the few victories she ever got over him.

'Did your uncle have the last rites?' asked my teacher, and I glumly nodded. Uncle Hughie had made a fetish out of having the last rites. Up till then he had celebrated each reprieve with a few choruses of 'Red Sails in the Sunset' and the odd bottle of plonk. 'Well that's all right then,' the silly woman replied, 'He'll be in heaven now.' It somehow failed to raise my spirits. I didn't want him in heaven; what had heaven done to deserve having him? I wanted him here to keep my world bright. Even though I hadn't seen him for over a year I knew he was still there and so the light of his lunacy had still illuminated the land. The last time I had seen him was just after Mickey had come out of hospital. He ruled the roost so much that neither Laurie nor I were happy to have him home. We were looking for ways to demonstrate our feelings, when we hit on the idea of joke soap to turn his face black. We had no money of course, so we had set off to find Uncle Hughie, who took us to his one-roomed home, his single-end in Bridgeton's Stevenston Street, listened to our story and gave us enough to buy the soap. Now he had truly gone and there was no adult left in the world who would understand the importance of spending money on black-face soap . . .

Hughie's funeral was preceded by a family conference to discuss his threats of long-term hauntings. To be on the safe side it was decided to have him buried without the trusty wooden crutch. As he had managed to find his way across the city on numerous occasions – and that while falling-down drunk – quite why they thought coming back from the next world without it would cause him any problems I have no idea. But then logic was never their strong point.

When the coffin, minus crutch, arrived at the church for the receiving service the day after Hughie's death, the O'Briens sat as far from each other as possible, because with very good reason they simply didn't trust one other. At the end of the service they all moved independently with one thought in mind, to touch the coffin in a last gesture of farewell, or as Skip insisted, to make sure the lid was on securely. There was a sharp intake of breath from the assembled congregation that always turns up uninvited at such events, as coincidentally the O'Briens reached the coffin at the same time. They surrounded it and each laid a hand on it, in a theatrical, almost cabalistic ritual. But the effect was nearly ruined when Tommy, who had no time for the Catholic church or the family's excesses, paused on his way out. 'Christ aye, that'll be right!' he said sarcastically from halfway up the aisle, 'Arise an' walk ya auld bastard!' Then turning to leave he obviously remembered the missing crutch and turned back. 'Or at least hop aboot a bit!' he added with relish.

Refusing to be put down by this interruption, the others were so taken with the effect their performance had created, that the 'laying on of the hands' became a tradition at every family funeral thereafter. A piece of genuine O'Brien folklore had been invented.

When Hughie died I was ten years old and beginning to show the effects of the dilution of the blood; some Clark sensitivity had crept in. At the wake I told Skip it was wrong that we should be having a good time while Hughie lay alone in the cold, dark church. Skip was aghast; no family member had ever mouthed such obscenities before in his hearing. 'Don't be daft!' he exclaimed, 'It's the first time in ma life that I've goat the better o' the auld bugger. An' if it'd been me insteed, him an' that crutch wid be up here the noo, dancin' aboot, as drunk as a monkey. An' besides,' he added, looking furtively about, 'How dae ye know he's no' here tae?'

Next day, the family, attired in their Sunday best, filed into the church for the final service before burial, and behind them extra mourners arrived unexpectedly. Every down-and-out and wino in the vicinity was there, and arriving last they left first after Hughie had been carried out to the waiting hearse. They took up position on foot immediately behind the hearse and along the route more joined in. This made it impossible for the posh cars provided for the family to take their rightful place of prominence because they were falling further and further behind. Eventually the cars were abandoned and the family had to follow the unofficial mourners, none of whom had been any too fastidious about their personal hygiene or attire.

'He's planned this!' I heard Skip mutter in delight, 'An' he's roon' the coarner noo, laughing at us!' The same thought seemed to strike the rest of the family and they all started laughing, which put a nice finish to a very odd funeral. I'm sure they were right too; no one had ever won the points from Hughie while he was alive, what possible difference could a little thing like death make?

'Ah'm sorry aboot yer Uncle Hughie hen,' said Peggy softly, and cuddled me to her. Then she pointed to the sky, where shafts of sunlight pierced the clouds. 'See that?' she said, 'That's God sendin' doon pathways tae heaven fur people that's jist died, mebbe Hughie wull be oan wannae thaim.' Even at the age of ten I had to smile at Peggy and her hopeless, undying romanticism. If I knew Hughie he'd be selling spaces on God's pathway to those bound in the opposite direction . . .

Pat, now alone in Stevenston Street, was haunted by

Hughie's 'twin' behind the door, but he finally summoned up the courage to dismantle Louis and then tried to lose his leg, the last artificial leg in existence. Not for him the formal handing over of the leg to the relevant authorities though, instead he tried to burn it, but it wouldn't burn. He left it in a hospital waiting-room and it came back to him next day. He abandoned it on a bus and it was returned the same day. He put it out for the binmen and they left it propped against the door, so that when Pat opened it the leg fell across his feet. 'Ah'm tellin' ye!' he wailed to the others, who were enjoying the whole business hugely as his paranoia grew, 'It's him! He's efter me!' Finally he tried Hughie's own solution to the unwanted second leg problem, and it joined the rest, filled with ashes at the bottom of the Clyde.

The hauntings weren't finished though, because Norah reported doors and windows opening by themselves. The others, delighted at the opportunity to add to the family collection of myths, decided that they had noticed the very same phenomenon. Soon every and any odd happening came to be attributed to Hughie, and so generations who were never privileged and fortunate enough to have actually known him, look up as the breeze blows a door open, or when they lock themselves out, or if there's a power cut, and say 'It's Hughie again!' He managed it after all, not just gone and not forgotten, but gone and very much still here. And if that isn't immortality, I don't know what is.

Chapter Sixteen

In my entire school career I only got the tawse twice, both times at St Laurence's. The first was for trying to help Bramble do his sums, but it would be years before I understood why I got it the next time.

I went home every day for lunch, partly to satisfy myself that Nan was all right, and partly because we couldn't afford school lunches, and Nan would have died rather than apply for free meals. Free meals were a badge of poverty and the kids who qualified for them were told to stand to one side, just to reinforce the point that they should be both ashamed and grateful, and to let them know that everyone else knew of their crime.

At the end of one lunch-break Nan had a fit and by the time I had got her to bed, where I knew she would sleep soundly for a couple of hours and then be fine, I was late for school. Late comers had to report to the deputy head, who invariably beat the living daylights out of them, but this time I thought I had the perfect reason. 'My mother had an epileptic fit, Sir,' I explained, 'And I couldn't leave her until she had come out of it.'

'You evil-minded madam!' he yelled, and went at me with the tawse like a man possessed. I hadn't a clue what had happened to him and simply assumed that he had gone bananas, as we all knew teachers were wont to do from time to time.

Something else happened at school that wasn't cleared up until the first incident was solved too, which also involved Nan. I had gone home on another lunchtime to find the house covered in blood and Nan staggering about almost comatose, begging 'Help me, help me.' A few days earlier she had been given new tablets by the GP, Dr Fields, who had been reminded at the time that she was already on medication to control the epilepsy. He had become quite annoyed at this, 'I'm the doctor here,' he'd said, 'You're only the patient Mrs O'Brien.' When I found her that day she had fallen semi-conscious against furniture and walls and her face was badly injured. I knew immediately that the new tablets were to blame. Growing up with a condition like epilepsy you develop an instinct for pitfalls and learn to identify problems quickly, but I didn't know what to do about it. We had no phone and neither did any of the neighbours, so I had to leave her while I ran back to school to ask the headmaster to call a doctor. I put Nan to bed first, which in fact was probably the wrong thing to do, but had I left her out of bed she would certainly have hurt herself more.

The headmaster was very sympathetic when I told him my mother was ill and rushed along to the school office to phone a doctor, while I trotted at his heels telling him the full story. When he heard that Nan had epilepsy he stopped in his tracks and refused to make the call. So I had to run home again, take money from one of Nan's secret stores and find a phone-box to call Mickey at work, the only number I actually knew because it was at the top of a letterhead that Nan had kept. Mickey called Dr Fields and we sat by her bed all day waiting for him to arrive, which he never did, and it was, I'm sure, sheer luck that she recovered. Dr Fields arrived the next day and took the new tablets away, but he didn't make any comment and certainly he never admitted his part or apologized for it.

Over the years I would replay the incident in my mind and wonder what had happened. Had I explained it wrongly to the headmaster, had he somehow misunderstood? Why else would a learned, educated man react that way except if he had misunderstood? I was an adult before I learned that epilepsy was regarded by the general public as a sign of being possessed by the devil, that epilepsy sufferers were thought to be mad, unclean or given to excessive sexual appetites, and I could hardly stop laughing. Then another mystery from the past suddenly fitted into place.

One day we had been going to see Peggy. We were about

to get off a tram in Parliamentary Road when Nan had had a fit. I was nine or ten years old, and there I was trying to prevent her falling off the platform of the moving tram onto the road, and no one would help me. The conductor and passengers stood back watching, but not one of them would help, and when the tram stopped they all insisted I had to somehow get her off. This was a situation I could have handled blindfold within our own four walls, but she had never fitted outside before and it took me ages to persuade her to go home with me. She was so confused that she couldn't cooperate and I remember her saying over and over again, 'Ah don't know whit tae dae . . .'

She had brought me up to believe that her condition was a nuisance, nothing more; for her it meant inconvenient fits and the necessity, the indignity, of depending on tablets. For me it meant coping with the fits and trying to make sure she didn't cheat on her dosage. Beyond that it curtailed our lives not at all. But to the good people of Glasgow she wasn't safe to touch, to the deputy head it was an insult, and to the head, well God knows exactly what he thought. Strange to think that Nan had so respected learning and education, yet a man who represented it so ably was a bigoted idiot and not one hundredth the human being she was.

Chapter Seventeen

In the Winter of 1958 we had a family wedding. One of my cousins was getting married, the son of Nan's sister Vicky, the eldest Fair Yin. Vicky had 'turned' to marry a Catholic and so her son had been brought up in the religion. Now he was marrying in St Mungo's, and much to Peggy's delight it was to be a white wedding. Nan, Peggy and I went out to buy wedding finery for the two of them at a club store.

A little man called Arnold White had come to the entire Clark family for as long as I could remember. For an agreed weekly sum he would issue a line to buy clothes from one of two warehouses he dealt with. The prices were high and so was the interest paid, and it meant there was little choice of where to shop, but it was the only way we could ever afford anything for the wedding. Mr White had issued Nan and Peggy with lines for both warehouses and off we went. It was a good day, full of fun and laughter, even though Peggy was pregnant again. They tried on everything in one warehouse and then tried on everything in the other, just for the fun of it. Peggy wanted Nan to buy me a fancy dress too, because she knew one of my 'Fair' cousins had a new rig-out, there was 'Dark Yin' honour at stake. I'd been given a pink dress for my tenth birthday a few months before though, and Nan was having none of it. Feeling sorry for me, Peggy gave me a necklace to wear, a cheap plastic popper of pink flowers with a glittery rhinestone in the centre of each one. Nan eventually settled for a blue dress and Peggy for a pink one with an all-over pattern of pale blue flowers. In the centre of each blue flower on the bodice was a glittery rhinestone, just like the necklace.

When the wedding day came around they had swapped, as they always did; Peggy was wearing the blue dress and

Nan the pink. Being Proddies they hadn't a clue what to do during the wedding service, and tried to follow my knowledgeable movements, kneeling, sitting, standing and generally bobbing about. Eventually it became too much for them and they collapsed against each other, laughing so much that the tears ran down their faces and the familiar creaks of merriment echoed all the way through the ceremony. And the more they tried not to laugh the more they did. They were like two schoolgirls, and I remember reflecting that had I behaved like that I'd have had a severe dressing down. Once outside at the end they mopped their eyes and told each other what a hoot it had all been, which set them off again of course.

That night, at the reception, after the bride and groom had gone, I went upstairs and heard singing coming from the room where the bride had changed out of her white dress and veil. And there sat Peggy at a dressing table, the wedding head-dress and veil on top of her curly hair, staring into the mirror and singing 'Mexicali Rose' very quietly to herself, lost in her dream of being a white bride. Somehow I knew enough not to disturb her; I left her alone to enjoy her fantasy and crept downstairs again, but the picture became imprinted on my memory forever and I see it still all these years later. Peggy as the bride of her dreams . . .

Chapter Eighteen

It was 19th December 1958; I know this because it's recorded in my ten-year-old script on the back of a plastic calendar, the kind you keep in a wallet. We were watching TV at home; it was a nature programme, something about birds, and the wind was howling outside. There was a knock at the door, and when I answered it I found Alexa Grimshank standing there in her usual agitated state. 'Thur's a fire through the wa'!' she said, and returned to her own house.

I closed the door and sat down again. 'It wis Mrs Grimshank,' I said, 'She said thur's a fire through the wa'.' Everyone nodded; Alexa was known to fly the odd kite and we all knew not to accept what she said as gospel. Still, something made me get up and look out of the window, where there was a lot of debris flying about, then I ran out onto the verandah, Laurie close behind, and Alexa had been telling the truth.

The top floor flat in the next tenement, which adjoined the Grimshank house, was well ablaze. We did what anyone would do in similar circumstances, panicked a bit, tried to figure out what to save, came to the conclusion that there was very little, then grabbed our coats and left the house, knocking on all the other doors on the way down. We stood outside in the cold, night air, watching sixty foot flames shoot into the sky, waiting for the fire-engines to appear. It was *déja vu*, shades of Balmano Brae.

The house belonged to the Ramsays, a family of shy, attractive children, two boys and a girl. They were a quiet, respectable family and both parents worked, so the grandmother, who lived with them, looked after the children. That night, it was thought that the youngest boy, who was about five years old, had been playing with matches in bed and had set the house on fire. The two boys and the grandmother were safe, but there was no sign of the middle child, Ella, who was the same age as me. Ella rarely played with the other children in the street. A pretty child, with blue eyes, short, curly blonde hair and a shy smile, she was always well dressed and we thought her mother wouldn't let her out to play for fear of getting her nice clothes dirty. We felt sorry for her because she was a pleasant girl and we all thought she would have liked to play with us more often.

The adults were knocking on doors up and down the street and in the facing block of tenements, trying to find her, while the rest of us huddled in the cold, watching the firemen being raised on turntable ladders with hoses going full-bore into the flames. A *Daily Record* reporter took Laurie and I into his car and gave Laurie a slug of whisky to heat him up, and from there I saw Alexa Grimshank. She had her hair in rollers and was wearing her fur coat over her nightie. On her feet she had an ancient pair of slippers over ankle-socks, and looped over her arm was a handbag containing all her money. In one hand she carried a budgie in a cage and clutched a dog on a leash, and in the other was the killer rabbit in another cage, plus the inevitable cigarette sticking out between two fingers. I wondered where she had secreted all the other animals, the cats with sore paws and the birds with broken wings, for I had no doubt that she had them with her too. It was the sum total of everything Alexa held dear enough to rescue from the flames, the clearest statement imaginable of what made her tick, and despite the drama being played out in front of me that night, the sight of her made me laugh.

The Ramsay parents arrived home within an hour or so and had to be held back from rushing into the burning building. I remember Mrs Ramsay's voice clear against the noise of the fire-engines, the crackling of the flames and the howling of the wind, screaming 'Ma weans! Ma weans!'

It was nearly 4 a.m. before the fire was out and the people in our part of the building were able to go back to their houses, but still Nan and the others looked for Ella. Then the firemen lowered a black box by rope from what was left of the Ramsay house. 'Whit's that?' Nan asked a fireman, 'It's the wean,' he replied, 'We found the wee lassie in her bed.' On the ground below the windows lay the Christmas presents the Ramsay children would have got in less than a week and I remember a doll lying there, grotesquely twisted from the flames and matted with mud.

The smell of burning was everywhere, a characteristic smell that lingers in the memory still, different from any other kind of smoke. Our house wasn't damaged but Alexa's house was. The room where I tortured the dulcimer was a blackened shell and water had penetrated the places that the flames had missed. The chimney was unsafe and part of the roof between us was open to the sky, so the firemen covered the hole with a tarpaulin and sat up for what was left of the night making the chimney safe so that the families below could go to bed. That night was the start of my admiration for firemen. During my working life I would have cause to admire them over and over again. They remain to me the finest human beings ever to draw breath.

Nan couldn't sleep and spent the night making soup and tea for the firemen. By the first light of morning she was on first name terms with them and when they finally left it was like losing friends we had known for years. I was allowed to sleep on into the day after the fire, which annoyed me, because I had badly wanted to go to school to tell everyone about it. As it was a Friday I wouldn't be able to tell them now until after the weekend. Being me, though, I had to write it down. I used the plastic calendar, the first thing I could find, to record the event in very small script.

Next day the basic details were on the front pages of every Glasgow newspaper and I was concerned that Peggy might think we had been hurt. After all, it was reported that an unnamed girl of my age had died in a fire at Halgreen Avenue, and maybe Peggy would think it was me. When we saw her as usual the next day, though, she said she hadn't been worried.

'Ah knew it wisnae you,' she said, 'Ah knew ye wur a' a'right.'

'How?' I asked.

'Ah jist knew hen, that's a',' she replied with a shy smile.

Later I asked Nan how Peggy could have been so sure.

'She tellt ye hen, she jist knew,' she said, smiling the exact same smile.

We never saw the Ramsays again, they were moved to another part of Drumchapel and never returned to Halgreen Avenue. Occasionally a neighbour would report bumping into Mrs Ramsay and that she had walked past them, and I found that very odd. With hindsight though, I can see that she just couldn't take any more reminders of what had happened on that December night.

Chapter Nineteen

Christmas and New Year 1958 passed in the usual mixture of family celebrations and drunken arguments with Skip. But I remember it particularly because of an incident that will remain with me for ever.

A few days after New Year Skip took me with him to see an uncle and his family. They lived with his wife's parents, because her mother had been an invalid for years and was totally bedridden. I liked going to sit with the old woman because the stories of her childhood were like history to me and I loved to hear them.

That night I left her bedroom and walked down the long, dark corridor towards the living-room, where the rest of the family were talking and laughing. Suddenly the old lady's husband stepped out of the darkness and grabbed me. He had obviously been waiting for me and pulled me against him, his wet mouth all over me, the smell of stale booze and cigarettes making me feel sick. One hand held me tightly while the other one was fumbling about in my pants and I could feel something hard pressing against my stomach. I froze completely. The living-room was inches away but I was so shocked and confused that I couldn't summon up the fight to get away from the old man to safety. What shocked me most was that I had known him all my life. He was an old drinking pal of Skip's and my cousins' grandfather. I couldn't believe he was doing this to me. Then the door handle turned and he pushed me away.

We both went into the living-room, where the party was in full swing. I felt physically sick and disorientated; everyone had been enjoying themselves without the slightest suspicion that inches away, on the other side of the door, the old man had been sexually assaulting me. When we were leaving he tried to give me money and I put it on the table and left it there. When he asked for a kiss I refused and Skip was annoyed, so once we were outside I told him what the old man had done to me.

Skip's response was a mixture of anger and annoyance, as though I had broken some unwritten social code by mentioning it. It wasn't that he didn't believe me, it was that he didn't want to know. It was as though these things happened, but they shouldn't be mentioned and he was ashamed of me for not adhering to that social nicety. His ten-year-old daughter had been sexually assaulted by someone she should have been safe with, but it would upset his life to acknowledge it or do anything about it.

I felt ashamed, dirty, unclean, and Skip's reaction had reinforced all of it. It must have been my fault, something to do with how I behaved or looked, or else Skip would have done something . . . wouldn't he . . . ? I didn't tell another soul, not my mother and not Peggy, who anyway, was now out of bounds. Peggy was expecting a baby in early May, my mother had told me, and I knew how sick Peggy got, so I mustn't annoy or upset her. So I kept my dirty, nasty, guilty little secret to myself. It had been all my fault, and even if I could have told someone I don't think I would have, I was just too ashamed of myself.

Every excuse was dragged out to explain why I couldn't sit the entrance exam for Notre Dame. Skip wanted me to go to Garnethill Convent near St Aloysius, because Granda Tom had had close connections with the school. Suddenly it seemed we were to honour the name of dear, departed Granda Tom, whose name hadn't been mentioned in years because no one cared anything for him. Couldn't I just try the exam? There was no point, I was told, even if I passed I wouldn't be going there, 'family duty' meant I had to go to Garnethill.

So the little clique of top girls at St Laurence's went to sit the entrance exam and returned with the papers. They had all passed. The teacher read out the questions and I was the only one, including the clique, who got all of them right.

And I'd have walked the composition too. I didn't think it was possible to be so unhappy, but I was only a child then; time would teach me that there are troughs and depths of unhappiness not even hinted at in the worst nightmares of a disappointed, almost eleven-year-old . . .

By this time Mickey had found a way of escaping from weekends in Drumchapel. Working at the University he had met up with a crowd of people who went to the hills instead of spending their weekends in the city. Being Mickey he soon amassed the equipment he needed to go with them and every Friday he would disappear and every Sunday night he would reappear. All of this was welcome in a way, because I now heartily loathed the sight or thought of him; the gulf between us had never lessened. He just wasn't one of us yet he controlled all of us. Nan still adored him unconditionally, I think she felt guilty about all those years he had spent in hospital, as though somehow she had been to blame.

Workmen had dug a deep hole in the road leading to Halgreen. Skip had been warned to watch out for it as he left for work that Friday morning, warned several times. 'Ye'd think Ah wis a drunk!' he protested indignantly. That night, coming home drunk as usual, he fell down the hole and couldn't get out for hours. Nan sat up waiting for him, but I had a feeling he was down that hole. He managed to scramble out in the early hours and we heard the familiar sound of him crawling up the stairs. He had broken his nose and his face was covered in blood mixed with the sandy-red soil, but he was in playful mood. As we tried to clean him up he would slip under the table and shout 'Peeka boo!' When we turned our backs he hid in a cupboard and shouted 'Ye cannae find me!' Next morning after his 'anaesthetic' had worn off he suffered. Apart from the broken nose he was covered in bruises from the fall and from falling back again everytime he had tried to clamber out.

   It was one of the few occasions when he didn't win the points. But Nan did, she went around smiling for days!

Chapter Twenty

It was around this time that Skip became a businessman. Looking back, it had all the elements of farce that were as necessary to his daily life as booze. Somehow he managed to rent a shop near Gallowgate and set up his own shoe repair business. He had no capital and of course had done nothing to find out whether such a business was needed or wanted in the area.

Every Monday and Tuesday evening Laurie and I would be sent around the doors of countless houses throughout Drumchapel, asking the occupants if they had any shoes to be mended. These would be carted home, often very late at night, and next day Skip in turn would cart them to his shop for repair. On Friday, pay night, we repeated the process, only this time returning the mended shoes and collecting the money. Again it would be very late by the time we got home and carrying the money laid us open to all sorts of dangers. There were times when we were scared, and one night we were certainly followed by two men. There were police houses nearby, so we sat in one of the closes for half an hour, knowing that if the men did intend to rob us they wouldn't do so anywhere near the police. When we came out the men had gone and we ran home. We never told Nan anything of this, she already disapproved of the arrangement but had been won over by Skip's assurances that all would be well, and it was only for a little while until business picked up. And anyway, the kids liked it.

Luckily for Laurie and I, the experiment into big business was headed for failure after only a few months. Skip had taken on someone to help him mend the shoes, but from what was coming in he could only pay one wage and that went to the other man. Together they would drink that, plus anything more that Skip might have, and soon he was back working for someone else again. All his life he insisted that if he had had another twenty-five pounds he could have made the business pay, but in truth it was like all of his fads, doomed to failure through short-lived enthusiasm and lack of thought.

Peggy wanted a home delivery. With her obstetrics history of difficult labours and haemorrhages, Nan had been sure that she wouldn't get it. The GP would tell her that it would be best if she went into hospital to have the baby, and Peggy would follow that advice. So it was a shock when he agreed to Peggy's request. It seemed impossible. Peggy was looking after Maw Clark, running the house, caring for three children under the age of five, one of them handicapped, and coping with McAvoy. Peggy was worried about leaving her children, so the other Clarks offered to care for them while she was in hospital. But McAvoy refused to let my mother, or any of the Clarks for that matter, take the children, either singly or together. Nan tried talking to him, and then arguing that Peggy needed to be in hospital, that she always had a bad time, and that she also needed rest. But the little man decreed that he would look after his own family.

When Nan told the rest of the Clarks they glanced knowingly at each other. 'When did he come up wi' this idea?' Uncle George asked sarcastically, 'He's never bothered aboot lookin' efter thum afore.'

'Leave it,' Peggy pleaded, 'Jist leave it. Don't annoy him, ye know whit he's like.' Anything for a quiet life, that's what she meant, she had to live with him and it was easier if he wasn't upset. And besides, the last baby, John, had arrived without any fuss or trouble, this one would too. Anything to keep the peace . . . It became another reason to despise McAvoy, as though another reason were needed.

George and Nan talked about how to deal with the situation, but they knew there was nothing to be done. McAvoy should've been thinking of his wife instead of using her to get one up on the family, they said, but their hands were tied. 'Ah'll tell ye wan thing,' George said darkly, 'This is the last wean. She shouldnae be hivin' this wan, bit it'll be the last yin!'

Something was wrong with Nan. It seemed as though one minute we were all talking, thinking and worrying about Peggy, and then without anyone noticing, Nan became ill. There were sobs and screams every night and often we would find her re-doing housework in the early hours, afraid to sleep and face whatever demons lay in wait for her. There was about her a frantic cheerfulness, a tendency to be jovial and talk too much, but never to meet your eyes. Then she would lapse into a deep silence, as if the pretence of communication was over, and having concealed whatever it was that she was hiding from everyone else, she could now brood on it alone. Dark circles appeared under her eyes, her skin took on a yellowish tinge and she aged rapidly, yet she refused to see a doctor. Every nightmare was explained away next day and became transformed in the telling into a funny story. It was as though she had surrounded herself with a protective wall of false laughter to deflect those who knew her and were close to her, a kind of emotional radar jammer.

'Ah hid this dream,' she told us one day, 'Aboot oor Peggy. She wis wearin' a long, white dress, an' cairryin' a big bouquet. Pink they wur, big pink roses. An' you wur therr,' she told me excitedly, 'An' ye wur fussin' roond aboot hur. Ah tried tae talk tae hur bit she jist stared straight aheed, widnae take any notice, it wis like it wis jist the two o' ye and yese wurnae botherin' wi' anybody else! Then she drapped her flooers and ye picked thum up, and she took wan o' the flooers oot o' the bouquet and gied it tae ye!'

Having lived all of my life with Peggy's wedding fixation, I was keen to tell her. 'She'll like that story!' I enthused, and was stung by the immediate change of mood. 'Ye'll no' tell Peggy! Ye'll jist leave Peggy alane!'

These spells of dark, brooding silence were followed by others of scaring hyperactivity, and she would hustle and bustle around, organizing, directing and then abandoning whatever she had been so engrossed in. She alternated between snapping viciously and greeting with over-enthusiasm anyone she met, and all the time there was that haunted, driven expression in her eyes.

There was no balance in her life or in her behaviour. Although I was about to sit my eleven-plus exams she would suddenly decide to keep me off school and we would set off together to visit Peggy, usually on the day of her ante-natal appointments with the McAvoy family doctor. For some reason Nan waited for the results of these appointments in a state of tension, but often after setting out on the journey to Blackhill we would turn back and return home instead, once only yards from 6 Moodiesburn Street, without seeing Peggy. There was never any explanation, probably because she didn't have one. I was barred from 'annoying' Peggy, now in the last three months of her pregnancy, so Uncle George was the only one I could turn to. 'She'll be worried aboot Peggy hen,' he told me, 'Ye know whit hur an' Peggy ur like. It'll be a' right when Peggy's better again.' Despite all this Skip didn't seem to notice anything wrong.

Easter Monday fell on 30 March in 1959, and at nearly eleven I could easily find my way alone from Drumchapel to Blackhill, so I had gone on my own to see Peggy. She was pale and quiet. The warm times, the funny times had gradually faded away during her pregnancy, but we still had our own private times together.

She decided we would walk to Hogganfield Loch, a mile or so away. I'd been there often with Laurie and David. We used to go on the pleasure boats or feed the ducks and swans, and we'd collect wild rhubarb for Nan to make pies or give us to suck raw with sugar.

It was overcast and chilly that Easter Monday, as Peggy struggled to fasten her coat over her growing belly before we set off. It was a green coat that had belonged to Nan, only Nan had become convinced that green was an unlucky colour, just as she was equally sure that keeping a lock of baby's hair would bring bad luck. Although she was by no means certain that the bad luck wouldn't follow the coat, reluctantly Nan had let Peggy have it.

Peggy was unusually quiet, in fact she didn't say a word as we walked along. I picked up a stick and started hitting stones along the ground and she made me stop. At the Loch I practised skiting stones; I was never any good at it, two bounces across the surface of the water was a major achievement for me, and I needed all the practice I could get. She stopped me doing that too. We had brought along some bread for the birds, but she wouldn't let me feed them. I began to wonder why she had wanted to come. On the way back she wouldn't even let me collect any rhubarb; it was as though she needed me to be there with her, not to talk, to play or pass the time, just to be there. It was something I nearly understood at the time, but not quite, like so much of what was going on. It was a time of restlessness, of waiting, without knowing what was being waited upon, somehow.

I was just reflecting on what a washout the day had been, when she did something truly puzzling. Our way home took us by Riddrie Cemetery, and she knew I was scared of it. Nan and I had to pass it on Saturday nights after our visits to Peggy, to catch a bus into the city centre, and to tease me, Peggy would laugh and make ghostly noises at me as we left her house. It was a place I would walk miles out of my way to avoid, and if I had no choice I'd hurry along with my eyes averted, breathing a huge sigh of relief when I was safely past. But on that Easter Monday, Peggy went inside, and I felt the hair on my neck bristle.

'Ah'll meet ye at the other gate Auntie Peggy,' I said, and made to hurry along the road.

'Naw hen,' she replied, 'C'moan in wi' me,' and with that she put an arm around my shoulders and propelled me into the graveyard. I was horrified. She knew I was scared of the place and I couldn't understand why she was doing this to me. I fixed my eyes on the the wall that separated the cemetery from the road and tried to calculate how quickly I could get over it, but again Peggy had other ideas.

As I hurried on, she dawdled, stopping to read the headstones on the way, and all the time I was struggling to keep my nerve and not bolt for home. I was torn; I knew I had to take care of her and go slowly because she was pregnant, yet every fibre of my being was screaming at me to run. I was angry with her, and the longer she took the angrier I became. She looked up at me as though she had heard my panic and laughed softly, then she put her arm about my shoulder again and hugged me to her. I was almost crying with the confusing mixture of emotions, fear, anger, hurt – feelings I wasn't used to having about Peggy, all mixed up with the closeness, the oneness, I always felt with her. Then to my huge relief, we left by another gate, and without a word of explanation from Peggy, we made our way back to the house. McAvoy was there when we returned. He looked at me. 'His she no' goat a hoose o' her ain?' he asked Peggy, 'She's aye here.' Peggy glanced at him and replied, 'You kin talk when it's *your* hoose she's in! She's merr right here than you!' I was amazed; I had never heard her answer him back, but she'd been tetchy all day.

Later, back home in Halgreen again, I told Nan about Peggy's detour through the cemetery, and she was as puzzled as I was. There was no one buried there that Peggy had known, she hadn't after all been raised in the area, there were no schoolfriends in it and no family either.

'Wis she wearin' that green coat?' Nan demanded, narrowing her eyes suspiciously, and I nodded. 'Ah shoulda burned that green coat!' she said with conviction, as though this explained everything, and Skip laughed.

'Did that green coat shove Peggy in the gates?' he asked in exactly the same suspicious tone of voice that Nan had used, 'That green coat's a bad bugger, a sneaky bugger! It aye goes lookin' in graveyairds so it dis!' He had narrowed his eyes too and was squinting about theatrically. Nan tried not to laugh but she couldn't help it.

'Ah jist don't like green!' she protested.

'Christ aye, we a' know that!' Skip laughed, 'Yur a' the same you Proddies, ye'd like the grass better if it wis blue, or orange mibbe!'

'Ye know whit Ah mean!' Nan was chuckling, but still trying to stand her corner.

'Aye,' replied Skip, 'Ye jist don't like green! Ye *tellt* us!' In the cold light of Drumchapel, it seemed funny and we all laughed.

Skip's greatest, and, perhaps, only talent was laughter and he could convert almost any situation into hilarious fun. This was a perspective the Clarks lacked; because they cared more deeply, they often took the world more seriously than was good for them.

Nan's superstition was already the subject of one of Skip's favourite jokes against her. Once his sister Norah, the family's self-appointed psychic, dragged Nan off to a spiritualist meeting. Nan wasn't happy as it was, but her discomfort had been increased when the medium had approached and told her she had an aura. Giving a detailed description of Da Clark, he urged Nan to come back to receive a warning message from her father. Nan was petrified and came home white as a sheet, but Skip was merciless and Nan's aura became a fixture. 'How's yer aura the day?' quickly became one of his sayings, 'Watch oot noo,' he'd say as she went downstairs, 'Don't fa' an' break yer aura!' In company he'd suddenly announce 'Did ye know ma wife's goat an aura?' He'd then go on to describe it, 'It's a wee thing, aboot so high,' he'd say solemnly, holding his hand a couple of feet off the ground, 'It's orange of coorse, wi' six legs an' it's covered in blue fur. It disnae bark or growl, it sings "The Sash". Bit it's a pedigree aura ye understaun', nae rubbish . . .' Given his way with Nan's aura, her thing about green was mincemeat.

Nan's dreams went on, and curiously, the more manic her behaviour became, the quieter Peggy grew. We saw her not only on a Saturday but also whenever the mood moved Nan, and although the two of them talked they didn't seem to communicate. I would watch these two women, who together had raised me, looking from one to the other as they spoke without connecting, trying to put my finger on what was wrong. Sometimes it seemed I nearly understood, then it would slip away from me before I could grasp it. In turn I would feel Peggy watching me, and smiling quietly;

as if she knew that we were all three of us part of the same restless, waiting, waking dream.

The 10th of May 1959 was my eleventh birthday and Peggy's pregnancy continued. She was now a week overdue and and as the month wore on she suffered the traditional remarks of, 'Ye still here yersel'?' 'No' better yit?' with her usual quiet, good humour. Nobody in those days referred directly to the baby or to childbirth; pregnancy was regarded as an illness that was cured by the totally unexpected appearance of a baby, and even that much was talked of in hushed tones. Children were left to understand by osmosis that the baby was inside in the growing stomach of a pregnant woman, and if this was actually mentioned by a child it was treated with great embarrassment. So hidden was the whole subject that I can remember wondering where babies did come from, because by the reactions of the adults around me, they obviously couldn't come from where they obviously did. If that wasn't the baby inside Peggy, I wondered, what was it and where then was the baby?

Monday the 25th of May was a public holiday and Nan had decided we were going into town together. Then she changed her mind and we ended up in Peggy's house. It was unusually hot that May and Peggy was sitting by the window, her folded arms resting on a small table in front of her. The sun was streaming through the window, putting her face in shade and lighting the outline of her curly hair in a fuzzy halo as she turned towards us. She was very quiet, becalmed in the final days of a long pregnancy that had tired and drained her even without the hot weather to help. So she didn't see us out, and we stood by the living-room door, winding up the conversation before we left.

'See ye oan Saturday,' Nan said, 'If yur still here that is!'

Everyone laughed.

'Cheerio Auntie Peggy,' I said. There was about her an air of fragility, of vulnerability and reacting to it I impulsively ran across the room to hug her. Everybody laughed again.

'Cheerio hen,' she smiled, holding me so that our two cheeks were crushed together, 'Ah'll be seein' ye!'

I rejoined Nan at the door and together we looked at Peggy, not seeing her smile because of the sunlight, but feeling it. Walking down the road to the bus stop I saw tears running down Nan's cheeks. I didn't say anything; I was by now used to all sorts of bizarre behaviour. Over that week her nightmares continued unabated and the weather remained too hot for comfort.

The following Saturday my mother suddenly decided that Peggy's baby was arriving, and much earlier than usual I was rushed along the road to begin the journey to Blackhill. Nan was very bright, her eyes shining.

'How dae ye know?' I asked, because we had no phone, few people did in those days.

'Ah jist know!' she replied cheerfully, and caught up in her excitement I could hardly sit still on the bus.

As we went in Peggy's door we were met by an aunt, one of the 'Fair Yins'.

'It's Peggy,' she said.

Nan and I looked at the closed bedroom door.

'His she hid it yit?' Nan asked, 'Is she a' right?'

As Nan sank slowly to the floor I was already moving away, our different movements in unison, triggered by the same knowledge. The aunt's arms closed around me, holding me so tightly that I could hardly breathe. I felt a terrible force rushing towards me, something was going to happen and she wouldn't let me go. So I punched and kicked, trying to get to the outside door, desperate to escape before it found me. I didn't hear the words, I felt them coming at me from a long, long distance before they were actually said, if indeed they were. In that split second I knew that Nan knew, had known all along, and I felt totally betrayed by her.

Out the door and leap down the eight back stairs to the backcourt. My ankles hurt with the jarring impact, but run on. *Run!* Across to the midden and dive behind the dustbins, lie flat among the garbage. Stop now to listen for them coming after me, only I couldn't hear anything because there was a thudding in my ears, drowning everything out. I turned my head to left and right then back again, but I could still hear only the pounding. Through a gap in the concrete I could see an illegal bookie paying out in the corner close, his minder at his side. The crowd milling around him seemed to be miming; heads thrown back laughing, arms waving, all normal except no sound apart from this thudding in my ears. The demons of hell were after me, the same demons that had pursued Nan all these months and I had to escape. Had to!

I crept out, zig-zagged between the air raid shelters and into a close to the left and sat down till the noise in my ears cleared and my chest stopped hurting. Think. *Think!* It was Saturday. Everybody came to the house on Saturday, so Uncle George would be here later. All I had to do until then was find somewhere safe to wait, somewhere the demons wouldn't think to look for me; so that ruled out the playpark and the pond.

Beside the bus-stop was an old ruined house that the local kids knew was haunted, we used to dare each other to go inside. The crisis had exorcised the ghosts, so I made my way there. I didn't think about anything, only waiting for Uncle George, that was all, not why. Hours must have passed, I was cold but it didn't matter; it was growing dark and he still hadn't come off any of the buses. Then I saw him, standing on the platform of an approaching 102 trolley-bus. I ran to meet him.

'Hullo wee yin,' he smiled, jumping off before the bus had stopped, 'Whit ye up tae?'

'Jist muckin' aboot,' I told him. I kept my eyes from his; if he read my eyes it would give him a clue and that might make it come true.

He looked at the grazes and the dirt on my clothes. 'Hiv ye been fightin' or sumthin'?'

I shook my head. He put out a hand and touched a long scrape down my arm. 'Christ hen, ye're freezin' cauld!'

'Ah'm a' right Uncle George.'

'Ye comin' in wi' me?' he asked softly, beckoning with

his head towards the house. I shook my head again, still looking down.

'Well, don't stey oot here too long eh?' He stood looking at me, puzzled. 'See ye then,' he began to move off, his cigarette half-raised to his lips.

'Don't go in there Uncle George,' I said.

'How no' hen?'

'Thur sayin' daft things,' I replied, still looking at the ground.

'Daft things? Who ur? Whit kinna daft things hen?' He stared at me for what seemed like hours, then his face seemed to freeze. 'Is it Peggy hen? Oh Jesus Christ! Is it aboot Peggy hen?'

The cigarette fell from his hand and he was running towards the house, the words still hanging in the air where he'd been. Later, as I watched from my cold sanctuary, I saw him set off to look for Skip, who was drinking somewhere. Uncle George was a 'Dark Yin', he had always looked like my mother; now he looked like the shadow she had become over the last few months. He had become part of the nightmare. Maybe it was true then . . .

Hours passed and he came back alone; Skip always knew how not to be found when engaged in his favourite pastime. We met up with him again as usual in High Street on our way back to Drumchapel. The 'Fair' aunt had come too because my mother was in such a state, which enabled me to sit well away from them on the bus, untouched by what had happened. I don't know what words they had used to tell Skip, I had walked away to look in a shop window, but my mother had collapsed again.

It was then decided to take her to the aunt's house for the night, because it was nearer and she couldn't have made the long journey to Drumchapel. At this news I threw an uncharacteristic tantrum. I hated staying in other people's houses; no matter what I always had to get home and especially on that night, to reclaim some kind of normality. So though I knew I couldn't win, I cried and screamed in protest. Nan was mortified that I should create such a scene, but I didn't care. I felt totally detached from everyone in the world and couldn't have cared less about Nan especially. She had known this was going to happen, had known it for months and had pretended she didn't. Well the nightmare was of her making and she could have it, I'd take no part in it.

Next day I sat as far away from my parents as possible on the bus home to Drumchapel and concentrated on the 'big hooses' I had first seen the day we had moved. As usual I gazed down the road that led to Notre Dame, trying to see as far along as possible before the bus passed and it was out of sight. At the Drumry Road bus stop I ran ahead of Nan and Skip and up into my bedroom. Laurie came in to ask why we hadn't come home last night and I ignored him. Later I heard Skip's voice in the room next door that Laurie shared with Mickey; it was muffled through the wall, but I knew what he was telling them by the tone. I climbed into bed and hid under the blankets, imagining myself somewhere else until it was over.

That Sunday morning we quickly changed our clothes and then returned to Peggy's house, where I eavesdropped as snippets of information were passed in whispers from one shattered relative to another. I wasn't being chased anymore I decided, the demons had after all accomplished their work, but if I kept my eyes down I discovered that I became invisible. That way I could hear without being told and could thereby not know if I chose not to. Only if I lifted my eyes would someone reach out to me, only then would I become part of their awful reality.

Peggy had apparently gone into labour on Saturday morning and the doctor had been called, but he wasn't there and a locum had come instead. In fact 'he wisnae a real doacter', and Peggy had screamed all day. The doctor had locked the bedroom door and only opened it to demand more towels and sheets. Maw Clark had to knock on neighbours' doors and ask for any they had when her own had been used up. I overheard her telling someone that 'the screamin' stoaped aboot four,' and she had gone out into the street and stopped two passing policemen.

The doctor who 'wisnae a real doacter' had refused to unlock the bedroom door, so the two policemen had broken it down, and when they saw what was happening inside they had sent for an ambulance. Peggy was barely alive by that time; the towels and sheets had been used to soak up a massive haemorrhage. At the Royal Maternity Hospital at Rottenrow she was taken straight to theatre in an attempt to save her unborn baby, but it was found to be already dead. Fifteen minutes later, so was Peggy. She was two months short of thirty-seven years old.

It was easy to avoid my mother over the next couple of days. She was locked in her own private world, but her eyes were docile now instead of frantic and her voice flat calm. It was like the end of a storm. Family activity centred on Peggy's home, now oddly quiet and empty, despite the rooms overflowing with people, and to my great relief they had little time for me. Now that Peggy was about to return once again to the room where she had suffered and died, the mirrors in the house were covered in keeping with tradition. This was to prevent her spirit seeing its own reflection and deciding to remain in the house. The white sheets covering the windows were a symbol of cleansing against the pollution of her death. It added to the unreality of the situation and helped me reject all of it. Nothing made any sense.

I spent most of my time on top of the old red-brick air raid shelter in the backcourt, out of reach of anyone, twelve feet above the ground. I lay on my back on that Sunday, determinedly concentrating on the clouds that were bringing an end to the hot spell. Some people see castles and things in clouds, but I never did; clouds were fine enough illusions in themselves. As I lay there, bright shafts of sunlight broke through, Peggy's 'pathways to heaven' and I told God what to do with them in no uncertain terms, and what I thought of Him just as candidly. I used every 'bad word' I had ever heard. 'Bastard!' I yelled, 'Swine! Git! Shite! Pig!', and then to make sure He knew I meant business, the ultimate insult, 'DRUNKEN IRISH PIG!' There was a sudden commotion and the door to Peggy's house burst open. Uncle Willie bounded down the stairs and was noisily sick in the backcourt, then he sank to his knees and wept, his forehead against the grey stone of the tenement. On top of my refuge I calmly turned my head away and my attention back to the sky; whatever was happening was part of the adults' world. None of it had anything to do with me and I didn't want to know . . .

On the Monday I had to endure a visit to a shop to buy shoes for an event I had no intention of attending. I still hated Nan and wouldn't talk to her or make her lot any easier if I could possibly help it. She tried coaxing me into conversation, but all I wanted was to be left alone forever. And I didn't want her rotten shoes either.

'There's a nice perra black patent yins,' she said, 'Try thaim. Ye *know* ye like patent yins,' hinting at the famous shoe quest when she had sent me with Peggy, who had been warned to buy only good, serviceable school shoes for me. 'Don't let hur talk ye intae anythin' fancy,' Nan had ordered, and Peggy had nodded firmly, full of resolve. We came back with a pair of bright-red patent shoes with ankle straps that fastened at the front with a single red button, and they made a clicking noise as I danced along the pavement. Sitting on the trolley bus on the way home to Blackhill I had kept my feet stretched out in front of me in case someone stood on my beautiful, magical shoes. As I stared at them in wonder Peggy laughed and kept repeating, 'Yur ma wull kill us, ye know! She'll kill the baith o' us stone deid when she sees thum!'

If Hughie was the only adult who understood about black-face soap, Peggy was the only one who understood that just once in every girl's life she needed bright-red, patent shoes that clicked when you walked. I became Ginger Rogers; for the duration of the red shoes I danced along the streets, the shoes didn't allow walking.

I wore the red shoes long after they fitted comfortably, and one day the local priest stopped me as I tapped along the pavement.

'These are awful red shoes ye have,' he said in his soft

Irish brogue. I wondered what he meant; awful red, or just awful?

'I suppose your Proddy mother let you have such vain things?' I hadn't a clue what he meant; they were red not vain, whatever that was.

'Naw,' I answered proudly, 'Ma Auntie Peggy, bit she's a Proddy tae!'

The priests always had a go at my Proddy relatives, who they knew for a fact were hellbent on destroying my good, pure, Catholic, eternal soul. Well, eternal as long as my Proddy relatives didn't win that was.

'Jist try thum,' Nan pleaded, holding the black patent shoes.

'Naw! *Naw*!' I shouted at her. I was behaving in a way that I had never dreamed I was capable of, but there were no boundaries any longer. Normal life had been suspended. Nan bought the patent shoes anyway, no doubt hoping to win me round. Next day, as I climbed the midden and jumped up onto the air raid shelter, I deliberately scraped the toes of the new shoes along the bricks. Then I lay down to concentrate on the sky, which was thankfully dull and overcast; God had taken the hint, not a pathway of sunlight to be seen. From there I could keep an eye on the comings and goings at Peggy's door, mainly callers in Brogan's vans delivering flowers. I remembered the Brogan's van that was always parked in Frankfield Street, on the route between Acrehill Street and Moodiesburn Street when we still lived in Blackhill. It had a huge basket of flowers painted on one side, and I used to run over, 'pick' the flowers and present them to Peggy when we reached her house. To tease her sometimes I pretended to forget and she would say, 'Where's ma floors then?' Then I would hand them over; it was our private game, our little bit of nonsense that no one else knew about, except Nan of course. Now Brogan's vans were bringing Peggy flowers that she would never see . . .

From the door I heard a cousin being dispatched by an aunt to find me.

'Yer waantit,' a voice said from below.

'Beat it!' I growled.

'Ye'd better come doon ur yur fur it!'

I jumped down from all of twelve feet, landed on my cousin and thumped him about the head.

'Noo beat it!' I snarled, and climbed back up on the shelter. He lay below crying, 'Yur daft you!' he shouted, 'Yur daft! Everybody knows it tae! Ma mammy says ye don't care aboot Auntie Peggy, yur jist oot here playin' a' the time because ye don't care!' I made to jump down again and he got up quickly and ran.

'Your mammy's a "Fair Yin",' I told him, 'So whit dis she know aboot anythin'? You go back in an' say ye cannae find me ur Ah'll get ye later!'

As I lay back down on the shelter roof I could hear him in the distance, obediently reporting that I was nowhere to be found.

Later I made another invisible sortie into the house to keep tabs on the situation. The 'fair' aunt pounced on me.

'They'll be takin' yer Auntie Peggy away soon hen,' she said, 'Dae ye waant tae see hur?'

'Naw.'

'It's a' right hen, it's no' frightenin' nor nothin'. It's jist like she's sleepin'.'

'SHUTUP! NAW!'

Her hands were coming towards me as I backed off in panic, making for the door and pushing past Uncle George as I ran, my aunt's voice protesting behind me.

'It's no' right! That lassie meant a lot tae Peggy! She should be made tae pey her respects insteeda playin' ootside a' the time!'

'Leave the wean alane!' Uncle George's voice was low and angry.

'An' she tellt me tae shutup tae!'

'Ah said leave the wean alane, ya stupid bitch!'

Chapter Twenty-One

From the top of my shelter fortress I could see movement out of the corner of my eye. Cars had arrived at the front of the house, and with a growing sense of panic I felt reality closing in. I wasn't ready for this; I'd thought I could keep it at bay by ignoring it, but it was happening anyway.

Still trying to maintain my cloak of invisibility, I slipped off the shelter and ran through a close at the side. A crowd had gathered outside Peggy's house, blocking the whole of Moodiesburn Street. Keeping my eyes down I found a way through and suddenly came upon my uncles and McAvoy carrying the coffin out of the close-mouth.

My instinct was to turn and run, but before I could I realized that though I was only inches away from them, they couldn't see me. I was totally detached, watching as though I had no more part in this than the huge throng of onlookers all around us. The muscles of Uncle George's pale, drawn face were working furiously, the way they did when he was trying to keep his temper. He stared at the ground, the coffin resting on his right shoulder, his eyes wet. Skip was in front of him opposite McAvoy, and behind was Uncle Willie, always the most emotional one, sobbing noisily, his face awash with tears. Keeping in step, I followed behind and watched them slide the coffin into the waiting hearse, the only sound Willie's crying.

An eternity seemed to pass and from inside the house I could hear Nan wailing as I watched the men pile flowers around the coffin. Suddenly aware that time was running out I instinctively put one hand on the coffin, the O'Brien farewell, just to say 'Peggy, it's me!' As I did so a bouquet fell off into my arms and as I put it back hands gently guided me onto the pavement again. I put my hand against the cool glass of the side window, and as the hearse moved away I felt it slowly slip across my palm. The car behind was filled with flowers, tributes from people all over Blackhill that they could ill afford. The whole community had turned out, many of the women crying softly, and with quiet dignity they saw Peggy off on her last journey.

The cortege didn't go into the nearby Riddrie Cemetery, it was bound for some place I didn't know. I stood on tip-toes to keep it in sight as long as possible, and as it finally faded from view, I felt something in my other hand. It was a single pink rose from the bouquet that had fallen from Peggy's coffin. Later, when I showed it to Nan she said the bouquet had been from me. She had ordered flowers from herself and had asked the florist to send something from me to Peggy. For some reason a bouquet of pink roses arrived. 'An' know whit?' she said, her voice flat and defeated, 'Peggy wis wearin' a long, white dress tae.'

I found that I no longer hated my mother, I realized that deep down I had known all along too; how could I not? And Peggy, watching me as I in turn watched the awful, unstoppable tragedy being played out between the three of us those last months, deep down did she know too? How could she not?

I remembered that Easter Monday, only two short months ago, when Peggy and I had gone on our odd walk to Hogganfield Loch. She had been wearing Nan's unlucky green coat tightly stretched across her stomach, and on the way back she had made me walk through Riddrie Cemetery with her. What had she been doing, I wondered, laying ghosts for me? If she knew then that soon I would only be able to visit her in a cemetery, did she also know it would take me more than thirty years to bring myself to do so? I took all those years to discover what had really happened to her on Saturday, 30 May 1959. I didn't find her again until I was an adult, older than she lived to be, standing by her grave with a bunch of pink roses, saying once again 'Peggy, it's me!'

While the men were at the cemetery the women removed the covers from the mirrors and the white sheets from the

My Auntie Peggy in 1943, aged 21.

always yours
nan
x x x x x

(Above Left) My father Laurie
(Skip) O'Brien Snr in 1942. This
photo made Laurie Jnr think his
daddy was 'a big man'.

(Above Right) My mother,
Joan Henderson Clark, shortened
to Nan for some reason. Taken
in 1943.

(Left) My parents' wedding day,
17th July 1936. Skip was 24,
Nan was only 17 and looks so
young you want to shout 'foul'.

... then the gable went

TOP FLOOR—CLARKS

SECOND FLOOR—TURNBULLS

FIRST FLOOR—McCREADIES

GROUND FLOOR—FITZGERALDS

(Above) Balmano Brae after the collapse in June 1951.

(Left) My cousins James and John Kelly, sons of Vic the 'Fair Yin' head, at Balmano Brae shortly before the collapse.

(Above) Peggy's wedding 27th March 1953. From left to right:
Uncle George Clark, Maw, Uncle Harry Clark, Mrs Brown (Auld Broon),
Uncle Willie Clark, Auntie Vic Kelly and Skip.

(Above) My maternal grandmother, Annie (Maw)
Clark, in 1943, looking deceptively angelic.

(Right) My paternal grandfather, Tom O'Brien,
ringing the bell at St Aloysius' College.

(Above clockwise from left) Uncle George Clark, Auntie Annie and their youngest child Anne at Loch Lomond. Uncle Tommy O'Brien and a friend (Tommy is the one standing). The photo Uncle Jim O'Brien sent of himself with a kitten, which caused my father to joke that it was taken 'Probably jist before he strangled it'. Uncle Willie Clark in the uniform of the Highland Light Infantry.

(Above) Me and my parents.

(Right) Me and Nan.

(Below) Me and my brother,
Laurie Jnr. –
*All taken in Edinburgh on
one of Nan's 'Guilt Trips'.*

(Right) Me and Nan in the early 60s.

(Below) Mrs Betty McGettigan, my teacher at the Marian school, who told the class that one day they would see my words in print.

(Above) Me and an immaculate fair cousin at a wedding. I'm the one in the dark dress with the hem taken down and dirty shoes. I was never a tidy child. Peggy gave me the necklace to uphold 'Dark Yin' honour.

(Above) Me in my first communion dress aged 8.

(Left) Rab at Loch Lomond.

My family.
From left to right: Rab, Debbie, Euan, Lisa and me.

windows and prepared a meal. I was safely back on top of my shelter again, and hours after the men arrived back another car drew up outside the house. A tall, dark-haired young man got out and I watched him knock on the door and then walk in. There was a wild roar of raw animal rage from inside the house and Skip emerged, pulling the young man behind him. He pushed him into the car and shouted, 'Git oota here son, ur sure as hell ye'll git killt!' Later I heard that the young man was the 'doacter' who had been with Peggy. He had wanted to apologize, but Uncle George had come within a few feet of killing him.

The day after Peggy's funeral I went back to school. Nan had written a note for my teacher explaining my absence; I didn't read it as I normally would have because I didn't want to know what it said.

'Your aunt died in childbirth,' the teacher said, 'That means she would go straight to heaven.'

'She's a Proddy,' I stated, defiantly.

'That doesn't matter. If she died having a baby she would go straight to heaven.' I thought she was the stupidest person I had ever come across.

'Would you like us to say a prayer for her?'

'Naw.' Like every other child in Scotland I usually spoke Lowland Scots outside and 'proper English' at school, but none of that mattered anymore and 'proper English' could go hang itself, along with this silly woman and her prayers. First I was supposed to be grateful that Hughie had gone to her heaven and now Peggy; if I ever came across this heaven I'd blast it to hell with the biggest gun I could find. Later it was noticed that I was withdrawn and quiet and the Parish Priest, Father Sheridan, was called in, the same one who gave me my First Communion.

'We're going to say a prayer for Margaret O'Brien's aunt and her wee baby who died last Saturday and are now in heaven watching over us,' he announced to the children, and I walked out of the class and out of the school. It was the only time in my life that I 'plunked' school.

*   *   *

With the eleven-plus over we were assembled in class and handed out notes with the name of our next school. I knew mine said Garnethill Convent; it was the alternative to Notre Dame for those who weren't quite good enough or rich enough. For a moment the thought surfaced that I'd tell Peggy on Saturday, then I remembered that I couldn't. There was a deep, black emptiness that stretched as far as I could see and feel and imagine . . .

Chapter Twenty-Two

The months after Peggy died passed somehow and are etched on my memory like an endless tunnel of pain that left the Clarks unable to think or act coherently. There was no conversation save for the occasional reluctant syllable when there was no alternative, and everyone seemed locked in their own distracted silence that didn't connect to any other.

There was no fatal accident inquiry into the circumstances of the death, as there undoubtedly should have been. Though the family were aware that there were questions to be asked, they were unable to summon up the strength to ask them. George, who had struggled with his emotions all of his life, now descended deeper into a preoccupied anger that he never truly emerged from, and Nan floated without direction, lost without Peggy.

At first we still visited Moodiesburn Street every Saturday, where McAvoy and the children continued to live with Maw Clark. There was no plan, we went because that was the pattern of our lives. Saturdays meant returning to Blackhill, it was that simple. I hated those visits and stayed outside the house as much as possible because there just wasn't any reason to go there any longer. Within a few weeks we stopped.

There was no way through the huge, awful void that Peggy had left, and the paralysis spread to everyone so that they simply could not function normally. There would be no recovery because the injury was too massive and life would never, ever be the same again.

On what was to be our last visit to Moodiesburn Street, though we didn't know it at the time, Maw Clark gave me the decoration that had stood on the top tier of Peggy's wedding cake. In 1953 I had waited outside the Proddy church and handed over a silver horseshoe to Peggy. To that small extent I had taken part in Peggy's wedding. I was also Peggy's favourite; perhaps Maw considered the cake decoration to be an appropriate memento. In the years since, it had stood at the top of the living-room press, the cupboard where the special china was kept, on the little triangular shelf formed by the way the press was built across the corner.

It had started out as a sugar bride and groom on top of a latticework dais, but Skip had made a cardboard horseshoe to stand behind the bridal couple, and painted it white and silver. It's an O'Brien trait to gild the lily, but it fitted in with Peggy's liking for all things extra-fancy, and she had been delighted.

I took it home to Drumchapel and examined it in my room. It had lost its sharpness over the years, the little figures seemed to have melted when you saw them close to. I didn't want it; it was a symbol of how, when and why Peggy's life had become a nightmare, so I smashed it to bits then threw the bits in the fire. I never, ever wanted any reminder of Peggy's disastrous marriage. To this day, whenever I see a decoration on top of a wedding cake, I can't help thinking of that one and what it signified. When I married, I decided, there would be no wedding cake.

Nan gradually withdrew after giving up the pretence of the Saturday visits, and by Peggy's birthday in August she had become a recluse. There were no more family gatherings; no decision was taken, it just happened. It was as though the heart and soul of the Clark family had been ripped out by Peggy's death and Nan's withdrawal, and the rest of them then withdrew in turn into their respective families. The pain of losing Peggy was intensified by being together without her, and it was simply more than they could bear.

Peggy's name was never used again, except as a means of fixing time. In the same way as people talked of events happening before or after the War, the Clarks talked of events before or after Peggy died, but she herself became a closed subject. Her laughter, her kindness, her gentle good humour and her hopeless romanticism, and by association the loss of these, became banned by an unspoken, mutual agreement. Better, they decided, to pretend that she had never existed than to accept her death, and Nan's self-imposed exile handed them another brick with which to build a wall around their collective pain.

It became accepted that 'Nan isnae well,' and therefore wasn't to be upset. They would cite this as a reason not to see her, because she did become upset at seeing them, as they did at seeing each other. Grieving together would have been the healthy way to deal with the pain, but it hurt too much. In that manner they contrived not to face it, and so it would remain a raw wound within them forever.

Nan, at barely forty years old became a shadow of herself, nervous of people, afraid to go out and cut off from her family, and so it would remain for the the rest of her life until her death at sixty-one. Nowadays her symptoms would be recognized as the grief of bereavement, but in the late fifties and early Sixties there was no diagnosis for what she was going through and therefore no treatment.

Skip was incapable of understanding what had happened to her because it was so foreign to his own nature. He was also incapable of getting help, even if he'd thought of it. Nan was the help-getter and always had been. Worn out with years of coping with the effects of Skip's drinking, she was now hit by the biggest blow she had ever faced. There was no one to turn to. Peggy had been her solace and support all of their lives, and Peggy had gone forever.

Had I been older I might have helped, but I was only eleven. With my brothers so much older and starting independent lives of their own, I was left to run the house, look after myself and my mother. I remember waiting for Skip to take over, but he never did. His life in fact was easier; he could stay out as long and as often as he liked, drink as much as he pleased and come home or not as he chose. Nan's attempts to bring order to his way of life had imposed some boundaries in the past, however weak. Now these were gone and he had a daughter to step in as housekeeper. He wasn't a bad man, he was a child and children think only of their own needs. Just as I had, till then . . .

Chapter Twenty-Three

Garnethill Convent came as a shock. Instead of the leafy, genteel avenues of the West End where Notre Dame was situated, Garnethill was a seedy, red-light area in the centre of the city, deprived in ways that Blackhill would have been ashamed to stoop to. Leaving the bus from Drumchapel at the main road, there was no alternative to the uncomfortable walk through the Garnethill streets to get to the school. There were in the city two shops that sold porn magazines, and I would walk miles to avoid passing them. There was something about the men who hung about outside that made me feel a kind of sick fear, and if I had to pass them I dreaded it all the way there and felt incredibly relieved when it was over. Walking through Garnethill gave me the same feeling; I never became accustomed to it and had to steel myself for that walk to and from school every day. If the nuns had come here to convert sinners I decided, then they had failed dismally.

The nuns were called the Sisters of Mercy and there again they failed dismally to live up to that description. One, Sister Annunciatta, carved her way through the children by lashing out at bare legs with the long, leather strap that hung from a belt around the nuns' waists. You could always tell where she had been from the weals on the children's legs, her own peculiar version of 'Excuse me please.' It always made me laugh to see the outsized rosaries falling from around the sisters' waists, accompanied by the thick leather strap, the sole intention of which was to beat the hell out of children: the perfect picture of their Christian values, suffer little children to come unto me, and by God you'll know you've arrived!

The headmistress was Sister Aquinas, a pale, skinny

Irishwoman of indeterminate age, with the palest blue eyes and thin lips which I never once saw break into anything resembling a normal, human smile. She had chosen to teach, and her starting point was the belief that all children were intrinsically wicked, evil, wily and permanently engaged in finding ways to sin. Her philosophy for dealing with her unfortunate charges, therefore, was simple: always be suspicious, always believe the worst regardless of evidence to the contrary, and always punish hard, whether warranted or not. I had her for English for one very long, hard year. While other teachers tried to draw from me any hint of imagination Sister Aquinas did her best to bludgeon to death any spark of creativity I had. Anything I produced was returned blue-pencilled to death and accompanied by detailed critiques in her tiny, pinched script, informing me that all my ideas and thoughts were 'sinful'.

'Kindly remember,' she wrote on one of my compositions, 'that your body is a temple created by God and must be treated accordingly and not defiled.' I didn't have a clue what she meant then and I still don't; I can only imagine she had been secretly reading *Lady Chatterley's Lover* and somehow got it mixed up with my innocent meanderings.

Eventually I worked out the kind of thing she wanted and wrote a morally uplifting piece of candy-floss about a straying Catholic returning to the fold. She loved it; it was the nearest I ever saw those martyred features and that thin, bloodless mouth get to a genuine smile. Having satisfied myself on her level of literary appreciation, I never descended to it again, and thereafter she should have bought shares in whatever company specialized in blue pencil production. She couldn't understand what had happened, kept saying I had shown that I could do good work, so why did I persist in producing such offensive material? For one so versed in the evil workings of children's minds it always surprised me that she never realized my sole intention was to offend her.

Another of Sister Aquinas' great obsessions was the monarchy. It was, she said, the Catholic church's last bastion against communism and we all had a duty to support it. This was an amazingly generous endorsement, given the prohibition on Catholics succeeding to the throne, a fact I loved to point out to her whenever she had worked herself up to her usual emotional frenzy when giving her anti-communism lecture. In her bid to keep the monarch dear to our hearts she kept a large, regal portrait of Her Majesty outside her office, and had the task of turning it right-side-out or wiping a moustache off it, depending on which mood I had been in when I passed by. Once I managed to hide it under the school altar in the main assembly hall. There, addressing the entire school, but looking directly at me, in her truly Christian fashion she called down God's curse on whoever had taken the portrait, and all the while it was no more than three feet away from her. What she didn't know of course was that God and his curses held little fear for me. He had done all he possibly could to me already and I had survived. After a fashion at any rate.

She also set herself up as a censor, telling us what books not to read and thereby ensuring a rush on them. DH Lawrence was right out, the man being morally depraved. Robert Burns was a fornicator and a Proddy, and James Joyce was even worse. Not only was he a Catholic, an *Irish* Catholic, but he was filth personified, though it was never quite clear where she stood on this issue. She could never make her mind up if being an ordinary Proddy was worse or better than being a filthy Catholic, so she did the ecumenically correct thing and heartily hated and despised them all, which managed to take in most of humanity. She seemed to me the opposite of the Irish people I had grown up among, a joyless, life-hating mutant, an O'Brien gone warped, and I couldn't resist taking her on.

'Have you read any of these books?' I would ask, 'And are you, a bride of Christ, now corrupted?' Her rage was a delight to behold.

'So Hitler was right?' I asked on another occasion when she was in mid-tirade against some other literary transgressor.

'Yes he was!' she spluttered. She was, without doubt, the

maddest, saddest, most repressed creature I have ever met, and she used to say that she had to be especially hard on me because I reminded her of herself at the same age. Apart from being a gross slander on me, this was, on reflection, a pitiful declaration of self-loathing, and the poor woman clearly needed more help than she would ever get in the convent, or from me.

Every now and again, when she could restrain herself no longer over one of my many indiscretions and was in danger of seriously attacking me, she would send for my father. After she had recovered HM's portrait and her world was thus safe once more from the influence of Marx, Lenin and Trotsky, he was summoned to listen to the details of my latest heinous crime. To my delight he put on his 'humble Irish Catholic' routine, which was almost as amusing as his sand-dancing.

'Bit Sister,' he said in deferential mitigation of my misdeeds, 'Hur mother's been ill recently.'

'My mother died when I was ten!' she raged, 'And I had to look after nine younger children!' This explained her hatred of children to my utter satisfaction.

'But Sister,' I said, 'You grew up to marry God, you're a saint, while I'm just a half-Proddy heretic.' Beside me I could hear my father trying not to laugh as Sister Aquinas performed spontaneous combustion.

'Your grandfather would be ashamed of you!' she seethed.

'Well that's OK,' I replied, 'I've always been pretty well ashamed of my grandfather as it happens. The Catholic one anyway.'

Later my father said reflectively, 'Ye mibbe went a wee bit too faur there.'

'She's aff hur heid,' I replied, 'She deserved it.'

'Aye,' he mused, 'Right anuff!' As I said, he wasn't a bad man, just a rotten father, but every now and again he got something right.

When school finished at four o'clock I would have to rush for the bus home and then immediately set off in search of the mobile grocery van that was prepared to give us tick. It had stopped outside our close earlier, but Nan wasn't able to get downstairs to it and anyway, she was so nervous of people that her speech wouldn't have made any sense to them.

Finding the van was pretty hit and miss, because I only had the vaguest idea where it would be at any given time, and there was always the fear that I wouldn't find it. If I didn't, then we didn't eat unless Nan had managed to keep a little cash back, which in those days was unusual. If there was money I would have to walk to the nearest shops some two or three miles away, join in the long queue and then walk back. At that time Nan could still manage to work around the house and to cook, but slowly she stopped doing even that. I found that I had little time or energy left for homework, and though I started out in an 'A' class at Garnethill, before long I had slipped down the 'B's.

Nan's withdrawal meant, of course, that she couldn't buy clothes for herself or anyone else, so I took that over too. The only way we could afford anything was with a Provident check, which was made out for a set sum, five pounds perhaps or ten pounds, with weekly payments plus interest, paid to an agent who called every Friday – pay night. The week's debts to the mobile van were settled then too, so though Friday night felt like money night, it wasn't by the time everyone was paid off.

Only certain shops accepted Provy checks and the goods in these shops were inferior and more expensive than elsewhere. So I found out early on how the poor are kept poor and felt the shame creeping over me if a shop didn't display its Provy sticker and I had to ask. If the assistant said 'no' then I felt even more ashamed to have revealed our poverty.

I was very young and at an age when I needed a mother to guide me and look after me, but instead I was looking after my mother. Nan took no part in buying my first bra for instance, in fact by that time I was buying hers, and no part in the agonies of puberty. She never asked about my periods and when they arrived out of the blue I was terrified but knew I couldn't confide in her. And of course there was no one else any longer for me to go to, so I learned from other girls at school, trying all the while desperately to put two-and-two together from the usual playground half-truths, and pretending I knew it all already so as not to look a fool. Looking back, it was the most confusing and dismal time of my life, more so than it usually is for any girl. I used to wonder why it was all happening and if it happened to others, and if it did, how come they coped so well?

Chapter Twenty-Four

We called Mickey's new friends the Crowd. They were part of a working-class movement to get into the hills and countryside during the depression of the 1920s and 1930s, when most were unemployed and penniless. Until then the outdoors had been the preserve of the gentry. With cheap transport and short working hours for those who had it, even shorter for those who didn't, and nothing to fill the endless days, the countryside became accessible to all. For the natives of Clydebank, the Old Kilpatrick Hills were the starting point, then the 'Bankies as they were known gradually moved further afield, forming the core of the movement.

Laurie had followed Mickey's escape route out of Drumchapel and our weekend hell to join the Crowd by the hills and the lochs. As soon as he had served his time as an engineering apprentice, Laurie had joined the Merchant Navy. Shortly afterwards Mickey had married at twenty-four. He had spent very little time with our family and had got out as soon as he could, marrying one of the Crowd. I was thirteen at the time and that's my first clear memory of Rab, my future husband, though I had been vaguely aware of his existence before that through stories I'd heard. Mickey and Rowena had married in a Registry Office and then had a ceilidh at her house afterwards instead of a wedding reception. My grandmother had been invited, but luckily she didn't stay long, because if she wasn't the centre of attraction she didn't hang about. If she had staged one of her dying swan acts in front of the Crowd they would have stepped over her and continued with the ceilidh. We had songs and chat, and sleeping-bags were put down in a separate room for sleeping off the effects.

It was 1961 and I had shopped for new clothes then managed with great difficulty to get my mother out of our house and settled down at the ceilidh. As the crowd assembled and the festivities started, she wanted to know one thing, 'Which wan's Rab?' I pointed to him standing against a wall, whisky glass in hand, and at that moment he slowly slid down onto the floor, one of the things he was most famous for. It was odd to think of my mother sitting there being entertained as I wondered how we could keep her calm among all the people. A few years before she would have run this show and revelled in it, she and – no, that era was all finished.

At five o'clock the next morning I was trying to persuade someone out of a sleeping-bag so that I could get in, when a voice said, 'Take mine.' It was Rab, the master of sliding down walls, and I gratefully accepted his offer. 'Fool!' I thought, as I snuggled down in the warmth he'd left behind and leaving him shivering on a couch I fell instantly asleep.

I had my first taste of how good weekends could be after that. Until then the Crowd were just names that I heard occasionally, but Laurie was home on leave for the wedding and he bought me my first pair of hiking boots. From somewhere I acquired a cast-off rucksack and an old sleeping-bag, and one Friday in late September we took a bus together from Buchanan Street to Drymen. From there we caught another to Balmaha on Loch Lomondside then walked the seven miles to Rowardennan, where the boatshed stood.

The shed was owned by the Scottish Youth Hostels Association and had as its commodore a little man called Freddy. He was English and looked it, with his long khaki shorts and knitted bobble hat, and he was unfortunately unable to pronounce his 'r's. So Fweddy he was to one and all, including himself. There was a strict rule banning sleeping in the boatshed, a rule made to be ignored, as indeed it was. So sleeping-bags were laid out on the floor between the canoes every weekend when the Crowd were in residence. Many a snap inspection was carried out by

Fweddy to make sure no one was sleeping in the boatshed, which of course they were. He never seemed to figure out what to do about this blatant flouting of the rules, so basically he did nothing and he therefore was held in some esteem by everyone, even if his authority was totally ignored.

That first Saturday morning we paddled up the loch to join another party who were camped halfway up, at the Major's Land. Then later we all paddled to Ptarmigan's Point at the head of the loch and camped there. I remember I was in the front of a double canoe, the first time I had been in a canoe in my life, as Laurie steered from behind. I was wearing one of his sweaters and the water that flicked off his paddles had soaked the arms, making them trail in the water. I was wet through, my arms and hips ached from the unaccustomed exercise of paddling and I was more tired than I had ever been in my entire life. While Laurie put the tent up I sat by the camp-fire with Ronnie, who had grown up with the wall-sliding Rab in Clydebank, as he made up a curry. I had never had a curry before either, and even if I had it wouldn't have been anything like this one. He just threw everything he had into a pot and tossed in an eye-watering amount of curry powder. I was tired, sore, wet, cold and hungry and I wolfed the curry down gratefully. I remember Ronnie watching me from behind his thick glasses and shrugging as I devoured his concoction, as though no one had ever done so before. Later I discovered that no one had . . . and why.

The deer were rutting and the night air was full of the throaty barks of stags; it was late to be at the loch. I think Nan had agreed to my going in the expectation that I would hate it, but if that was her plan it back-fired. I was captivated. It wasn't just getting away from the especially awful weekend drinking bouts of my father, it was the silence of the loch early in the morning that hooked me, a silence so loud I could hear it, and it was the Crowd. Pyschologists say that if you have bad family experiences it is possible to offset the damage through a substitute family group – and that's what the Crowd was. I was the youngest by some years and was therefore treated as a younger sister, but one who was accepted and quietly protected, much more than I had been with my natural family.

The only problem for me was my brother Mickey. I was always on trial with him, over-conscious of what I said, did or looked like. He was forever on the lookout for something to criticize about me, and his sarcasm could be stinging. He even had Skip's frown of impatience, and whenever I made a mistake there it was. The others in the Crowd often stuck up for me when he zoomed in on one of my many imperfections, laughing and telling him to leave me alone. It was as though I only existed in Mickey's eyes as a reflection of himself, and he saw me as a constant embarrassment.

It was many years before I saw that he acted as he did because of his own insecurities, but even if I had realized it at the time I could have done nothing about it because of my own. Behind me was the great, yawning wound that Nan had disappeared into and all I had to do was look out of the corner of my eye to see it clearly. My life had become a constant struggle not to be swallowed up too, yet no one else seemed aware of this and, therefore, of the effect it was still having on my life. I suspect that it would anyhow have come under the heading of 'pull yourself together', whether I could or not.

Chapter Twenty-Five

Laurie married six months after Mickey, only his wedding to Ellen, also one of the Crowd, took place in a Catholic church. It seemed to me again to be an attempt to win Skip's approval, at least in part, though I'm still not sure if Laurie realized it at the time. I found weddings a drag, I was never a creature made for ceremony and protocol, and a Catholic service provides lashings of both. The Crowd assembled afterwards at what was a fairly traditional wedding reception, and Skip maintained tradition too, by disappearing to the nearest pub so that he could drink at his own speed.

For Nan the very long day had held more terrors than the more homely, relaxed wedding ceilidh that Mickey and Rowena had chosen. She regarded Laurie as her weakest cub, the one who had to be given extra care and consideration, so she was already more on edge. None of this deterred Skip from abandoning her among strangers though, which made me so angry that I went to the pub to drag him out again to support his wife. It was raining when I found the place and even my resolve and anger were held in check by the convention that females, particularly young females, did not enter pubs. Then I heard Rab's voice.

'Where ur ye gaun?'

'Ah'm gaun' tae drag that auld swine oota there!' I replied, 'He's left ma mother sittin' at the reception by herself!'

'Leave it,' he said quietly, 'Ah'll get him oot.'

He went into the pub and then came out again, saying that one of the Crowd would bring Skip back to the hall. Then he took his jacket off and put it around my shoulders and walked with me up the road in the rain. I didn't know how to react to this. Giving me his sleeping-bag at Mickey's wedding was one thing, but his latest gallantry puzzled me. What puzzled me even more was my own reaction of no reaction. I was used by now to having to rely on myself. After thirteen years of living with the reality of Skip, there were no fairy-tales in my mind about men and chivalry. To say that I could be prickly if patronized would be an understatement, yet I accepted Rab's protection and I couldn't have explained why, not even to myself.

After his marriage Laurie took to his in-laws with a vengeance, they were the best people who had ever drawn breath apparently, and we saw considerably less of him. It was understandable, of course, he had escaped and now he had a fresh start with a new family where he had never been hurt or found wanting. We all do what we must to survive.

Garnethill Convent was suddenly interested in world politics. The reason was simple; in 1960 John F Kennedy was elected and in 1961 he had been sworn in as President of the United States. JFK was a Roman Catholic!

I was in Art class when news of the election result was conveyed to the entire school by a specially selected messenger who ran round every room. I sniggered and the Art teacher assumed I was smiling with pleasure. 'Yes,' she said, 'Isn't it wonderful? A Catholic President!'

In fact I was quite taken with JFK but like most of America I had to overcome anti-Catholic prejudice to keep supporting him. Here was a politician who seemed to listen to what young people said and thought, who rehabilitated idealism while the older, supposedly wiser lot shook their greying heads and told us we'd grow out of it eventually.

None of this mattered to Garnethill though. To them he was simply a Catholic and could therefore do no wrong. During the 1960 campaign, while old Joe Kennedy wisely trusted in securer methods like buying votes, Garnethill was offering daily prayers for JFK's success, and on that cold January day in 1961, when he was sworn in, the whole school was allowed home early.

★　　★　　★

My favourite teacher at Garnethill was Miss Johnstone. She taught Geography but had been forced to teach English as well, a subject at which she did not shine. We all grew up caught in the dichotomy of language, speaking standard English to teachers and the Glasgow version of Lowland Scots to each other and at home. Miss Johnstone though had failed to absorb the particular rules governing this and spoke her own peculiar pidgin version that strangely encompassed the two. 'I'm giving oot forms about the school trip,' she would announce, 'And I waant youse to take them home, fur tae be signed. Youse'll see that the train has a buffet,' which she pronounced as in 'tuffet'. To emphasise her little local dialect difficulty we of course spoke to her only in the best BBC English.

Miss Johnstone was a tiny, bird-like soul of about sixty, with badly dyed blond locks and thick glasses. The glasses put her at a disadvantage when it came to applying make-up and nothing ended up where the fashion magazines recommended. Lipstick was applied lop-sided, halfway up one nostril on one side and nearly to her chin on the other. Eye-shadow was always a disaster, landing anywhere between her forehead and nose, and we avoided a lot of work by helping her sort it out. There was about her a disorganized, distracted air, as though she was permanently in a rush to be somewhere else, and her black academic gown invariably hung off one shoulder and trailed on the ground. She would come in determined to work very hard, after a lesson the day before had deteriorated into a beauty session instead, then someone would produce a new eye-liner. 'Noo, put that away,' she would say, full of resolve, 'We huv goat to work today!' 'But it would suit you Miss Johnstone,' the devious one would say, 'I bought it specially for you!' 'Oh well,' she'd say, her eyes by now glued to the item, 'Mibbe jist a little look, and then we must git back tae the lesson!' We could have sent Miss Johnstone out into the world like a painted hussy, but the truth was that we were fond of her, and though we frequently distracted and teased her, we wouldn't have hurt her.

Another ploy we used was to muse out loud about

the number of unmarried teachers we seemed to have at Garnethill. 'Funny how all our teachers ended up old maids,' someone would say with a theatrical sigh, 'I'm *sure* it wasn't because nobody fancied them,' another would chime in, 'I mean some of them are still quite passable . . .' Miss Johnstone knew what we were up to, but she could only take so much before launching into a spirited defence of her feminine attributes. 'Ah've hud my chances!' she would shout, 'Don't you worry hen! I have hud them lining up oot there! A twenty-inch waist I had, and a perra – a figure like an oor-glass!'

She married a farmer when she was in her sixties, the widower of a friend, which provided us with unlimited entertainment. 'Did you always fancy him Miss Johnstone – sorry, Mrs Crane? Did your friend know, or did you keep it secret?' She would get herself into all manner of predicaments trying to explain that love had blossomed amid the pong of manure only after her friend had shuffled off, and were we suggesting that there had been something going on while her friend was still alive? No, no, we'd say, we just hoped it wasn't on the rebound for him in that case, and it was a pity she had to settle for someone second-hand, that was all . . . she had had all those suitors waiting in line, unused so to speak, a bit of a come down . . . And was she having any, you know, difficulties adjusting to married life? 'Like whit?' she would demand, eyeing us suspiciously. Well, it must be difficult adapting to certain things at her age, doing certain things that she hadn't done before, or that we *presumed* she hadn't done before when she was *Miss* Johnstone, especially as Farmer Giles had been used to having certain services for so long . . . 'Whit do youse mean?' Well, cooking for more than one, for instance, washing smelly socks; why, what had she thought we meant, what else *could* we have meant? Next day she would deliver a little sermon before work started; she was having no distractions today, she knew exactly what we were up to and she was having no more of it. 'You're looking tired this morning Miss John – sorry, Mrs Crane,' someone would remark, 'I don't know *what* you've been up to, but look at those shadows under your eyes!' 'Noo, I'm no' having that!' she would smile slyly, thinking she was right on top of the situation, 'I know whit youse is up tae . . . shadows ye say?' A make-up bag would immediately be produced and the rest of the lesson would be spent repairing her ravaged countenance. It never failed.

At home life continued. Nan became more settled in her isolation and Skip, more entrenched in his drinking. I went away every weekend possible, after Nan said she didn't mind. It was of course exactly what I wanted to hear, and I'm ashamed when I look back now and imagine what her weekends were like. She would be alone with the TV while Skip was out drinking, with no one to talk to and nothing to do, and when he came in he would be in whichever mood the booze had produced. That was how she would spend the days and nights when I was away enjoying my freedom, enjoying missing what she was forced to endure. If I felt guilty at the time I can't recall it, being away was like breathing fresh air for the first time.

Skip's family was dying out now and more than once I was required to attend the funeral of someone on the O'Brien side that I had never met because of one of their many feuds. O'Brien funerals were fun though, totally unlike the other one I had gone to in 1959, the one we never talked about. Then Uncle Pat died. Inevitably, after all the years he and Hughie had lived and fought together, he too had contracted and died of TB.

Their sister Norah was there in a flash, laying claim to everything in the house, each item being apparently tailor-made for some niche or other in her own home. In fact, if she wasn't very much mistaken, this or that, and probably both items had been long-promised to her. The remaining O'Briens exchanged disapproving glances but said nothing; there was more than one way to sort Norah out after all, and they knew them all.

Uncle Tommy arranged the funeral, and after what was known in O'Brien talk as the creamy-tartar and to other mortals as the cremation, he assembled the survivors to go over the financial details. At the end of the discussion he slapped a half-pound slab of lard on the table in front of his sister.

'An' that's fur you Norah,' he said.

'Me Tommy? Whit fur?'

'Well Norah,' he said with relish, 'Ye claimed everythin' else, so we thought ye might as well hiv whit wis left when we burned him tae!'

After the laughter and jollity of the funeral, something happened that was to scar my relationship with Skip forever. Coming back later that night with a long-lost cousin, Skip walked with him into the Crystal Bells pub, a favourite O'Brien haunt in the Gallowgate, leaving me outside. There was no warning, so I had no chance to protest. It wasn't the safest area to leave a thirteen-year-old girl to stand alone and it was getting dark. I was already feeling scared and humiliated, when a man suddenly came out of the pub and tried to talk to me. I ignored him, my heart thumping, and to my great relief he walked off, but then turned again to watch me from a short distance away. I was desperately watching the pub door, hoping Skip would come out, willing him to come out, but even when the man came nearer again I had absolute certainty in my mind that nothing would happen. He wasn't watching me, I was imagining the whole thing. Only, I wasn't.

He grabbed me from behind, his forearm across my throat, and dragged me backwards through a close and into a derelict tenement. I have heard of women fighting bravely to protect their honour, but with me it was blind panic, not a thought-out response. As I fought against him, some mad desire to keep my dignity stopped me from screaming. Some Clark point of decorum told me I had to get out of this not just alive and as unharmed as possible, but without drawing attention to myself. The only reason I got away from the man was because he was drunk and that had made him less coordinated than a panic-stricken, teetotal girl.

I immediately ran into the pub, unheard of behaviour for a female of any age at that time. Everyone turned and stared in sudden silence as I entered. The cousin had gone and Skip was drinking alone. He looked up, calmly drained the remains of his whisky into his beer, drank it and walked out with me. As I told him what had happened he said impatiently, 'Ye know no' tae go intae a pub, yur auld anuff tae know better than that!'

I tried again to explain what had happened, but I was wasting my time. He had no intention of listening or of going after the man. Instead he kept walking towards John Street, where the Drumchapel buses left from, all the time keeping up a perfectly normal, but one-sided conversation with me. He went over the events of the day, laughed at the jokes and insults, made comments of his own, and carefully edited out any reference to the minor fact that his daughter had been attacked and assaulted while in his care.

I couldn't think of anything to say. My mind whirled with the twin shocks of what had happened to me and Skip's surreal reaction to it. Then gradually I felt the physical things, like the bruises and gashes. My clothes were ripped and torn and my hands were stiffening up because the skin across my knuckles had been scraped off; my knees were grazed and the hardened, dried blood stood out like shiny rivers down my legs. There was blood running down my throat from my nose, and over my chin from my split lips, and one eye was so swollen that it was closed. As Skip ignored it all and fell asleep on the bus, I could see my reflection in the window and could well understand why the other passengers looked at me curiously. My obviously distressed appearance also explained the sudden silence when I ran into the pub earlier. As we got off the bus to walk the short distance to Halgreen Avenue, Skip made his only reference to the incident, then or ever. 'Ye'd better tidy yersel' up,' he said disapprovingly, with that characteristic frown expressing his distaste, 'An' we'll tell yer Ma that ye fell doon the stairs oan the bus. Nae point in upsettin' hur, is thur?' No; no point at all really . . .

Just as in the earlier incident with his old drinking pal, my uncle's father-in-law, I felt ashamed, but not this time of myself. I was ashamed that this man was my father. Curiously, all his life he liked to pretend that there was a special bond between us, but if there was, it was a bond of shame forged during those terrifying incidents. I found it impossible to meet his eyes after that time, because I had such contempt for him. For the rest of his life, whenever we talked about anything, I always thought of the assaults with a kind of furious wonder that he had managed to wipe them from his memory.

Adult perspective later brought some understanding, though I have to say no forgiveness. To have taken the incidents seriously he would have had to address the cause, which was his drinking, and to have done that would have threatened the man's very existence. He was an addict, he needed booze to live, and everything else came after that. This included the health and well-being of his wife, the care of his family and the protection of his child. Somewhere in his soul I think he knew this, and he didn't have to see the contempt in my eyes to know that it was there, because I'm sure he held himself in the same contempt.

Like any child I had a right to better. The world may not have owed me a living, but Skip owed me care and protection, and I never got it. Though all my life I have tried to be logical and place the blame where it belongs, my self-esteem has remained dented by those assaults and the fact that Skip didn't care for me as much as he cared for the bottle. No matter what happened later, regardless of what I achieved or what others may have come to think of me, the shame and the guilt of being so debased and worthless in the eyes of the first man in my life, somehow linger on.

Chapter Twenty-Six

Garnethill had its share of sexual incidents too. The area around the school was frequented by prostitutes of both sexes and the ugliest, least convincing transvestites I have ever encountered. Because of this there was a constant police presence and we were encouraged by the Sisters to report any suspicious characters we saw hanging around. Unfortunately, when we did so they invariably turned out to be undercover policemen, and we then embarked on games of 'spot the polis' instead. This prompted a request from the police that leering convent schoolgirls should desist from sidling up to their officers and offering them a good time.

The Sisters had a curious mixture of attitudes towards us. On one hand we were pure, innocent, vulnerable Catholic maidens who had to be protected from men at all costs, because men were evil. On the other hand we were scheming madams, who given half a chance would tear off our chastity belts and fornicate in the middle of the street whilst wearing a school tie. Regardless of which was true we had to be kept away from any temptation of the male persuasion and convinced that men were the enemy. The image they tried to create for us was of men as sexual time-bombs, ready, willing and able to explode into sexual activity at any moment and without much encouragement. We were therefore advised not to make eye contact with any male, anywhere at anytime, and not to wear patent shoes, lest the creatures caught sight of the reflection of our knickers and be inflamed beyond control. It was little wonder really that Convent schoolgirls had the reputation of being sexually active at the earliest opportunity and promiscuous with it, there being no fruit so sweet as that which is forbidden. And there was another embargo that I have never understood, on whistling, which for some reason made the Virgin Mary cry . . .

On one occasion, the Sisters seemed to be proved right about our 'wickedness'. There was a flasher in the cobbled lane between the school and the convent who was somewhat surprised, it must be said, to attract an avid audience shouting, 'Show us yer willie!', 'Fling it ower yer shooder!', 'Is that the best ye kin come up wi'?', and other such maidenly encouragements. Out came the Sisters of Mercy, whipping everyone in sight with their belts, including the unfortunate star turn, who was attacked with such ferocity by these paragons of virtue that he would certainly have been rendered unable to raise as much as a smile for some considerable time, if ever. They beat the holy bejezus out of the poor creature and he limped off, bent double and with grounds for charging the Sisters with GBH at the very least. This incident gave Sister Aquinas a most welcome, and some might say a Godsent, opportunity to become quite flushed of face and hoarse of voice from denouncing the lustful, sinful nature of the male of the species, and it was noticeable that she did so with unnecessary frequency. I never did discover if she had personal experience of the male transgressions that she spoke of with such eloquence, though it was not for the want of asking. Taking deep offence she would then send for Skip, to remonstrate with him about the sexual nature of my questions, which from every point of view was a bit like taking coals to Newcastle. Apart from his contribution to my knowledge of the subject, wasn't he, as a representative of the lustful, sinful crew the wrong person to stop such questions?

I was as much a puzzle to the other girls at school as they were to me. It was the swinging sixties after all and they spent all week talking about boyfriends, pop music and fashions while waiting for the weekends to get to discos. I went through my weeks waiting for the weekends too, to get out of the city and off with the Crowd. Every Friday I took my hiking gear into school and come four o'clock I changed in the toilet into trousers, boots, anorak and rucksack and dashed down to Buchanan Street to catch the bus. My schoolmates considered this to be bizarre in the extreme and never shrank from telling me so. Needless to say I found their preoccupations every bit as bizarre, but then, I had been too well brought up to say so.

During the summer months we headed for Loch Lomond and the eight mile walk to where the boatshed stood. Inside, the canoes lay in tiers along both sides of the long shed, supported by wooden struts. At the top was the stove, that roared so loudly that from the outside the boatshed looked and sounded like an enraged, wheel-less, abandoned steam train. Inside there were two tables covered in leftover paint from numerous canoes, and painted on them in bright blue were the words, 'WUR TABLE' and 'PEASANTS' TABLE'. We still laid our sleeping bags on the floor between the serried ranks of canoes, except for Ronnie, who slung his hammock from two beams above.

We went away for the peace and to act the fool where civilisation couldn't protest. My favourite time at Loch Lomond was very early in the morning, when the silence and the light had a special quality that seemed to extend the senses. I would creep over the sleeping figures, like giant, snoring maggots, and make my way to a rock beside the water and there I would sit until sounds of life came from the boatshed. A maggot would shuffle and hop onto the pebbly shore and collapse again, having been kicked enough times to make it move out of the way, or needing to escape the smell of cooking.

Once Rab, the wall-slider, who was a shipyard worker in 'real life', lost his way in the forest. In his befuddled state all the man knew was that he had to keep going upwards, because the loch could become suddenly and dangerously deep in parts and he was a non-swimmer. He was discovered next morning, twenty feet up a Caledonian Pine, fast asleep across a bough, and an animated discussion took place underneath about how the best use could be made of this diversion. Some suggested yelling loudly in unison so that he would fall out in shock before he realized where he was, and though this plan held undoubted attractions it was decided to leave him alone, after taking photos, of course. There wasn't the slightest chance that anyone would climb the tree to save him, in fact the possibility wasn't even raised. When he finally made his way down no one mentioned where he had spent the night and neither did he, until the photos were developed.

Rab's main contribution to the Crowd was to cause furious anger and severe irritation whenever possible. Every topic was debated around the camp-fire for however long it took, and the disagreements were bitter and noisy. Rab would start out with a belief that was guaranteed to be at odds with the majority and at the end of several hours of serious discussion he would say with a grin, 'Ah don't care, Ah still think the same!' He did this even when his argument had been comprehensively demolished and proven invalid hours before. He had never been known to change his mind on anything, so he was a constant challenge that the others couldn't resist. Invariably the night would end with frustrated oaths being screamed into Rab's impossibly smiling face, as we all crawled into sleeping bags at 4 a.m. There was no doubt about it, the man understood about scoring points and he won every time. I went away every weekend hoping he would be there and would be disappointed when he wasn't. I felt this about other favourites, but though I thought nothing of expressing my hopes or regrets about them, I kept quiet about Rab.

Chapter Twenty-Seven

Just after New Year's Day 1962 Uncle Willie turned up in Drumchapel; I opened the door and there he stood. It seemed a lifetime since I had seen him – but then it was. We greeted him with delight and settled down to a night of laughter and jokes. Skip put a record on our ancient radiogram, an old 78, and Willie said, 'Ah like that!' Skip said 'Dae ye Wullie?' removed the record from the turntable and smashed it over his head. Willie smashed one over Skip's head, and so the evening continued until we had a heap of black jagged shards on the floor and Willie was laughing and mopping up the tears. Sheer vandalism, in fact, and we lost a lot of the records I had learned to sing to. Hours of my childhood I had spent by that old radiogram, duetting with Mario Lanza in 'The Drinking Song' from *The Student Prince*, John McCormack singing 'Danny Boy' and of course, 'Red Sails in the Sunset'. Now they were all gone in one mad evening.

It all ended in tears, of course, because it reminded us too clearly and poignantly of similar occasions in years gone by. When the bottle had been spun and the party-pieces trotted out, the thought in each head was of the song that wouldn't be sung, that night or ever. 'Mexicali Rose' would never be heard again, but it hung there more strongly than those that were. We always recognized that the sentimental words had fitted Peggy perfectly, but since her death they had taken on a deeper significance. 'Mexicali Rose, I'm leaving . . . Mexicali Rose stop grieving.' They echoed through every heart and mind, so that we each withdrew deeper into our separate shells with our memories.

During the evening I heard Skip complain to Willie in a serious tone that I wasn't up to scratch as a housewife, that I didn't devote myself entirely to scrubbing floors for instance. 'It's a' fits an' starts,' he said, in the tone of a man sure of getting support for his complaints. 'Fur Christ's sake Laurie,' said Willie angrily, 'She's only a wean, she shouldnae be daein' hoosework at a'!'

At the end of the evening he and Nan clung to each other and wept. It had been an all too painful, bitter-sweet reminder of life once upon a time and it wouldn't be repeated.

Sometimes, however, my godmother, Auntie Annie, came to see us and occasionally there would be a spur-of-the-moment visit from a group of three or four of the family, in a desperate attempt to recapture what they had lost. She stood there between them all though, the one who would never be there again, and no matter how exciting and happy the reunion had been, there was a sadness, a shared poignancy at the end, and no words were needed to explain why. Once my brother Laurie's wife asked who Peggy was. 'I keep hearing about before she died or after she died, but who was she?' To my amazement I found myself giving her the Clark treatment, by behaving as though she had made an unfortunate social gaffe. From Nan there was icy silence as she turned her head, staring into the distance, and I had to force myself to reply, 'She was an aunt, Nan's younger sister. She died young.' It answered the question she had asked, but it didn't begin to explain the raw, painful world that we had been trapped in since. Somehow there were no words for that.

Shortly afterwards we heard that McAvoy had placed Peggy's children in care. The two boys went to Quarrier's Homes at Bridge of Weir and the girl to Eastpark Home in Maryhill because of her handicap. It was the final twist of the blade. The only person who could have coped with the three children and would once have fought McAvoy for the right to do so was Nan, and Nan was no more. She knew this too and I watched her wilt further into herself at that time. It was to be a guilt Uncle George would carry for the rest of his life too, that he hadn't taken Peggy's children as his own. But he shouldn't have blamed himself. He and Annie already had three children all closer in age than Mickey, Laurie and I, and he was just an ordinary working man with an ordinary pay packet. Quite apart from that, McAvoy was the only one with the right to make that decision and he would never have let any of the Clarks have the children. Rather than do so he chose to place them in institutions for their entire childhoods.

For myself, at thirteen and too young to be able to affect what was happening, I could only feel that I had let Peggy down by accepting what was being done to her children. Nothing had gone right for her in life and it seemed that even in death she wasn't getting a fair deal. Something took hold in me then, a determination to get the kids out of the institutions McAvoy had sent them to, a resolve to put things right some day.

At Garnethill I was struggling. Looking after the house, Nan and myself obviously took its toll on my schoolwork, but I never told my teachers why I wasn't coping with work I was really perfectly capable of doing. Keeping secrets is normal life for the families of alcoholics and this was just one more. To the Sisters of Mercy I was simply a non-trier, except in English, History and Art, the subjects I liked.

Stressed in every aspect of my life I had subconsciously decided to rely on the things I found easy, rather than struggle with the ones I found harder or less interesting. In a twisted way, too, I began to accept my position as fair payment for the years of being feted as 'one of the bright ones'. I had always felt acutely embarrassed by the glory I received for excelling at what came naturally, when I knew from my sufferings in Maths that it was possible to work hard for little or no result.

By the third year I had gone down to a 'C' class, much to the annoyance of my English teachers (apart from Sister Aquinas) who knew I read books voraciously and scored consistently high marks in their classes.

My classmates had all been in 'C' classes from the start and had been learning shorthand and typing from the first year, regarded as only fitting for the lowest form of academic life, while I had been learning Latin. Sister Aquinas had reeled with shock and horror when I explained in first year that I wanted to learn shorthand and typing too because I wanted to be a journalist and a writer. My request was denied with all the disgust she could muster, and the good Sister could muster a lot. Two years on, those regarded as natural low-achievers were thus better off than I, and as I dropped Science, Latin and French, I had the gaps filled with more English and Art. It seemed that just like Granda Tom, I was escaping from my home life by immersing myself in Literature and Art, and I became so good at design and screen printing that the Art Teachers and School Inspectors bought my work. Endless discussions then ensued about whether my work was mine to sell, the school's or the Education Department's. Not that it really mattered, because characteristically I lost all interest in the finished article and gave it away to whoever wanted it.

'I don't understand you!' I remember one of my Art teachers saying, 'You have this talent and so many people recognize it, but you don't seem to care!' I didn't understand it either, but now I do. It was low self-esteem; whatever I achieved wasn't up to much, because I wasn't up to much in my eyes. If it was mine, it had no value. It was that simple. For similar reasons I was doing what Laurie did with his Maths ability, making it mean nothing because it was my skill.

My excellence in a few subjects was enough to make me top of the class, which understandably irked the others, because I didn't compete at all in the subjects they were good at. Looking back, it should have been obvious that this was a bright child in some sort of trouble, but the Sisters' minds didn't work like that. I was different from the others and that was as far as their insight reached. The aim of the other girls was right on target, to get married as soon as possible to a good Catholic boy and to start a good Catholic family with all due haste. This wasn't my ambition and I resented the constant attempts to force it on me; I resented the relentless religious bias of the school in a way that the Sisters and the good Catholic girls understandably objected to.

One week out of every year was dedicated to Nun Recruitment. We would be subjected to non-stop propaganda about what an exciting life lay ahead of us in a convent, a career second only to giving birth to hordes more of the faithful. We had talks in which we were urged to search the deepest recesses of our souls for the merest shred of a vocation, and endlessly shown films of nuns taking their vows at different stages of the process. While the others found the wedding ceremony, complete with wedding attire and gold bands, but minus a groom, a thing of beauty, I could barely contain my astonishment.

Missionary Nuns would arrive to tell us of their good works among natives of various descriptions, and how these people had been made into good Catholics as a result. Couldn't the good works be done without conversions, I wondered; was it strictly necessary to be a Catholic in order to be saved from starvation? Soon they were warned to accept no questions from the unbeliever, so that avenue of discussion was cut off. I was only trying to cause trouble, I was told, which suited the situation perfectly: for discussion read trouble. For the hell of it I would seek out Sister Aquinas and express an earnest belief in a vocation. She would glare at me, as she had done the previous year, and the one before that, and tell me that mockery was a sin, for which God would surely punish me. I thought He had already done so in advance, by sending me to Garnethill.

Newly ordained priests were regularly sent to us to get used to being adored, but in reality it was a baptism of fire. The idea was that we would anonymously submit questions and receive replies wise beyond reason, and these sad young lads would stand before us in their new outfits, which were always several sizes too big, trying to look confident, paternal and pious. It never worked. The girls saw them as the nearest thing they would ever get to human sacrifices and the *double entendres* flew. They were only lads and the girls knew it, so they would flutter their eyelashes, lick their lips, suck their pencils, wink – anything to put the new priest completely off his stride.

I, on the other hand, had to take them on in earnest, which spoiled the fun for the others. If the Pope was against the Pill for destroying human life, why didn't he join CND, to stop mankind being wiped out by nuclear war? By the time I got on to the holocaust and the blind eye turned by Pope Pius XII, the fledgling had usually flown to Sister Aquinas for protection against the anti-Christ. My classmates were quite rightly furious, because they had every right to their fun and I always cut it short, which was my fun. Then I would be hauled before Sister Aquinas and castigated for questioning The Will of God, which in turn led me to question the existence of her God, leading to the old argument about communism and the monarchy.

She beat me on the young priests, too, eventually, first of all by censoring the written questions in advance to eliminate the O'Brien ones, and then by banning me entirely from attending the sessions. So instead of talking seriously about serious issues, the young priests reverted to being the sexual playthings of the *good* Catholic girls, the girls enjoyed themselves again and all was right with the world. Me? I went to Art or the library, which were of course enormous punishments to fit my terrible crimes, and I suffered mightily.

Though Nan had no time for any religion, all of my pagan thoughts were of course put down to my having a Proddy mother, and prayers were frequently sent heavenwards, entreating some saint or other to arrange for Nan's immediate conversation to The One True Faith. Only then would my good, pure, eternal Catholic soul be saved.

The Catholic faith permeated every subject and minute of school life. Indeed it was the Maths teacher who was most devout in her entreaties for Nan's conversion, more so than in the teaching of Maths. Her method of enlightening us into the mysteries of her subject was to write some obscure formula on the blackboard and have us copy it down. If she was asked to explain she would exclaim, 'I've just written it on the board!' Little wonder really that she never succeeded in having Nan turn into even a nominal Catholic. I'd go home and tell Nan that any minute now her entire life would change, that the divine power of St Someone-or-other was about to strike, and she'd laugh uproariously.

At least twice a week the entire school would be marched down to St. Aloysius church, where Granda Tom had received his pantomime send-off, for whatever religious service was in season. It became clear well before I reached third year however, that if forced to attend I could, and would, put on such a convincing performance of choking from the pungent smell of incense, that I might well expire from over-acting. A tacit agreement was therefore reached that I could instead make my way to the nearby Art College to watch the screen printing in progress. This left both the school and myself to our own individual acts of worship, but it really did annoy Sister Aquinas. Had she been a different kind of Irish she would have understood the Game and not let her annoyance show. There was no real satisfaction in beating someone who didn't know about scoring points, but I was so dismally unhappy at Garnethill that I'm ashamed to say I took what little was available.

Chapter Twenty-Eight

JFK was killed in November 1963. Garnethill went into mourning for a martyred prince of the church, cut down in his prime. With hindsight there were elements of farce and irony about the Sisters' reaction, because had they but known it, JFK was an especially fine example of the lustful male whose sexual appetites were out of control, the kind of male they spent so much of their time protecting us from.

I was inconsolable; it felt like the end of the world, and as I watched events unfolding on TV I identified with them so much that I felt I was actually there. Even all these years later and with Camelot uncovered as Shamelot, the memory of those events still affects me. That JFK was just the same as every other politician I have no doubt, in fact I now think he was worse. A generation's ideals and the glimmer of hope that JFK represented, that those ideals could be made to count for something died that day on Dealey Plaza. I get that same lump in my throat when I hear the old pacifist folk song, 'The Strangest Dream', because it represents the same age of innocence as JFK did to us then.

Everything that we know now about JFK wasn't of course common knowledge at the time. He was a young, handsome hero who had been cruelly murdered in front of the world's appalled gaze. We were given time off school to watch the funeral, of course, but Garnethill's reasons for mourning JFK were not mine. I wrote a great deal of very bad poetry about it, and won new respect from Mrs Crane, neé Johnstone. It was so excruciatingly bad that she thought it was good and at first refused to believe I'd written it. Thereafter she regarded me with deference as a genius and often asked me to read and explain the significance of poems by real poets, as though I had something in common with them. I got away with a lot, because she was not a good English teacher and had very little understanding of words, spoken or written. So I used to make up ludicrous explanations that made a travesty of great works and she agreed with every one.

It was a valuable lesson to me of how easily fools can be made to look like sages. Since then of course I've seen it happen many times. You only have to look at any area of public life, especially the House of Commons, to see living examples of that particular phenomenon.

I had my only serious illness in 1963. It started up at Loch Lomond and at first it seemed like sunstroke. My head ached all Sunday, but when I got home it eased off and then on Monday it got worse again. Within hours I was vomiting and light hurt my eyes. The GP arrived and asked me to touch my toes, which hurt my back, but I told him that it was the strain after a weekend in the canoe. Luckily he listened to his own instincts rather than me and diagnosed meningitis, and almost before I knew it I was taken by ambulance to Ruchill Hospital.

The Clark attention to dignity won out even in this situation and I refused to be carried on a stretcher. Before the ambulance arrived I struggled upright, washed and dressed, and when the crew knocked on the door I walked past them to the ambulance, leaving them in the house looking for this seriously ill patient. Nan looked desperate, but still she couldn't summon up the strength to leave the house, so Skip went to hospital with me. Despite my bravado I felt really ill in the ambulance, but Skip typically turned away from me as we drove to the hospital, unable to handle any human attempt at communication.

In the hospital meningitis was quickly confirmed, which struck fear into Nan's heart. One of my cousins had had it when he was a child and had been treated with the new wonder drug, Streptomycin. In those early days the dosage of the drug wasn't certain, and he got too much, destroying his hearing and leaving him completely deaf for the rest of his life. I only had the viral strain of the illness, but it was bad enough. Within a week I was home again, but weaker than I would have believed possible. I wasted what energy I had getting angry because I had so little of it. During my week in hospital Skip had been run off his feet doing all the chores I usually did, and despite my weakness he instantly and gladly handed them all back to me.

I went back to Garnethill for my fourth year to take my O levels. The Education Department had given me a grant in the form of a cheque to buy a uniform, and as we didn't have a bank account Skip took the cheque to one of his pubs to have it cashed; naturally that was the last we ever saw of it.

I have no idea why Garnethill put up with me in what was to be my final year. Skip had decided that as I would just get married anyway there was no point in staying on any longer. What he meant was that if I was earning he would have more to spend on drink, but my mother, who once would have fought such a nonsense, was no longer able to do so. I remember looking at her for some sort of reaction as he announced his decision, the three of us knowing what he was really saying, but all she could do was lower her eyes. Though she had long ceased to function as the woman and the mother I had known, sometimes I still had expectations and so was often disappointed. It was illogical of course; like expecting her to live without a beating heart. All of the problems she had were symptoms and without diagnosing the source she would never get well again, but facing the cause would be too painful. What if she died from the cure?

At lunchtime one day one of the Crowd passed my school on his motorbike and stopped to chat. I was aware of one of the Sisters watching us, and assumed she was ready to attack him if he turned out to be easily inflamed and exploded into a sexual frenzy. Later I was told to report to Sister Aquinas, who wanted to know who he was. She couldn't handle the fact that he was a friend; males couldn't be friends, they were sexual time-bombs or they were nothing. No other kind of male existed.

'You were seen touching him!' she seethed. I hadn't a clue what she was talking about, but then that wasn't an unusual experience, as far as I was concerned she spoke Sanskrit with a Russian accent most of the time.

'Touched him?' I asked, wondering if his masculine powers stretched to hypnosis of a maiden in order to make her unwittingly commit obscene acts in front of a nun.

'You put your hand on his arm!' she stuttered, 'Don't deny it! You were seen!'

I could think of nothing to do but laugh, in fact I didn't even think, I fell about in front of the wizened old crone and shook with mirth. She didn't know it of course, but the weekend previously, and many more before, I had slept beside him and numerous more males, our sleeping bags actually touching for hours on end! She didn't know how to handle laughter, so she stomped up and down her study, delivering a lecture on morality, then she ordered me to go to confession. I'd had enough of her over the past four years. 'Get burnt,' I replied, and walked out, fully expecting, indeed hoping, that she would expel me this time and let me out of the madhouse for good. But she didn't; I have no idea to this day why not. Maybe I was her challenge, sent by her God to test her, maybe she just liked touching fire by associating with my extreme brand of evil. But it wouldn't be long before she was rid of me and I of her. As soon as I took my O Levels in English, History and Art, the only subjects I now studied, I left Garnethill forever.

Chapter Twenty-Nine

I didn't fight Skip's decision that I should leave school after my fourth year because I hated Garnethill so much, so I can't lay all the blame on him. Having said that though, I know perfectly well now, as I did then, that any protest would have failed.

Before I left I saw Sister Aquinas for the last time, by accident on my part at least. She wanted me to consider something: that those who are the strongest rebels often have the strongest vocations and are trying to fight their destiny. The shallowness of the woman's understanding still surprises me and I'm more than old enough now to know better. It was one of those occasions when I actually did have the right reply instead of thinking of it later and wishing I'd said it. 'See you in hell,' I said as I walked out.

The sad, not to say tragic, thing, was that a fair proportion of my schoolmates did become nuns, most joining the Sisters of Mercy, brainwashed by the false glamour that the nuns deliberately projected. Most of them left later, once years of their lives had been wasted in discovering that there was no such thing as the much-vaunted vocation that we heard so much about during the annual recruitment week. In my opinion it was no better than the kind of indoctrination tactics used by the Moonies, tactics the good Sisters would rightly have condemned. Together with the nuns' silliness, their insensitivity and dislike of humanity in general, the wasted years of those young girls remains my lasting memory of the unhappiness I associate with Garnethill Convent.

Many of the girls who didn't become nuns married quickly as soon as they left; one, a bubbly, vital girl called Anne-Marie, married the following week. All through our school years she had come in with gifts and enormous cards from her boyfriend, for her birthday, Easter, Valentine's Day, Christmas or whatever. I met her a few years later, pushing a baby in a pram and holding a toddler by the hand. She was nineteen-years-old. She appeared happy, but all I felt for her was profound pity, and anger at those who pushed Catholic motherhood as a gift from God and a duty to Him.

There was yet another group who had always seemed so much more worldly-wise than the rest of us. Their zest for living had been held in check so long that any fool could see the danger that it might one day burst forth with unknown consequences. Girls like Jan, who had been at every school with me since the days of the Marian, a slim, pretty girl who knew it all. Her group were the ones whose skirts were just that bit shorter and who wore make-up so discreetly that it was undetectable, even to the nuns who had a sixth sense for anything on their banned list. While the majority of the girls lived for discos and dates, Jan's little group of sophisticates had gone further along the path to adulthood and had left such childish things well behind many years before.

I used to envy Jan and her little group their knowledge of life, their easy acceptance of all the things that made me feel awkward. They didn't experience puberty, their bodies simply caught up with their existing mental maturity without any apparent trauma or effort. They had no problems with males, in fact they had mastered the art of manipulating men very early on and had a confidence years beyond mine, and certainly light years beyond anything the Sisters could have dreamt up in their worst nightmares. For that little group marriage and kids had never been an option, but unlike me they hadn't made it a battle-ground; they had simply served their time as quietly as possible until they could leave it all behind them and start their adult lives.

As soon as they left school they disappeared into the upper reaches of city life without any discernable pause in the transition from the schoolgirl stage. Jan went to London and became a model, and every so often I'd see that pretty face with the secretly knowing expression smile at me from the pages of magazines. Garnethill had done nothing for Jan except contain her till the age of sixteen, but at least she had survived it, she had made a successful life for herself and done what she wanted. I had never been close to Jan, she had always been too mature for me, even when we were both eight-year-olds in Mrs McGettigan's class, but I always envied and liked her and I was secretly pleased that she at least hadn't fallen for the lies and become a nun or a breeding machine. I had this mental picture of Jan in my head for years; she was wearing black patent shoes, staring men straight in the eye, and I could almost hear her whistling!

In the Summer of 1964 I left school at the age of sixteen, and we also moved away from Drumchapel, one of the worst decisions for my mother. At 48 Halgreen Avenue she had neighbours who, if not quite in the Balmano Brae class, were as near it as possible. On the bottom flat lived Mrs Boyce, who regarded the entire close as her own property and dashed out to shoo away anyone who lingered on the stairs for longer than she found acceptable. Across from her were the Hannahs. Mr Hannah, as everyone knew, was hen-pecked. He was a tall, thin man with steel-grey hair and a quiet, long-suffering manner. Everytime he entered his own home he had to take his shoes off at the outside door, and we were all used to his wife's screams if he actually touched anything inside. Then one day he disappeared and we discovered that for years he had enjoyed a secret romance with a much younger, and richer woman, and they had now left together for a new life in Spain.

Mrs Hannah, now left on her own, showed no outward sign of grief and continued in her houseproud ways, refusing as ever to admit anyone into her shrine. No one noticed very much that she hadn't been around for a while because no one saw her normally. Then the smell alerted the other inhabitants of 48 something was wrong. When the police broke down the door they discovered that Mrs Hannah had been dead for a couple of months at least.

On the first floor lived the Williams family. Mr Williams

was severely disabled but he still managed to father seven daughters and only stopped when Mrs Williams' reproductive life did. Next door were the Wilsons, who mysteriously changed their name to Connor, which did nothing to improve the life of Mrs Wilson/Connor, who was a slim, beautiful woman of incredible sadness. Below us lived the Baillies, another family of girls, three this time, all vivacious, dark females, one of whom was addicted to Elvis Presley and for some reason Rennies antacid tablets, which she chewed like sweets. I don't know which aberration amazed me most, though these days I certainly rank curing heartburn above listening to Elvis.

Beneath Alexa Grimshank, on the third floor, lived the Rankins, and it was Mrs Rankin's proud boast that her husband had not been allowed his conjugal rights since the conception of their fourth child fourteen years before. Sexual relations were regarded by her as indecent, and any respectable woman would be morally bound to bring them to an end as soon as possible. She disappeared too, under a huge coat that covered her from head to foot, before she tearfully confessed to Nan that at the age of fifty she was about to produce Rankin offspring number five. Mrs Rankin never came to terms with being caught out as a lying fornicator, much to the amusement of the other women in 48, and made up all sorts of stories to cover what she maintained had been her only lapse in fourteen years of unblemished purity. There were dark hints that she had been ravished, which gave us all a new perspective on Mr Rankin, a quiet, unassuming electrician in Singer's sewing machine factory, who didn't remotely resemble Rudolph Valentino.

So 48 was a place where people still knew other people to varying degrees, and when Nan became unable to leave the house the other women continued to come to see her and bring her up to date with the news. With both Laurie and Mickey now married, the house was one bedroom too big, but I don't know whose idea it was to move out of Drumchapel. After eight years, the conviction took root that we lived too far away from the centre of

Glasgow and were too isolated. If we lived within the city, or so the argument went, the family on both sides would visit more; Skip's argument I'm sure. My mother had a different agenda of course, she hoped that by moving to the city again Skip would come home more often. Nan was still looking for Utopia. Both hopes were unrealistic of course. After she heard that we were moving, Alexa Grimshank sobbed every time she saw Nan, and on the day we moved out of Halgreen she took herself off to her mother's at the crack of dawn so that she wouldn't have to see us go.

A few miles north-west of the city centre a new housing estate had been built on the site of Maryhill Barracks. It was a mixture of high rise and of the traditional tenement blocks that existed in Drumchapel and elsewhere. The boundary wall of the Barracks had been retained, which proved that whatever lack of judgement and imagination governed the design of homes for people to live in, someone, somewhere, must have suspected there were things from the past worth keeping. Part of the old barracks' wall ran along Wyndford Road, so in a ludicrous attempt to give the estate an upmarket image, it was called Wyndford Estate, though to everyone in the area and all who came to live in it, it was known simply as The Barracks.

Twenty-four families lived in our block of one and two bedroomed flats in Kirkhill Place, and we never came into direct contact unless we met in the lift. There were no young families, indeed most of the new tenants were OAPs, so there was little life about the place, and none that could penetrate the vast number of doors separating the flats. It was like a maze.

The days of washing greens had long gone, but the memory lingered on in the token provision of a small area on the roof that could be used for drying clothes. It seemed so unnatural, though, that no one ever used it, and it was troublesome too because it meant going through the inevitable labyrinth of doors, up in the lift and then unlocking the door leading to the drying area. The flats were heated by electricity that was too expensive to use for long, and there was a large, heated airing-cupboard, like a huge tumble-dryer without the tumble, that was equally costly. If they didn't have washing-machines and tumble-dryers of their own most people went to a laundrette. Comparative affluence, it seemed, was bringing a breakdown in social contact in the city, but the collective folk memory remained somehow, and the laundrette served as a meeting place for those reluctant to give up that contact.

For Nan the move to Kirkhill Place was nothing short of disastrous, because for a start Maryhill was an area of the city we knew nothing about, it was as foreign to us as Drumchapel had been but without the attractions Drumchapel had at first. She knew no one and because of the way the flats were laid out she got to know no one. She saw no other soul and spent all of her time staring out of the kitchen window as traffic and life passed her by two floors below. When I went out her face was at that window, and regardless of when I came in again, it was still there. There were many pubs in the area, too many for Skip to contemplate passing, so his drinking habits didn't change significantly. He'd come out of work, head for a pub, hop on a bus home and head for another pub. He usually slept some of it off for a couple of hours before heading out for the pub again in the evening. In some ways his frequent non-appearances while we lived in Drumchapel had been a blessing, because now he was just as drunk but he was around more, and it was impossible even to think of bringing anyone home. This of course bit deeper into Nan's isolation; I at least met people during the day when I went out.

I often asked my mother why she had married Skip and she'd reply, 'Ach . . .', and turn her head away; I don't think she understood why herself. He had been looking for a mother I think, and who better than Nan Clark, a famed earth-mother? He was just another sad, lost child who had found his way to Nan but unfortunately no one had arrived to claim him back again. And how was she to judge? She was seventeen when they married and had no other relationship because he had always been there, waiting, needing to be mothered. She hadn't a chance.

The world it seemed wasn't wide open to receive a sixteen-year-old journalist/writer with O Levels in English, History and Art, even if I threw in Mrs McGettigan's special prize for composition into my application. It was all I wanted to do, although my Art teachers had been keen for me to go on to Glasgow School of Art to study textile design. This would have meant staying on at school to take more exams, which had already been ruled out, of course. In any case, no matter how much I enjoyed Art, it was never in the same league as writing. It was more 'something to do' when not writing. A pastime, not an instinct.

By this time Mickey had built up a good career in medical electronics and he mentioned that jobs were going in the Eastern Infirmary. I had absolutely no hankering to do hospital work, but it could bring in a few pennies while I waited for my great literary skills to be discovered, something even I had to concede might take a while. Meantime I had to find money to live on, cash for the necessities of life, like a tent, a groundsheet and some climbing socks. When I turned up for the interview I hadn't a clue what I was being interviewed for and cared considerably less. If I got it that would be fine for a little while, if not then something equally temporary would do.

The Consultant Cardiologist interviewed me with the Hospital Secretary, who it was clear didn't matter greatly in the proceedings.

'I see you went to a convent school,' said Dr Alexander Cunningham, 'Presumably this means that you are of the Catholic faith?'

'Does it hell!' I replied, 'It means that my father is. I had no choice in the matter of where I went to school but I see no reason why I should take his religion any more than his politics. It's bad enough that I'm lumbered with his Irish Catholic name without an intelligent man like yourself making objectionable assumptions!'

He smiled politely. 'And the assumption that you are a Catholic is objectionable, is it?'

'In other circumstances you might well have been invited outside to settle the insult with claymores drawn!'

Just as well I didn't care about the job I thought. As I left I had a mental picture of the two of them immediately dropping to their knees, rosaries in hand, to offer up hundreds of Hail Marys to cleanse them from listening to my blasphemous outpourings. Next day a letter arrived asking me to start within a week. Dr Cunningham, it transpired, was a mite anti-Catholic, and he was to turn out to be the nicest, least prejudiced bigot I have ever met. I wasn't remotely qualified for the job, I had no Maths or Science qualifications and would have to study at night school just to get what I should have started with. I'd have to go to college to take the standard technician's course, all while working in the hospital. Because of my anti-Catholic remarks Dr Cunningham decided I could do it, while I didn't really care, because long before I had to do it I'd be a famous writer . . .

Sandy Cunningham was a very shy man and a brilliant doctor; a man of deep passions and even deeper moods. He had fallen foul of the medical mafia that ran the health service in Glasgow and had therefore been denied both power and influence. His brilliance remained, but he regretted that he had never mastered the art of dirty dealings and in-fighting essential for a successful career in medicine. Had he learned to be as unscrupulous as the rest he would have advanced further and as he saw it, could have achieved more, 'got things done', as a result. He was a very humane man though and could no sooner have fought dirty than applauded a goal scored by Celtic Football Club; it simply wasn't in him, he was too decent.

To get him through board meetings, where he was inevitably in a rebel minority of one – doctors forget loyalty to friends when it means being looked upon with disfavour by those above – he took the odd tipple. This of course only gave the mafia another weapon to use against him. 'Blown it again!' he'd mutter, 'I've blown it again!

What a bloody fool I am!', and he really didn't object if you agreed with him. Then he'd brood in his room for however long it took for the mood to pass, until the next time.

Chapter Thirty

On my first day as a Student Cardiological Technician, I was taken by an experienced technician to 'Thor's ward'. As we entered the huge swing doors, Marie let them go again ever so quietly, and tiptoed around the ward. 'It's OK darlings,' said a voice, 'The old bastard isn't here yet, you're perfectly safe!' Marie sighed with relief. 'Thanks Dr Patel!' she smiled, and as we walked on down the ward she whispered, 'His name's Patel, but we all call him Petal. He's a bit, well, you'll find out!'

We stopped at the bedside of a man in his sixties and Marie rubbed a gel on his ankles and wrists, then fixed rubber bands around, and screwed wires to the small, hooked metal plates holding the bands together. The wires ran to an ECG machine, and when the dial was flipped, various different tracings spewed out of the machine. They made no sense to me, but Marie explained that the patient had suffered a heart attack a few days before and the leads recorded the electrical activity in different parts of his heart. By comparing the tracings taken over the last few days it was possible to chart the rate of damage, recovery or otherwise. Then another lead attached to a small suction device was moved to different positions across the patient's chest and more tracings spewed out.

When we had finished we removed all of the equipment, placed it back in the drawer under the machine, re-made the bed, and then just as we were about to pull back the screens we heard an army of footsteps marching across the long ward. Marie winced, put a finger to her mouth to silence me and then very carefully, like mime artists, we crept out of the ward, pushing the ECG machine in front of us. I let the door go behind us with as much care as

Marie had when we went in, but from inside the ward a voice bellowed after us, 'Who's that crashing through my ward? Who is it? I know there's someone there! Come out you bugger!'

Marie grabbed my arm, propelled me and the machine down the corridor, turned right down another and through a doorway. Behind us feet crashed along in pursuit as the voice continued to yell demands and threats, but whoever it was hadn't been quick enough to see us go in the door. With great aplomb Marie walked out again, humming gently and going very slowly in the direction we had just come from at high speed. We passed the owner of the voice, a very tall, thin man with thick, steel grey hair and a hawklike face. He was striding along the corridor with several other white-coated males in tow, going in the opposite direction to us.

'Good morning Dr Murray,' Marie said smoothly.

'Good morning, Miss . . . er . . . Did you by any chance pass some blighter coming from the direction of my ward?'

'Why no,' she replied, all calm innocence, 'I don't think so. Did you notice anyone Meg?'

I shook my head dumbly, wondering what in hell was going on.

'Are you sure they didn't use the other lift Dr Murray?' she offered helpfully, 'The one beside your ward?'

'I . . . um . . . don't think so, Miss . . . um . . . But then again . . .'

'I think it's disgraceful,' Marie continued, 'Disturbing you like that Dr Murray. I'd never go into your ward during rounds!'

'And I appreciate your consideration,' the voice boomed, 'Not everyone in this hospital is as professional and considerate as yourself, Miss . . . um . . .'

With that he barked us another good morning and we made our way to the lift 'the blighter' might have used, passing Dr Patel on the way. He wrapped his white coat around him, folded his arms theatrically across his chest and said, 'Nice performance darlings, your secret is safe

209

with me!' He was the campest act I'd ever seen, as he disappeared down the corridor, half-heartedly 'searching' for whoever had upset Dr Murray.

'Now you know why we call him Petal,' Marie sighed, 'And it breaks my heart, he's so gorgeous and he's out of reach, unless you're six-foot-four, have a beard and happen to be a bloke!'

'Who . . . What was that all about?' I asked.

'Oh *that*?' she said, 'That's Thor, he's the chief of this unit and he hates people being in his ward. In fact he hates people, to be honest. No one is allowed to *think* loudly when he's doing his rounds, but if we don't have an up-to-date ECG to show him he blows up.'

'Well what are we supposed to do?' I asked, 'How do we get tracings for his ward rounds if we can't go into his ward?'

'Well we do go in silly!' she replied, 'Then we get out while his back's turned of course! Haven't I just shown you how to do it? Don't you think Petal's gorgeous? I'd give my all for him, if only he'd take it!'

'Why is he called Thor?'

'Oh him. Well his name is James Thor Murray. He was born nine months after his parents' marriage and honeymoon in Iceland. They met this good-looking young man there, called Thor, became friends, and when the monster arrived he was called James after his father and Thor after this good-looking friend.' Marie laughed, 'Well that's the story Thor tells, because that's the story his mother told his father and him, but we all think the original Thor was probably much more than a good friend, and mummy gave him both names to cover all options. It would certainly prove what we all know to be the truth anyway.'

'Which is?'

'That he's a complete bastard of course!' She continued humming as we walked into the lift and pressed the button to close the doors.

'D'you think it'd be possible to turn him?' she asked, her mind still on the unattainable Dr Patel, 'I mean, surely if Petal experienced the love of a good *woman*, someone just like me? Of course I'd have to get him drunk first and talk in a deep voice. What do you think?'

Nan had been delighted that I was going to work in a hospital, it was so respectable, so learned, so close to all those single young doctors who came from 'big hooses'. If only she knew, I thought, if only she knew . . .

It was in the hospital that I was first called Meg. There were already two other Margarets in the department, a third would cause too many problems, it was decided.

'We'll have to call you something else,' said Sandy Cunningham, and I kept quiet about being called Rita, because I hated it. 'How about Peggy?' he asked.

'NO!' I almost shouted.

'OK, keep your hair on! It's a perfectly decent name, but if you don't like it we'll think of something else!'

'It's not that I don't like it . . . it's just . . . I'd rather not . . .'

'OK, OK! Meg then, how about Meg?'

And Meg it's been ever since.

Going to and from work at the hospital every day I passed Eastpark Home, where Peggy's handicapped daughter had been sent five years before. The sign on the main road outside, with breathtaking tact announced 'Eastpark Home for Infirm Children', and though I loathed cigarette smoke I always went upstairs on the bus so that I could look through the windows. I don't know what I expected to see, a small cousin, perhaps, holding a placard proudly proclaiming our family link. It was on my mind constantly as the months passed, then one day I got off the bus at the Home and went in.

I explained to a nurse that I was Anne McAvoy's cousin, that I'd only recently moved to the area and could I see her please? Anne was ten years old by then, and she slept in a long dormitory. There was a locker by each bed, and in hers she had every birthday, Christmas and postcard that she had ever received. She had on display every present and every postal-order – uncashed – that she had ever been sent, a gesture of reassurance to her that she existed, that she mattered. I found her bright and cheerful, showing off her visitor to the other kids without the slightest suspicion that her visitor felt ashamed of being accorded the honour.

Seeing her was incredibly painful on all sorts of levels. Firstly there was shame that I hadn't been to see her before. She was, after all, Peggy's child. There was also the awful frustration that she simply shouldn't be there. This thought, of course, skirted the edges of the reason, the unspeakable reason that we still hadn't faced, the loss so unacknowledged that we couldn't mourn it. I still hadn't shed one tear over the events of 1959.

She was still there you see. Peggy. As a way of coping the family had unconsciously decided that she hadn't lived, therefore she couldn't have died. Their logic may have been tortuously faulty, but it was understandable. *I* knew that she had lived though. Peggy and Nan had made me what I was; I was the living proof of her existence. So I had secretly kept her alive somewhere deep in my soul, suspended in an emotional infinity. She was just as I last saw her on that Monday in May, and every now and again I would check that she was still there, smiling at me, her hair lit by the sunlight behind her. I suppose I must have known by some kind of instinct that we all had to let her go some day, and we could only do that by mourning. Sometimes, without planning it, I would push against the edge of the wound until it became too painful, then I would back off, returning her to where I kept her, until the next time.

This was to be the only time I saw Peggy's child. When I went back to the home McAvoy had been told about my first visit and had banned any more. The Eastpark staff were embarrassed but I was relieved, though it still makes me ashamed to admit it. However much the visit may have meant to the child the awfulness of the Home and of the situation had paralysed any good intentions I may have had. I was no better than the Clarks, my latest push had reached the painful area and it was just too much.

But the scenario stayed etched in my mind no matter how I tried to flush it away. Peggy's child shouldn't have been raised like that, not Peggy's child, not any child. When the children had been placed in Homes I had decided that one day I'd get them out again, but reluctantly I accepted now that I never would. I amended my list of things to be done in the future though: one day I'd find out the truth about Peggy's death, and added to that aim was a determination to get children out of institutions. All children in Homes became Peggy's children to me and though I never mentioned the items on my list to anyone, they lived quietly in my mind. They weren't ambitions or exciting goals to reach, but certainties that would happen, one day.

Though I had drifted into medicine, I found to my astonishment that I worked well with sick people and coped in a stressful world where crises were routine. I didn't have as many Saturdays free to go away with the Crowd, but that turned into a minor irritation rather than a disaster. Besides, the others had started to pair off and get married, so those of us still single met in the couples' houses. I saw Rab in Laurie's house sometimes and he was one of the few it was safe to allow into my own house. He would arrive out of the blue and whether I was there or not he would stay, making Nan laugh. She admired his clear, blue eyes, saying for some reason that they were 'sailor's eyes.' 'Naw thur no',' Rab would reply, 'Thur mine!' and Nan would giggle like a girl.

What kept me in the hospital was Glasgow, or rather its citizens. Like every Glaswegian I had always been of the opinion that it was the finest city in the universe; it didn't matter if the universe didn't agree, we took no offence, we were that sure of ourselves. It was only when I worked in the 'Eastern', as it was known locally, that I saw why Glaswegians were so special though. They will lay before complete strangers the most intimate details of their lives; if they feel a story coming upon them, then a story you will hear. Out-patients that I would see at a clinic for perhaps ten minutes of their lifetime, treated me like a member of the family, privy to all aspects of their personal lives.

One woman in her late forties came in for a routine ECG, and as I was explaining the procedure to her she said, 'Stockport! Whit dae ye think o' that? Stockport!'

I knew better than to make any comment at this early stage. She undressed and lay on the couch, and as I started to attach the electrodes she got down to the tale.

'Ma man's goat hissel' a joab in Stockport! Stockport! Whit dae ye think o' that then hen?'

I made a non-commital noise; I had no idea yet where this story was going.

'That's oota Glesca, in fact oota Scotland!' I marvelled at the breadth of her vision; Glaswegians rarely acknowledge that their city is actually a part of any land, even Scotland.

'Naw, naw,' she stated, 'Nae Stockport fur me, he kin go if he waants, Ah'm steyin' whaur Ah belang! Mibbe that'll pit an end tae a' these weans!' I had a fleeting vision of hundreds of xenophobic children clinging to every inch of her, all of them refusing to go to Stockport.

'Ah've goat wanna twenty-five,' she continued, as my little machine churned out her paper heartbeat, 'Wanna twenty-three an' wanna five! Terrible intit?' She was overcome by a spasm of laughter that destroyed the ECG, so I waited till she had recovered and then tried again. 'Y'know,' she continued thoughtfully, 'Ah've oaften thoaght, if Ah'd hid some Kit Kats in the hoose that day he'd probably have settled fur a cuppa tea instead! That'll teach me tae forget the biscuits, eh hen?' I could see a whole new Glasgow advertising campaign on family planning, with hoardings throughout the city proclaiming, 'Gie's a brek – hiv a Kit Kat.' With that she put her clothes on again, said 'Ta ta hen!' and disappeared forever, leaving me still wondering after all these years, what became of her and her Stockport-bound spouse. Her ECG incidentally, was clear.

If Glaswegians are communicative at the best of times, I discovered that illness rendered them positively verbose. Being sick stripped them to their raw best and characteristics I had been aware of became somehow enhanced, making me look at them again, surprised that I had passed over them so lightly before. Working with ordinary Glaswegians, if there is such a thing as an ordinary Glaswegian, took me back to Blackhill, and in a way that made sense, because the people of Blackhill had been fighting for their survival too.

A large part of my working day was taken up with acute heart attacks and we drew many of our patients from the Clydeside shipyards and the heavy industrial works in our part of the city. I was constantly surprised by them and surprised at being surprised too. A welder from Browns turned out to be an expert on Spanish poetry, a riveter from Fairfields was an authority on Renaissance Art, and Charlie, a shipyard electrician, knew everything about the works of Robert Burns.

He was in his fifties and his face was grey with pain. The ECG showed a massive heart attack, yet apart from his pallor he was showing no real signs of discomfort.

'Are you OK Mr Thomson?' I asked, always a silly question but it opens the score sheet.

'Ca' me Charlie hen,' he grinned, 'Mr Thomson wis ma faither!'

'OK Charlie; how's the pain?'

'Bloody awful hen, bit Ah've goat ma ain wey tae deal wi' the bugger.'

'Eh?'

'Well, ye know thaim wimmen that concentrate oan sumthin' else when thur havin' weans? Ah'm gaun ower in ma heid everythin' Rabbie ever wrote. Mind you, it's gettin' a bit cheeky oan it noo, Ah wish Rabbie hid wrote a bit mair!'

'We'll give you something for the pain then, give Rabbie a rest.'

Over the next few days I got to know Charlie and learned more about Burns in the process. Charlie's knowledge was immense, because he loved every line the Bard had written. I used to try to trip him up, regarding myself as a more than passable Burns buff, but he came through every time. 'Ye'll never beat the champ!' he'd grin, and I never did. If he had some pain he'd call to the nurses, 'Wee, sleekit, cowerin', tim'rous beastie!' and as the pethidine

215

hit home he'd serenade them with 'My love is like a red, red rose.'

A week after the first heart attack he had another and we could do nothing for him; there was too little left of his heart muscle. He died reciting 'A Man's a Man for a' That.' As we worked on him, knowing it was utterly hopeless but having nothing more than effort to offer, his voice trailed away, '. . . the man's the gowd for a' that . . .' From a poetic point of view, and doubtless also from Charlie's, it was a fine way to go, but I never got over the feeling that we lost something special everytime someone like him died. Yet a few weeks before we would have passed each other in the street without a second glance.

They were the kind of people I had grown up with and the more I knew about them the more I respected them. I was always the last to give up on cardiac arrests. 'Christ Meg!' the rest of the team would argue each time, 'You *have* to accept it, we've lost this one!', but I always wanted to keep trying and afterwards I would analyse the whole event for something we could have done that we hadn't.

The doctors were representatives of the monied classes, everything about their backgrounds kept them far removed from the people they dealt with. As a rule, unlike the vast majority of their patients, they had gone to fee-paying schools, had lived all of their lives in wealthy, high-amenity areas and they spoke differently. Living on a different level they often missed the true worth and richness of the people that Charlie represented, while I was one of them and so I knew exactly what was being lost. Maybe that was why I hated giving up and why I fought harder each time; it was after all what I had been brought up to do, to fight for those who couldn't fight for themselves.

Chapter Thirty-One

At this time the Crowd would meet up every Thursday night to decide where we were going the following weekend. For years our meetings took place at the Continental Café in Sauchiehall Street, until it was raided and we discovered that it was a notorious centre for drug dealing. We'd never noticed what had been happening around us as we argued over who was paying for the espresso.

Every August the diverse strands of our weekend life met up at the Cowal Highland Games in Dunoon. Even if we had gone in very separate directions throughout the rest of the year, we always met up at Cowal. The main attraction was the rolling ceilidh from the camp-sites through every pub and hotel in the town, taking in the famous march-past of hundreds of pipers after the Games. For the tourists the march-past was the climax of the day, but for us it was all just beginning.

The Crowd would swell as we walked about the streets picking up people we hadn't seen since the previous year. We didn't even actually have to see each other. Once, walking past the George Hotel we heard the strains of 'Morag's Faerie Glen' sung in a fine tenor voice. We knew that only one man sang that song and in that voice, so he was collected and on we went. We ended up that year at a ceilidh given by the Rose Fletcher Women's Pipe Band from Dagenham. It was held in the Innellan Village Hall, a few miles outside Dunoon and I have clear recollections of several of the Crowd being up on the stage singing, and the usual 'lasting friendships' being struck between strangers destined to remain so.

In the early hours of the morning we were to be found making our unsteady way back on foot and in the rain to the camp-site some miles away. Inevitably we lost some along the way, who had 'decided' to sleep it off in ditches or wherever, but the triumphant band who were able to continue suddenly remembered as they approached the camp-site that it was inconveniently situated on top of a hill. As we struggled upwards to the comfort of the tents, singing raucously and dragging the more moribund behind us, a voice shouted 'HALT! WHO GOES THERE? GIVE THE PASSWORD!' High above us, silhouetted against the skyline, were four Highlanders, Pringle's Nightwatch.

Nobody knew much about Wullie Pringle, though it was rumoured that he was a failed welder from Govan. Nobody knew either how he and his followers got from A to B; they just appeared then disappeared. There was a theory that they were the result of a failed 'Brigadoon' experiment, that they had once been perfectly ordinary half-wits but had wandered along just as the button was pressed to start the process. They were thus trapped in time, condemned to roam the earth for all time, dressed like Highland clansmen and transformed into tartan half-wits.

Wullie believed himself to be the reincarnation of Bonnie Prince Charlie and therefore always dressed in full Highland regalia. More curiously, his band of followers also believed his claim to the throne and they gathered around him, all dressed in heavy caped coats over kilts, with long feathers attached by silver clan crests and pinned to the glengarries they wore on their noble heads. Wherever Wullie went they arranged themselves around him, long cromaks at the ready, *sgiann dhus* sharpened, prepared to protect the royal personage from any insult or injury.

Not only did these retainers cook his meals, but they tasted them too, presumably in case they had inadvertently spiked them with arsenic. Before the Prince entered a pub, two of his senior followers would check it out for the presence of enemies, and once inside they would stand around him, eyeing the company suspiciously, just in case. At night they mounted a guard around his tent as he slept, four men at a time for four hours each, through wind, rain, hail and snow. Needless to say they were a bizarre bunch, and they wore their very warm clothing all year round. For some reason on that Cowal weekend, they had honoured us by pitching camp next door while we were having a jolly time in Innellan with Rose and her girls.

'FRIEND OR FOE?'

'Whit the f—?' somebody demanded of Wullie's protectors.

'STATE THE PASSWORD OR DIE!' boomed the caped half-wits, cromaks in one hand, drawn *sgiann dhus* in the other.

'Away tae buggery!' suggested a half-asleep, wholly inebriated voice, and above us the spiritual remnants of the '45 still barred the way to our tents. In the darkness it was difficult to judge with any accuracy what happened next. There was a claim later that it had all been a ghastly accident, but I know that I heard giggling in our ranks first. Someone, or two, certainly grabbed Wullie's guards by the ankles and pulled them down on top of us. Naturally this had a domino effect, and we all rolled back down the sodden hill we had only just managed to climb up, landing at the bottom in a large heap. There was a great deal of laughter, several of the company being in that peculiar stage of intoxication where everything seems funny, even rolling down a hill in the rain and dark, with large sticks and *sgiann dhus* about.

'Wait a minute!' shouted a voice, 'Wanna Pringle's mob is wearin' Y-fronts under the garb! That's no' right!'

'Yer lucky!' yelled another, 'Ah've goat a big bare arse stuck in ma face!'

A bloodcurling scream rent the air as the said big bare arse was soundly bitten. It took some time to sort the situation out, because everytime we climbed up the hill the memory of what had happened the last time overcame us and we all ended up laughing and falling down again. Meantime, of course, the Prince was unprotected in his tent.

Next morning, or whenever we awoke, the Young Pretender and his following pretenders had slunk off in disgrace as we slept. Whenever we spotted them again after that embarrassing contretemps, we never mentioned their defeat at the hands and teeth of a bunch of drunks and a teetotal girl; that would have been unnecessarily cruel, and possibly treasonous. Perhaps the humiliation had some effect though, because not long afterwards Wullie emigrated to Australia, leaving his stunned henchmen to mourn for their 'Prince across the Water'. They wandered about, still in full theatrical garb, lost and lonely, looking for someone to follow, like extras in search of a Scottish Tourist Board film.

Some time after Wullie's emigration, on a sweltering hot day, one of the Crowd, Calum Young, happened upon Tam the Druid, on the walk to Rowardennan. Tam, a devoted member of Wullie's entourage, was in his twenties and had a serious heart complaint. As a matter of honour he refused ever to remove his caped coat, which was a warm item to cart around on top of a kilt, especially in the middle of summer. Normally pale to the point of translucence, Tam the Druid had the extremely disconcerting habit of coughing and turning blue. To be fair to him this was hardly his fault, but it could be frightening for bystanders, especially as Tam's honour also prevented him from resting. He may have had no Prince to protect anymore, but that wouldn't stop him dropping dead for the cause, whatever it was. And that was exactly the performance he seemed about to visit upon poor Young that Saturday when Tam the Druid suffered a harsh fit of coughing.

With sweat running down his blue face and presumably the rest of his anatomy as well, Tam refuted Young's suggestion that he remove the topcoat. 'I never take off my coat!' he stated, staring enigmatically towards the horizon, as heroes are wont to do, then he collapsed in another coughing bout. Young had had enough; the last thing he could have coped with was a dead Druid, so he jumped over a wall and found an alternative, solo route to the boatshed.

Tam survived that episode, but the last we heard of him and his fellow abandoned Pringle-ites was that they were trying to raise money to bring the Prince back from the Antipodes, where, it was said, he had become incapacitated by homesickness. Apart from being barking mad that is.

Chapter Thirty-Two

Youth Hostels weren't quite our scene, except for the 'Den', where one of our own, Jack Savage, was Warden. Jack kept 'K' Dorm for our exclusive use, something the average hostelite resented but could do nothing about. If Jack said 'K' Dorm was fully booked, then 'K' Dorm was fully booked. Apart from this justified and perfectly understandable little foible, Jack was the most honest man ever to draw breath. Every forgotten item, no matter how small, insignificant or useless, was carefully logged and kept in the store in case the owner came back to reclaim it someday. Even discarded bottles were collected and the deposit of a few pence redeemed, the money joining the rest of the lost booty in the store. We all nagged him about this – and then came victory day:

In the store lay an old pair of disreputable white sandshoes that had been left behind years before; anyone else would have assumed they had been thrown away, not forgotten. Anyone except Jack. The day came when Jack needed a pair of 'sannies' and the shops were miles away. 'Dae ye honestly believe the bloke's gonnae come back fur thum?' we nagged, 'Be serious Jack, a tramp wid refuse tae wear thum. Ye take these things tae the pointa fetish Jack!' We condemned his elitism, his determined show that he was more honest than the common man, knowing that this would really hurt, because Jack was the purest communist ever born. Eventually, under attack from all sides, he caved in and proved us wrong by donning the old white sannies. Two days later a bloke turned up, 'Ah left an auld perra white sannies here a coupla years ago,' he said, 'Ye don't still huv thum by any chance?' Jack, his toes curling up with shame inside the stolen sannies, had to deny that he had ever seen them, and he never got over the guilt. Especially as we used to ask after his white sannies for years afterwards and mutter, 'A thief *and* a liar, tut, tut. Ye used tae be such an honest man Jack. Whit happened tae ye?'

It was a normal day in the hospital. There was a general examination room just inside the main entrance, where patients were examined and then dispatched to whichever department their ills demanded. It was a barn of a place with curtained off cubicles, and behind one a surgical houseman was faced with a problem posed by two homosexual gentlemen. They had 'married' each other and then become too hooked on the symbolism by placing the gold band on a very original extremity.

'It was all right at first,' suffering one wailed, 'But when it began to swell the ring got stuck, now it's *very* sore!'

'We'll have to cut it off I'm afraid,' said the bemused houseman, and the bridal pair screeched as one. 'Well we can't leave it on!' said the houseman in exasperation, 'Gangrene could set in very quickly!'

A terrible howling was heard this time, then the houseman realized what was wrong.

'I mean the ring you idiot, the *ring*! Not his dangly bits!' He left a nurse spraying the be-ringed appendage with cold water to reduce the swelling and sent for someone with pincers. Outside he wrote up the case notes, 'Months I've been qualified,' he muttered, 'And I haven't met one yet! Where are they?'

'Who?' I asked.

'The normal patients!'

'This is as normal as it comes!'

Behind another curtain the medical houseman was struggling with a gentleman who had collapsed on a train. He was refusing to remove his city uniform of pinstripe suit and bowler hat to be examined.

'Let me talk to him,' I suggested, 'I know what's wrong.'

'Now you mustn't be embarrassed,' I cajoled, 'I know what the problem is and I promise you no one will say anything about it.'

'You won't laugh at a silly old man?' he asked, clipped military moustache quivering and his arms tightly crossing his chest.

'Of course not! Now you must let us do a couple of tests and then you can most probably go home.'

He then removed his shirt to expose a lovely little red silk bra trimmed with black lace; it was too small for him, no wonder he'd passed out on the hot, crowded train. They always wore such exquisite things, far nicer than most women thought practical and more expensive than most could afford. No doubt he had the full matching set of panties and suspender belt underneath too.

'How did you know?' asked the houseman.

'I didn't for sure,' I replied, 'It could've been chains, or rubber.'

Sometimes I wondered at the wisdom of letting these young lads loose, straight after their Finals, when they had no experience of the big, bad world; it didn't seem fair on them somehow, or on the rest of us. Outside another cubicle a more Glasgow-wise Senior House Officer was explaining to another puzzled houseman why his patient kept worrying about her brown kittens instead of helping him with her symptoms.

'I ask her what's wrong and she just goes on about these damned brown kittens! I keep telling her someone will look after her cats, but it's all she'll say to me!'

'Well son,' said the SHO, 'She *is* telling you what's wrong with her. It is her considered opinion that she is suffering from bronchitis. "The Broon Kittens" is Glasgow slang for bronchitis. By the sound of her cough she's probably right. It's your task my boy to apply your mighty stethescope to her rib cage and confirm it. Go to it!' Two years ago someone had probably given him the same teach-in. A normal day, and into this normal day came a porter pushing a trolley.

'Joe's fainted,' he said to no one in particular, 'So Ah've jist pit 'im in cubicle four till he comes 'roond.'

From around the assembled medics there came a collective growl.

'You can put him in the incinerator for all we care!'

someone said, and there was a bitter laugh of agreement all round.

Joe was the car park attendant for the main forecourt and he kept his forecourt for 'those and such as those'. Senior consultants were assured parking spaces and all others were pounced upon and threatened if they as much as stopped to let a passenger out. He even resented the ambulances stopping in their own bay to bring patients in. Our main point of contention was that the forecourt was the quickest way into the hospital, and it made more sense for genuine workers to get inside fast, rather than consultants who were hardly on the front line.

People like the infamous Dr Thor Murray for instance, who drove a beautiful white vintage Lagonda that would have financed the building of a new hospital, were waited on with due and sickening deference by Joe. Thor had his own reserved space that Joe shepherded him into every day, with much bowing and his own weird combination of a salute and a tug of the forelock. Thor would then sweep off to his luxurious suite deep inside the hospital, where he would see his private patients, using every NHS facility available. This was against the rules, but Thor was stuck way back around 1920, and the board turned a blind eye. This was most appropriate, because the board were all Thor's private patients. Most of them were non-medics and mistook show for substance; they had no way of knowing that Thor had ignored every piece of medical progress after 1920 as well as all other aspects of normal life. So the resentment we all felt for Thor and his like applied to Joe, who fawned over him and them, and tales of Joe's treatment of generations of ordinary, mortal hospital staff regularly did the rounds. Now here he was, snoozing in the examination room.

'I don't like the colour of him,' said another tech, looking behind the curtain.

'I hate every one of his rotten cells,' said someone else, 'So what's new?'

'He looks a bit blue.'

'Let us know when he turns black!' Everyone laughed.

'He's arrested!' shouted the tech, feeling for a non-existent pulse. Everyone laughed again. 'Next you'll be saying that Santa does exist and that there really is a tooth fairy!'

Then we realized that she was serious, dropped what we were doing and the resuscitation routine took over. All the way through voices could be heard muttering, 'I can't believe I'm doing this!' and 'We'll never live this down even if he doesn't make it!'

Sod's law really is an odd thing. You can work on patients deperately for hours, with everything going for you and nothing going wrong, and still you lose them. Joe we got back. He was lying on the floor, pink and breathing again amid much cursing from the assembled company. The SHO glared at the tech who'd looked behind the curtain and said, 'There is no hope for you, you understand that, don't you? For a start everyone in this room will never forgive you, but the rest of us must all swear a blood oath here and now. We must all promise to deny any involvement in this obscene act and any knowledge of who took part, even under torture, OK? If the rest of the hospital hears about this we're all done for!'

Just then the door opened and in thundered Thor. 'The porters told me the car park Johnny was here!' he yelled, and catching sight of Joe lying on the floor with tubes and wires attached all over his body, he bellowed, 'Is that him? Where's his hat? Don't know him without his hat! Hey you! Car park Johnny! Get up! Some bugger's taken my space! I want his arse kicked out *now*! Get up! D'you hear me? I want you to get up!'

'It's a little tricky at the moment Dr Murray,' said the SHO very smoothly, 'Five minutes ago he was dead. You see we've only just resuscitated him.'

Thor stopped mid-roar and took in the scene around Joe for the first time, then said with utter contempt and distaste, 'My God, will you people stop at nothing? Why don't you let people die in peace?' With that he swept out and off to his suite, leaving the Lagonda parked in the ambulance bay.

A couple of months later I was helping to get a patient out

of an ambulance as Joe watched in disgust. The SHO was there too, and as we turned towards the hospital together, the white Lagonda swept past in style. We watched Joe go through his usual odd salute-forelock tug routine and as Thor disappeared inside Joe approached us.

'That Dr Murray,' he said, 'He saved ma life y'know.'

'Really?' said the SHO with total uninterest.

'Aye, sure enough,' said Joe, his horrible little eyes shining with tears of admiration, 'Ah hid this bad turn, nearly died so Ah did, an' he saved me. Ah heard this voice an' opened ma eyes, and there he wus, telling me Ah hid tae get up! Saved ma life he did, a wunnerful man!' Overcome with emotion he sniffed loudly and hirpled over to assault some innocent soul who was trying to find somewhere to park. The SHO shook his head. 'I'd rather that old bastard Thor took the blame than us,' he said, 'But ain't life an absolute bitch sometimes?'

Chapter Thirty-Three

One day I was walking through my own unit's female ward when I spotted a familiar face. I looked at the ward list, and it was, it really was. It was Jan.

'What's wrong with her?' I asked the houseman.

'Do you know her?'

'I went to school with her.'

'Really? That might be helpful actually, she won't say a word. Maybe she'll talk to you. We got her in last night, an overdose, and she nearly managed it too. We want her to see the shrink, but she won't even tell us to bugger off.'

'She was working as a model the last I heard of her a couple of years ago, I always thought she'd got it made.'

'Well she won't work as a model again,' he said, 'She's only held together with chewing gum and pills these days.'

I walked towards her bed, noticing how thin she was, the dark shadows under her eyes and the pale, almost transparent skin; it was Jan, but it wasn't the Jan I had known.

'Hello Jan,' I said, and she looked up at me with total indifference.

'You probably don't remember me,' I continued, 'We went to school together.'

'It's Margaret,' she said, pointing at me and smiling, 'Margaret O'Brien! What are you doing here?'

'That's my line! What are *you* doing here?'

She shrugged. 'I took an overdose.'

'Why?'

'Because I want to end it all.' She wasn't upset and she didn't even seem sad; it was a statement of fact. I sat beside her bed.

'But Jan, you had it all stitched up while the rest of us were still playing with dolls, what went wrong?'

'Me? I had it all stitched up? Me? Are you kidding? You were the one who knew all the moves!'

'Are you sure you *do* remember me?' I asked.

'God! Do I remember you!' She was laughing now, a good sign I supposed, but I hadn't a clue what she meant.

'How you handled all those mad nuns,' she said, 'You drove them even crazier than they were! Do you remember the time that second year got pregnant and had to leave the school, and they were lecturing us about it? And you said she should just say an angel had appeared announcing a virgin birth and before she knew it she'd have her own flock of nuns! I thought Sister Aquinas was going to explode in flames!'

'I don't remember that,' I said, 'But it sounds like me.'

'And the time you told her Jesus Christ was just a local politician who had offended the establishment, and before she could get up from the floor you said in fact he was probably a communist!'

Yes, it was definitely me she remembered, that was certainly one of mine.

'I used to envy you!' she said, 'You knew just how to get them going! Where did you get all that stuff?'

'From books,' I replied, 'Where else?'

'That's right,' she laughed, 'You always had a book in your hand. I always thought you'd be a writer, how come you're wearing a white coat?'

'I wish I knew,' I replied, 'I still write, but just for myself. But what happened to you? I used to feel so smug knowing this famous face on the front pages of magazines.'

'I couldn't handle it,' she said, 'You have to be really in control in that game, and I wasn't. Seems to me I've spent my entire life trying to get control of it. I ended up taking pills to keep me awake, pills to make me sleep, pills to keep me thin. And men! Around me like flies they were, and I always chose the wasp!'

She was on the brink of tears now, lying against her pillows, staring at the ceiling.

'Jan, it might help to talk to someone.'

'A psychiatrist? Forget it Margaret, it's too late now. Besides, do you think I haven't talked to them before?'

I decided to leave it till another time, so I changed the subject to the one thing that had made her smile before, our schooldays. As I left she said, 'I always admired you Margaret, you were always so confident, so sure. You didn't need a group around you, you were always yourself and you said what you thought. I never had that courage, but every time you scored a point against the nuns I felt like cheering!'

Funny the impressions we make on other people. All through my childhood I'd been a loner, keeping the awful secret of my father's drinking and the shame of how poor we were from the rest of the world. Since 1959 my mind had been constantly in turmoil and I'd looked at Jan and her little group, thinking they were sophisticated and so worldly-wise compared to me. Yet there was Jan trying to end her life at the age of twenty, having tasted success, messed around with drugs and been involved with who knows how many men. What had I done? I had wanted to write, it was the only thing I had ever shown any aptitude for, yet here I was, in a demanding job to be sure, but given that I could do it, it was as safe as houses.

As far as the swinging Sixties and the drug culture were concerned, they might as well have not been happening. I avoided going out with men on a one-to-one basis, and those I had dated lasted one date; I couldn't bring myself to get involved with anyone. Part of that was a natural reluctance given the one marriage I had any close knowledge of, but it was also partly because the earlier assaults had left me with a dislike of being touched. I used to think this dated from the time of Peggy's death, when one of my aunts had held onto me as I tried to escape hearing the actual words, but that incident had only compounded the dislike. It was really rooted in the first assault just beforehand, and the later incident outside the pub.

There was another reason though that lurked at the back of my mind, one I hardly dared think about because it was so impossible. That reason was Rab. I realized even then that anyone I dated reminded me of him in some way, a similar way of laughing perhaps, or 'sailor's eyes', but they weren't him. At the time I didn't admit any of this, even to myself, but whenever I saw him I felt more alive than at any other time. Our meetings were no more than verbal duels as we slagged each other off with insults; he was at least ten or twelve years older than me, well out of my reach and I knew it. He hadn't shown the slightest interest nor had there ever been the merest hint that he might regard me as anything other than the kid of the Crowd. The possibility of romance had never been considered. Rab was completely unattainable, but while he was there I couldn't sustain interest in anyone else.

Sod's Law, which had dogged me all of my life, even operated here. There were plenty of girls dashing around looking for Mr Right and bemoaning the fact that their relationships never came to anything. I, on the other hand, wanted only friendship, so naturally I attracted the kind of men who wanted to settle down and raise families. I never saw the warning signs. I'd have some perfectly nice chap I considered a friend proferring a diamond ring and I wouldn't have a clue how or why the situation had sneaked up on me without my having any inkling of it. I then reacted badly, out of embarrassment and confusion, hurting them in the process without actually meaning to. There were the others, whose only crime was to remind me of my father in some way so that I had to get rid of them as brutally as possible. There was nothing wrong with them, it was nothing they had done, and looking back I still cringe at how I treated them. If Jan thought I had all the answers, I was obviously a better actress than I had given myself credit for.

Next day, when I went to the ward Jan had gone. She had signed herself out and disappeared. I couldn't shake off what she had said though. Why was I here when I should have been writing? Had I drifted into the safe haven that the NHS was in those days and settled for that safety? In thirty years time would I end up as a long-serving chief technician, wishing I had struck out and at least tried to write instead of playing safe all my life? That thought joined all the other uncertainties and confusions in my head, rumbling around and crashing into each other but never coming to the surface or to the remotest prospect of a conclusion.

Chapter Thirty-Four

My father's main preoccupation, apart from drinking, was his Eighth Army connection. He had spent six years away from home as a gunner in the Royal Artillery and every Saturday he still met one or two of his old comrades in a pub in the centre of Glasgow. The outcome was entirely predictable of course, he came home barely able to stand, but then he spent a lot of his time like that. Every year there would be a reunion in London, and off he would go in his black blazer with the gold buttons and the Eighth Army badge on the breast pocket. The badge was a yellow silk cross on white, all outlined with real gold wire; no expense was spared if it was something for himself. Those weekends when he boarded the coach to London were heaven for Nan and me. He would leave on Friday, drink himself senseless for three days and arrive back on Sunday night. But we had the sheer bliss of knowing that he wouldn't come falling through the door at any moment, so we didn't waste time and nervous energy waiting for the sound of the key missing the lock that usually heralded his arrival. The trouble was that we never knew what kind of mood he'd be in, screaming abuse, fighting mad or hysterically funny, at least to himself. So when he went to London we spent a relaxed and happy weekend together, and I used to say to her that if only she had left him years before it could be like this all the time. If only.

Of course by this time Nan wasn't physically or mentally capable of making a fresh start. Anyone meeting her for the first time would never have believed the kind of woman she had been, I had trouble myself relating her to the crusading earth-mother I had known as a child. There were odd flashes of the old Nan, when she read a newspaper item that described some kind of injustice perhaps and she would become quite articulate with anger about it. She had a healthy dislike of all politicians and would roundly berate them whenever they appeared pontificating on TV, regardless of what party they represented. But it was all from her armchair, she never showed any interest in re-entering life again.

Sometimes I would try to persuade her to see a doctor, but she really didn't want to; her life, the one she wanted, had gone with Peggy, and she didn't want what was on offer without her. What I didn't know at that time was the manner of Peggy's death and how it had destroyed all Nan's belief in justice, natural or otherwise – it nullified the code of honour she had lived by. There was a feeling of marking time, of waiting for the day she could go too. She had grandchildren by then from both Mickey and Laurie, but there was no rebirth through them. There was a distance, a preoccupation about her, as she sat in her armchair and simply waited.

It was a holiday Monday and things were slack. Our prospective patients either kept their crises for ordinary times or else they took them on holiday and visited them on resort hospitals. Either way we had little to do. I was summoned by one of the three housemen our unit employed and found two of them waiting for me. They manhandled me into a prepared bath of cold water, partly to pass the time and partly in response to what I had done to them, which was doubtless payment for something they had done to me first. A few weeks before, I had got revenge on one by pouring a jug of cold custard down the back of his trousers while he was doing a ward round with various professors. I then put the other one's name on all the coupon applications in every magazine I could find and his few free hours had thus been filled with calls and visits from double-glazing salesmen and kitchen installers. As I emerged soaked to the skin I ran into the other houseman, the one who had admitted Jan.

'Oh Meggie, I was meaning to talk to you. We got your

friend in again last night, whatsername, Janet Wotsit? No go I'm afraid.'

'She still won't see the shrink? I'll talk to her again if you like, but I'm not sure it'll help.'

'Well it won't as a matter of fact; what I meant was she was dead on arrival. Sorry.'

I was used to death by now and I knew that overdoses far outstripped all other admissions to medical wards. It was considered a cry for help, though we knew there were many more we never received, they were DOAs – they had finished crying, they meant it. But still I felt stunned: twenty years old, the same age as me, and so sick of her existence that she had made the calm, considered decision to die. It gave me a few more questions to add to those already rattling around inside my head. If there was a lesson from Jan's life and death, what was it? Was it to go for it at all costs, to at least try, or was it to play safe and keep whatever you had? In the back of my mind too was a thought that I kept to myself, the thought that my mother was doing exactly the same as Jan had done, only more slowly and painfully. As some guru once said when all other words were superfluous, ain't life a bitch sometimes?

Chapter Thirty-Five

One evening I was in someone's house, one of the Crowd. In the back of my mind was the chance that Rab might be there, a small chance, but it was better than nothing. He wasn't. It was a good night though, we talked about what had happened since we had last met, then someone said,

'Oh guess what? Rab's gone to work in New York!'

'Has he?' a voice said calmly, 'Good for him!' It was my voice.

My mind whirled and my stomach churned as I fought the blankness for some means of keeping the conversation flowing. The world had just collapsed, the moon had disappeared and the sun had fallen from its orbit, and all I could think of was how I could keep talking as though everything was normal. The conversation turned to something else and somehow I managed to keep up with it. It was all thanks to the NHS training that I could act normally in the deepest of disasters, and at that moment I thanked all manner of non-existent gods for it.

Later I escaped to the toilet to lean my forehead against the cool tiles of the wall and make myself take deep, even breaths. I remembered the arguments between my mother and father when I was a child and how I had learned to divert my attention from the mayhem that was all around me. I would lie under my blankets and mentally transport myself somewhere else to drown out the voices, and I told myself that that was what I had to do now. I had to concentrate all my attention on appearing my usual self, and keep talking normally until I could leave. Then and only then, could I scream and sob, when there was no one to see me or hear me. All I wanted to do was get under those blankets and never come out again. Later, on my way home, feeling empty and hollow inside, I caught sight of my reflection in a shop window and I couldn't believe how ordinary I looked. Anyone seeing me would have thought everything was fine, that the world hadn't stopped turning, that I wasn't falling apart. God, but I was good!

There was no way I could ask anyone when or why or for how long Rab had gone to America, at least not without arousing the suspicion that perhaps I gave a damn. I decided that I couldn't risk hearing the answer anyhow, so I avoided the Crowd for a while. I could admit to myself that he had gone for good, but I wasn't sure I could hear it actually said by someone else without throwing myself on the ground and howling like a kicked dog. I tried to rationalize it, to bring down the inflammation. It didn't really matter did it? Even if he had stayed at home forever he wasn't interested in me, so what possible difference could it make that he had gone thousands of miles away? He had been no more attainable at home, had he? No, but at least I could see him sometimes, talk to him. Then the awful thought occurred that he might have gone away with some woman and that the next thing I'd hear was that he was married. Well, said that infuriatingly calm, medic's voice, that was always on the cards, here or in America, so what was the fuss about? He hadn't even told me he was going, that was how important I was to him. Face facts. He had told the important members of the Crowd and hadn't given any particular thought to the kid; didn't that tell me something, if not everything? But what if I never saw him again? Well what was different, asked the voice. Everything. *Everything!*

After he'd gone I concentrated on my exams and work. The Crowd was virtually finished for me now and weekends at the loch were a thing of the past. I still occasionally saw my brothers and the others and sometimes someone would produce the latest letter from Rab and read it aloud as I tried to appear uninterested. I sneaked a look at the address on one and copied it down, calling myself every kind of fool under the sun. Even as I picked the postcard, wrote it out and then sent it off to him, I knew I was being as stupid as it was possible to be. He didn't reply, but some weeks later he mentioned in a letter to Laurie that 'Your sister sent me a postcard.' That was all. The medic's voice was growing weary of going over old ground; how many ways did the man have to spell it out? Get lost was get lost! I headed for the refuge of my blankets again and tried to transport myself somewhere else, somewhere it didn't hurt. But everywhere did . . .

I had to do something with my life I decided. It was the beginning of 1969, I was nearly twenty-one years old and I could see no future. I was stuck in the mould of the dutiful daughter and as far as my father was concerned, I was a ready-made housekeeper. At work I was a Senior Technician and had passed all my exams; I could do everything on automatic pilot. If I decided to stay I could indeed be here in thirty years time, having gone nowhere, done nothing and had no life of my own. There was marriage and motherhood of course, but that would mean settling for second best and I had never done that, never would. I had no idea what I wanted, I only knew I didn't want what I had.

The idea of going abroad started gradually. I had nowhere particular in mind, but I didn't want to go to America. And what of Nan? How could I leave her? I wrestled with the questions constantly, trying to come up with answers and not succeeding very well. There were sisters-in-law now, wasn't I due some time off, a life of my own? I knew that Nan as she had been would not have tolerated her daughter sacrificing her life, but she wasn't as she had been, she was as she was and I felt I was abandoning her. But still the feelings of frustration, of suffocation nagged at me. America was where the money was, but America was where Rab was too, and I knew myself well enough to know that if I went there I'd try to find him. That way lay humiliation and tears. Besides, I was Nan's daughter; if I went abroad I couldn't go for the money, I had to go on a crusade. I thought about Voluntary Service Overseas and wrote off without telling anyone, that way if I was rejected or decided not to go ahead with it, who would know? Then I relaxed and put it out of my mind.

237

Chapter Thirty-Six

Allan Forsyth was a brilliant surgeon; he was dashing, handsome and he had that gleam of danger in his sparkling eyes. He was the stuff of heroes, a devilishly dark man made to be a swashbuckling pirate, and every other doctor in the hospital hated him. He existed on research grants, an uncertain way to earn a living and one that most doctors wouldn't touch, especially one of his ability. His team wandered around the hospital dressed casually in open-necked shirts, slacks and desert boots, not for them the obligatory old school tie, the pinstriped suit and the well-polished black-leather shoes with the regulation three laceholes. They laughed a lot and showed no signs of respect and this added to the reasons why Allan Forsyth and his mob were so disliked by the ultra-conservative medical profession. Needless to say, anyone who didn't quite fit the conventional mould admired the Forsyth team, the man cried out for renegades to join him, and we cried out to sign up; it was, naturally, one of my dreams to work with him.

One wintry lunchtime I was sent to a disused theatre recovery room on the second floor and told to report to Mr Forsyth. I was walking on air, I was one of the chosen, and I longed to tell everyone I met along the way. I'd say very casually, and with a sigh that denoted a blasé manner, 'Allan Forsyth's just asked me to come along,' – if anyone asked that was, which no one did. The patient was a down-and-out who had been brought in with hypothermia and he was in cardiac arrest. It was my own unit's receiving day, so Forsyth must have been asked to take this one over, and I was in dreamland, because I was part of it.

His entire team of bright young things had been assembled and my job was to record tracings at various times and monitor the effects of what was being done to bring the patient back. There was a heat bath over the man, a metal cage lined with light bulbs to warm the body, because the heart couldn't be restarted below a certain temperature. Forsyth had opened the sternum from throat to navel and was pouring warm saline over the exposed heart; it was exciting stuff and it was happening before my star-struck young eyes. The brilliant members of his disreputable pack were doing things with fancy equipment, buzzing around the patient like so many industrious bees around a particularly luscious flower, and the room was full of people watching or helping.

A blood technician leaned across to take a sample from the patient and the man's arm pushed her, though of course he was dead. She looked up at Forsyth, who smiled below his mask so that those dangerous eyes crinkled and sparkled above. 'It's just a muscle spasm,' he laughed, and we all laughed too at the tech's reaction. Then I tried to replace an electrode that someone had moved and the patient pushed me too.

Unlike the blood technician I was used to handling arrested and newly-dead bodies and I knew this wasn't a muscle spasm; the man *had* pushed me. I remembered a paper that Dr Cunningham had insisted we all read, about a doctor who had arrested in his own hospital and afterwards was able to recount everything that had happened and what had been said by whom. The theory was that if the brain was well enough supplied with oxygen during a resus attempt, then it remained aware of events, even though the patient was unconscious and clinically dead. The black humour that we needed during life-and-death situations could, it was suggested, be heard and understood by the unfortunate patient, and Sandy Cunningham wanted us to think about that in future. In the instant that the man on the table pushed me I remembered this and I looked up at Allan Forsyth. He held my gaze for a moment and then he looked away; he didn't try to laugh and reassure me. But still, we were trying to save this man's life, weren't we? Even if we had to do unpleasant things to save him, it was worth it.

Hours passed, countless samples and readings were taken, and then suddenly Allan Forsyth called a halt, thanked everybody and swept out with his motley crew, all laden down with equipment and bits of paper. He stopped briefly by my machine, took all of my tracings, muttered his thanks and gave me one of those heartmelting smiles. I was totally bemused. What about the patient?

'Why aren't we going on?' I asked a houseman attached to Forsyth's team, and he shrugged.

'He's got all he needs,' he replied.

'What do you mean?'

'Well Allan is doing research into hypothermia at the moment . . .' he said, and left the light to penetrate my grey-matter without any further help. I had worked for hours in the hope of saving the patient, and all that time Allan Forsyth had been collecting data for his latest research project. Once the glamour of the event had cleared I realized that the patient's chances of survival had been almost neglible to start with, so Allan Forsyth had used him for his own purposes and when those had been satisfied he'd let the man die. I felt sick. I remembered the man pushing me away, and I felt sicker still. Later I discovered that the patient was being taken by a houseman and a porter to my own unit when Forsyth had come across him in the lift as he went to lunch. So he had simply pulled rank and stolen a live lump of research material, who being a down-and-out, just happened to have no interested relatives who might have asked questions. It was ideal; how could he have passed up such a gift from hell?

A few weeks later, engaged on another research project, Forsyth passed the word that he was looking for stroke victims in medical wards, the terminal, deeply unconscious cases, preferably without any troublesome relatives. Obviously impressed by my work, not to mention my devotion to him, I was one of those chosen to inform him of appropriate cases I came across. One of the old consultants, one of the less academically minded sort who simply made patients better, approached me. My admiration of Allan Forsyth was well known and the old boy didn't beat around the bush. 'You're not going to do this awful thing?' he demanded, 'You're not going to help that terrible young man are you?'

Remembering the man in the recovery room I replied that I had absolutely no intention of helping Forsyth.

'Good Meggie,' he replied, 'I know he's attractive to females, though God knows why, but he isn't at all a nice man.' He patted my shoulder and started to move off, then he stopped and said, 'And another thing, I wish you wouldn't wear trousers in the ward you know. It quite makes my day to see the odd inch of black lace under a white uniform as you bend over a bed!'

A few days later he caught me in the ward again.

'Has Forsyth been in touch with you?' he asked.

'No.'

'Well he spoke to me and I told him I wasn't taking part in his gruesome experiments and neither were you,' he said angrily, 'And d'you know what the jumped-up little bastard said to me? Said we were holding medical research back for decades!'

The thing was, he was undoubtedly correct, we were. But I still feel sick when I remember the patient who pushed me away when he was dead. Not surprisingly there was no longer any possibility of my joining Allan Forsyth's team after that, they had changed from free-wheeling swashbucklers to tacky, cynical quacks in my mind. It added to my growing disenchantment about everything around me and strengthened my need to get away.

Funnily enough, I saw Allan Forsyth on TV recently. He's Sir Allan now of course, an important, influential man, and how could anyone ever have doubted he would be some day? The dark hair is edged with grey now and he is possibly more handsome than he was as a young man, and that gleam in his eyes that I once found so irresistible, remains strong and bright. He has a long list of letters after his name now and an even longer list of achievements and is universally admired and feted. Gone are the days when he had to steal patients or ask for favours. And I wouldn't dream of letting him near any of my family.

★　　★　　★

The letter from VSO invited me to an interview in Edinburgh in March. All I knew about the organization was that it had been set up to provide help for the Third World by providing professionals who would train people to work in their own countries. It pre-dated the Peace Corps, which being American naturally got all the publicity. For spending one or two years on a specific project the payment was board and lodging and the local equivalent of £3 per week. Sounded just my thing. Other people with my qualifications could clean up financially in the developed world as well as the Third World, but if there wasn't a whiff of doing good and *not* making big money about it, I couldn't be interested, could I?

The day before the interview, which I hadn't mentioned to anyone, I got a cardiac arrest call from one of the operating theatres. The average surgical response to any and everything is to grab a scalpel and cut, and so it had always been in surgical arrests. Patients who could have been brought back using external cardiac massage were invariably opened up, the heart grabbed and manually pumped and the whole unfortunate episode complicated by the introduction of major surgery. There had even been cases of patients dying from the unnecessary surgery rather than whatever had ailed them, and we dreaded a call from a surgical unit, because it inevitably meant they had done the damage and had now run out of ideas.

Usually we would arrive to find the patient in the latter stages of rigor mortis, having been subjected to perhaps an hour of surgical 'help' and so dead that Jesus on a good day couldn't raise him. The surgeons would then say that calling the medical cardiac arrest team was a waste of time, they'd called them the other day and they were useless. So I was very pleasantly surprised this time to find the patient lying on the table, untouched by surgical hand, having gone just as the anaesthetist put him under. I ran through a series of tests and found the heart beating normally, so as befits a medic in the position of putting down the surgeons, I hammed it up. The odd breathing problem isn't unheard of as a patient goes under, together with a slight disturbance in heart rhythm, and usually the anaesthetist stops for a minute, puts in some oxygen until the patient stabilizes and then the operation can continue. In this case though the anaesthetist had played it cautiously. Perhaps he didn't really want to do the op I mused, maybe he had a date to play golf and was calling foul to make sure he got there in time.

'Well there you are chaps, a perfectly normal heartbeat,' I said grandly, 'Don't blame yourselves, could happen to anyone, and you *are* just surgeons after all. How could you be expected to know anything about a difficult subject like whether or not the patient was alive? This is medicine after all, not some knife and fork job!' It was standard procedure for us to put the surgeons down as it was for them to put medics down. All the same, they were being very submissive about it, you could usually count on some opposition, some vengeance at least. I had taken the electrodes off and was heading for the door.

'And don't hesitate to call if you're ever in difficulty again,' I said, 'You know we don't mind helping you lads out, even if it is a waste of our valuable time.' I always had to gild the lily.

'Mmm, Meggie,' said the anaesthetist, 'I'm very worried about this patient.' He looked it, as he leaned against the tiled wall, idly reading his paper. 'I think if you don't mind, I'd prefer you to stay for the operation. In case he goes again, and we can't handle it.'

The two surgeons sniggered. It was my own fault, entirely my own fault. I should have quit while I was ahead, several sarcastic insults ago.

It was an exploratory stomach operation and the finding was gangrenous colon. The smell of gangrenous colon is beyond anything dreamed up by the Hammer House of Horror. There is nothing I can think of that even approaches the stench. It clings to you, smears itself over your respiratory system and hooks into every crevice; it is so thick and strong that you can almost see it and feel it. So bad was it that one surgeon worked for fifteen minutes alone, while the other one had fifteen minutes outside, breathing real, beautiful air. The anaesthetist suggested the same arrangement with me and we tried it once, but the shock of coming back in again convinced me to stay put throughout. Sixteen feet of reddish-purple intestine, together with its putrefying contents, was removed, but I still hadn't suffered enough. The theatre orderly put it in a plastic basin which he then took great pleasure in placing on top of my machine. It lay there, inches from my nose, glistening horribly with slime, the fumes rising from it.

'There y'are Meg,' he said, 'Some link sausages for your tea!'

Medical honour, as well as my own, was at stake. I swirled a finger in the awful brew and said casually, 'No thanks, I prefer the sliced variety myself!' Everybody laughed. Slowly I dismantled my equipment from the patient, whose heart and breathing hadn't faltered throughout, and took my time over labelling the tracings. Then I sauntered out of the theatre, singing to myself as I went. 'Oh Meggie!' came the anaesthetist's voice as I left, 'You handled that so well that we'll be sure to call you whenever we have trouble again!'

'Anytime chaps!' I replied, 'I know how often surgeons get into trouble. It's so refreshing to meet the odd one or two prepared to admit it!' They all laughed again.

Down the long corridor to the lift I went, pushing my machine ahead of me, still singing – you never knew what deceitful surgeons might still be watching. Into the lift and down to my own department. Still singing. As soon as the door closed I grabbed a large bottle of Lysol and scrubbed the finger that had swirled so nonchalantly through the feet of revolting colon, then I scrubbed the entire hand and then the arm. Finally I went upstairs, had a shower, brushed my teeth, sprayed myself with enough perfume to give a tart's boudoir a bad name and finally changed my clothes before I felt clean. It was standard procedure to keep a change of clothes in your locker, because you never knew what would happen, from a patient being sick over you to being thrown into a bath of cold water by some idiot houseman, but I had never been so glad of it as I was then.

At the VSO interview next day I was faced with a panel of three people, an elderly man, a middle-aged woman and a tanned young man. I have always liked interviews and never feel nervous, which probably says a great deal about me that doesn't bear closer investigation. This one was par for the course. I didn't desperately need them to accept me and to be honest I was finding out as much about them as they were about me; it was entirely possible that I could turn them down and go looking for the big money instead. Then the tanned young man put his foot in it.

'I wonder if you have any idea of the kind of smells you can get in an African hospital,' he said in a very superior tone of voice. He was a VSO himself and obviously knew it all. 'I mean they do differ considerably from the antiseptic smells you are used to, I just wonder if you could take it.'

'Listen chum,' I said, 'Have you ever been inches away from a gangrenous colon?' He shook his head.

'Have you had any experience whatsoever of gangrenous colon, even from a very great distance?' He shook his head again.

'Well until you have, don't bother me with your African hospital smells, because I can guarantee that they just don't begin to compete!' That showed the little twerp! I seemed to have this way with interview panels, I thought as I went out, I kind of grabbed them by the scruff of the neck and threw them around my head a bit. Oh well, nothing lost really.

A week later the letter arrived saying if my references checked out I would be accepted and would then undergo courses in tropical medicine. I really was going abroad. Now all I had to do was tell Sandy Cunningham that he was giving me a reference.

And Nan of course, I had to tell Nan . . .

Chapter Thirty-Seven

Norah was the only one of my father's family still alive. She was a tiny lady, certainly under five-feet tall, and by now into her seventies, but she kept in touch, visiting the Barracks on the odd Sunday. She sometimes came with her husband, Uncle Harry, a tall, quiet, straightforward soul whom she'd run rings around for nearly fifty years. The hats for which she was famous were still very much in evidence, and the deceit for which she was infamous was still there too. Behind the latest millinery creation lurked a mind sharp enough to cut unsuspecting victims to the bone, not that this let those of us with well-founded suspicions off the hook.

I had at that time a collection of blouses in every material, colour and design, and much of her efforts were directed at getting her hands on as many as possible. This one was for a very sick friend, that one would suit her daughter so well, the daughter who'd had such a bad time lately. Not that her daughter knew she was being used for the pitch nor would she ever set eyes on the blouse – other than on Norah's back. She never came empty-handed of course, I was always offered a pair of shoes that didn't fit, suit or interest me, or some awful pair of earrings she had doubtless conned out of some other defenceless individual.

Hughie, her main adversary was dead and gone, in the flesh at least. Doors and windows still opened but it was difficult to compete for points unless he actually made an appearance, and so far he had decided to win his points while invisible – cheating though it undoubtedly was. Jim was off looking for good, honest, non-violent crime to commit, on one side of the great divide or another, though Norah, the great mystic of seances and teacups, always insisted that she 'felt' Jim was still alive. While he was otherwise engaged he wasn't around to provide her with entertainment, so the nonsense with the blouses was mostly a diversion for her. I at least knew the basic rules of the Game, and even if we both knew I could never seriously hope to win the points, the tantalizing prospect of a lucky draw forever hung in the air between us to amuse her. Her acting talents were still prodigious, so I was never really sure if she'd had the three heart attacks she laid claim to, chiefly when negotiations for the latest blouse were going against her. A hand would go to her chest and a pained expression would take up residence across her features, together with an earnest entreaty 'No' tae worry aboot me hen . . .'

Then one Sunday she seemed to be in real pain that didn't even respond to the lashings of brandy that usually did the trick. My mistake was to take this seriously, because once I had she lost all sense of reality and the theatrical performance took over. I phoned the hospital, arranged for the receiving physician to see her and took her, Uncle Harry and my father down by taxi. By this time she was in danger of having a heart attack from the fear of having a heart attack, so I ran the tests myself; her latest hat remained firmly on her head throughout. Her heart was as strong as an extremely robust ox, there wasn't the slightest sign of any of the three previous attacks, and all that ailed her was indigestion. She carried this news off beautifully by simply ignoring it, and informing one and all that this attack had been every bit as severe as her other three. The medicine given to her by the doctor, a common antacid available over the chemist shop counter, she hailed as a wonder drug, and that was that.

While we were waiting for a taxi to take her and her husband home, I opened up the cardiology department and made them coffee. I wasn't aware of having created any impression until I realized that Norah and Uncle Harry were looking at me with a certain awe. Then I saw what they were seeing: their niece with all this clout, having access to this impressive looking world of technology, being on first name terms with the godlike doctors – it far surpassed any interest my latest blouse might have aroused a few hours earlier. Then I looked at my father, who sat sipping his coffee beside them. He was completely unaware of all the things that had impressed his sister, and the contrast was startling. The thought popped into my mind that perhaps he should have been more impressed than Norah, and that if I had been Mickey instead he would have been beside himself with pride. I wasn't aware of competing with Mickey, but I did have a sudden insight into how difficult it must all have been for Laurie, who was in the same category as myself; the one marked 'Not Mickey'. We would never match up: no matter what we achieved we would forever remain in the 'Not Mickey' section. The thought made me smile to myself, but it also made me feel sadder for Laurie than I had ever felt; he was a male after all and throughout his life he had tried in all sorts of ways to matter to my father. In that moment I knew it had all been useless and always would be, yet I also knew it wouldn't stop Laurie from trying. Laurie was like one of the Clark 'Dark Yins', forever trying to win affection from a parent incapable of giving it and without realizing that it wasn't worth much even if it had been forthcoming. Laurie was always much more of a Clark; if only he could see the true value in that.

The following week Norah turned up again and brought me a pair of nylons. By this time every female I knew was wearing tights, but I appreciated the trouble she had gone to and wondered who had been conned out of the stockings for my benefit. She left with my best blouse. Well, what could I do? She had now suffered four heart attacks and I thought a little kindness was in order. It was the nearest I ever came to that lucky draw with her and I didn't have the heart to go for it. That's what distinguishes the truly great Game players from the second leaguers like me; being able to go for the kill!

Sandy Cunningham was sitting behind his desk when I went in.

'Chief,' I said, 'I need a reference.'

'What for? Are you leaving?' He said it as though an

affirmative answer would book me straight into a psychiatric appointment. Leave the Eastern Infirmary? Could this be the action of someone who claimed a passing acquaintance with sanity?

'I'm going abroad,' I replied.

'Where? America?'

'No, to one of the developing countries, Africa probably.'

His expression suggested that I was already speaking Swahili and his eyebrows were having problems disentangling themselves from his hairline.

'I'm going with VSO, Voluntary Service Overseas.'

'Aren't they the lot who do it for nothing? I mean you don't get any cash?'

'Well you get some, but it's voluntary, yes.'

He sat staring at me.

'There's a man in this somewhere isn't there?' he demanded, with the conviction of one who believes he's hit on the truth.

'No,' I said, 'I've just got to get out of here.'

'I knew it! There *is* a man involved! It's not that large houseman upstairs is it?' His face wrinkled with disapproval.

'There's no man, and the chap upstairs is just a pal.'

'That's not what everyone else says,' he said, 'Everybody knows he's keen. I'd hate it to be him, can't stand these religious maniacs, can't stand him!'

'You know what this place is like for rumours,' I smiled, 'It's nothing to do with the religious maniac houseman upstairs. I shouldn't be here though, I don't really belong in medicine, it just sort of happened.'

'But you're good at your job!'

'I know that,' I replied, modest as ever, 'But all I ever wanted to do was write, it's my only talent, and if I stay around here much longer I'll end up trapped for life. I've got to get away somewhere to think about what I really want to do.'

He smiled a fatherly smile. 'Oh Meggie, we all want to write when we're young! It passes! We all grow up! I could show you reams of poetry I wrote when I was still a normal human being, that would do my reputation as a bastard no good at all!'

'I'm going,' I said, 'And you must give me a decent reference.'

'OK,' he said, 'But I still say there's a man involved in this and I intend to give the religious maniac a bloody hard time on principle.'

'Another thing Chief, could you keep it very quiet? I don't know where or when I'm going yet, I don't want to talk about it to everybody for months and months.'

'You know me,' he smiled his determined smile, 'The soul of discretion! Not a word!'

As I was leaving he called me back and pointed to a calendar on the wall. It was the kind the drugs companies put out, filthy or funny for the younger doctors, pseudo-arty for the older ones like Sandy Cunningham.

'Is that the Pope?' he asked.

I looked at the title underneath. 'It says the Doge.'

'Yes, but is it really the Pope?'

'Why would it say the Doge if it was the Pope?' I demanded, 'And why are you asking me anyway? I wouldn't recognize the Pope if I fell over him in Casualty!'

'Yes, but you'd recognize a Pope-ish look, wouldn't you? I can't bear it, the eyes follow me everywhere. If it is the Pope he could be putting the evil eye on me, don't you think?'

'It's the Doge!' I said, 'It says it's the Doge, so it's the Doge!'

'OK. Right. Fine.' He looked at it with an uncertain smile on his face then reached forward and tore off the picture. 'But just in case, I'll get rid of the ugly bugger anyway!' he said, catapulting himself a month forward. 'You see how I depend on you? Who else could help me with problems like this? You are very selfish, just going off into the wide blue yonder like this without a thought of the effect on others!'

Next was Nan. She was sitting in her usual chair by the fireside, and I started by saying that I had the chance to work abroad for a year, maybe two.

'Ye hivtae go,' she said firmly, 'Ye hivtae say ye'll go.'

'But what about you Mum? How will you manage with him? You'll be losing my money too.'

'Look hen, Ah married him,' she said, 'You didnae. A' these years Ah've been worried sick that ye'd gie up yer life tae look efter him. Ye've made somethin' o' yersel' wi' nae help frae him and no' much frae me since, since . . . Ye've no' tae throw a' that away.'

She sounded like my mother, as though the clock had been turned back years. Any minute now Peggy might walk in. I didn't know what to say.

'Ah always waantit ma weans tae see the world,' she said proudly, 'Ah waanted ye a' tae make a decent life fur yersels and no' tae grow up tae be like him. So ye've tae go hen. Don't stey away mind, come back hame sometimes, but get as faur away frae him as ye kin. If ye don't it'll a' hiv been fur nothin'. See?'

It was a conversation I was to go over in my mind all of my life, so often in fact that I memorized it. After she had retired from the world in 1959 there were times when I had blamed her for deserting me at the very age when girls need their mothers most. Yet she seemed to be saying that she had lived these last ten years to make sure that I didn't end up trapped by duty to my father as she was. It hadn't occurred to her that I might feel a sense of duty towards her, that I might stay at home because she needed me. If I hadn't been there, if she'd had no reason to go on, she might not have survived Peggy's death. Only then did I really appreciate how severe that blow had been, but there had to be more than I knew, and my resolve to find out one day was underlined in my mental notebook.

Devastating as the loss of Peggy was to all of us, and my mother in particular, there had to be another element to it that had destroyed her faith, her hopes and her belief in everything. It had shaken her to her very roots, but far from giving up, she had summoned the courage from somewhere to hang on until the moment when I decided to leave the nest. I remembered how upset I had been as a child when I realized that I would never fly like a bird; maybe that had prepared her for the day when I would spread my wings in one way or another. I'd been dreading telling her, but she was quite delighted; it had made her effort worthwhile.

The entire hospital knew; everywhere I went someone wanted to talk to me about going abroad. Sandy Cunningham had obviously thought the whole thing over and decided that my going reflected some sort of glory on him, and he made a point of touring the hospital and telling staff and patients alike. It was quite a let down when I told them I had no idea when I was going and no idea where. Then slowly and thankfully life returned to normal.

In July 1969 Neil Armstrong became the first man to set foot on the moon. I watched it live on TV in the early hours of the morning, wrapped in a sleeping-bag, with chicken sandwiches and a flask of coffee beside me, as Armstrong took his giant leap for mankind. At the same time Rab was doubtless watching it in New York and when the tickertape parade was held to welcome the astronauts home, he would probably be in the crowd. Rab was rarely mentioned these days, the Crowd had become used to the fact that he'd gone, and I couldn't ask.

Hospital life was full of ordinary days that were jam-packed with tedium. To the patients we were admitting, every day was a personal crisis, but even crises can be handled on automatic pilot; I needed something to do. One day the cardiac arrest bleeper sounded and announced 'Cardiac Arrest, Orthopaedic Theatre,' and all over the hospital, crash team members wondered if it was April 1st, then yelled into their bleepers 'Are you sure?'

The Ortho Theatre and wards were only yards along the corridor from our department, but we rarely saw the Orthopods. They just got on with whatever it was they did with bones and things and left the rest of us to get on with real medicine. We passed them in the corridors or in the canteen, friendly, smiling faces that we didn't know well because we had never worked with them. As we hadn't worked with them we therefore hadn't fought with them, so they remained friendly, smiling faces. The

Orthopods were so far removed from mainstream hospital life that they weren't quoted on the gossip hotline.

The theatre block housed identical operating theatres on every floor, one directly above the other, and so the Ortho one wasn't really different, it just felt different because we had never been in it before. And there were the friendly, smiling Orthopods, standing back from the patient on the table to let us get at him. Usually there were so many hands eager to help and getting in the way that harsh words had to be spoken, but the good old Orthopods weren't to know that. And the patient was cooperative too. Our success rate was very low; the real world wasn't a bit like those impressive TV soaps where with one dramatic shock the patient immediately gets up and starts raising money for hospital equipment. But this chap had obviously watched enough of those to know what was expected of him; one such dramatic shock and he was back in normal rhythm. It made us look so good, and we were all acting a shade smug, but then it was nice to be able to put on a slick show in front of the surgeons, and the Orthopods *were* surgeons, of a sort anyway. I got quite carried away and decided to run a completely unnecessary series of tracings that could have waited a couple of hours. It would look impressive in the case notes, so professional and efficient, quite unlike the usual chaos on these occasions. Then the tracing went off. It was the theatre orderly, he was fiddling with the electrodes. I had seen the old chap around and I'd often thought how typical it was of the Orthopods to keep him on at his age, but then nothing much happened in the backwaters. Still, he must have been about a hundred and of limited use to anyone else. How kind the Orthopods were not to throw the old boy on the scrap heap.

'Do you mind,' I smiled, still flushed with success, 'If you touch the electrodes the tracing goes off.'

'Sorry, I didn't realize.'

'It's OK, no problem,' I replied. Who could be angry on a day such as this? I flicked the dial back and started again, and once again the tracing went off, because Methuselah was fiddling again.

'Whatever you're doing,' I said, 'Could it wait just a few minutes please, until I get this done?' I asked, going back to zero again.

'Oops! I really am sorry!'

'No, no, not at all, don't give it another thought.' Regular members of the crash team were by now standing back in amazement; under this amount of provocation bodies had been forcibly removed in the past. But this was different, this was me under the glow of success. Then the tracing went again, and I sighed heavily and swore loudly.

'Dear me,' said the old orderly, 'I've done it again haven't I? I really am sorry!'

'You said!' I replied through gritted teeth, but before I could start once more he was at it again. The time had come for those harsh words. I leaned over the patient on the table, grabbed the orderly by the lapel of his white coat and pulled him down to my eye level.

'Listen chum,' I snarled slowly and patiently into his face, 'Your friends here made a muck-up of this patient, and we had to come in to sort it out. Now until we hand him back so that you can trim his toenails or whatever it is you pass your time doing in this dump, we are in charge, and what I'm doing is infinitely more important than whatever the hell you think you're doing. So if you even think of touching those electrodes again there will be two small, spherical objects bouncing around on the floor, and you'll be singing falsetto! Do I make myself clear?'

There was a sharp intake of breath all round the theatre. They were such a pleasant bunch the Orthopods, they had probably never heard harsh words spoken before; they didn't live in the real world like we did.

'Yes, oh yes,' the orderly said, 'Crystal-clear!' and then he did the decent thing and left.

An hour later, with our cooperatively alive patient safely installed in coronary care, I wandered back to the department to be told that Dr Cunningham wanted to see me. Congratulations coming my way!

'Come in Meg,' he grinned, 'There's someone here you

should meet.' It was the Ortho orderly, no doubt sent over by his chief to apologize.

'No need for apologies,' I told him grandly, 'Just remember to keep out of the way in an emergency in future.'

'Meet,' said my Sandy Cunningham, 'The Professor of Orthopaedics.' Orthopaedics *had* a Professor? Well they said that attack was the best method of defence, I only hoped 'they' were right.

'In that case he *should* apologize!' I said, 'Even a Professor of Orthopaedics should know that when you call in the pros you stand back and let them get on with it instead of getting in the way!' I'd just seen the film 'M*A*S*H', and I'd lifted the dialogue straight from Trapper John. They looked remarkably like fish, sitting there with their mouths hanging open as I headed smartly for the door.

Then I went to the toilet, switched out the light and did some serious cringeing in the dark for half an hour. How was I to know? Who would ever have dreamed that there was an Orthopod Professor? And he did mess around with the electrodes, didn't he? And for all he knew he could've been doing some serious damage, couldn't he? So it was all his own fault, wasn't it? He thoroughly deserved to be totally humiliated . . . in front of his entire staff . . . by someone young enough to be his grand-daughter . . . didn't he . . . ?

Later I saw Dr Cunningham again. 'I suppose the silly old sod is going to have me shot?' I asked.

'No,' he replied, 'What he actually said, and I quote, was "God, if I were only fifty years younger I'd bed that wild young thing! What a woman!" The silly old sod is in love, and you live a charmed life if I may say so.'

Whenever I saw the Orthopod Professor after that he leered at me, licked his lips and blew kisses, loudly exhorting his team to prove they were real men by bedding 'that wild young thing' and telling everyone in earshot exactly what he would've done in his youth. 'You'd have the best sex of your life!' he'd roar, 'Trying to tame that one!' I blushed to the roots of my toenails at every encounter, and the rest of the hospital enjoyed themselves by whistling 'Wild Thing' whenever I was around. It followed me down corridors, in the lifts, the operating theatres and in the wards, and to this day, whenever I hear that song on the radio I hide my head and blush scarlet.

I never did find out if the Orthopod Professor meant it, or if he had some O'Brien blood coursing through his body and had found the perfect way of paying me back. But he succeeded in putting Orthopaedics on the gossip hotline for the first time in living memory and he certainly won all the points. No question.

Skip came home one Saturday afternoon, in his usual state, and announced that he was going to bed. He had met a friend who was coming later to collect him for another drinking session and naturally he wanted to be fresh for the event. The friend was Jim McAvoy. Nan and I exchanged looks of anger and disgust. It was as low as Skip could stoop; we knew he'd drink with anyone, but McAvoy wasn't counted as among the human race. He was actually expecting us to invite him into the house and be sociable to him!

Silly man. Whenever Skip slept off the booze he heard nothing, it was like a mini-coma, so he didn't hear McAvoy hammering on the door a few hours later. Nan and I walked past it, making no attempt to hide the fact that we heard him and were ignoring him; at one point he even looked through the letter-box and shouted to be let in. We ended up laughing so much that we could hardly stand, and clung to each other for support.

When Skip got up he fretted about McAvoy's non-appearance as we fought to keep straight faces, and eventually, with good drinking time passing, he went out again. He came back hours later freshly reinebriated and with McAvoy, but I got to the door in time to push his 'friend' out again and lock the door behind Skip. He drew himself up to his full five-foot-one-inches and tried to act out the master of the house routine. This was his house apparently and he'd say who came in, then he ruined it all by being too drunk to negotiate the opening of the door. Nan sat in her chair, weeping with laughter.

'Jim tellt me he looked through the letter boax an' ye baith ignored him!' he yelled, plainly aghast that such deceit could exist within his own family. McAvoy listened outside the door.

'He's bloody lucky we did ignore him! My Uncle George wouldn't have ignored him!' I replied for McAvoy's benefit, 'We remember the life he gave Peggy! Ask your wee pal if he remembers someone called Peggy. Dark-haired, attractive, a pleasant woman, too good for him! Ask him if that rings any bells.'

'Ah invited him as a guest! You apologize tae Jim!'

'He's a rat! And you only get in because you're married to my mother, otherwise the embargo would apply to you too!'

'Ye think yur sum'dy!' he screeched pathetically, falling back on the old insult that no doubt he and McAvoy had been discussing all night in whatever pub they had met up in. But it awakened something in Nan.

'Aye, ye're right,' she said savagely, 'Thur's mair Clark in hur than O'Brien, she *is* sum'dy!'

Eventually McAvoy gave up and went away and Skip yelled himself to sleep like the baby he was, but it was a kind of turning point. Instead of trying to placate him for the sake of peace we had laughed at him, and he hadn't known how to deal with that. It gave Nan some form of upper hand for the first time in many years and I began to believe that she could cope while I wasn't there. It was a new low for Skip in my eyes though, I was disgusted that he'd have anything to do with McAvoy and the thought that we'd have him in the house was beyond belief.

Later, out of the blue, Nan said quietly, 'Dae ye remember Peggy?' It must have been triggered by my jibe at McAvoy earlier. She really didn't think I had forgotten her, it was simply the only way she could manage to bring up Peggy's name after having avoided it for so long.

'Of course I remember her Mum!' I replied, 'It's like it was yesterday! I could never forget Peggy!'

'That's good,' she said, 'The three o' us wur good pals, wurn't we?'

'It was like we were one Mum, the three of us were so close.'

She nodded. 'It's no' the same withoot hur,' she said, 'Ah jist feel kinda . . .' The words ran out. It was the first time she had ever talked about Peggy and I held my breath, hoping she'd go on.

'Like a part of you is missing,' I said, 'And a part of me too.'

'Aye,' she said, 'That's it. Missin'. Dae you feel like that tae?'

'All the time. I've felt like that ever since. Sometimes I feel as if I'm still looking for her, though I know I won't find her.'

'Dae ye think there's another life efter this wan?'

'And we'll all meet up again? No, I wish it could be true. Sometimes I'd do anything to see her again, I can't believe she's really gone.'

'It's jist that sometimes Ah wake up in the middle o' the night, an' Ah'm sure Ah've heard hur sayin' ma name. Ah aye heard her sayin' "Nan" when sumthin' was happenin', it wis like that a' oor lives.'

'I remember,' I smiled, 'The two of you didn't need to talk.'

'A' they months while she wis expectin' the last wean, Ah kept hearin' her sayin' "Nan". An' a' that Seterday, Ah heard it tae, an' Ah knew she wis hivin' the wean. Then it stoaped, an' Ah knew . . . Bit noo I still think Ah hear hur, an' sometimes during the day Ah get this feelin' that she's there. Y'know, right there beside me. Dis that sound like Ah'm daft?'

'Of course you're not daft!' I said, 'You're just keeping her alive in your mind, same as I am. I can't really believe she's not there any longer either. Peggy was always there . . .'

My mind was working frantically, making sense of the memories of those months when Nan couldn't sleep. She was hearing Peggy calling for help, and that was normal for them, it worked both ways. Only when she rushed to Peggy's side there seemed to be nothing happening. But there was something happening, of course, and the prophetic dreams had tried to sound the warning that Nan didn't want to hear, so by morning she had converted them into funny stories.

But she hadn't fooled herself, and she hadn't fooled me, either. I had known something was wrong, even if I couldn't put my finger on it. While she spoke I was hoping Nan might say something about how Peggy had died, but I had a feeling that if I asked questions she wouldn't be able to carry on. Each word came out sounding fragile, as though the slightest pressure could blow them all away forever. There was a silence and then she said, 'Dae ye mind that seance Norah made me go tae? The wan where the man said Da Clark hid a warnin' for us? Ah've aye thoaght Ah shoulda went back tae see him.'

'You don't believe that do you?' I asked, 'If Da had a warning about Peggy he wouldn't have needed some stranger to pass it on, would he? And how would Da have known? We were the closest to Peggy, and we couldn't stop it happening, could we?'

'Ah wis wearin' that green coat that night,' she said, 'Ah couldnae wear it again efter. Ah shoulda burned that green coat . . .'

'No Mum,' I replied, 'We should've burned McAvoy! Or better still, we should've burned McAvoy's old man, just to make sure!' She laughed, but then she said sadly, 'Still, Ah shouldnae hiv let her hiv that green coat . . .' Ten years on and still all that longing and 'if onlys'. All that pain and misplaced guilt. She never spoke of the events leading up to Peggy's death again, and I never asked because I knew she couldn't tell me whatever was still hidden. I was convinced that there was more to the story though and one day I had to know it all.

The news came at the end of August; I wasn't going to Africa, I was going to India. The hospital I was being sent to was in the former French Protectorate of Pondicherry, just outside Madras in the south of the country. In the Sixties France had been trying to get rid of its empire and had built a huge complex in Pondicherry along the lines of an American campus. The hospital, called the Jawaharlal Institute of Post-Graduate Medical Education and Research, JIPMER for short, had its own staff accommodation, post office, school, shops and snake-catcher. What it didn't have was trained staff, and I was to train a technical team to run their own department. I had been expecting Africa probably because of the sun-tanned young man who had challenged my ability to cope with African hospital smells. India was more exciting, and I would leave on 30th November, St Andrew's Day.

The months between would be filled having vaccinations for smallpox, cholera and all manner of other nasties, and at least I didn't have to pay any doctor a professional fee for wielding the hypodermic; they were fighting each other for the chance. I also had to assemble a completely new all-cotton wardrobe for the different climate. I was going in the Indian winter, but compared with a blisteringly good Scottish summer it would still be tropical. Sandy Cunningham bustled around taking an interest in every detail, reading books on India and passing on information and generally taking charge whether I let him or not. Having come to the conclusion that my wonderful altruism was really a feather in his cap, he had ensured that not only the hospital but the entire medical world knew all about the great adventure too. He arranged for me to go to London, to watch advanced cardiac surgery at Guy's Hospital, where unfortunately neither patient made it off the table. Well at least it laid to rest the myth of London superiority.

Next were the farewell parties, which worked out about one a week at the hospital. At each one Sandy Cunningham got up and gave an emotional speech about how the Scots were seasoned globe-trotters, and how I was following in a great tradition. This took him, for some reason, onto the disproportionate number of island fishermen who had died during the last War protecting shipping convoys, men who were never recognized as the heroes they were. For that reason I should avoid Germans at all costs, and the English, which went without saying, even if he did say it anyway. Foreign travel was clearly a wonderful thing, as long as the foreigners were weeded out of the experience.

The Crowd had to have a ceilidh too, any excuse was seized on for a ceilidh now that most of them had settled down with wives, children and mortgages. The invitations were individually written in as near copperplate script as I managed to learn in the time available, and put in language meant to suggest the Raj.

'You haven't done one for Rab,' someone said, going over the list with me.

'I hardly think he'll come all the way back from America!'

'He's back. He only went over for a year.'

'OK, I'll do one for him,' I replied, in that calm, casual voice, though my heart was thumping like, well, like a wild thing.

The excitement was short-lived though, because that cold, analytical voice in my head quickly reminded me that even if he was back, he'd hardly gone out of his way to let me know. Nothing had changed. He went without bothering to tell me and he'd come back the same way; it remained a pointless business. But I could still see him sometimes, I thought. With his wife, probably, the voice suggested. That was something I really couldn't face. Imagine bumping into him and him saying 'This is my wife . . .' It would certainly happen sometime soon, if it hadn't happened already, and I didn't want to be around when it did. I wrote out another invitation and sent it off to him, because he was one of the Crowd and it would have looked odd if I hadn't.

Nan seemed to have a new lease of life. There was no miraculous transformation, but she was taking notice of everything that was happening, inspecting all the new clothes for the tropics and talking more than she had in years. I was playing it all down a bit though, I didn't want my leaving to be a great big event. I still had work to go to and time to fill before I left, so a fever pitch of excitement would have been hard to sustain.

The ceilidh was set for the Saturday before I left, to give those attending all of Sunday to recover. I opened the door to the first arrival; it was Rab. The medical report given by some nervous houseman would have been, 'Please Sir, the patient's heart leapt clean out of her thorax and it was last seen dancing on the ceiling, singing "Happy Days are Here Again" . . . I fear the patient's condition is hopeless.'

'Oh,' I said, 'It's you, the Yank.'

'An' it's you,' he replied, 'The ratbag. Ah need tae get some booze, ye'd better grab yer coat an' come wi' me an' show me the nearest boozer.'

It was the first time I'd been alone with the man in years, since the time he had taken his jacket off and walked with me through the rain when I was no more than a child. Now I was sitting across a pub table from him, drinking coke and fending off insults.

'Ah'm embarrassin' ye, go oan, admit it,' he grinned.

'I admit it,' I replied, 'It's like being with neanderthal man.'

'Good,' he winked, 'Ah've never met the bloke, but he must be a stoatir if he's like me. Ah love tae embarrass ratbags!'

When we got back the ceilidh was in full swing; the Crowd didn't stand on ceremony, it didn't matter to them that the hostess wasn't even there. Rab disappeared into the throng and I got caught up in a sing-song somewhere else. When the first wave retired to sleeping-bags on the floor upstairs, another wave arrived and took over, and so it went on all night. At one point Rab demanded that a woman be brought to him, to shouts of derision all round about who would take him. Well at least that proved there was no Mrs Rab on the horizon.

'I hear you're looking for a woman,' I said.

'But no' a ratbag,' he replied, and was once again lost in the Crowd. Arguments that had lain dormant since the last time we were all together were resurrected and re-argued, and songs were sung without the aid of a campfire, until the call was heard, 'Goodnight Rab!' Rab couldn't drink a lot of whisky, in fact after one glass his eyes gleamed and his banter scintillated for an hour or so and then he fell asleep. This was common knowledge and the Crowd waited for the moment at each gathering and yelled out in unison as he dropped off where he was or crept off in search of his sleeping-bag.

Slowly the night drew to a temporary lull and I lay down beside Denis, who also came from Drumchapel. He had a well-earned reputation for being a stud, but I had grown up knowing him and considered him to be nearly a brother. Much to my surprise, as I lay down beside him he grabbed me and instantly launched into a love scene from *The Thomas Crown Affair*, a film that was all the rage at the time. He had cast himself as Steve McQueen and I was Faye Dunaway apparently, or I would have been if I hadn't laughed. I got up and went upstairs, smiling wryly to myself. Sod's Law again. The only man I wanted had gone to America, which was at least partly responsible for my going to India. Only he had come back and I was still committed to going. The only man I wanted was lying snoring in a sleeping-bag in front of me, while one I didn't want was grabbing at me. I aimed a kick at the sleeping figure and muttered 'Sod you Rab!' He stirred mid-snore, turned onto his side and resumed snoring where he had left off. I lay down beside him; I wouldn't be able to say I had slept with him of course, but I figured it was as near as I was ever likely to get. Downstairs someone woke, started singing and the ceilidh swung into another phase. I stayed where I was.

The Crowd began to disperse around lunchtime. Rab didn't know where to get a bus home so I volunteered to show him; to my annoyance a few of the others came too, 'for a breath of air'. On the way nothing of note was discussed, and as Rab boarded his bus he said to me 'Well cheerio. Remember to write, and don't gobble too much rice!' If Humphrey Bogart had had that little to say to Ingrid Bergman, *Casablanca* wouldn't have been worth making; as romantic farewells went it didn't exactly rank way up there with the best. But then it wasn't a romantic farewell, was it?

Chapter Thirty-Eight

It was my last week in the hospital. While I had been at the ceilidh one of the surgical housemen had attempted to murder a patient; it was the talk of the place, and no one could talk about it without laughing, of course. It was not just any houseman, but John Alexander, one of the pleasantest, easiest to work with chaps in the history of the sub-species. I had known him as a medical student and as a medical houseman before he had gone on to do his six months with the surgeons, which admittedly could turn anyone into Frankenstein's monster.

John had been on casualty duty, the worst ordeal anyone can ever undergo, and apparently it had been a particularly bad go. His wife had given birth to their first child the day before and John hadn't managed to see her or their son yet. He had been awake for over twenty-four hours, then he had been presented with a Chinese cook whose brother had tapped him on the head with a knife in the family restaurant. The knife was sticking out of the cook's head and all he wanted to do was kill the brother who had put it there. The knife didn't seem to be bothering him, but the reason for the argument, that he kept a dirty kitchen, still did. So while John had been trying to deal with the kind of injury he had only encountered before in his worst nightmares, the injured man was trying to get at his brother. At one point he had succeeded and the two Chinamen were wrestling on the floor, and John could see his career disappearing before his very eyes. It wasn't every doctor who lost a patient by allowing him to scramble about the floor with a knife imbedded in his skull, after all.

He had just finished dealing with that when the next one arrived, a pleasant, calm little man in his late forties, with a fireside poker sticking out of his chest. John's weary eyes watched in horror as the poker jumped in time with the man's heart-beat, and he listened as the history unfolded. The little man was a bachelor who lived with his mother, and as they had been watching TV together he had stirred the fire with the poker and then left it in the coals. When it was glowing red-hot, he had lifted it out and plunged it into his chest, so that as John could plainly see, it had come to rest against his heart. The patient was clearly feeling no pain and was polite and helpful. John then made the fatal mistake, he asked why he'd done it. The little man replied amiably, 'It seemed a good idea at the time.' No one could do anything other than sympathize with young Dr Alexander; it had been a tough year, a tough twenty-four hours in particular and of course there had been all the anxiety leading up to the birth of the son he had yet to see. The fates had clearly conspired to get at him and it was little wonder that he felt off form. The first the rest of the casualty staff knew that there was a problem was when they heard a kind of gurgling sound behind the screens, and when a curious nurse looked she found nice, pleasant John Alexander with his hands around his patient's throat. John had had enough, he had flipped and it took three of them to prise his fingers off the man's windpipe.

I saw the patient a few days later. He had inflicted a serious injury on himself, or rather, series of injuries. First of all he had a neat hole burned through his chest, through which you could watch his heart beating; that would clearly need a few goes of plastic surgery to close up. He had also inflicted a burn on the outer surface of his heart that would leave a scar similar to a heart attack, and there he sat in bed, courteous, smiling, grateful for whatever was done for him. Happily the slight bruising around his throat was fading. I was tempted to ask John Alexander's question – it seemed such a totally demented way to kill oneself – but I wasn't at all sure that I trusted myself to refrain from John's solution if the little man gave me the same reply; so I didn't.

If Indian medicine could top this, I'd be very surprised.

* * *

On my last day at the hospital I was asked to see a patient called McGettigan, a man in his early sixties. I knew little about him except that it was a routine check, there was nothing wrong with his heart. Was he, I wondered, any relation to a Betty McGettigan who was a teacher? Yes, she was his wife. Did she teach at the Marian school many years ago? Yes, she did. Before I left the ward I asked the houseman what was wrong with the patient.

'It's the nervous system,' he said, 'Incurable I'm afraid. We've just told the family.' He screwed up his face and shook his head, it was a rotten part of the job. Losing patients was bad enough, but telling their relatives we'd lost them was worse. As I left I saw them sitting outside the ward, Mrs McGettigan and her two daughters, their heads close together, deep in conversation. Her hair was as I remembered it, swept back with a deep wave on either side framing her face, and caught in a French roll at the back of her head. It was exactly the same, only now it was pure white. I stood at the lift watching her with her daughters, tempted to go up to her and talk, but there is a time and place and now wasn't the right one for a reunion with a former pupil. What could I have said anyway?

'Hello, I know you've just had devastating news about your husband, but guess who I am?' It seemed strange to be close to her and not to talk to her, but if I'm honest there was also a feeling of relief. I should be writing; she'd always said so. 'One day you'll see her words in print,' she'd told the others on the last day of the Marian school. Yes, I knew she needed time with her family right then, but another factor was that I really didn't want her to know I was working in medicine. If I had any nagging doubts about going away, seeing her settled them somewhat.

It was 30th November, 5 a.m., time to go. There were no emotional goodbyes as I left the house in the early morning darkness for Glasgow Airport. My father had got up for some reason to see me off and as I turned to go he made a movement that suggested he might be about to hug me. He couldn't do it though, it wasn't in the man to show

266

emotion, if that was what he was thinking of. Instead he patted my shoulder, which made me smile; the truth was that I couldn't have taken a hug from him anyway, it was years too late for that. As I closed the front door I heard Nan's voice coming from her bedroom, 'Cheerio hen, hiv a good time.' I might have been going for a night out. I knew even then that I would regret for the rest of my life not telling her all those things we all leave unsaid until it is too late, but all I said was 'Bye Mum.'

Peter, Paul and Mary were singing 'I'm Leaving on a Jet Plane' as the shuttle took off for London; I made a mental note to one day find that record and jump up and down on it, for threatening my stiff upper lip.

Glasgow is a corruption of a Gaelic word meaning 'dear green place', and from the air a surprising amount of greenery was still visible. My mind was in turmoil as I watched it fall away below me, all my doubts had returned and they now seemed like sound sense. What was I doing? Was I running away from all the parts of my life that didn't work rather than sort them out? Rab was down there somewhere, unaware and uninterested, but that was a fact I would always have to live with, so how did going off to India help that? Nan was down there, and Peggy too, buried with all sorts of questions I wouldn't find the answers to in India. Just what did I think I was doing? Nan had spent her entire life, and mine, searching for Utopia; it was just over that far-off hill, just beyond the next house move. Perhaps I was doing the same, taking on Nan's quest without really thinking it through. Whose search was I going on and just what did I think I was doing?

I didn't realize it at the time, but as I flew off from Glasgow on my great adventure that St Andrew's Day I was already planning my return.

Utopia, after all, is where the heart is . . .

Epilogue: Voices, Dreams and Searches

Rab and I had been married for eight and a half years and lived with our three-year-old son, Euan, on an island off the West Coast of Scotland. It was 4th February 1980 and it had been snowing heavily most of the day. Nan was in hospital on the mainland. She had burned her leg, nothing serious, but the dressing needed changing three or four times a day. To save time for the district nurses she had gone into hospital for a few days.

I had arranged to visit her on the Wednesday, but I had taken a notion to go across instead that Monday. The blizzard struck as I was negotiating the farm-track with Euan in his buggy. The local postie stopped me at the road end and told me it was blocked further along, so I couldn't get to the ferry terminal. Reluctantly I turned back, annoyed at myself for being so stubborn. Wednesday was only two days away and Nan wasn't expecting me till then, so why this determination to get there today? I had a young child to consider after all, why subject him to howling winds and snow too thick to see through?

All that day Rab drove a snow plough in an attempt to keep the island's one road open. He came home briefly to refill his thermos and to grab a bite to eat, then dashed out again at 8 p.m. I was getting Euan ready for bed when I heard a voice say 'Rita'. Assuming Rab had forgotten something, I went to the front door, wondering as I opened it why he had called me Rita. He disliked the family name and like everyone else these days he called me Meg. When he wasn't at the front I went to the back-door, annoyed now that I had to leave the baby. Why couldn't Rab use his keys for heaven's sake? The snow plough had gone; there was no one there. Outside there was nothing but swirling snow.

268

Without thinking about it I went straight to the phone and called the hospital.

'Can you please tell my mother to call me?' I asked the staff nurse on Nan's ward.

'Have you spoken to anyone already?'

'Yes, I spoke to the ward sister the other day,' I replied, 'Tell my mother to reverse the charges and none of her nonsense. I'll worry about my own phone bill.'

'Have you spoken to anyone today?' she persisted, and for the first time on that freezing cold day I felt a chill.

'What's wrong staff?' I was aware that I was holding my breath and forced myself to let it out again, slowly and easily.

'She's had a relapse.'

'Look staff, I'm stuck on this island and I can't get off. I'm a medic, tell me in medical jargon what's happened and I'll understand.' There was a pause as she wondered whether she should tell me on the phone. I concentrated on my breathing.

'She's had a full systemic collapse. She has double pneumonia, septicaemia and renal failure. Five minutes ago she slipped into a coma.'

'She's dying,' I said, moving up a gear in crisis mode, 'How long?'

'I really can't say.'

'Come along staff!' I said in my most officious medical voice, 'My mother's dying and I can't get to her! Kindly stop playing with words and tell me the truth!'

'I shouldn't tell you this over the phone, but I'd say a couple of hours at the most.'

It was just after 8 p.m. I put Euan to bed and sat down, my mind totally concentrated on Nan. Exactly two hours later I called again and she had just died. I was perfectly calm, thanked the staff nurse for caring for Nan and for being honest with me. Then I sat down again to wait for morning. I couldn't be there with her, it was the nearest to a vigil by her side that I could manage.

To this day I have no explanation for the voice calling my name as Nan slipped into unconsciousness, all I know is that I heard it. It was neither male nor female, just a voice, but plain and clear. Neither do I know why I went straight to the phone, because I had made no conscious connection between the voice and Nan. And the thing that has haunted me ever since is that I had thought whatever bound us closely together had weakened and died after 1959. If she was calling me then it had still been there, and I hadn't even known. All those years when I had needed her and missed her, yet she had been there all along . . .

The dreams started in 1985. Night after night I would wake up covered in sweat and shaking with terror, and soon I was finding reasons to avoid sleeping. I was thirty-seven-years-old, happily married with three children; nothing was wrong. Yet out of a clear blue sky I was having nightmares. And they didn't fade in the cool light of day, they remained crystal clear afterwards, and still are today.

In one I was walking down a road with beautiful gardens on all sides, all filled with pink roses, nothing but pink roses. I kept looking around, in a desperate attempt to find some other flower, but everywhere there was nothing but pink roses. When I woke I couldn't understand why I should find pink roses so distressing, but soon I was watching for them wherever I went during the waking day, and hoping not to find them. And I couldn't understand why.

In another dream I was in a room I didn't recognize and Jim McAvoy was standing beside a closed door, looking down at the floor. I was facing the door, and the Clarks were behind me on all sides. There was something awful behind the door, but I had to open it and I knew somehow that the family didn't really want me to. I turned the handle and as the door swung open, there stood Peggy, her face solemn, almost reproachful, as I had never seen her. Her dark-brown hair was swept up in a sophisticated, smooth style that was all wrong; Peggy had a mass of curls. She was wearing a long dress of heavy, powder-blue satin, plain, simple and beautiful, but nothing like Peggy would have chosen. She loved pink, and nothing could be too fancy, no amount of lace and frills was ever enough, everything had to be a riot of

over-the-top, cheerful nonsense, or she considered it plain.
None of the Clarks spoke in the dream, but they seemed
to be showing Peggy to me and telling me everything was
fine. Only it wasn't Peggy, not the real Peggy, and nothing
was fine, and the look on her face terrified me.

Then I was sitting in a booth in some fashionable
restaurant. It was thick with tropical plants and music
played softly in the background, some vaguely familar
tune I couldn't quite place. I had a cup of coffee in
front of me as I chatted to someone. I could, she was
saying, get the information fairly easily, there was the new
freedom of information legislation for instance, and I knew
where to start, I knew the date in 1959, and I had enough
medical contacts. The place to start, she was saying, was
the Registrar's Office, which seemed logical to me and I
was agreeing. Then as I turned to look at her I found it
was Peggy, but before I could say anything she disappeared
and I sped around the fancy restaurant desperately trying
to find her. Then I noticed that the tropical plants had
turned into pink roses and the music in the background
was 'Mexicali Rose'.

Next I was walking along a familiar road near to the
Eastern Infirmary and I saw someone I knew coming out
of the flower shop carrying a bunch of flowers. She was
wearing a beige wool coat and expensive black patent
high-heeled shoes, and she carried a plain black clutch
bag. Her jewellery was discreet, but quality, and her hair
was beautifully swept back from her face. I touched her
sleeve, and she turned towards me; it was Peggy. Once
again she looked at me with that solemn, reproachful stare.
Then wordlessly she handed me a single pink rose from the
bunch she carried and disappeared before my eyes.

These dreams kept recurring and terrified me for no
reason that I could understand. I had never been scared
of Peggy in my life and if her ghost had appeared before
me I would have been delighted. I had never truly known
what had happened on 30th May 1959; whatever else the
dreams might mean, they were reminders of how much I
didn't know about a tragedy that had changed the entire

course of my life. In my new, happy life I had attempted to put it all behind me, I had crammed it all into a mental compartment and put up a notice saying 'Finished. Do not open.' Only it wasn't finished and now it was leaking out, forcing itself into my life, and I couldn't get it to go back into the compartment again.

After a few sleepless months I gave in. There was only one thing I could do. I had to go back to 1959 and find out everything that had happened, I had to know why Peggy had died to understand what had become of us all afterwards. The dark, yawning abyss had to be filled in, no matter how painful it might be, or it would remain there, seething and furious for the rest of my life.

I planned it carefully. First of all, even if I did succeed in uncovering the events of that day after twenty-six years, I was so close to the story that I might misinterpret whatever I discovered. So I found Ian Cameron, a Consultant I had known in the Eastern who was also a psychotherapist, and one of the wisest men I had ever known. I told him the story and he agreed that the dreams were pushing me into investigating Peggy's death. 'Isn't that funny?' he said, 'When I was a medical student in the forties we had to do home deliveries, and Blackhill was my area.'

So the streets where I had played as a child in the fifties were the streets he had walked as a young man, delivering babies in the forties. Then I had grown up to work with him and later to involve him in my quest over an obstetrics death in those same streets. Dr Cameron agreed to help evaluate whatever information I turned up, he would be my thread through the labyrinth.

The first thing I did was to visit the Registrar's Office in Martha Street, Glasgow. This was the area where the Clarks and O'Briens had lived. Their births had been registered in this office, just as mine had been and Mickey's and Laurie's. Peggy's death had been too, and it was where Rab and I had married. In the next street was Rottenrow and the hospital where Peggy had died, and further along was the Brae. So all around were reminders of events in my life.

I asked the clerk for Peggy's death certificate and gave him the date. When he came back he took me into a side room. There had apparently been a change of cause of death. The first was signed by a Dr S A Collins at the hospital, citing 'Obstructed labour ¼ day. Rupture of uterus. Severe Haemorrhage.' Then there was a police post-mortem by a Dr W P Weir, and he'd changed the cause of death to 'Rupture of uterus and intra-peritoneal haemorrhage following forceps for foetal distress,' clearly blaming the use of forceps.

I paid for a copy of the certificate and wandered back down the road. W P Weir was Walter Weir, a well-known pathologist, and luckily someone I knew, albeit slightly. Another coincidence; like Ian Cameron I had known him professionally without suspecting that his shadow had crossed my life years ago. When I phoned him he told me he had just retired and I explained what I wanted to know. He had no difficulty in remembering Peggy, despite all the PMs he had carried out.

'It was a bad case,' he explained, 'I had seen very few like it, a real mess.' In my experience medics only remember the bad ones.

'You seemed to blame the forceps,' I said, 'And you dropped any mention of obstructed labour from your findings.'

'Yes, that's right. I was very clear about that. There was no obstruction, and the use of forceps would have been wrong anyway, an obstructed labour needs a Caesarian section. Whoever used the forceps that day killed the woman and the child. The haemorrhage was well-established, if I remember correctly there was very little blood left in her body, she had virtually bled to death before she reached Rottenrow. They wouldn't have been able to do anything for her by that time. I'll have a look, I might have my notes still, I'm sorting stuff out now that I've retired. Give me a call back and I'll see what I can find.'

I found Dr S A Collins through the medical mafia. Though he wasn't in the medical directory, the list of doctors in this country, I found his brother. Steven Collins was now a Professor of Obstetrics in Malaysia. I immediately wrote off to him and planned my next move. It had to be the family doctor, but I didn't even know his name, only McAvoy would know that. I picked up a Glasgow telephone directory and called up every McAvoy listed. The McAvoys were a large family and the GP had been their doctor, if I could find one of them I might be able to avoid actually talking to Jim McAvoy, if he were still alive.

It was surprisingly easy. I quickly found one of McAvoy's brothers, who told me the name of the GP, Dr James Hammond. McAvoy was apparently living with his – and Peggy's – youngest son in Glasgow. All attempts to find Dr Hammond then hit a brick wall. I tried the medical mafia and the word came back that Hammond was dead. I tried every medical organization and the reply was the same: there was no record of a Dr James Hammond. I discovered that he had had a partner in the sixties and I called that man's home to discover that he had been dead for years; his widow told me that Hammond had too. She gave me the number of the practice they had shared, but when I called I was told the same story. I don't know why I kept going down that road, perhaps it was just a natural cussedness, but somehow I didn't believe what I was being told about Hammond. I had a distinct feeling that he was alive. I went back to the Glasgow telephone directory once again and called every Hammond I could find. And there he was. I could hardly believe it, but his voice was on the other end of the line. I told him that I was writing a book and one of his former patients came into the story – totally untrue at the time, but I didn't want him to know Peggy and I were related, or he might clam up.

'Her name was McAvoy,' I said, 'I think she died around 1960, I wonder if you remember her?'

'Margaret McAvoy,' he said, 'Six Moodiesburn Street. 1959.'

Instantly I knew that what had happened was out of the ordinary; you only remember the bad ones. Twenty-six years later and Hammond could still remember Peggy's address; it must have been very bad. I had caught him off guard, so I asked him if I could see him rather than keep the conversation going on the phone and arouse any suspicions. In the flesh I'd be able to judge how honest he was being in his answers too, and it would be harder to throw me out than it would to hang up the phone. He agreed to see me in two days time and I hung up without leaving my number, so that if he thought better of it he wouldn't be able to contact me and cancel.

Over the next couple of days I tried to compile a list of questions and settle on some strategy for dealing with both Hammond and the situation. I was finding it very difficult sometimes to think about Peggy in a detached way. While I was talking to Walter Weir I had struggled to keep my mind from picturing the scene in the bedroom that day. Long-hidden memories kept intruding and putting themselves in context, making the picture more complete. The more I found out the more I had to feel emotional about and I couldn't afford that if I was going to get to the bottom of the story. So if the two days before I met Hammond were an eternity, they were also an opportunity to put some distance between the truth and my feelings.

Hammond lived in Newton Mearns, in the affluent south of the city, in 'a big hoose'; I smiled to myself as the daily woman let me in. His home was a typical Victorian mansion, with large airy rooms and high corniced ceilings. The decor was ultra conservative, antique furniture and a cream and beige colour scheme, the kind of house that gave the feeling of permanence. Nothing had moved from its allotted spot in a very long time here, a house where children had never lived to disturb the quiet gentility. There was only one picture of a baby and it had that indefinable look of having been taken many years ago.

Dr James Hammond was sitting by the fireside in an elegant armchair with curved, wooden legs. He was a small, portly figure with receding white hair that had once been sandy-red. Dressed immaculately but soberly, his cuff-links bearing the entwined initials of his name, he sat smiling. His clasped hands rested in his lap, and a gold tie-pin bearing the same monogram held his dark maroon tie. I thanked him for seeing me, and to put him at ease I told him of my medical background and we talked of doctors we had both known. He was delighted to have someone to swap gossip with and told me a little about his days as a GP during the setting up of the NHS. He'd had a single-handed practice for most of the time apparently, until the early sixties, in fact. I asked him how he had coped with the demands this must have made on him and he bristled with pride and said he simply sacrificed himself for his patients, not that they deserved it in the main of course, but it was the kind of man he was.

He'd been a widower these last five years and he often looked back now and regretted how much time he should have spent with his wife that he'd spent instead with his demanding patients. He took out a monogrammed handkerchief and blew his nose. Then I told him the story I had prepared, that I was writing something about Mrs McAvoy's sister, who had saved the lives of her neighbours when Balmano Brae had collapsed. He blew out his cheeks derisively.

'I should be very surprised if we're talking about the same family!' he laughed, 'Those people weren't capable of anything notable apart from prodigious breeding, believe me!'

'Really?' I said, 'I wouldn't know. I just stumbled across this story and felt I had to follow it through.'

'Well for a start they came from Blackhill,' he said, 'Now a young lady such as yourself wouldn't know anything about Blackhill. It was a hell-hole, a den of thieves and murderers, but as we used to say in those days, if we kept them all together, at least we knew where they were!' He laughed merrily at his little jest. 'Many of my patients came from there. They had to be looked after like children, told whether they were ill or not, and more often they weren't. Too much booze and too little solid food, that was their trouble in the main, give that sort money to feed themselves and their children and they followed a liquid diet if you know what I mean! I was the only person who could go into Blackhill in a car and not have the wheels stolen while it was still moving. I was strict with them you see, let them know who was boss!'

'Weren't there any decent people there?'

'Not a one my dear, decency wasn't something that counted in Blackhill. It must be very difficult for someone like you to understand, but those people were barely human, the absolute dregs of humanity at the most.'

'And Mrs McAvoy?'

'Oh she was just like the rest, a big, blowsy, coarse-spoken creature.' I wondered for a moment if he had actually known Peggy, if he'd ever set eyes on her.

'Didn't know her well, mind you,' he continued, 'I was the McAvoy's family doctor, only saw her after she married Jim McAvoy.'

'What was he like?'

'Pretty much par for the Blackhill course. Low intelligence, no education, but with a kind of animal cunning.'

'And did you see Mrs McAvoy throughout her pregnancy?'

'No, no, you didn't see that sort until they went into labour, then it was a knock at the door and "Please doacter',"' he mimicked a Glasgow accent, and as I looked at him I remembered Peggy going to ante-natal appointments. Nan and I had waited for her in Moodiesburn Street once, on one of my mother's sudden desires to see her, and as Peggy came in she smoothed her cotton smock over her belly and said, 'If Ah'm no' away by Monday Ah've tae go back tae see him.' At that time she was already overdue and only weeks from death. This was Peggy, who had longed for motherhood, who adored babies even if she was having too many. Peggy kept her ante-natal appointments.

'And was she overdue?'

'Overdue? No, no; not that I remember.'

'And who was at the birth?'

'I was.'

'You were? That's lucky, you'll have all the details. I had been told that someone else attended that day.'

'No, it was me.' We were having no more amusing detours

into the backward ways of the Blackhill natives I noticed, he was too busy paying close attention now.

'And what happened?'

'Well McAvoy called me, I went to the house and the labour progressed.'

'But she died in hospital didn't she?'

'Yes.'

'Well how did that come about?'

'Oh, it was taking a long time and she was getting a bit tired so I decided to send her in.'

'Who else was there?'

'Nobody, just me.'

'No nurse?'

'No.'

'Who called the ambulance then?'

'I did.'

'But I understood that the nearest public phone was some distance away.' I knew exactly where it was. I had a clear recollection of being squashed in the phone box listening as my mother called the hospital to be told that Peggy had just delivered her first live child.

'I took my car.'

'So you had to leave the patient to do that?'

'Well she was OK. As I said, she was just a bit tired. There was no danger as such.'

'No sign of bleeding?'

'No . . .' He thought about it for a moment and said, 'Perhaps her pulse was a little fast.'

'But there was no outward sign of bleeding?'

'No.'

'Did you go with her in the ambulance?'

'No. If she had been in any danger then of course I would have, but she was just having a long labour and was tired.'

'So who went with her, if you didn't and there was no nurse present?'

'I think McAvoy went.'

'Was there anyone else in the house?'

'No.'

278

'But there were children weren't there? Who looked after the McAvoy children?'

'Well perhaps there was someone else there too, I can't quite remember, it's so long ago . . .'

'When did you hear that she'd died?'

'A couple of weeks later. McAvoy came and told me.'

'Didn't you call the hospital after sending her in?'

'Well I would have if I'd had any reason to be concerned of course, but it was all quite straight forward you see, so I didn't bother.'

'And when you heard she was dead?'

'Well I was shocked of course. I don't know what Rottenrow could have done to her, they must've made some sort of mistake.'

'Didn't the Fiscal contact you about a Fatal Accident Inquiry?'

'No.'

'And didn't you hear the cause of death?' He shook his head and I read both causes out to him.

'Well Rottenrow must've done that,' he replied, 'I didn't use forceps at all. She was tired, that was all.'

'I heard that you had treated McAvoy very kindly afterwards,' I said, testing a family suspicion that McAvoy had been paid for not causing a fuss, 'I heard that you had given him some financial assistance.' He was a little unsettled by this.

'Well I did feel sorry for him, rogue that he was, with his wife dead and three children to provide for, so I did give him a few pounds. When you've been a GP for so many years you find yourself giving more than medical care to these people sometimes. When I retired a few years ago my patients were in tears, begging me to stay on. They're not bright you see, it's like dealing with very dim children. McAvoy was like that, I just helped him out at a bad time and told him not to say anything to anybody.' He gave a conspiratorial laugh. 'The last thing I wanted was a line of Blackhill spongers at my door every day looking for booze money!' He had paid McAvoy off; the family had been right.

I wasn't going to get anything else from Dr James

Hammond. He was lying, I was convinced of that, but pushing him would be useless, so I steered the conversation back to mutual medical acquaintances and he visibly relaxed. I could see how nervous he had been just by the difference in him. He was obviously a lonely man and he was enjoying the conversation so much that he didn't want me to go.

'I'm sorry I couldn't help you more with the McAvoy case,' he said as I was leaving.

'Oh please, don't worry,' I smiled, 'I thought it was all a wild goose chase, at least you've confirmed that.'

We were at the outside door when he said it. He said it all.

'And besides, what difference would it have made if she had lived?' he asked, 'My wife only had the one, a girl who died of heart disease, and my wife was a lady, she would have made a wonderful mother. Those women, the Margaret McAvoy sort, they had them like shelling peas. If she had lived she would have gone on spawning them, year after year, more thieves and murderers from Blackhill to terrorize and pollute the city.' It was the bitterest, blackest, most chilling little speech I had ever heard. His voice seethed with distaste and venom. I wondered what kind of childhood he had had, what awful experiences in his life he could have suffered to fill him with such poisonous bile. I gave an involuntary shiver as I walked back down the road to the railway station.

Everything was jumbled up inside my head, all sorts of feelings and emotions jostling for position alongside the logical dissection of what I'd just witnessed. I felt like running away from Hammond and his 'big hoose', I had to get away as quickly as possible. I felt dirty in some way, tainted by hearing his putrid little speech. When there was no train due I almost panicked, I *couldn't* wait, I *had* to get away. I ran outside and stopped a taxi, not entirely sure where I wanted to go. I asked to be taken to the Royal Maternity at Rottenrow then sat back and tried to calm down. I felt as though I had been beaten up, I was aching all over and my insides felt as though a huge, long-taloned claw had reached within me and ripped me apart. I couldn't believe I had sat still and listened to such savagery against Peggy and my family, such blatant lies about them and about Hammond's part in our tragedy. A pure Clark couldn't have done so; my Uncle George would have hit him and Nan would have delivered an impassioned, articulate speech then wept for hours on Peggy's shoulder. Whatever else I had to thank the O'Briens for I now had to acknowledge that their policy of never showing their emotions, and their facility with the tactical lie, could be very useful skills. But the Clark emotions were churning around and I was feeling very fragile.

I walked around the maternity hospital, unable to explain to myself why I was there, then I decided to go to Blackhill, so I hailed another taxi. The driver was less than impressed by my destination.

'Blackhill hen?' he asked, 'Ur ye sure? Hiv ye no' made a mistake hen, Ah mean dae ye know whit Blackhill's like?'

'I don't want you to stop, I just want to drive past.'

'Well a'right hen, bit it's no' the kinda place where ye staun' aroon', understaun'? Ye really need sumb'dy tae ride shotgun fur ye!'

The chemical factory had gone, but the gasworks was still there, the two gasometers now painted a nice shade of blue, the Gas Board's attempt at improving its image. If you can't be 'green' then blue is nearly as valid in 'green' terms. There was no hint in the air of gas emissions though, filters had been fitted, so the gasworks no longer 'came out' in a solid lump of lung-stopping fumes. My old school had gone, so had Paddy Doyle's, where my happiest memories of my father were rooted. Even today the slightest whiff of leather can bring those early days back to me, and I see him again, a little figure hunched over his last, mending shoes as I sat beside him drinking hot, sweet tea from his old army mug. Happy memories of when I was too young to know what life was really like for my mother and so had no reason to suspect what it would become for all of us in time.

I directed the taxi driver from Royston Road to Craighead

Avenue which had bordered St Philomena's School. There used to be a high metal fence all the way along, over which the enemy Proddies threw clods of earth at us in our mutually satisfying lunchtime battles. Past the pond and right, to where Craigendmuir Street joined Acrehill Street. There we had met up with David and his pals at the end of the school day, and thrown insults at each other all the way home. Past the gap in the tenements where we had watched the paratroopers jumping from the blimp we never found, and the house of the little man who had murdered his wife.

David's house was there on the right, and a couple of closes further on was where Bobby, the mentally handicapped boy had lived. Between the next gap was where Jamie had been killed by the train, nearly in the backcourt of his own house. Across the road was Mrs Logan's house of plenty, courtesy of her gangster nephew, Billy Fullarton, and our close was two along. Only it wasn't there anymore. Instead, huge concrete pillars rose hundreds of feet above, carrying the M8 motorway. All those times I had driven over that exact spot, never suspecting it was the site of 34 Acrehill Street; over where Fullarton had made us walk home alone, and where Santa had rushed through the air one magic night on his way to deliver presents to other children. I asked the taxi driver to take me to Moodiesburn Street and he feigned ignorance, so I firmly directed him and made him wait outside number six.

'Dae you know who lives in that hoose ower the road?' he demanded, and I shook my head. 'Arthur Thomson!' he said, 'Arthur bloody Thomson, y'know, the Godfather o' Glesca crime! This isnae ony place tae linger hen!'

Thomson, Fullarton, names I had grown up with so they held no terrors for me, and I smiled at his nervousness. I went through the close and paused at Peggy's door. It felt the same as it had after her death, as though she was there, just beyond the corner of my eye, and if I turned my head quickly . . . Down the eight back stairs I went, half expecting to meet myself. I'd only managed to jump them once, on a Saturday in May long ago, with the demons of hell after me.

The air raid shelters had gone and the backcourt was a backgreen now, with real, green grass. The middens had vanished, given way to more modern means of disposing household rubbish. It all looked smaller, of course, shrunk by the years, but that apart it was as I remembered it. I went back to the taxi, where the driver was sweating with unease. When I asked him to head back to the city centre he became verbose with relief. Did I know this part of the city, how did I know the street names, was I looking for someone? But I didn't reply, I was deep in some rite of passage, taken beyond words by an instinct to touch base. I had known it all so well as a child, my footprints would be there somewhere, along with generations of others, indelible, invisible, but there. I just had to see it all one more time before I could put it away. We passed the cemetery where Peggy had made me walk with her only weeks before she died, helping me lay ghosts. It occurred to me that that was what I was doing on this day: that I was making my peace with the ghosts of my childhood.

During that night I thought through everything that Hammond had said about Peggy, my family and the people of Blackhill, and his awful, bitter outburst as I left him, and I was physically sick.

It took me a couple of weeks to settle down enough to think through Hammond's story. He hadn't been with Peggy that day. I remembered lying on top of my shelter after the men had come back from burying Peggy. Another car had drawn up and a young man had got out and gone into the house. He was the one who had been there, the doctor who 'wisnae a real doacter', a tall, dark-haired lad in his late teens or early twenties who had towered over the much older figure of my father as he hurried him away from George's rage. Hammond was barely five feet tall, the same as my father, he was in his seventies, which meant that in 1959 he would have been in his late forties, the same again as my father, and his hair had been sandy-red. Hammond hadn't been with Peggy.

I called Walter Weir again and repeated Hammond's version of Peggy's death.

'Hammond's lying,' he replied, 'He has a lot to lie about. I don't think he was the attending doctor that day.'

'Why?'

'Well what I saw wasn't the work of an experienced GP, and Hammond was certainly that. What I saw was the work of a complete novice, to put it kindly.'

'Don't put it kindly.'

'Then an apprentice butcher could have made a better job of it. Let's go back a bit. Firstly, there's a tendency towards bigger babies with each pregnancy, and this lady had sub-acute rickets. She didn't have the disease, but no doubt her mother did and Mrs McAvoy carried the marks of that. Most Glaswegians of that era were very small, like all poor city-dwellers her skeletal growth had been retarded. So her pelvis wasn't roomy; it could've coped with a smaller baby, but this one – it was a male foetus – was bigger, partly because it was also overdue. She was thirty-seven and she was getting tired. Any experienced GP would've sent her to hospital, she'd have had a section and all would have been well. Whoever was there that day didn't know what he was doing. Tiredness or obstructed labour, it doesn't matter, either should have meant a section, but instead he tried forceps, and he wasn't experienced with those either. The bad luck just piled up from there on. He probably applied the forceps just as a strong contraction struck, stretching the uterus paper-thin, and it all ruptured. Then she began to haemorrhage and he made the wrong choice again. Instead of sending for help he tried to stop it, and he had no chance of doing that. It all smacks of lack of experience and panic. You have to ask why he didn't try to get help when he was in such desperate trouble, and the likeliest explanation is that he couldn't.'

'Why? What do you mean?'

'My guess is that he wasn't a doctor, so he couldn't send her to hospital and risk being found out. Once she ruptured she needed to be in hospital pretty damn quick, and he still didn't send her. He tried to handle it all himself because to do otherwise would've risked discovery. And he couldn't contact Hammond because Hammond wasn't at home. So he panicked.'

'If he wasn't a doctor, what was he?'

'Probably a medical student who'd agreed to cover for the GP for less money than a fully-qualified locum would accept.'

'That's illegal isn't it?'

'Yes, then as now. The medical fraternity would swear on a stack of bibles that it couldn't and didn't ever happen, but you and I both know they'd swear to anything on a stack of bibles. It did happen.'

Ian Cameron listened as I told him the story. 'So how do you feel?' he asked.

'Overwhelmed, mixed up. Tell me, what kind of medical student would have put himself in that position do you think?'

'Most likely one who didn't have daddy's money to see him through. After the war we began to see more working-class boys coming into the profession, not many mind you, but the odd one. And I'd imagine that he probably thought nothing much could go wrong in one little day. If, as you say, Hammond was concerned about spending so little time with his wife and wanted a day off from his single-handed practice, he probably thought the same. He'd get cheap cover for the day and what could possibly go wrong? At least what could possibly go wrong that couldn't be covered up, anyway?'

'Nothing. That's just it. Nothing went wrong that wasn't covered up. Just the death of a young woman and her child and the destruction of an entire extended family.'

'And you have to remember that the NHS was still in its infancy in 1959. I used to deliver babies in Blackhill when I was a medical student only ten years or so before, the GP probably did the same. It wouldn't have taken much for him to persuade himself that all these new-fangled rules were nonsense, and more so if it saved him money.'

'Especially as the people of Blackhill were so worthless and undeserving of proper medical care.'

'Yes, awful, isn't it?'

'Do you know what would have happened if it had all come out at the time?'

'Well the guilty man was the GP, but I suspect if there had been an investigation he would've come out of it looking like a hero anyway. You must remember that in those days, even more than now, doctors were gods. If he couldn't be got out of it he would've been suspended on full pay for perhaps six months.'

'Is that all?' I asked incredulously.

''Fraid so. And the family would have had to fight bloody hard to get even that, bloody hard. It wouldn't have been seen as in the public interest to pursue anyone involved, the establishment would've covered all tracks.'

'Would the police have covered up for Hammond? Two of them broke down the door and sent for the ambulance.'

'It would've been out of their hands, they couldn't have questioned the "doctor's" professional qualifications and very likely they wouldn't even have entered the event in their notebooks. I would imagine sending for an ambulance wasn't exactly an uncommon occurrence for policemen in Blackhill.'

I wondered what had happened to the medical student, if he had gone on to qualify. If the lad who'd been with Peggy was around twenty years old when I was eleven, he would only be in his forties now. For all I knew I could've worked with him. I couldn't help feeling sorry for him. Everyone makes mistakes with patients, but his must have marked him for life. What had happened in the bedroom of 6 Moodiesburn Street was a nightmare for him too, and it must still be keeping him awake, wherever he was. The lad wasn't to blame, Hammond was.

I couldn't stop the picture of Peggy's dying. Awake or asleep it played in my mind like a film endlessly repeating itself, as I tried to change the ending.

'Well you must remember,' Ian Cameron explained, 'The eleven-year-old child you were, has been secretly keeping Peggy alive all these years in the hope that the ending could be changed.'

'But I'm an adult for God's sake!'

'An adult with a child inside, still running through the backcourts and hiding in the darkness, desperately trying to hold on to the fabric of her normal existence. Now she's been brought face-to-face with reality and it hurts. That's why the dreams scared you so much. In themselves there was nothing frightening about them, except the fear of facing up to the pain that had to come. There was no grieving for Peggy at the time and supressed grief will find a way out, someday, somehow.'

There was still something missing, the picture wasn't complete, and no matter how I tried to ignore it, it bothered me. I needed to know absolutely everything, to confirm it in every way that I could. I tried to get out of it by wondering if I was turning the knife, making it hurt more for some reason. The missing piece was McAvoy. The thought of seeing him again, of talking to him, made me feel angry, sick, a mixture of all sorts of feelings, none of them positive. But he *had* been there throughout. I put the idea into cold storage for a while then I got up one day, caught the morning boat to the mainland and went to see him.

McAvoy was living with his younger son, John, and his family in Johnstone, another housing estate with a bad name. He didn't know me at first, then I saw recognition dawn on him along with the horror. I don't suppose he ever thought he'd see one of us again, and clearly he wasn't anymore delighted at the prospect than I was at seeing him. He had faded with age, he looked as though he had melted in some way, his features were so indistinct. I thought of the groom on the wedding cake decoration, the one I had smashed after Peggy's death. The eyes were the same though, showing what Hammond called his animal cunning.

I told him I wanted to know about Peggy's last day and he looked as though he wanted to run out of the room. He couldn't remember. I said I remembered every second, so surely her husband must remember something, hadn't he been with her to the end? I had come a long way, both in miles and in emotion, I wasn't about to let him off the hook, so I stood my ground until he believed that I wouldn't go away until he talked. I asked him how he'd met Peggy and how long he had known her before they married. He told how they'd met at work five years before and because they lived near each other in Blackhill they'd travelled on the same bus. Another reason to curse the collapse of Balmano Brae. He couldn't remember the date of their marriage, Peggy's birthday, the date when she died or what sex the child had been. I was trying to keep the conversation neutral so that he would give me whatever information he had, but already I could feel my anger rising. Peggy had gone into labour around 8 a.m., he told me, and the doctor arrived soon after. It was Dr Hammond. 'I've talked to Hammond,' I said, 'He was on holiday that day so it couldn't have been him.' McAvoy looked uncomfortable.

'Oh aye, that's mibbe right anuff. Ah furgoat. Ah think sumbudy else came insteed.'

'When did she die?'

'Aboot five o'clock, hauf an 'oor efter we goat tae the hospital. Ah wis sittin' ootside an' the doacter came oot and tellt me.'

'And was there an Inquiry afterwards?'

'Aye. Ah went doon tae the court a while efter an' they tellt me tae wait ootside. Then they came an' tellt me tae go hame, that Ah wisnae needed.'

I remembered my mother saying that McAvoy had told the family to stay away, and they had been so destroyed by the months since May that they couldn't fight back. McAvoy was the only one able to function with any purpose, and he should've been the one most affected by her death, surely? I asked if he'd told the family any of this.

'Naw. It wis nane o' thur business! They hated me the Clarks, aye causin' trouble atween me an' Peggy,' he snivelled, 'Thoaght Ah wisnae good anuff fur hur, ye'd think she wis royalty ur sumthin'! They wur a' like that, thoaght they wur sum'dy!'

'They were somebody,' I said, 'And Peggy was better than royalty. She deserved a lot better than she got.'

He glared at me with his bright little eyes, but he was too intimidated to say more. There he was, a shrivelled little nothing, and there I was, young, healthy and a Clark.

Later my cousin John walked with me to the train station. I could hardly drag my eyes from him. Every expression on his face, every movement of his head, even his laugh, it was all my mother. It was like seeing a male version of her. He told me that he and his brother and sister had grown up in care, and that his father had always refused to talk about Peggy. In fact he had believed that his mother had died giving birth to him. But he'd been just over a year old when she died and he hadn't even one memory of her, neither did his brother or his sister. I tried to tell him what she had been like, but I was talking to a stranger about another stranger who meant much more to me than to him, much, much more. He gave his father a home, he said, because there was nowhere else for him to go and he had remained in some contact throughout the years he and his brother and sister had been in children's homes. Protecting his future meal tickets Nan had always said. John obviously had no idea that McAvoy had discouraged the Clarks from seeing them, and of course no idea of how Peggy's death had affected us all.

None of Peggy's children had any real curiosity about their mother, she might never have existed, and I found it very sad. Had she lived we would have been as close as brothers and sisters, because our mothers would have been joint mothers to us all, and instead we had nothing in common. Nothing, that was, except a noticeable physical resemblance to one another and in John's case a staggering likeness to my mother. Our life experiences had made us strangers, and I couldn't see any prospect of changing that. It would remain a major regret of my life that I would never know Peggy's children. There was no feeling there between us, and it would have been pointless to pretend that there was.

Looking back on my day I thought about the differences

between us. I had survived the trauma, I had found my way out of poor housing, bad job prospects and an unhappy life, but only because I had Nan, and even a subdued Nan had been enough. The motivation and drive towards education had come from Nan and Peggy, and my cousins had lost both and so they hadn't achieved what I had. The only real difference between us was that my mother had lived and so had her dreams for her children, while for my cousins, both had died.

The months of searching for the truth about Peggy's death had left me feeling angry, but had brought no relief, no peace. I was angry at McAvoy, because he couldn't remember anything about Peggy because he simply didn't care. He could at least have loved her a little bit . . .

And I was angry at Dr James Hammond on so many fronts that it was hard to separate them. Mainly because of his attitude to the people of Blackhill, who had provided him with his 'big hoose' and his standard of living and had doubtless given him respect over the years, respect that he didn't earn and didn't deserve. How could he have worked so closely with those people and have no understanding of them or their situation? And his attitude to Peggy made me seethe with rage. Peggy had died because she lived in Blackhill. She had no money and came from the poorest orders of the working class, therefore she wasn't worthy of Hammond's personal or professional care.

But it went further. In reality her fate was sealed before her own birth. She died as she did because of the family she was born into. Before I set out on my quest for the facts that possibility simply hadn't entered my mind, and now I wondered why it hadn't. How could someone of my background and experience fail to have spotted it? The more I thought about it the clearer it became. I had been brought up among the Clarks and the people of Blackhill. They were decent, honest people with a basic belief in what was right and just. Even though they were treated shabbily and unfairly by those in power over them, they *knew* that treatment to be wrong. Which had proved to be my handicap; I hadn't been taught to look for the indecent and dishonest, so I didn't. That had been the case all my life; it was doubtless why when I did find it I was so outraged, and it was that outrage that had made me a crusader like Nan.

Amongst all of this personal grief was anger that *any* woman should have died as Peggy did, that the medical and legal world could regard a woman's life to be of so little consequence that they so quietly and effortlessly covered up the circumstances. They should have been appalled, shocked, enraged, that in 1959 any woman should have been so mistreated. I learned that the Procurator Fiscal had informed the Crown Office of the death in September 1959, a month after McAvoy had gone to his office in the court building and been sent away without being interviewed. No information had been collected from the others involved either, and the story emerged of an unfortunate woman who had died in childbirth, so an FAI wasn't required.

Even without the information I had uncovered after twenty-six years, Walter Weir's report would have been enough to alert them that something wasn't right. But the last thing anyone wanted to do was to hand the working-classes a stick of injustice to beat the good guys with – though of course that would not have been how it was put. No, it would have been represented as in the best interests of the family, that they had already suffered enough, best not upset them further, simple souls that they were.

The truth was that Peggy was of no importance and neither was the family. They came from Blackhill after all, so what did they matter compared to the reputations and careers of upstanding, educated, professional men? Justice? What was that and what understanding did the Blackhill element have of it anyway? After all, it wasn't as if they felt the same about their families as the educated classes, was it?

So my dreams of Peggy were replaced by violent dreams of shootings and warfare, angry dreams that were every bit as disturbing. I often wondered how much my mother had known. I realized that subconsciously I had waited until after her death to do my sleuthing. Had Nan still been alive, how could I have told her all I had found out, and yet how could I not? Uncle George was still alive, though I hadn't had any contact with him in many years. I toyed with the idea of talking to him, dropped it, then toyed with it again.

When Auntie Annie answered the phone we went through a potted history of the years since we had seen each other, then I asked her if she thought Uncle George would talk to me about Peggy. She doubted it; he hadn't spoken to her about 1959 in any detail. She remembered the doctor who 'wisnae a real doacter' coming to the house after the funeral. 'Tall, young, dark-haired,' she said, 'He wis upset, wanted tae say he wis sorry how things turned oot. Geordie wis sitting by the fire facin' him an' this doacter wis by the door. An' Geordie jist went fur him, he wis acroass that fast, an' the roars o' him! If yer Da hidnae goat tae the doacter first Geordie widda killed him. Yer Da shoved him ootside and the rest o' us hung ontae Geordie tae he wis away.' All my life I remembered Auntie Annie's voice in any family crisis, 'Watch Geordie!', that familiar warning to everyone present that he was near boiling point. I spoke to Uncle George.

'Hullo therr wee yin,' he said, 'How ye daein'?'

'Fine Uncle George, but I need to talk to you. I need to talk about Peggy.' There was total silence at the other end. 'Uncle George, can I come to see you?'

'Aye, a'right hen,' he said quietly.

He was sitting in an armchair by the fire, his hands clamped on the arms, looking down. He was white-haired now, but still a striking man. I had a glimpse of how Nan and Peggy would have looked in old age, had they lived to see it. I told him what I had found out, and as he listened the muscles in his face kept tensing and relaxing.

'Ah know a' this hen,' he said quietly, still looking down.

'Then why did the rest of you let it go?' I asked, 'This wasn't just anybody, this was Peggy!' He was silent for a long time.

'Ye don't unnerstaun' hen,' he said, 'Ye don't know whit it wis like.' Another long silence, then the words came from him slowly, dragged out over twenty-six years. 'Fur Peggy Ah mean. Me and yer Da an' Wullie hid tae clear the room oot efter. Thur wurr piles o' sheets and towels everywhere, a' soaked wi' blood. It wis like a . . . like a slaughthoose.' The knuckles of his hands were white and he had the facial expression I remembered that told you George was having problems with his emotions. I thought of the three of them, all returned from war combat some ten years before, men who had seen terrible sights, cleaning out the bedroom after Peggy died. My mind went back to when I had been lying on my shelter and I had watched Uncle Willie rush out of the house and down the stairs where he was sick in the backcourt. Now I knew why.

'It wis oan the wa's tae,' he continued, 'An' the smell. Even years later Ah could smell it in the hoose, an' Ah coulda pointed tae where the marks hid been oan the wa's.'

'And the doctor, the one who came to the house after the funeral?'

'He wis jist a boay,' he said, 'Jist a big boay, nae mair than twinty. Ah cannae mind a lot aboot that, Ah kin jist remember everybody haudin' me doon . . .'

'But why did you let it go?' I persisted, 'You knew she hadn't died, she had been killed.' He sighed.

'We didnae waant people tae know,' he said, 'Me an' Nan, we talked aboot it, bit we didnae waant people tae know.'

'Know what Uncle George?' I asked puzzled.

'Whit it wis like fur her hen, fur Peggy.' He was looking at me, willing me to understand because he couldn't go on. Then slowly it sank in. Nothing could bring her back, but they had been trying to preserve some sort of dignity for Peggy. They didn't want outsiders idly conjuring up mental pictures of gentle Peggy's agony as she died in a welter of blood. It was the best they could manage. The story was that she had died in childbirth, end of story. A tragedy to be sure, but the less people knew the less they had to talk about. The 'dark yins'' sense of self, their dignity.

'How much did my mother know?' I asked.

'Nan knew it a',' he said, 'We didnae tell the rest everythin' an' Ah don't know whit they f'un oot fur thursels.'

I thought about Nan carrying it for all those years and never being able to tell anyone. All that poisonous knowledge locked up inside her and no one to share the horror with. That's what had come between us and opened up an unbridgeable gulf, the awful truth that she couldn't share. I had been convinced that whatever closeness we had died in 1959, until the voice calling my name before she died had made me wonder.

'Ah blame masel',' Uncle George said, 'Ah've thoaght a' these years that Ah coulda stoapped her marryin' McAvoy. He didnae gie a bugger fur her, Ah coulda pit him aff the idea mibbe. Thur wis wan time, afore she wis expectin' the last wean, Ah hid him by the throat an' Ah coulda squeezed a bit harder, Ah coulda ended it. Ah've sometimes wished Ah hid, an' Peggy wid still be alive. Ah widnae hiv minded gaun' tae jile, Ah shoulda done it while Ah hid the chance.'

'Uncle George, you couldn't have stopped Peggy,' I said, 'She was desperate to get married and anybody would've done but he was the only one around. Nan told her, I remember them talking and Nan telling her that the family would never accept him and if she took him she took him knowing that. Peggy had no illusions, she knew nobody approved, but she thought it was her last chance.' He nodded his head sadly.

'Bit ye aye wonder, dain't ye?' he said. 'Efter he pit Peggy's weans intae care Ah wis that angry that Ah went up tae Moodiesburn Street an' pit him oot, did ye know that? An' Ah thoaght tae masel', "By Christ! An' urn't you the Big Man? Ye shoulda did it afore!" It wis easy, he wis sich a wee weasel. Ah shoulda went up there while she was still alive and pit him oot.'

We had all gone our strange, separate ways after that awful day in 1959, yet we were thinking the same things, feeling the same guilt and desperately fantasizing a different ending. Nan never said it, but I felt her regretting that she hadn't tried to persuade Peggy into a hospital birth. And she could have done it, we both knew that, she more than anyone could have changed Peggy's mind. And Nan had always felt guilty about giving Peggy the unlucky green coat . . . that she hadn't heeded the medium who told her she must come back . . . that she hadn't acted on the dreams.

For myself, I had often day-dreamed about it. If some power had given me one chance to go back in time, what could I have done? I could have gone back as an adult to that morning when she had gone into labour, and passed myself off as Dr Henderson, Hammond's locum. It would have been easy to send the boy who 'wisnae a real doacter' away. I could have used some sort of disguise to cover the family resemblance, and anyway, Peggy wouldn't have known the adult me. Then I could tell her that she would have to go to hospital to have her baby and she would obey, because she respected and trusted doctors as people of learning. I knew enough about hospitals and doctors to have carried it off far better than the scared, panicky 'doacter'. And while she was being sectioned she could have been sterilized so that there would be no more pregnancies, no more threats to her life. Then I would have disappeared, mission accomplished and returned to the present time, having had all those changed years with Peggy, Nan and the family. It was the stuff of dreams. The other fantasy was that if only I had been older Peggy would have listened to me because I worked in a hospital, in her eyes I would have been someone of importance and so I could have influenced events. That was my illogical guilt, being too young to stop what was unfolding before me, the guilt of a powerless child.

After speaking to Uncle George I began to appreciate the depth of the blow to Nan. The loss of Peggy was terrible, but it went beyond that. All of her life she had believed people to be equal in worth and had thought it was a universal belief. The people who brought their problems and their letters to her weren't inferior in any way, through no fault of their own they just weren't able to solve their problems.

I remembered once complaining to her that she had sent

us out into the world armed with her beliefs but minus the knowledge that most of humanity didn't think the same way. She looked puzzled for a moment then said, 'Bit that's their problem, no' yours. They jist don't understaun', bit you know whit's Right.' There was only what was Right, that tangible, unshakeable and undeniable central pillar of all she lived by. But Peggy's death, and the manner of it, had shaken her beliefs to their foundations. Not only was it Not Right, but the educated people whom she had always respected and wanted her children to join, were exposed as frauds. An intelligent woman, she would have finally understood that Peggy had died because Hammond had regarded her as worthless, and that the legal establishment had covered it all up. 'The boys' had protected each other. Who knew better than Nan how much work it took to right a wrong, and that this one could never be righted? It was too big, too comprehensive, and at the end of the day she would still have been left without Peggy. For the first time in her life she had to accept that justice did not always prevail, and the best she could achieve was the protection of her sister's dignity in death.

Her final surrender had come that August, when it became clear that the Procurator Fiscal in Glasgow wasn't going out of his way to inquire. When that became clear, where was there for her to go but inside herself, demoralized, confused and wounded to the core of her spirit? The one duty she had left was to see me grown and on my way to independence, and looking back at those years when she had come so near yet never quite given in, I realized what an effort it had been for her to keep going. There was no one to confide in, no one to help her shoulder the burden. My father was incapable of that level of understanding, or if he did understand, his addiction to booze had long since rendered him incapable of acting upon it. My brothers hadn't shared the unique relationship she had with Peggy, and although I had, there was that old problem, I was too young. The world could ill afford to lose someone as good and gentle as Peggy, but it had also lost the wonderful, shining idealism and zeal of Nan, that was the real tragedy of 30th May 1959.

The light didn't completely die though, and perhaps she suspected that, or at least hoped for it. It's there still in me, and as I get older I see myself reacting as she did to situations and I hear myself using her words to explain to my children that Right is all. Peggy's death and the aftermath have made that belief stronger. It's why I'm a journalist after all, a small modern-day attempt to right wrongs. I happen to have a facility with words, so as Nan would have said, I do it because I can. I have often wished that my own children could have known Nan and Peggy, but now I realize that they do. Because of what they taught me, Nan and Peggy live still in me and so they will live in my children.

The letter with the foreign stamps on the outside arrived many months later, long after I had given up on Dr Steven Collins. Yes, he did remember Mrs McAvoy as it happened, she was his first fatality after leaving the army and taking up the Rottenrow obstetrics post. The GP hadn't been able to be there apparently, he had a single-handed practice and had taken the day off. Whoever had been left to cope wasn't as knowledgeable or experienced and had made rather a mess of it – he had never known who that was. They had no hope of saving Mrs McAvoy by the time she arrived, the haemorrhage had been too great, but they had hoped to save the child by performing an emergency Caesarian section. They didn't get that far though, the child's heartbeat had gone and it was obviously too late. Mrs McAvoy should have been brought in much sooner, the child had been in distress too long and Mrs McAvoy had died very shortly afterwards. The worst possible outcome to lose both, all very sad. The GP had turned up next day full of remorse that he hadn't been there himself, but no one pushed it because it seemed he was well thought of as a GP. No one blamed him, it was just one of those things. If you wanted to lay blame, lay it on inadequate medical care in the poorer areas of the city, the legacy of poor nutrition over generations, poor education . . .

It was only the simple piece of information that connected all the others, but the effect of Dr Collins' letter on me was like a barrier finally being breached. In whatever secret corner of my heart I had kept Peggy alive, the illusion began to crumble. Peggy was dead and it was now time to let her go. It was as if she had died that day, and I cried as though I had just been told. Adults don't cry, they leak tears, but children sob till the pain recedes and I was wracked by an eleven-year-old's grief. After a long, difficult search I had found her again, but in finding her I had also to lose her. Finally able to grieve for her, to acknowledge all the horror of her death, I found that the good memories had been released as well as the bad.

I remembered how she cried as she laughed, the way her eyes shone and the way she encircled you in her warmth as she spoke to you, giving you a feeling of total security. I remembered her wearing a full-skirted dress, white it was and covered in deep pink roses. She had looked so beautiful, the most beautiful creature I had ever seen. Whole conversations between Nan, Peggy and me came flooding back, I could hear her voice again in my head and I smiled at the sound. It took several months, but very gradually, the terrible event that had broken the Clarks as a family, that had destroyed Nan and decimated my childhood in one fell swoop, began to shrink in proportion. It became one terrible event, but it no longer threatened to destroy me. With the brake off, life could go on.

I wanted to talk again to Walter Weir, to thank him for his help and to tell him his analysis had proved correct. When I phoned his number his son answered and I discovered that he had died only months after I had first spoken to him. I also wanted to see Dr James Hammond again. I wanted to tell him who I was, and more importantly, who Peggy was, to make him understand the consequences of his brand of patient care and the fact that the ripples were still going on, two generations later. I didn't want revenge, there was no point in that, but perhaps Nan's belief in anything that went wrong being a misunderstanding that needed to be explained had taken stubborn root. At any event I wanted to state my relationship to Peggy as I couldn't when we talked, to let him know that I was proud of it. His dark, bitter tirade against Peggy, my family and the people of Blackhill had stayed with me and perhaps I wanted to see him again to help me come to terms with that, a kind of cleansing of the psyche. But he too had died, even before Walter Weir. If I had left my search much longer I wouldn't have found out anything.

When I told Ian Cameron all this he smiled his wisest smile.

'I don't believe there's such a thing as coincidence you know,' he said, 'I think we all carry some instinctive means of communicating on a universal timescale. You didn't know Walter had done the PM and you didn't know about Hammond, but something made you look for them at that precise time. And when everyone told you Hammond was dead already, some instinct told you he wasn't and that you would find him. There's only one thing left that you *have* to do. You know what that is, don't you?' I shook my head, but I was lying.

'You must find out where Peggy is buried and visit her.'

'I know where she's buried,' I said, 'Uncle George told me.'

'You must go, you'll find it very healing.'

'No,' I shook my head again, 'There's no point. It's not as if she'd be waiting for me there, it's just a piece of land after all.'

'You're making up excuses,' he smiled, 'You're sensitive and instinctive, you'll go when you're ready, but you *will* go.'

Granda Johnston had bought the plot from a John Dunning, who funnily enough had lived beside Uncle Hughie in Stevenston Street. For all I know the Dunnings could have been frequently treated to 'Red Sails in the Sunset' long before I was. The story was that the Dunnings had gone to find a new life in America, but maybe they were just moving out of earshot. A child was buried in the plot, twelve-year-old Christine Dunning, then the family had sold it to Granda Johnston and gone. It was very fitting I thought, that a lost child should be lying beside Peggy.

Next to be buried, in September 1916, was thirteen-month-old Catherine Clark, a well-kept family secret. No one had ever spoken of a dead child, so it was there from the start, this means of dealing with tragedies by pretending they hadn't happened. Catherine had died from 'catarrh of the bowel', which in a baby would have meant gastro-enteritis. She died when George was a month old, so she would have been weaned from the breast to let the new baby feed. In those days of poor hygiene such deaths were commonplace, as they are in the Third World today, and there would have been no money for a doctor or for the medicine that was available.

What, I wondered, if Catherine, the firstborn child of Annie and Henry Clark, had been fair and blue-eyed? George had been the first 'dark yin'. Was it possible that the death of that little one could be linked to Maw Clark's preference for 'fair yins'? Common though child deaths were at the time, there is no reason to suppose that she was any less affected by the loss of her baby than any mother would be today.

Next to be buried was Da Clark followed by Granda Johnston, then Peggy and her baby and finally Maw Clark. In 1985 I didn't want to go there, not ever. Then one day in October 1992 I went. People who don't know me think I'm impulsive, but I'm not that exciting. Before I do anything I have it fully mulled over in my mind from every direction but because I don't discuss my thoughts it looks like sudden impulse to outsiders.

It was a nice, autumn day and I took with me a big bunch of pink roses that I'd had to search for at that time of year. All the way there I thought that this was the route Peggy had been carried on all those years ago, this was where she came after I had watched the cars out of sight that day, her gift of a pink rose clutched in my hand. Along this same road she had gone, past these houses, turn left into the lane and through the gates. Turn left again and up a little hill, follow the path to the right and it was third from the roadside. I had been scared that it might be awful, that Peggy might be lying in some desolate, ugly place, but she wasn't. There was no headstone; to have erected one would have been to admit that she had gone, and besides, there had never been money in the family for that kind of thing. I decided that she would have one soon. It was well-tended and there was a weeping willow close by, its branches sweeping over where she lay. On either side there were headstones, one for a young man killed during the War. It wasn't at all traumatic, it was a very peaceful and an almost happy visit. I felt that I was with her again. I imagined the scene; my uncles and my father gathering around for the final service, and all those flowers, so many that an extra car had to be provided to carry them. In my mind I could see it as though I had been there. I laid the pink roses on the grass and said, 'Peggy, it's me. I love you.' And standing there beside her I started to laugh, it was not after all the kind of language one working class Glesca lassie uses to another, even if they are related. In my mind's eye I pictured her laughing with me, and Nan too, I could hear the three of us laughing together again. Ian Cameron had been right. It was a very healing experience.

This is a story of a working-class family in Glasgow, and the ordinariness that made them extraordinary, because if I have learned one thing about working-class Glaswegians it is that. But it is also the story of any poor family in any big city at that time. They all had their tragedies, it came with the poverty. It's also the story of those two strong women who were the most important influences in my life. Ironically, both perished, but it's still their story, their standards, that will be remembered, and looking back at my childhood Nan and Peggy stand out like brilliant stars. The hardness, the sadness and the suffering pale into insignificance as well as those who caused it, while Nan and Peggy remain clear and proud.

As I lay on top of the old red-brick air raid sh
that became my haven during those days that chan

course of my young life in 1959, I have a clear memory of deciding not to bother with what was unfolding behind the white-covered windows of Peggy's house. But I promised myself that one day I would find out everything, I'd tell our story . . .

None of the Clarks or the O'Briens were to become rich, famous or influential. They were better than that, they were ordinary and had to struggle to survive, so their story is more courageous and inspiring than anything the nobility ever achieved. Not all ordinary family stories are traced to source, nor all the heroes and heroines acknowledged and celebrated for the sheer guts they showed in surviving. But they should be.

THE END

NO MEAN CITY
by A. McArthur & H. Kingsley Long

The classic novel of the Glasgow slum underworld

No book is more associated with the city of Glasgow than *No Mean City*. First published in 1935, it is the story of Johnnie Stark, son of a violent father and a downtrodden mother, the 'Razor King' of Glasgow's pre-war slum underworld, the Gorbals. The savage, near-truth descriptions, the raw character portrayals, bring to life a story that is fascinating, authentic and convincing.

0 552 07583 3

A SELECTION OF RELATED TITLES
AVAILABLE FROM CORGI AND BLACK SWAN

THE PRICES SHOWN BELOW WERE CORRECT AT THE TIME OF GOING TO PRESS. HOWEVER TRANSWORLD PUBLISHERS RESERVE THE RIGHT TO SHOW NEW RETAIL PRICES ON COVERS WHICH MAY DIFFER FROM THOSE PREVIOUSLY ADVERTISED IN THE TEXT OR ELSEWHERE.

All Transworld titles are available by post from:

Bookpost, P.O. Box 29, Douglas, Isle of Man IM99 1BQ

Credit cards accepted. Please telephone 01624 836000, fax 01624 837033, Internet http://www.bookpost.co.uk or e-mail: bookshop@enterprise.net for details.

Free postage and packing in the UK. Overseas customers allow £1 per book (paperbacks) and £3 per book (hardbacks).